Sons
of
Bear Lake

Sons of Bear Lake

A Novel

by Douglas D. Alder

Springville, Utah

Copyright © 2003 Douglas D. Alder
Alder@dixie.edu

All Rights Reserved.

No part of this book may be reproduced in any form whatsoever, whether by graphic, visual, electronic, film, microfilm, tape recording, or any other means, without prior written permission of the author, except in the case of brief passages embodied in critical reviews and articles.

ISBN: 1-55517-667-4
e.2

Published by Salt Press
Imprint of Cedar Fort Inc.
www.cedarfort.com

Distributed by:

Edited by Marilyn Brown and Elaine Alder
Typeset by Kristin Nelson
Cover design by Nicole Cunningham
Painting of Bear Lake by Steven Songer
Cover design © 2002 by Lyle Mortimer

Printed in the United States of America
10 9 8 7 6 5 4 3 2 1

Printed on acid-free paper

Library of Congress Cataloging-in-Publication Data

Alder, Douglas D.
  Sons of Bear Lake : a novel / by Douglas D. Alder.
      p. cm.
  ISBN 1-55517-667-4
  1. Bear Lake Region (Utah and Idaho)--Fiction. 2. Depressions--Fiction. 3. Brothers--Fiction. I. Title.
PS3601.L345 S66 2002
813'.6--dc21
                         2002014752

Chapter 1
Everett

The grave was fresh, the sandy soil of the cemetery loose and dry under the bunchgrass. As the October sun burned off the heavy dew, the starlings chattered in the morning air. The curled autumn leaves blew across the grave, whispering a warning of the coming snows, snows that would dampen them into the earth.

It was silent in Bear Lake Valley. Harriet glanced across the familiar expanse—the flatness of the glazed lake beside the low, barren mountains. Folks said that it looked just like the Sea of Galilee, calm against the arid hills.

It was quiet because at last the 1932 harvest was over, the alfalfa and hay gathered in against the austerity of the Great Depression. The few tourists had gone, the rowboats had been stashed away for another season; the campgrounds and cabins had been nailed shut.

And the funeral was over.

The town folk had returned to their tasks, driving the Herefords down from their grazing on the high Wasatch range, stacking wood for the fierce winter to come, canning preserves—mostly apples, the only survivors of the biting late frosts of spring.

It was silent and Harriet was alone.

She needed the solitude, a vigil. Just a year ago today they had knelt across the altar, dressed in white, clasping hands and speaking sacred words that had bound them together. Now Everett Proctor's body, in those same white clothes, lay rigid in a pine encasement beneath this parched sod.

Grown men wept while they pounded a casket together from fresh siding intended for his new barn. Everett had been their pride, born and raised in this valley—an example of what they stood for: muscle, virtue, hometown. Taking the gospel message to the state of Virginia, he had preached from door to door and returned a man at twenty-two. He had found himself a wife over in Ovid. She was a wit with pluck. Strong and loving. Together they embodied Bear Lake.

Passing the gospel from father to son had worked well in his case and that is why these people were here, here in the Rocky Mountains, here at Bear Lake.

There was no good reason to be here otherwise. When the winters came and the lake froze over, it was obvious that this icebox was hostile to all humans. Even the Shoshoni knew that long ago, never wintering at Bear Lake. Only the Mormons would take that chance. However, the Mormons were doing something more than building these isolated towns. Everett was the product of that something more. He and generations of others who sprang from the soil of these mountain valleys were building a Kingdom of God.

Harriet concentrated on the parched soil of the grave. Now he lay under that soil, a buried October leaf. His caress, his tight embrace as they slept, were gone. Gone.

Just a mile from here, up Jacob's Canyon, was the site of their first kiss. Tethering their horses, they had left the stream and climbed a treeless bluff to the lookout. There they had a view of the entire lake—twenty miles long, half as wide. With his arm around her waist, he had drawn her to him. She had responded warmly to that embrace.

They had been courting in public for two months at the Friday night dances. The elders had made sure there were only two slower waltzes in among the square dances and polkas—none of this fox trot stuff with body contact for the youth of St. Charles. Sitting on the back row at Sunday meetings they had held hands secretly, but not outside of the church where the whole congregation might see. The after-meetings seemed as long as the preaching ones. No one wanted to leave. All the talking, the sizing up, the plans for the week, they happened in the foyer or, in good weather, out on the lawn. It was hard standing around when you knew you were getting powerfully interested in each other. But waiting for the right moment was Everett's way.

Often he had talked to three or four girls together when Harriet was nearby. That could make it look safe without drawing attention. But the other girls were canny. They knew what was happening between Everett and Harriet, so they slipped away. Soon there were just the two of them again trying to look casual.

Up on that bluff it had happened, surrounded only by the clear blue of the big sky. No longer could they be coy. She wanted the kiss and he did too.

The kiss was long. It sealed them for eternity.

The next Sunday they held hands in the foyer, a public declaration. In private there were more kisses, more hikes, but that was all. He had earned her trust. It would just be a matter of time—not even much time.

To legitimize their informal engagement, Everett drove to Ovid to ask Olie Nielson for his daughter's hand. Harriet had warned her dad that Everett was coming to visit, but Olie made no special preparations for it in any way. When Everett Proctor arrived the next Sunday evening, dressed in his missionary suit, Olie had changed back into his overalls and was headed out to milk their four cows. He took Everett along, gave him a milking stool, but told him just to sit.

But Everett was not one to sit by and watch people work. "I can milk in my suit. I've done it before," he said.

"No, what I've got to say will probably last four cows," Olie pronounced.

Everett wasn't really surprised. "Then you know why I'm here?" He hesitated.

Olie grinned. "Harriet's not one to keep secrets," he said.

"Well, do you approve?"

For a moment Olie was quiet. "I have great respect for Harriet's judgment," he said.

Everett caught the inference. Obviously her dad was going to brag her up, and well he should.

But Olie had more to say. "I need to help you be successful in living with Harriet."

Of course. And Everett felt ready to be instructed.

"I've thought all week what would help you the most. You already know some things and you'll soon discover more. What you might not know is that she is not used to criticism."

"That's interesting."

"We decided to avoid that in raising our children. We felt they would thrive if we didn't knock them. You likely know already that she is confident. She will tackle anything, even dry farming."

"Oh, so you've heard about that." Harriet must have told her father he had been thinking about it.

Olie continued milking. But he stopped for a moment and turned his head away from the cow. "Yes. It scares me. I wouldn't dare try it. But if you are going to do something brash, now's the time. You don't have anything to lose."

They talked for nearly an hour. The milking was finished well before that, but they just sat and conversed, mostly about farming, some about Ovid. When he left, Everett knew he had a real friend.

Once it was official they almost quit dating. They certainly did nothing that cost money. Instead Everett drove to Ovid almost every night where they sat in the porch swing snuggling and talking. Everett figured they couldn't get into trouble if they courted in sight of her parents.

One Saturday he decided to splurge a whole dollar and take Harriet on a tour of Minnetonka Cave, up St. Charles Canyon. Because it was so close to his home, Everett had been there many times, a favorite outing for Boy Scouts and youth groups. Somehow Harriet had never seen the cave; perhaps the twenty-mile distance to Ovid made the difference.

Late Saturday afternoon they gave the Forest Service employee their entrance fee, fifty cents each. There were also two middle-aged couples and two teenagers, one belonging to each family. That made eight of them plus their guide who appeared to be about twenty-six years old, a summer Forest Service worker Everett did not know.

As they went through a large wooden door, the escort locked it from the inside after he switched on the string of small lights attached to the cave wall along the narrow steps. Descending the damp, slippery steps, they walked cautiously. The attendant began his lecture about stalagtites and stalagmites. Soon the formations were in sight, some with water dripping from them, feeding the nearby pools, some with lights behind them, illuminating their colors of pink and rust. It was quite a marvel to think how old the formations were.

Then the lights went out. One of the women screamed. Harriet assumed it was part of the show, to illustrate how really black black could be. Nonetheless she grabbed for Everett and he willingly held her.

"Funny, they didn't do this the other times I've been here," remarked Everett.

"Really, is something wrong?" Harriet questioned.

"Folks, please don't move," the guide said, reaching for his flashlight. "I'm not quite sure why the lights went out. It will be necessary for me to go back to the switch box next to the door. You can either remain here or come back with me."

"You're not leaving us here alone," replied one of the women. "This is nonsense, I want my money back."

"I'll be glad to refund it, ma'am. In fact, I think it would be best if your boys do not stay here."

Both families turned back up the trail—even the boys, who were glad not to be left in the dark.

Everett looked at Harriet a moment to appraise her nerves and then said, "We'll wait here for you."

"Are you sure? It's pretty cool in here. Let me give you my jacket," he said, handing it to Harriet.

"Yes, I've been here before."

"All right."

One of the men chuckled, looking at Harriet, "Do you trust him?"

So they were alone in the darkness. The pitch black enveloped them. Everett held her so tight he could feel her heartbeat.

"Are you afraid?" he asked.

"Well, I wouldn't do this alone."

"That means I have a purpose."

"Oh, this is just one of them," she joked.

Everett laughed and kissed her gently. She responded and he kissed her more passionately.

"Well, this could get interesting."

"Oh, I'm not defenseless," she laughed.

"Maybe," he argued. "Especially not if I defend you from the beast here at your side."

"Does that mean I don't have to worry about you?"

"Not if I keep up a good record of safe behavior," he laughed.

Harriet began to sing children's songs. He joined her, proving that they had both been in primary classes, even if they were in different towns.

Then the lights came on.

On the way home that day Everett said, "You know, that might be the best dollar we will ever spend."

With the wedding now pending, Everett had much to do. Corrals had to be built, steers bought, the north forty plowed, winter wheat seeded—enough to make a spare living. There was already a cabin that could be turned into a starter home but the soil came first.

Turning ranchland to farmland was risky. This new thing they called "dry farming" was catching on, thanks to the county agent from the state college, but it was daring. No one in St. Charles had made a go of it yet. Skeptics argued that the winters here were too cold for the wheat to survive under the snow. Planting in the fall instead of the spring seemed suicidal. Everett intended to give it a try. It meant that the winter moisture would sustain the wheat in the spring without irrigation and by fall it would ripen, producing almost as much harvest on the dry land as on irrigated land.

In October both families drove across the mountain to Logan—parents, aunts and uncles. They all dressed in white and climbed the spiral staircase of the pioneer temple to the wedding chamber. There inside the thick stone walls, the temple president sealed them to be an eternal family, a new household, with Everett as patriarch and Harriet as the nurturer—both to raise a righteous generation to the Lord. It was the apex of their lives, the fulfillment of the plan. It stirred them both, she to tears and Everett to a confident grin.

For their honeymoon they steered Everett's rickety Ford throughout Cache Valley's west side to look at dry farms near Cornish. Meandering casually for three days, they reached the narrows where Bear River breaks through the pass into the valley of the Great Salt Lake. There they turned toward Tremonton and more dry farms, going even as far as White's Valley. Veering north they reached Preston, catching Idaho's Emigration Canyon to re-enter Bear Lake Valley near Ovid. Their trip was retracing the same 1870s route the first Mormon settlers used to penetrate to the shores of the lake, the same lake which the Indians had called Sweetwater and the fur trappers later dubbed "Bear Lake."

Now she was alone. She had spent her first night without him. The dying had been quick. Meningitis they called it. It struck suddenly. First he grasped the temples of his head as aching pounded inside his skull. Then he vomited and lost his balance, perspiring profusely as his body burned with increasing temperature. He lay prostrate on the bed with rare will to talk. He lingered five days, not long enough to maim his body, not even to fade his tan. He sank each hour until he slipped from life.

Compelled to return to this dedicated spot, Harriet chastised herself. She chided her own doubts; she knew these cemetery remains were not her Everett. She had to believe. What else was there? She had to know that they would live again, together. This was not the end; she and Everett were sealed for eternity.

She had been stalwart so far, yet she came here to weep. Abandoning composure, she fell across his mark in the soil and sobbed. With fear, with pain. For the loneliness that would be her reward. Their year had been tender, their work fruitful. The harvest had come. And now he was gone.

He was one of those who did things right, who believed and acted with verve. And everything had fallen into place. Virtue and vigor had worked.

She had never intended to be strong alone, to preside or to manage. Instead she had become just what she wanted—a partner, a team member. He loved to assert. It was perfect.

But now he was gone.

She was beginning to worship him.

The October warmth turned her sobs to slumber. Though the sun shown with unclouded brilliance, she slept—in the cemetery on the hillside, near the place of their commitment.

On awakening she was nauseated again. She had decided to wait to tell him. It was too early. And then he had become ill. So she had disguised her discomfort. Surely he would want to know that his seed would continue, but he spoke only of recovery until his last day. Then he was so apologetic for abandoning her. He worried for her care as the fever drove him in and out of consciousness. There was the mortgage and mostly the loneliness; she would likely not find another husband because she was sealed to Everett. No one worthy of her would want a wife he could not take to be sealed for eternity. She might live alone. That haunted him; she silenced his attempt at nobility. No, she would not consider being sealed to another. She was his and would remain firm to her commitment. One year together was a testament—she would wait for eternity. Without a tear she bore him that witness. She was brave throughout and chose not to tell him that their child would come in seven months, just prior to her twentieth birthday. He would know. He would be there. No need to worry him on his last day.

Gathering her thoughts and herself together, Harriet stood up. She chose a bouquet of white roses from among the flowers at the grave. They were too beautiful to wilt there.

The Ford coughed all the way to the cabin. The engine would be the next casualty; Everett had said he would get to it soon.

The night was hard. She heard sounds that had not been there before. She wept and wanted to leave the bed. But she did not dare. *There might be a bat. Would the door blow open? What if a wolf prowled too near? What if a strange car came up the road?* Such thoughts had never plagued her.

She had not been much afraid since her twelfth birthday when she decided ghosts were an invention of Uncle Abe. He delighted in her wide eyes as he told stories, especially those attributed to the fur trappers who were legendary in the tall tale department. On that pre-teen day she realized she had never seen a ghost. A twelve-year-old in Bear Lake Valley is just as good as grown up. That's when handouts ceased and allowances began. It was a time to say farewell to ghosts and to being frightened.

Tonight there were no ghosts, but Harriet cried and cried. She had never felt so alone, had never trembled like this. Her fear mounted. The wind whined, a sandy, wheezy whine. Far away a coyote howled. She lay gazing at the caulking between the logs as never before. The rows swirled in her consciousness through the light of the flickering candle she and Everett had always placed beside their bed. But tonight, with her mind alternating between sleep and delirium, she forgot the candlelight and began to lose control. Her head was throbbing and she trembled. It was as though she were still seven years old, at a time when the attic was full of the supernatural.

Drugged with exhaustion and helplessness, she fell into a fitful sleep, finally unaware of the dawn. Her body wanted to separate from her spirit. She seemed to be spinning, falling. It was not a dream. And it was not dying. She just could not get her pregnant body and troubled spirit back together. Sweating profusely in a cold, sticky sweat, she felt she was standing aside and watching her body shake. Terror and surrender seemed to be pulling at each other.

A clamor of confusion drew her toward semi-consciousness. It seemed like screaming—the shrill clanging shook her from her bed. Eyes half open, hands outstretched, she groped forward. Three steps woke her to the realization that she was staggering toward the bell banging on her door. In the habit of civility she answered, clearing her throat: "Yes, Sister Pugmire, I'm all right."

"Harriet, I just wanted to bring you a fresh loaf of bread and check on you."

"I know I look awful. I just overslept a bit. I feel fine."

The kindness shook her into action. She realized how close she had come to a careless collapse. Without reason she responded automatically, turning to her toilet, to dressing, to surviving. She did not weigh the arguments of having lost purpose against the need to live for the baby. How close she had come to the abyss.

As mid-day announced itself with the shift of shadows, Harriet heard another motor car climbing the last bend to the cabin. It was the familiar high pitch of her parents' well-tuned vehicle. Old but well-cared for, it obeyed her father's will.

Without knocking, he unlatched the door and entered softly, as if he were expecting her to be asleep. Without apology he admitted, "I felt you needed me."

Harriet paused, attempting to keep up formalities. Then she burst into tears. She sank into her chair, body limp, head and hair sliding down to the chair's high back. He rushed to her, kneeling beside and surrounding her with his huge arms and chest.

For many minutes he just held her. She trembled without crying. His hardened muscles tensed but held the position firmly. Then he slid an arm beneath her legs and rising, carried her to the bed. He reached in his overcoat pocket and withdrew a tiny bottle.

"I have come to give you a blessing, Harrie. Do you want a blessing?"

She assented with a nod of relief. Then closed her eyes.

He gently poured one drop of oil from the bottle to the crown of her head. Setting the bottle aside, he placed both of his hands on her head—as Moses anointed Aaron. His words rang like scripture too, speaking of her courage to come, her mission to live, her womb to deliver a son, her life yet to be fruitful.

He finished and knelt again, kissing her face. Tears dropped freely from his eyes. He placed a blanket over her, then rose.

Walking almost silently, he went back and forth to the car, bringing in boxes and sacks of food. Then he sat beside her again, holding her hand until her breath came rhythmically and her eyelids closed.

Chapter 2
Harriet

The winter was long, and harder than she had expected, which raised questions about Harriet's determination to stay in St. Charles. Returning to Ovid would be like quitting. Her parents understood, though hesitantly. The life within her gave purpose, courage to be a family, to keep a house, to be an entity on her own. But the silence was fearful. There was no way to escape it at night.

The tales of Siberia made sense now. Uncle Abe claimed that winter in Bear Lake was like Russia's frozen Northeast. Severe cold—sometimes thirty degrees below freezing—and winds that doubled the chill factor, were so standard that weather was no excuse for inaction. Schools seldom closed, church meetings defied the elements, farmers fed their cows alfalfa and continued to milk them every day. But the chickens went on strike, their feet and combs stiff with frost. Highway 89 was kept open by the constant tedium of plodding snowplows, a vital north-south line since the Oregon Trail was forged out by trailblazers in the 1840s. It had to be open for the nation's sake.

The lake froze solid on December 12th, a month earlier than usual. No one had to tell Harriet; she could sense it as the fog lifted. The freezing cold from the night did not change in the day. The winds just swept across the ice and wound around the encircling mountains. It was like living inside an ice chest.

That's when she carried unchopped logs into the house for splitting. Even with the vigor of swinging an ax, she worked up no sweat. The wood sustained a fire in the stove, the heat rising quickly to the loft beams. The floor remained cold, as though the ice were creeping in.

This cabin had not been intended for human habitation, rather for tools and tractors. But Everett had hoped it would do for a season or two while they tried their hand at dry farming.

Living there meant they were not really in town. In fact, they were nearly a mile up the hill. The structure had been built above the canal, amid the foothills. No irrigation water could flow to it. One could claim they were defying Brigham Young's admonition for all families to live in the village. Of course, the danger of Indians had long been gone, so there was no real urgency. But Everett had intended to stay in the cabin for only two seasons. Then he had planned for them to try for a place in town and be back in order.

Harriet knew the wood supply would hold out until spring because Everett had not scrimped in gathering it from the foothills. She also knew that lumbering such full-sized logs and bringing them to the cabin for another winter could not be just a sideline task for her as it had been for him.

Then there was the Ford. Even with a blanket left over it all night and hot water poured over the radiator, it started only on alternate days. She felt panic edging closer when the car failed, but on another day when it chugged into action, she pretended it always would.

The women in St. Charles Ward were ingenious, sensing her isolation. No one suggested that she needed help. It was the other way around. They asked for her aid.

"We need you for a part in the Christmas pageant."

"Could you come to my house for three days and take my children while we go to Ogden for the cattle auction?"

"How about joining our literary club? We meet monthly and hear book reviews from one of our group. You can choose any book you like for your report."

"We need you to handle the cash register at the ward bazaar."

"Will you teach the seven-year-olds in Sunday School?"

"The ward dinner is next week. We'll be cooking turkeys and pies all day. Could you come?"

On one Sunday Sue Pugmire came up to her in the church foyer. "Harriet, would you mind if I dropped over to your house tomorrow, this time for a chat? I think of you every day and have decided that we two should get better acquainted."

That caught Harriet off guard. She didn't really know why this lady, twice her age, would be thinking about her, beyond the obvious. It didn't matter though. She had to admit she had been very lonely. Sue seemed so solid, so sensible. Mother of six, she knew the ropes of parenting and at the same time was involved in most town activities.

Besides that, Sue could tell a good joke. And she really knew how to laugh.

Harriet wanted Sue to come. Nevertheless, she was tentative. "That would be great but you must realize that my house is just a cabin. I live like the pioneers. It was fun when Everett was with me—one great campout. But it's nothing to look at."

Sue responded with her hearty laugh. "Hey, first homes are supposed to be simple; otherwise they spoil you. If I come by about one o'clock will that be okay?"

"Great. I'll have the chores done by then."

That was the arrangement. It seemed comfortable, so Harriet didn't worry a bit. She knew that the ward members in St. Charles wanted to make her pregnancy a pleasant one. All of them felt they had a stake in Everett's offspring. Everett had been their pride and joy. And of course they would want to be part of the parenting.

On Monday, right before one p.m., when Harriet heard an approaching car, she felt glad to have a visitor. She welcomed Sue as though they were old friends.

As they settled onto the old couch Everett's folks had given them, Sue said, "Harriet, perhaps you don't know but I was Everett's teacher in Primary for three years and became especially fond of him. Selfishly I wanted him to be around our house as an example to my boys, so I hired him to dig our garden and pick apples with my three boys who were five years and more younger."

Harriet basked in the words of praise. "I didn't know that exactly but Everett often pointed out your orchard," she replied.

Sue continued, "It worked just as I wanted. My boys latched onto Everett. They thought they wanted to be just like him and that was fine for me. I became more and more attached to Everett, wanted him to be part of our family. I even liked to play jokes on him to test whether he could catch them. One day I sent the boys to weed the garden knowing that our neighbor would soon switch the irrigation water and they would get flooded.

"Everett figured out that it wasn't an accident and helped the boys plot to get back. So they filled the wheelbarrow with mud and dumped it right on the back step and then went on an unauthorized hike."

"So I took him away from you, didn't I?" Harriet smiled a half-smile.

"Yes, but that was fortunate too. It served to show my boys what a courtship was to be for them. It came as they reached their teenage years—just in time."

Harriet was happy to remember. "Well, I realize that most everyone in St. Charles loved him. I often feel like an intruder, having won his heart."

Sue replied, "That's what you did all right. He adored you."

Harriet hesitated. "Yes, but I know that most folks in town had their own candidates for his match."

Sue put a hand out and grasped Harriet's fist in her lap. "Probably so, but we quickly adjusted and feel like you are our own."

Harriet felt her feelings spilling out now. "I wish I could feel that way. I still seem like an interloper—a maid from peculiar Ovid who stole her way into the upper crust."

Sue seemed surprised. "What makes you say that?"

"Well, I realize that Ovid is a different kind of town than St. Charles. We are Danes and you are English."

Sue leaned back with a pleasant reassuring laugh. "Oh Harriet, that was three generations ago. We're all Americans now. No one in Ovid speaks Danish, do they?"

"No, but they feel a bit unwelcome."

"Do you sense that yourself?"

"I'm not sure. I can't quite figure it out. Tell me how your generation feels about us."

Sue settled back with a smile. "Well there are some differences. But we share the same cold weather and the struggle to survive. We believe the gospel alike. We meet together in the Paris Stake Tabernacle. We go to the same high school. We are mostly alike."

But Harriet wasn't ready to give up her point. "Yes, but there is still something different. For example, I'm sure that no one in St. Charles had me in mind as a wife for Everett. They had lots of candidates but not someone from Ovid."

There was a pause before Sue spoke again. "You are perceptive, Harriet," she admitted. "I think everyone in town is pleased with your marriage, your devotion to Everett and especially your pregnancy. But you are right, they wouldn't have thought of you."

"And it is because I am from Ovid?"

"Well, probably. But you've got to realize that it is not a big issue. We work in the same church and that matters a lot. We are part of the same world together. Our community is not just St. Charles. It is at least all of Bear Lake, but really far beyond that, all of Utah and southern Idaho, all of Mormondom. That expands to Europe and beyond."

Harriet returned Sue's smile, but she was so glad to have a listening ear, she continued to ask questions. Since coming to Bear Lake she had felt an unspoken sense of isolation from Everett's people. "I just don't understand it, because we don't speak Danish any more in Ovid. Is there some sort of secret about us that I don't know? I don't mind if you tell me truly. Why are folks in this town reserved about us?"

"Harriet, you realize, don't you, that I'm sort of an outsider too," Sue began. "At least I come from Laketown. I crossed the state line to marry into St. Charles. From my point of view that is not much of a leap because that is Bear Lake country too, even if it is in a different county and a different state. That old Utah-Idaho state line east-west through the lake causes some differences. But I didn't feel like an outsider. Never did."

"Well, one can't see the lake from Ovid," Harriet said. "But we consider ourselves Bear Lakers and think everyone else should. We are not sure they do, even if we are both in Idaho."

Sue smiled vaguely, looking off into the room. She was ready to admit there were differences. "Harriet, that old language thing lingers on, just like it does in other parts of America. The Germans in Wisconsin are a tight group and the Norwegians in Minnesota cling together. It should be different here because we have all molded together faster. We have all learned English. The church leaders here urged it and have not wanted congregations to conduct services in the mother tongue."

Harriet knew that. "Right. As far as I know, we never held meetings in Danish even though some of the old timers' English was slow in coming."

"Everyone made the transition pretty fast, within one generation. Perhaps it happened because they needed each other so much," Sue replied.

Harriet wasn't ready to give up her quest for understanding. "Yes, but some folks have long memories," she said. "Ovid still seemed different somehow."

Sue's gaze fell to her hands in her lap. She would discuss the subject if that was what Harriet wanted to do. "I haven't given it much thought but perhaps the difference nowadays has to do with what Ovid kids do after high school. Take Everett for example. There was just never a question in his mind that he would go to State College after high school. That doesn't seem to be the case with boys from Ovid. They go to work as soon as they can. Do you know why?"

"I'm not exactly sure. The college recruiters tried to get me to go over there but I wasn't really interested," Harriet paused. "Having a family was much more my plan," she admitted.

"Yes," Sue smiled. "Which brings me to another thing." She continued with courage. "The folks in Ovid had a bigger struggle than the ones in

Bloomington and St. Charles. It wasn't because life here was easier, not at all. It was because the English arrived in better shape. I don't know exactly why or how. But the original Ovid people had families that were fragmented. There were more orphans. It was common for one or both parents of those early Danes to have died on the plains or after arriving. Lots of those orphans were forced to support themselves by the time they were ten. Unfortunately some of them never quite got established or never got really absorbed into schools, church, or towns. They worked hard, but it took a full generation more for families in Ovid to get their roots down."

As Harriet listened, Sue's explanation rang true to her. "I know what you are talking about," she replied. "I have a couple of uncles who roamed all their lives. It scared me." Now she looked off into the room and twisted her fingers. "I never thought it through like this but I knew that what I wanted to be was a mother and a farmer's wife. Everett was that guarantee for me. I never wanted to go to State College for my world. I was afraid it would lead me away. Bear Lake and family are my vision. Folks are suggesting I go to State College now but that is not me. Everett was to be me. And he's gone."

Sue took Harriet's hands and pressed them. Then she drew her close and held her for a moment. "Let us be your friends," she said.

Harriet had to admit that Sue's visit opened her eyes.

That next Sunday, Charlotte Squires, also twice Harriet's age, stopped her in the foyer. "I don't know if you quilt, my dear, and I don't know if you mind a bunch of old ladies. But won't you come to my house tomorrow? We have a quilt on in the living room and there will be a half dozen of us working on it."

Harriet had agreed to Charlotte's invitation, mostly out of politeness. In reality, she was uncomfortable about actually showing up. Once there she saw why. It took more patience than she expected to make her stitches sufficiently petite to satisfy Sister Squires, a prize winner at Idaho's Bear Lake County Fair. Charlotte had gambled to let a newcomer have a try. The patterns were intricate, the lines had to be straight, the stitches even, but Harriet was determined to learn. She knew she needed activity. The alternative was silence and that, she was quickly discovering, was unbearable. She decided to take every invitation, even if it was with grandmothers.

Besides, quilting was only the by-product. Talking was the main fare. When she was a teenager Harriet made fun of the continuing pregnancy talk among married women. Now it had a ring of authenticity. So after a couple of weeks at learning, Harriet returned the favor and invited the women to bring the quilt to her cabin for an afternoon's work.

On this particular day Abigail Allen from Laketown, at the Utah end of Bear Lake, was in town. Charlotte Squires invited her to accompany them to Harriet's. Bringing a wealth of Laketown newsiness with her, Abigail was a favorite at quilting bees. She had been at the Paris Tabernacle that morning to conduct a women's choir practice for the coming stake conference. Charlotte prevailed on Abigail to stay for two hours of quilting before turning south for the twenty-mile drive to Laketown.

A natural matriarch, Abigail presided over the chit-chat with good-natured firmness. The sisters had been admonished in Relief Society classes to avoid gossip, so the conversation had to be steered to uplifting themes. Still the talk came naturally to pregnancy and deliveries.

It didn't take much coaxing for Abigail to recall the mothering experiences that made her a favorite guest. The eldest daughter of thirteen children in Laketown's second generation, Abigail helped rear her siblings before she began her own brood. She was to repeat the pioneer life when she and her husband, Gordon, homesteaded at South Eden, an oasis on the east shore of the lake. Though she could have gone to Montpelier, twenty miles to the north, Abigail insisted on having her babies at home rather than seeking the safety of a fledgling hospital. On one occasion, when road construction blocked the highway, the doctor had to hire two husky boys to row him across the lake, arriving just fifteen minutes before the delivery.

Harriet enjoyed the women's stories. But alone at night she had to face the fact that some of that flitting about doing busy work was an escape. She could not afford to attend quilting bees forever. There had to be a more relevant use of her time. Often when she came home there would be a sack of potatoes or a package of meat on the table. Anyone might have brought it in because she never locked her door. No one did. The gifts were given out of kindness, but they were gifts of welfare, too. Perhaps the Bishop planned them. Perhaps they were spontaneous neighborliness. But she knew that her dependency had to end soon. Her pioneer heritage had established in her a fierce self-reliance as well as a desire to be part of the community.

The rush of adulthood was falling in on her all at once—not just parenthood, but self-sufficiency. How was she going to make it work? She had forty acres and a mortgage, the mere beginning of a self-sustaining farm.

Fifty years ago her plight had been common. Polygamous husbands set up many wives with forty acres in Bear Lake Valley. Although the wives had to work unceasingly, the irrigated fields, as opposed to dry farms, could support a family. The wives often plowed the fields themselves because the husbands only came four or five times a year. If they had growing boys, they were fortunate. If not, they worked as men. The valley's well-known leader, Preston Thomas, for example, was away from his family during three missions. Even when he returned, he had to spend the winters in Salt Lake City in the legislature. His wife raised seven children nearly alone. The Riches and Budges and Pugmires all had similar stories. Why couldn't Harriet make it like her ancestors, the Danes of Ovid, who won against many odds?

The mortgage.

Pioneers had no mortgages. They pulled together, shared the harvest, built canals in teams during the winter, responded to bishop's calls to build the Tabernacle in Paris or even the Temple in Logan. And they made it. Never above the poverty level, they nonetheless had milk and meat, apples and carrots, potatoes and berries—all grown in the short Bear Lake season. They traded any surplus for flour, and somehow subsisted.

Mortgages were an invention of modernity, two generations after the first attempt at survival. Such irony. In complete poverty the pioneers relied on themselves. The next generations turned to banks. How would Harriet ever make mortgage payments? Forty acres of dry farm wasn't enough to generate a profit even if Harriet could plow, harrow, plant and harvest from a tractor.

On their next encounter in the ward foyer, Harriet sought out Sue Pugmire's opinion. "Am I being even half realistic?" she asked. Sue paused a minute and then returned with a tough question: "Is farming woman's work?" Harriet thought a moment. She couldn't find a single picture in her mind of a woman in her generation who was farming all alone. Working out on the land, yes. But not alone.

Sue pressed a bit, "Harriet, I know you are resisting it, but why don't you consider the idea of going to Logan to State College?"

Harriet looked at her. For a moment she was speechless, until her words came tumbling out. "Well," she said, "some of my high school graduating class have gone on scholarships. But it's not really my yearning . . ." She quickly recovered with a positive note. "I'm not dumb. I could get good grades. I did in high school. But I know what it really means—leaving Bear Lake for good. The girls over there meet someone, marry and move beyond Bear Lake, sometimes marrying outside the church. They seldom come back, even for a visit and when they do, their fancy ways don't fit. Somehow it seems disloyal."

Sue had been such a good sounding board. She smiled now. Harriet felt the love Sue's words were meant to convey, though she made difficult suggestions. "Well, I know what you mean. You have seen things as they are. You have also realized that those forty acres of dry farm won't support you. The other option is to move to Ogden or Salt Lake. Every year many farm families give up the land and move there to find jobs in the smelters and railroads. They get paid real money, something we seldom see."

"Wow, factories sound even less enticing than State College."

"I know. I've seldom talked so pessimistic. This sounds like man talk. There's got to be a way for you to do what you want to do. So stick with it."

Driving back to the cabin, Harriet mulled over Sue's advice in her thoughts. *Even as a teen I never wanted to chase after Hollywood actors or be carried away by some salesman. Escape was not attractive. It is not only Everett's grave but his land I want to tend.* She had faced into the wind so far in her life, knowing how to weather winters. That was what she could do and wanted to do. She was strong and stubborn. Physical work wasn't foreign to her. For a full decade she had ridden her father's haywagon and hefted bales. The cows were accustomed to her milking. The tractor knew her control just as much as her brothers'. She could also cook up a meal for a dozen folks. No one thought of her as a tomboy, but there was never a suggestion that Everett would have had to do all the physical labor. She felt right about planning to stay put.

In January the Stake Conference was held in the Paris Tabernacle. Ward congregations from all the westside towns—Laketown, Pickleville, Garden City, Fish Haven, St. Charles, Bloomington, Paris and Ovid—gathered at the cathedral-like structure for a winter festivity with no equal. Visiting dignitaries from Salt Lake were there. All day Saturday there were Sunday School and Primary conferences for teachers and some performances by the children. Apostle Melvin J. Ballard with flowing mane and sonorous voice, instructed the youth leaders on the theme "Shall the Youth of Zion Falter?" His traveling companion, A. Hamer Reiser, suggested effective teaching methods for Sunday School teachers. By using the refined English of one who knew literature and scripture, he seemed to elevate the mundane to elegance. Together they were almost Olympian in their three-piece suits, homburg hats, their watch chains crossing their vest pockets.

Amy Brown Lyman, serene and refined, directed the women's Relief Society meetings. She gave instructions for enlivening each of the four women's departments—Spiritual Living, Cultural Refinement, Homemaking and Compassionate Service. She pled with the women to remember that their weekly classes did not replace their chief goal—compassionate service, to the sick, the lonely, the poor. It seemed somehow incongruous to hear such words from a woman attired in silks.

Abigail Allen's choir sang. The biggest bazaar of the year was held all day. Teachers from all the wards along the west side met to share ideas and there was a huge banquet held in the school gymnasium Saturday evening, followed by the traditional dance.

Harriet was betwixt and between. Her unmarried classmates lived for the dances and the sparking. She didn't miss the dance, but she planned on leaving early. By sitting on the sidelines she forced the kindly middle-aged men to ask her for a dance, a politeness that hurt. The young married elders found it wise to steer clear of her, as did the unmarried single fellows, deterred by her obvious pregnancy.

The wind howled outside, drifting the snow so fast that people were joking about sleeping in the gym that night. Watching the snow, she realized this wouldn't be one of those times she could leave early. Gazing about, she thought she could ask any of a hundred people here to let her stay at their home for the night and she would not even be embarrassed.

During the fox trot Bishop Clark sat down beside her and made small talk. "Let's see, the baby is due when?" he smiled at her.

"Mid-April, as best I can figure," she hesitated.

"Well, that's just about right," the bishop mused.

"What do you mean, just right?"

"That will give us until then to do some thinking before the spring planting has to start."

She didn't know what he meant by thinking. But she believed she could guess. "Yes, I've been doing a lot of pondering already."

"Okay, let's both do that. Then after the baby's born we'll need to have a right good talk."

With that he got up and went off to chat with another of the flock, leaving Harriet puzzled.

For a moment she had to gather her own thoughts together, to admit that "what she had been pondering" was quite mixed-up. The bishop had been savvy enough to know she was confused. And she needed counsel. She had been feeling obligated to tend Everett's farm, but she could keep skepticism away only by suppressing it. She had never followed any good ideas to a conclusion. There was a certain comfort in realizing that Bishop Clark was thinking about her, yet some relief that their next "chat" was a few months away.

In early April, when the time for the baby's delivery drew near, Harriet intended to pack the Ford and drive to Ovid. It was only twenty minutes from there to the Montpelier hospital. The baby would come attended by the family doctor and supportive parents. That much she allowed. Even wives with living husbands sometimes went home for the first birth.

By March 17, the lake ice had been breaking up for a whole week. Fierce winds blew the cracking sheets to the shore and packed them like huge books, upright, against trees, even pressing the beach houses. Some slabs were ten feet high. The season change was announcing itself with furor. Then after a week of warming and winding, a spring storm came. Snow poured like a thunderstorm, wet and heavy. There was actually thunder as though this were a July cloudburst. But it was plain to see that the blizzard would not cease in a half hour like the welcomed July rains. Such spring snow squalls were almost an annual guarantee. She knew what they would bring, and it was so. Within an hour there was a foot of heavy, slushy snow. The sky continued to blacken. It could last through the night, maybe bring three feet by morning up here in the foothills.

The labor pains began a half hour into the snowstorm, three weeks early. Harriet had been reading prenatal care articles; she knew about pre-labor pains. Intense labor should be several hours away. She thought about Abigail Allen's births. The snow made Harriet equally isolated. But if this were the real thing, she could surely hold out for a few hours.

Wait or go? The snow was so fierce. She was frankly frightened, perspiration coming as much from fright as from pain. The contractions subsided. She relaxed. She could make it until morning and then the main roads might be cleared. But how could she get the Ford down a mile of country road to the highway?

Another pain, crunching and tightening her whole belly.

She had better seek help. Everett's mother was here in St. Charles, close, but it would be so embarrassing to bring her out in this blizzard for false labor. Her own mother was fourteen miles away. How could her parents ever get through on roads they could not see? They could be marooned in this mess; their errand of mercy could become a tragedy.

Her heart raced. As blood rushed to her head, she felt her temples pulse. Her forehead beat as though she were in a fever. She felt panic. It was nearly a mile to the nearest telephone at the Morris home.

There was no certainty that the baby was coming now. Perhaps it was a day away. But if it were to come during this storm, she must lay her plans now. Visions of Indian women, the Shoshoni and the Bannock who roamed these very hills, came to her mind. They went off to the bushes alone and delivered their babies. She had heard how they made stools about eight inches high and eighteen inches wide to sit on like a saddle on the ground. They took cords to bite on. It was legendary that they didn't yell out when the pains came.

No midwives, no screaming, no halting of the tribe's travels.

And many died.

Then the pains came more sharply, gripping her body and halting her breath. She had thoughts that death did not seem so unwelcome. Longing to be with Everett would be easy if it were not for their child. Even if this was to be her only child, she wanted to bear it and raise it to be like him. She must not give up; she must be sensible, let her body follow its natural inclination, just as the Indian women had done in the brush.

She thought of Abigail Allen who chose to have her babies at home. But Abigail had not been alone. So Harriet might be halfway between the Shoshoni and Abigail—not in the woods, but alone in her cabin.

The pains came again. The perspiration flowed hot this time. She shivered. Then she set her jaw and started carrying water to the stove. She filled her largest pot and several small ones. She stoked the fire. The pains came again. She bit her lip and looked for a towel to serve as her rope, still shivering. Then she gathered several sheets, stripped the bed of its blankets, put an oilcloth on the mattress and laid six sheets, neatly folded, near to it.

The pain was long and sharp. She cried out, grabbing a towel to thwart the sound. Why, when there was no one to admire her propriety? She sat on the bed and tried to think of each step ahead, asking herself why she had not seen a birth. Why hadn't she asked her mother what happened? Darned all this modesty. It was just one of those things one wraps in confidentiality and sends off to the hospital. You can talk about it at quilting bees but only obliquely. Why not frankly with your own children?

The wind was churning to a crescendo, howling like a chorus of coyote. Though it was early afternoon, the clouds and snow drenched the light away. The pain came constantly now, with little time to recover between contractions. She pounded back against the pillow, her eyes closed and her teeth biting through the towel. Suddenly the cabin door burst open. Snow blew in and Harriet thought to rush against the door. She held her breath, closed her eyes, and then started for the door. Lunging toward the wind she fell against two figures—her parents.

"Oh Harrie, I just knew your pains were coming. Somehow I felt it." Even the wind could not drown out the message.

Chapter 3
Bishop Clark

The first Sunday in May was "Fast Sunday" in St. Charles. In the routine ways of ward life, Fast Sunday afforded a ritual high point. On that day at the meetinghouse people came fasting, new babies were blessed and given their name, eight-year-old children were confirmed following their baptism in the lake the day before. The bulk of the meeting time was devoted to the bearing of testimonies—spontaneous statements of faith and thanksgiving from members of the congregation who stood in place, Quaker-like, and addressed their peers, often about Christ's influence in their lives. Though children generally dozed, they somehow caught the gist of the messages, because they later made light of the tearful speakers or the broken brogues of immigrants who vibrated with fervor about their own conversion and trek to the "tops of the mountains."

The obvious concern of the adults was to extend the zeal of the pioneer epoch, now several decades in the past. For teenagers whose heroes were coming more and more from the "Hit Parade" and the World Series, the pioneer image could seem completely out-of-date. Not a few of the youth harbored longings to escape from Bear Lake, to be discovered, to be in the world of high fashion—or at least to wear the uniform that would head them out to exotic naval ports. Such escapes unsettled many a Swede or Swiss immigrant who fervently told of their parents' flight from poverty to what they considered celestial coves in Bear Lake Valley. They welcomed the opposition of wind and winter in replacement for the corruption of Europe's Babylon.

On this festive Fast Sunday Harriet was the center of attention and ritual. She dressed the baby in a blue outfit, tenderly crocheted by Everett's mother, Grandma Proctor. Everett Junior was a healthy baby with his father's countenance. Harriet chose to wrap him in a white shawl of her own making, partly to advertise the blue and partly to symbolize the baby's father. She had worked its threads with her knitting needles in the cabin's snugness which Everett's supplies had provided for her during the cold nights of the winter.

Now with firm pride she was announcing their son's entrance into the community. She was launching their offspring in the direction set by his model father.

Grandpa Proctor was the "mouthpiece" in the ring of men who held the babe in their arms. Nielsens and Proctors all held one hand under the child and the other hand on the shoulder of the next fellow priesthood bearer in a circle of relationships and authority. Even though Harriet would like to have heard her own father's rich tones and sober words, she asked Grandpa Proctor to substitute for his son whose death had come too soon. Everett would have had it so—the Patriarchal Order.

There was never a question what the name would be, so there were no surprises for the congregation. Nonetheless the scene was symbolically impressive. Grandpa Proctor was still in the prime of manhood, his thick blond hair testifying of his British lineage while his smooth Bear Lake drawl revealed his second generation absorption into America.

With Harriet's tears, she expressed a silent prayer of longing that this boy would someday be allowed to speak the words of a father's blessing. The blue eyes and the blonde hair of the babe seemed to guarantee he would match Everett's handsome frame. She knew it was her challenge to win him into the goodness of his father.

Among the many who stood later to testify, the most penetrating words were from Harriet's father, Olie Nielsen. Though he was a visitor, it was his right, even his obligation to speak of Zion, of how people in St. Charles had loved and supported Harriet, of how he and his companion, Harriet's parents, felt anguish at her parting from them, yet trusted in her neighbors' good caring. He stood and testified that the Saints were one people, being sifted in their Maker's hand, sent here to build Zion. And this was how it was done, by pulling together and building a righteous generation. This was the Lord's way.

Brother Nielsen spoke of the unknown future that Harriet and little Everett faced, with many on the sidelines wanting to steady the ark, but that it was Harriet's right to set the path for the two of them. He knew of Harriet's values, of her determination, of the rightness of the plan Christ had set. Somehow they would follow their Savior's plan. All else would fall into place. Everett Junior was in good hands.

Harriet was moved deeply by her father's words. She could feel the tops of her ears turning red, even burning with tension. She read through his motive to express so much trust in her that she could find her needed confidence. She thought of standing to speak herself. Having so recently been a teenager, she was reticent because she knew how she would look to her peers with the tears running down her cheeks. But she could not stop the tears, so she wept for her husband, for her parents too far away, for the farm, for pain still within her, for a baby who had no father to romp with him.

After the meeting Harriet and the babe could hardly rise from the hand-carved bench in the St. Charles chapel. The whole congregation wanted to see the child, to touch Harriet's hand, to express intentions of support. The uncles and aunts wanted to greet one another. The young cousins tried to avoid the family kisses, when they saw the aunts were intent on delivering them. The extended family was a clan of huggers. Even Uncle Abe Nielsen came from Ovid for the occasion. Now he would likely spin a yarn. By the time Junior was grown he would already be a legend—the offspring from a dry farm.

Finally, when Harriet was about to leave, she felt a hand on her shoulder from the pew behind her. Turning, she saw the weather-worn face of Bishop Clark and his white forehead, shaded by years of wearing a hat. His many seasons of plowing and harrowing and harvesting into the sun branded him as a Bear Laker. "Harriet, I was wondering if I could get you to take a ride with my wife and me to Laketown on Wednesday?"

"To the south end?"

"Yes, I've got some business at the Kane ranch down in Round Valley, and my wife wants to visit Abigail Allen. I thought that would give us a chance to have that chat we talked about."

Harriet realized that this was not an invitation, but more of a gentle command.

"Well, what time did you have in mind?" she replied, not wanting to offend his authority.

"Oh let the sun get to its warming angle. I'll come for you after the chores are done, about ten."

Harriet actually felt a relief that the time had finally come. "I'll be ready. Is there anything you want me to bring?"

"Yes, bring the baby, and just you."

Whoever he might be, Harriet had always respected her bishop. Bishops were just somebody everyone needed. It didn't matter his name or occupation so much as the fact that everyone respected his office. It was nice when the bishop was popular as a person. But if he was a little slow or spoke broken English, everyone just pitched in and made him a folk hero anyway.

Bishop Clark was exceptionally considerate, always dependable, and very much in charge. Fortunately, he was also a seasoned Solomon. His boys were ranching on their own, making him right proud of them. His two daughters were also well-launched, one into marriage, the other as a beginning school teacher in Randolph, the county seat of the Utah half of Bear Lake Valley. The bishop's own farm was exemplary. And he was always gentle—gentle with people's confidence and gentle in making requests. So it was not hard for Harriet to trust this man who bore the mantle as Judge in Israel. It was just that she had grown up knowing Bishop Jensen in Ovid. If Jensen had been in St. Charles, she would have gone to him every week of the past winter.

Bishop Clark awed her a bit. She eyed him closely each Sunday, his blue serge tightly buttoned to hold back his portly paunch. She attended to his presiding, but she couldn't always tell how he felt about her personal hopes and dreams. She let him initiate the conversation. She found he sometimes had something in mind that she hadn't put there. It was confusing. She had never really wanted to challenge him by demanding an explanation, yet she was apprehensive. Because she did not have a clear plan for herself, she wasn't about to dig in her heels and insist on making her own decision. At least a Laketown journey with the Clarks wouldn't be like going away to college.

With both determination and desperation mixed together, Harriet slid into the back seat of the Clark's Chevrolet on Wednesday morning. It was far from new, but it had the smell of scrubbed carpets and waxed leather. She was impressed when the bishop opened the car's back door for her and waited to close it until the baby was safely settled in Harriet's lap. As he walked around the shining hood to his side, she rehearsed what she planned to say.

It was hard to explain how she felt because each idea countered the previous one. She was determined to stay on Everett's farm. But she had no idea how to get the spring plowing done. The winter wheat on the low foothills looked right encouraging. If it ripened to harvest in September, Everett's experiment would be a major victory. The whole county would be talking about it. But she would have to hire the next plowing and seeding out. And with what money? There were monthly payments to make on the mortgage. Everett's father and her own dad had been making them on alternate months.

How long could that last? There was the logging to do and the cattle to drive to the west range. Who would do that? Of only one thing was she certain. She did not want to abandon Everett's dream.

All this flashed by in the time it took the bishop to get into the driver's seat in front beside his wife Violet.

As they rumbled down the country road, there was little talking. Driving on the gravel lane was too noisy for convenient conversation. When they finally reached the town, the Clarks began chatting about St. Charles, how it was bursting into spring. The apple trees were in bloom. The bleak hillsides were ablaze with the color of alpine wildflowers. Sister Clark pointed out that the bees had been industrious among Indian paintbrush, sego lily, purple thistle and especially the large serviceberry and chokecherry bushes. Harriet had not noticed; she was caught up in decisions, not scenery.

The Bishop turned south when he reached Highway 89, grateful for the oiled surface. In six miles they came to Fish Haven. Violet Clark joked about the big dance pavilion there where the dances were anything but square. In fact, Fish Haven was hardly a real town. The swimming resort with its huge bathhouse for changing clothes attracted the tourists—some of them not so desirable. There were even cabins for overnight guests and three stores packed with souvenirs. Bishop Clark remarked, "No, it isn't a real Mormon town, yet there is a ward meetinghouse and a four-room school right next to each other." Harriet thought, *Maybe it was St. Charles' loyalty that made Fish Haven somewhat suspect.* Violet continued, "Certainly the looseness at those dances, where 'outsiders' and beer were frequently mixing, set a tone for Fish Haven."

Between Fish Haven and Garden City the bishop cleared his throat. Without asking Harriet what her plans were, he simply plunged ahead, beginning with a very formal, "Sister Proctor." He paused. "I ran across an opportunity for you recently."

Harriet could hear something hesitant in his voice. "An opportunity?"

"Yes, an opportunity for employment."

"For employment?"

"Yes, employment. Now I can understand that you feel duty-bound, even downright desirous of staying on Everett's experiment. This employment has the disadvantage of taking you away from his land. But I thought you ought to at least consider it as sort of an alternative to help you decide about the farm."

Garden City whizzed by with its turnoff into Logan Canyon. The acres of raspberry bushes on Hildt's land looked as impressive as ever, trimmed and ready for the new season. The whiteness of the new wooden church, which gave this junction importance, attracted their glance as they drove on.

"What kind of employment?"

"Well now, I hope you won't dismiss it out of hand until you see it."

Things were becoming clear now. This ride was not to be just a chat. She knew it all along. Harriet could see that Bishop Clark had been doing some homework. He had probably already talked things through with her parents and the Proctors. She wasn't sure that she liked them all planning things for her. She worried that she was being put out to sea like an indentured servant.

"There is a situation down in Round Valley that calls for immediate attention by a resourceful woman," Bishop Clark continued.

Harriet thought, *That's where I come in. He's at least being complimentary. But I still suspect he's trying to talk me into something other than staying on the farm.*

"You know where the Kane Ranch is, in Round Valley?"

"Actually I don't, though everyone has heard of it. For some reason I've only seen Round Valley from a distance when we came to Ideal Beach. Look there." Harriet pointed toward the lake. "There is the octagon roller skating rink we came to as kids. It was great to roller skate. We felt like Bear Lake was pretty fancy to have a skating rink. Not many towns have that. Then when we sat on the beach to eat baloney sandwiches with mustard, Dad told us the stories of the fur trappers who held their rendezvous in 1827 on that very spot. He said the Indians came by the thousands to meet the fur company supply train and the trappers. There was a week of gambling and trading and drinking and shooting, he said."

Finding that her words tumbled out faster and faster, Harriet knew she was nervous, like a child going to the doctor's office. Somehow she was trying to forestall the possibility that she might be moving to Round Valley. "At night the Indians would disappear into Round Valley. When the trappers would climb the overlook next to Ideal Beach, they could look into Round Valley and see what seemed to be thousands of campfires burning," she continued. She took a breath and tried to slow down. "I guess ever since then I've almost been scared of Round Valley," she admitted. It seems so isolated, so silent, so full of those Indian legends. "I didn't realize that it was even inhabited, except that I knew Kane's ranch was there. Somehow I didn't put them together."

Harriet looked at the Bishop. She might have stamped her feet, announcing that she wouldn't move from Everett's land. But she had tried that stomp all winter and there were lots of reasons why it wasn't very convincing. She was gradually discovering that her youth was past. This decision was what adulthood was about.

She had often heard adults talk about "sorrows." The word seemed to characterize old folks. There had been so many setbacks in Bear Lake Valley, so many frosts that killed crops, so many cattle that died on the range and so many young people who moved away, both physically and spiritually. There had been so many bodies to put into frozen graves that they had begun to dig rows of pits in the fall to avoid the necessity of shoveling into frozen ground when winter took the weak. It was the adults who did the sorrowing. The dances and swimming and roller skating and hiking and going to school, the courting—the fun things—happened to youth.

Harriet realized she had now passed her youth. Impetuosity wouldn't work. Everett Junior had to be in steady hands. Her father's blessing that day in October and his testimony last Sunday told her she could do it but she would have to abandon dependency. She would have to get going, using the lineage that throbbed in her veins. So she might consider the Bishop's "opportunity."

After they passed Ideal Beach, the highway dropped down to the shoreline and ambled around to the lake's south end. The shore was so full of pebbles and rocks, one couldn't easily lie there in a swimming suit. The water was clean, so clean that the rocks were visible twenty feet out from the road. But this year the lake was low because of a two-year drought. The ground water sources were receding.

When the highway turned east, it meandered through meadows where budding cattails and tall sunflowers mingled with swamp grass. Five minutes more brought them to the Laketown Junction. To go on straight would lead to the steep canyon that lifts one to the plateau toward Randolph, the center for ranching. A right turn brought them in four blocks to the Laketown Mercantile, the town center.

Somehow the two-story stone structure, the town's most imposing commercial spot, got misplaced a block. By rights it should have been either across from the high school or opposite the ward meetinghouse. As it was there were two centers, the Merc, and the ten-acre town square hosting high school and the church. Brother Brigham would have been pleased with their planning, but might have chided them about the separation of the two areas. At least he would have been glad that Laketown was a right proper Mormon town, checkerboard square with broad streets doubling as firebreaks, with irrigation ditches on each side.

Both the Merc and the meetinghouse were built with red sandstone that stood unadorned as the pioneer craftsmen had cut and laid them. No stucco, no frills. The Merc was shaped like a two-story shoebox standing on end while the meetinghouse had an oval design with a towered entrance attached to the thin end at the east. The church occupied the northeast corner of a ten-acre city square. The rest remained free for a baseball diamond and meadow and school. One structure broke the meadow's vista, a tiny Relief Society Hall. It had been used to store wheat in pioneer times and as late as World War I when the wheat was used for the war effort. Finally it had been converted into a women's midweek meeting place. Harriet was examining all of this closely, wondering if this might be her new world.

The bishop answered her questions enthusiastically. "Oh my yes, there are people in Round Valley. Meadowville is in Round Valley too."

Harriet was still uncertain. "Meadowville? Somehow I didn't realize it was in Round Valley," replied Harriet. "I just thought of Meadowville as somewhere south. How big is it?"

"Well it's a rip snortin' place. I'm sure there are at least six families."

Six families. Harriet wondered. "And I suppose this opportunity you speak of is in that overpopulated community."

"How did you guess? Yes it is. As I was saying, Kane's ranch is west of Laketown, right in the center of Round Valley, with lands going south to the top of the foothills. Between the ranch and Meadowville there is the land homesteaded by Lyman Ridges. Grandpa Ridges has had a stroke and is in a bad way. He is essentially an invalid. His daughter, Carmen, was taking care of him. She married a young cowboy from Wyoming, Hank Grossberg, who came through here each summer driving cattle. Lyman tried to discourage that marriage because Hank's free-ranging lifestyle was not what he envisioned for a Mormon girl. But when the courtship grew more intense, he finally compromised. If they would be married by the bishop, instead of running off, he would offer Hank a job with rights of inheritance for staying in Round Valley."

Bishop Clark waited, then slowly continued. "I'm telling you all this because Carmen died last winter, leaving Hank with a two-year-old son and her invalid father to care for. I'm told that Hank is looking for a housekeeper to cook meals for the family, tend his son and care for Grandpa Ridges so he can work his fields and tend his cattle. Abigail Allen says you can sleep at her home in Laketown."

Abigail Allen had been the guest storyteller at one of Harriet's first quilting bees. How well Harriet remembered the sister's recital of winter pregnancy and birth. She might have much to share with Abigail. Harriet surprised herself by rather quickly saying yes, she would take up the project the bishop had felt would be good for her. She smiled. Suddenly her life was on a different course.

Chapter 4
Hank

For five months Harriet drove Hank's pickup truck the four miles from Abigail Allen's Laketown home each evening and the four miles back to the Round Valley home early in the mornings, arriving early enough to begin preparing breakfast by 6:30 a.m.

On many counts it was awkward. She was sponging off Abigail, who wouldn't accept any rent. One time she got stuck in the snow and had to trudge a mile back, carrying Everett, Jr., to get Hank to bring his tractor and pull the pickup back onto the road.

Nonetheless that was their arrangement—days at the farm and nights with Abigail in town.

For Harriet those nights at Abigail's were like going to college. After Junior was asleep they spent an hour or two talking. It was a seminar on folklore as the matriarch told the stories of the valley. She loved mentoring Harriet and she went about it with determination. She knew that residing in Laketown could be miserable or exciting for the young woman, depending upon their evening sessions. There was so much she intended to transfer to Harriet, to assimilate her into the south end of Bear Lake Valley. The whole heritage of Laketown flowed through Abigail's genealogy and she had a clear vision that Harriet was to stay.

To begin with, there was quilting. Since Abigail had met Harriet through quilting in St. Charles, and knew the therapeutic value of that handwork, she kept a quilt up in her living room so they could spend a half hour some evenings stitching and doing the talking Abigail had in mind. The stitches somehow pulled the ideas out into the open.

Harriet often asked good questions. "Tell me about growing up in Laketown. I know what it was like in Ovid. I want to know if it was different here."

"I don't think the difference was the location; it was time," Abigail responded. "I'm thirty years older than you are, Harriet. We grew up before money, it seemed. And there weren't any conveniences. For example we had to drive the animals down to the lake every day to water them. The CCC dam hadn't been built and the big ditches weren't in."

"Life must have been much harder than now."

Abigail smiled. "We kids didn't know it. We thought we were living in the Garden of Eden."

"Didn't you suffer like the pioneers?"

"Oh my, no. We had all the food we needed, but we raised it all—vegetables, potatoes, corn. And we put it all in a pit with ice cut from the lake and straw to cover it. The cold storage lasted until August when we had fresh vegetables again."

"What about meat?"

"We killed pigs and put them in brine for salted pork. There was plenty of beef and we had scores of chickens and eggs, of course. We just had to work to get it all. But we thought that was fun."

Harriet still had questions. "What did you use for flour?"

"That was the great thing about Laketown. There was a grist mill here. People came from many towns to grind their flour and put it in sacks. We took the shorts home to feed to the chickens. We didn't know we were poor because all this was done without cash. The only time in our life when we kids needed money was at Ideal Beach."

Harriet knew about Ideal Beach. "Did you go there for boating?"

"Well yes, row boating, but the big thing was dances. Of course we girls didn't have to pay but the boys had to pay fifty cents."

"I thought you held your dances at the church. We did in Ovid."

"That's right. We had dances there every Wednesday and Saturday. But they were rather mild. You know they were for the entire family—moms, dads, babies and us kids. And the music was always the same—Joe Hansen chorded on the piano and Boots Riddle did the same on the guitar while Mable Sparks did the fiddling. That's what made it, the fiddle." Abigail was still smiling at her memories.

"So where did Ideal Beach come in? We didn't have a resort in Ovid."

"Well, you know that dance floor has springs underneath it. That place is special. It was for dates. And they had a real orchestra, often from Evanston. In the summer there were lots of people there, but mostly dates. Lots of tourists. It was a cash matter and just for adults, not families. Between the church and the resorts I think we danced almost three times a week."

Harriet pictured her mother at the dances. "My mother still has some of those dance booklets. Did you use those?"

Abigail nodded. "Oh, you bet. Your date would take the little pencil attached to it and write himself in for the first and last dance and maybe some in the middle. Before the first fifteen minutes you'd have your book all full and the evening went by in a whirl."

"I've heard that some of the boys went outside and drank beer."

"Well, it happened. But if they didn't behave, if they were causing any ruckus, the chaperones would escort them out and wouldn't let them back in. We were pretty straight and quite proud of it. It was a lot more fun that way. Our parents never worried about us going there."

Abigail was presenting a fairly rosy picture, Harriet thought. "So are you telling me that you and your friends liked growing up in Bear Lake?"

"We loved it. There was so much fun. For example, winters were the best time. People got out their horse-drawn sleds with runners on the back. We kids would jump on the runners and hang on for a great ride."

"Didn't the drivers shoo you off?"

"Gosh no. They had been kids. They wanted us to enjoy life."

"What about the cold?"

"For us kids it didn't seem to matter. The cold is what made ice. And ice was fun. We went to the lake and skated all over. Sometimes there were big parties on the lake. They dragged cedar trees behind the sleighs clear across the lake from the Rayburn Ranch and built big bonfires on the ice. We cooked hot dogs and sang songs."

"Didn't that melt the ice?"

Abigail laughed. Her gray curls shook, and she had a pleasant way of pursing her lips. "I don't know! Anyway, we never fell in." She grinned. "The ice was pretty thick."

"You seem to be telling me that no one was suffering, that life was easy."

"Well these are just childhood memories. Now I know that there were lots of difficulties. But we kids didn't realize it. Our parents loved us and wanted us to have a great time. They made us think that working with them was fun. Most of all we had great friends to be with and we did the dancing and singing and fun together. Now I realize that the parents kept a close eye on it. But it all fit in. We lived together. I can't imagine a better childhood."

As well as her childhood tales, there were recipes Abigail wanted to perpetuate, and particularly local stories about the town's families, the farms and the general ethic of pulling together. She hoped that Harriet would absorb it all and then she could approach a more important topic: "How's Hank coming along, dear?"

Harriet was taken back. She was not sure what Abigail meant. But she wanted to say something. "He seems satisfied with me as his housekeeper."

Abigail didn't mince words. "I mean are you civilizing him? You know that's our job. Table manners, reading books, clean language, good shaving, haircuts, brushing teeth, saying prayers—that's our role—to set a standard."

Harriet thought she could answer that, so she listed a few things on her fingers. "Let's see—his table manners must have come from Wyoming cattle herding." Abigail had a twinkle in her eye. "He's not much for reading, his language is improving, shaving and haircuts and tooth brushing were accomplished before I arrived. The surprise is prayers. He takes his turn as though it is natural to him." She saw Abigail nod. "I suspect that is Carmen's legacy. But I walk cautiously. I'm not anxious to get fired."

"What do you mean fired?" Abigail mock-scolded her. "You are a lot more than an employee. And yes, I agree, Carmen was a very positive influence on the Wyoming drifter."

"I'm household help," Harriet wanted to emphasize.

But Abigail was pressing for something more. "Not on your life. You are a genuine Saint. Your genes and your spirit are central in Meadowville. His plan has come back to life."

Harriet could feel herself sitting up straighter. "Now wait a minute. I just took employment there. Nothing more."

Abigail lowered her face so that Harriet could not see the smirk on it. "That's a fine fiction, dear. We'll both live with it for a while."

"For a while?"

"Yep."

Harriet didn't want to press that one. Even she had limits.

One day Hank interceded. Though he was not a man of many words, he knew this would be a major discussion. He entered Harriet's arena only after considerable planning.

He approached her hesitantly after the supper dishes were cleared. "Harriet, it just doesn't make sense—you driving to Laketown to stay overnight."

She wasn't quite sure if Hank was talking as her boss or as her suitor. She tried to act like this was the first time the idea had come to her: "That's how we set it up."

Hank was a large man, with a heavy head of sandy-colored hair. He hid his face from her by pulling his fingers through his mop of hair. It didn't seem to be an activity to perform at the dinner table, but he was gathering strength, she knew. "I know, but things are different now."

Harriet tried to look surprised. She remembered their agreement clearly. "It made sense then and the same reasons fit now."

Hank steadied his hands on the table. With surprise she saw that they were shaking. "No they don't," he said. And after a moment, "We need you at night, too."

Harriet felt a chill at the top of her head. *Now what does he mean by that?*

But words didn't come to her. Harriet was not sure she wanted to know more. But she let him fumble for words. "When Peter is sick, he wants you, not me. And when he is well, he still wants you."

It was an admission that had probably been hard for him to make. Harriet sensed this. "You're there with him at night. You can horse around with him. You ought to tussle each night together—father and son," she replied.

Hank was sober. "I can't do it as well as you do," he said quietly. Then he brightened slightly. "And what's more, Grandpa wants you near too."

Harriet was stumped. Well, he had admitted the young and the aged needed her. But what about Hank? She hadn't been hired for night work, but after five months she knew this was not just a day job. In fact it wasn't just a job. It was family and she was fast becoming its mother.

When she hadn't replied, Hank continued. "We need you here at night, almost as much as during the day."

There it was again—double meanings, she thought.

She dodged by saying, "Hank, Peter needs you to put him to bed; you should read to him and tell stories. I can do it. But he needs a dad to be big in his life."

"Maybe so," replied Hank, "but I'm no good at it. He and I fit while chopping and stacking wood. He rides the tractor with me. That's man's work." He cast a glance around the room nervously, then returned to his gaze. "I'm telling you that we'd be better off if you slept here at night and you would get a lot more rest without tripping back and forth to Allen's."

Harriet knew at this point that he was going to push her to the end of the argument. So she might as well take it up. "That may be true, but it isn't right for two unmarried people to be sleeping in the same house. It isn't right and I can't even consider it. It is not a matter of what people would think or say. It is just not right." When she finished her speech, she waited for a moment, wondering what he would say. The room grew silent and breathless.

"Okay," said Hank. "Then I have a proposition." The chill in her head grabbed another inch of her scalp. And then she had to laugh silently. "I will move out and you move in," he finally said. He looked so proud of his solution.

Shaken, Harriet tried to maintain her composure. "So . . ." she hesitated, "Does that mean you will ride the truck to town at night and come back in the mornings? That doesn't accomplish anything."

Hank shook his head. "No, it doesn't mean I'll drive to town. I'll sleep in the bunkhouse just like I was hired help. Some farms have seasonal hired help. I was one such a guy for years. It's proper even if you don't think grandpa is a sufficient chaperone. I can be a camper again."

Harriet had not seen that one coming and was caught off guard. So after consulting Abigail, Harriet allowed herself to give in.

At first, Harriet was fully occupied with the two boys and grandpa, and cooking and washing and everything else. She began to see herself suddenly becoming like her mother who got up early every day and started in on an endless list of domestic chores. She seemed to have not a minute to think about anything else.

But her growing role did not trouble her. Unlike some girls in her high school class, she was not put off by her mother's occupation with domestic matters. Some of her friends openly decried that kind of life. They boasted that they would escape such a harness; some did by leaving the valley and belting themselves to a factory or a traveling salesman. That didn't seem to be much of a graduation. No, Harriet had always accepted the fact that she too would be living in a kitchen and on a farm and in a town right here in Bear Lake country.

But she would never have guessed she would be acquitting herself in her situation. It was so unorthodox. Here she was taking care of four males and she was only related to one of them. She was living in the same house with them. What surprised her is that she did indeed have time to reflect. The more she did, the more puzzling it became.

She felt life on a farm was just fine—the smell of animals and of growing things, the open sky, the wind and the range. She even liked farm equipment, the odor of oil. These had captivated her since girlhood—the sights and smells of the land. She and her dad, Olie Nielsen, had been buddies in the barns, on the tractors, and alongside the haystacks. Never a tomboy, she knew she was a girl. But that hadn't kept her from the alfalfa and hay and the barn and the cows. She had never resented any of that.

Living in Laketown was pretty much the same as living in Ovid, especially because the lake was nearby.

That kind of reflecting settled her mind instead of upsetting it.

The strange component of the puzzle was Hank.

He was surprising her. Initially she was delighted that the two of them were so different. That had made the situation seem safe. He would just be her employer. Then her reflections surprised her. She couldn't ignore him. She was bound to be pleasant with him. And he never presumed to be her boss. But her thinking about him uncovered something she had missed. He reminded her of Ovid's detached orphans who grew up and spent their life roaming. Driving cattle to the Montana mines or being freight teamsters satisfied them in their teens and twenties. They seldom settled down until their middle years, and when they did, they never quite bought into village life. Once they found a niche, it somehow took a good while for them to gain acceptance in community celebrations and then to finally become "churched."

Hank was not a Dane who was kept at arm's length, but he was a second generation German (they called them "Krauts" in Wyoming). Harriet surprised herself that she was becoming comfortable with second generation immigrants. Those two uncles she had known earlier, who had never seemed quite civilized, had eventually married. Now she could see for the first time that their wives had probably not been "strange" to live with them.

She was amazed to realize that Hank could be trusted, even if he was not a "square." She had known only men who were classified as "straight," conformists who could be fun, lots of fun, despite their somewhat formal exterior. In addition, they were dependable. She was offended by the town beer drinkers who poked fun at people such as Everett and her dad and Ovid's Bishop Jensen for their straight talk and obedient behavior. But now she was spending part of every day with one such unorthodox interloper, an unchurched, unrefined outsider.

Hank has been decent with me right from the first day. I am amazed to admit that I can trust Hank even if he is not a square like my Everett or like our neighbor Woodruff Kane. I know that Hank will go on cattle drives; he lives for them. I'm not comfortable about that, but I don't intend to go with him to be his chaperone. I am not willing to mix with the kind of fellows who are on that drive. Hank will be gone only two weeks a year and I hope he will come back decent. The other fifty weeks he seems a lot like those Danish orphans who gradually backed into our village life.

Harriet was surprised at her reflections. *It gets things figured out.* Maybe that's what her mother had been doing, and Harriet had missed it. *Mom wasn't just doing the laundry or the cooking. She was mapping out her life. That's why she was usually calm. She had figured it out and I just didn't realize it until now.*

On December 20, 1936, Harriet married Hank Grossberg. The ceremony took place at the Ridges/Grossberg home in Round Valley. Bishop Jaggi from Laketown married them "until death do you part." From their home in Ovid, Harriet's mother and father, the Nielsens, followed a snowplow the length of the valley from Ovid to be first through the drifts that morning. All of Meadowville was there, packed into the parlor of the Ridges' two-story saltbox homestead, the product of Grandpa Ridges' own hands. The women of the Laketown Relief Society prepared cakes and hot cider for the guests.

The courtship had been so different. They had never really had a date. But they knew each other—so much more than first-time couples do. She knew how he chewed his food, how he split logs, how he built fires in the stove. She knew he didn't do dishes or make beds or sweep floors. All of those later realizations, those mundane things most couples never discover until marriage, she knew without any of the artificial behaviors of going on a date. She knew exactly what daily life with Hank would be like. What she didn't know was how to edge him her way—into Zion. She would not allow him to pull her out. But could she bring him in?

Nearly everyone was pleased with this new arrangement. Hank quipped that he was glad to move back in from the bunkhouse where he had been sleeping since Harriet gave up on driving back and forth to Abigail Allen's in Laketown five months ago. Grandpa Ridges had taken to Harriet right off because she could almost understand his throaty squeak, the remnant of his speech. Bishop Clark's plan to get her here had been taken right over by Bishop Jaggi, whose ward boundaries encompassed Round Valley and who had long laid plans to ensnare Hank into the gospel net. He had employed Carmen's goodness initially and would try again through Harriet. The two boys would certainly benefit from this consolidation. And the Ridges' half section would continue to thrive.

Harriet's acreage in St. Charles would have to be sold. But it had barely been a starter farm anyway. Harriet would find good use for the profit, if there was any. Likely she would bank it toward Everett Junior's future mission.

Harriet was reconciled.

Unlike Everett, Hank was not at ease with words. His was a calm, if not even reticent demeanor. Listening and observing were his tools, which sometimes baffled Harriet, who could not always know what he was thinking.

But she had come to love Hank Grossberg, a surprise to her. He would never replace Everett. That was best because of the Temple. Everett was Harriet's for eternity and Hank was for mortality.

Mortality fit Hank best anyway. Even at thirty-five, Hank already had parched and cracked skin from living in the open—open air, open roaming and open lifestyle. He was brown from the sun which beat on him every day in a land where it seldom rained. He was brown from his old behavior of living halfway between heaven and hell. But he wouldn't pull Harriet his way. He respected her determination to join with the Saints in their attempt to be virtuous. He knew that Harriet would draw his son Peter in her direction. That was all right, if she could convince the self-willed strapling.

Hank liked his beer. He could cuss with the best of ranch hands. He was a free spirit from the northern Wyoming mountains who was hardly attached to family or town. He had somehow got stuck to Round Valley like a fly to flypaper. He had married land and couldn't tear himself away. It was good land and he knew it. He had never been able to get Lyman Ridges' land into the profit column very far, and he was often haunted with the prospect of failure, but every day he rose before daybreak to crystal clear air, to pristine mountains adjacent to his own land, to the sun he could have all to himself. Deer and elk were his daily companions, and the West Range was in full view, awaiting nearly limitless cattle herds.

Hank was hooked on Round Valley. He was at his best on horseback, driving cattle on that range, keeping the war going against the coyote, dreaming of someday killing a bear. Everybody said that Old Ephraim, killed in 1923 by Frank Clark, was the last grizzly of the Wasatch, but Hank was still looking, still hoping. Just fifty yards from the Ridges' property line Hank could enter U. S. Forest Service domain. There he could look for twenty miles without the invasion of a building. That was a satisfactory compromise for Hank Grossberg. He would farm, though his heart was not in it, if he could ride that range regularly.

That was the convenient compromise for Harriet—a companion who would settle for her in this life only, who didn't trouble his head about eternity and who had learned to co-exist with Mormons without becoming one. She would be in Bear Lake Valley with her people, fighting the elements for mere survival and living the communal style of Zion.

That was her life—the Gospel and God's people. That would shape Everett Junior in the mold of his father. And maybe Peter too.

It was a convenient compromise to start with. Secretly both of them hoped it would become more, and feared it might be less.

Harriet had surprised herself. She was married to a "Gentile" as Mormons called those outside the fold. Not in the farthest reaches of her mind had that ever been a possibility. But here she was and with the approbation of two bishops, all of Round Valley and even those in Laketown who had kept up on the situation at the Ridges. The only holdouts were her in-laws, the Proctors, who feared their grandson was being distanced from them, that his new father was questionable. Their anxiety was that Harriet would drift Hank's way, pulling Everett Junior out of the priesthood possibilities they all envisioned for him.

How strange it was. First she had married with the highest aspirations. Everything had gone according to the plan. But the plan stopped short. Now she was going into a marriage that wasn't even second choice. Hank wasn't a backsliding Jack-Mormon who could be reactivated. Nor was this a quick "have to" wedding that could be reabsorbed into the community with time. This was an outright, willful union outside the faith, but it had been marginally acceptable because it could only be "until death do you part." That was understood by all, though no one mentioned it. Even the Proctors felt some comfort in that. As a result, what would have been considered rebellious if Harriet had married as Carmen had, now ended up with the approval of almost everyone. It was a union of outside and inside.

The next day was Sunday. Hank went to church with Harriet, each of them carrying a child. During the meeting the new Grossbergs, who had been the object of merriment yesterday, stirred more sober thought among the Laketown ward members. *His being here means that he will likely allow Harriet to continue coming*, thought Sister Williams, the chorister who depended on Harriet's alto. *With our good behavior he will let those two boys be baptized at eight, become deacons at twelve and maybe even missionaries at twenty*, thought Woodruff Kane, Hank's Round Valley neighbor. Member of the High Council and one of the few men in the ward who saw a handsome return from farming, Woodruff intended to keep the friendly pressure on Hank to get him baptized. It was for his own good in this life and the next that Woodruff willed it.

Hank is not really an outsider, mused Brother Erwin, the Merc storekeeper, *even if he only comes to church on his two wedding days. Sure he chews and spits at times. But he pays his bills. And above all, he stays here, here in the valley that many deride. He's right among us every day.* Brother Nielsen, the ward scoutmaster, worried that Hank could be done in by the Thompson brothers who gambled and told filthy tales about Mormon polygamy on their occasional visits here. He hoped that eventually Peter and Junior would be in his scout troop. But he knew that Hank's hunting and roundup buddies were often full of whiskey. That was not what scout camps offered.

Bishop Jaggi wondered mostly what was going on in Hank's head: *Does he see us as a bunch of old-fashioned Puritans? Can he overlook our faults all gathered here in this room, mixed with aspirations none of us can fully perfect? Can he see beyond conformity, beyond authoritarianism? Does he see only what we do or can he have some interest in our vision? We will have to work on him from several levels—as heir to that land, as neighbor, as customer, as father, as husband, as tiller of soil, as range rider. We are all those, too, and we need each other. Actually,* thought the Bishop, *Hank may do more for us as an outsider, to cause us to be what we claim, than if he were comfortably inside.*

Harriet tried to see the meeting from Hank's eyes. Though he sat quietly, he was not absorbed in the proceedings. Somehow he knew to bow his head for the prayers, but he did not close his eyes. He recognized Bishop Jaggi, sitting on the stand with a counselor on either side. The bishop made several announcements—that a youth outing was scheduled for Friday evening, that a temple excursion would be held on Saturday in Logan, and that the choir would practice at 4:00 p.m. each Sunday.

When the chorister stood up to lead the congregation in the next song and the young men arose at a side table, Hank acknowledged that the sacrament ritual would be next. As the twelve-year-old deacons walked throughout the congregation bringing small pieces of bread and tiny cups of water to the members, he did not partake. No one seemed concerned at his abstention.

The first of the three speakers was a fifteen-year-old girl he did not know. Her words lasted three minutes, taken from a paper she placed on the pulpit and had obviously written herself. The two men who followed took about fifteen minutes each, farmers from Laketown he knew from years of contacts at the Merc. Their words were homespun, including folksy stories interspersed with scripture readings. Hank seemed to miss the point of either talk. Certainly neither moved him. He almost dozed but fortunately avoided it. To his credit.

During another song by the congregation, Harriet held the songbook for him to see. He didn't even hum—music was not one of his talents. After the closing prayer was pronounced by the storekeeper, Fred Irwin, the organist then played a festive piece, its tones growing in power to cover the sound of the members arising, leaving the chapel and bidding one another good-bye.

As they got into the truck, shuffling the two boys in also, neither Hank nor Harriet commented on the service. Both were treading lightly, but it was clear that this church thing was part and parcel of the marriage, exciting or not. Harriet feared that Hank had missed much of the meaning. For example, the youth speaker was a young person pretty much on her own. Her parents had dropped her off at the church as they headed to Evanston for their monthly shopping spree, not even coming in long enough to hear their daughter. They were nominal members but did not participate, not even to the extent of helping her prepare the talk. Despite this, she was doing well so far. Her friends and teachers were her support. Harriet knew she would have some challenges ahead and took every opportunity to encourage her.

The first farmer to speak, George Hail, had also achieved a victory. He had an intense fear of speaking in public, a leftover from his general lack of confidence. Harriet knew George had anguished about his talk, but she was proud of him because he spoke without making any excuses or even hinting at his anxieties. The last farmer frustrated Harriet. It seemed he had not taken the assignment very seriously, appearing to have given it only a cursory thought that morning. He was comfortable and confident, but said nothing of significance when he could have used his talents to cap the meeting with sound insights. These realities Hank likely missed, Harriet mused.

The ride home to Round Valley drove in the stakes of permanency. By this marriage both Hank and Harriet had tied themselves to this land, to Bear Lake Valley. They would never get it out of their sinew now.

Hank was nothing without this land. As a roving cowhand in Wyoming he would never have earned the money to buy a farm. His marriage to Carmen had not been bribery to get this land, far from it. Initially Grandpa Ridges did everything he could to keep Hank from it, to persuade his daughter to reject Hank's marriage proposal. When he saw that he was driving them away, he reversed directions and it was effective. Hank and Carmen took up his offer to live on the farm well before Grandpa had his stroke. It was a fortunate negotiation and a landfall for Hank. Yet he saw it only as a base so he could be a free man, free to ride the range, free from debt.

Carmen's sudden, if not mysterious, death threatened Hank's lifestyle. Now the marriage to Harriet freed him from obligations to nurse Grandpa and from raising his own son alone. She had been very delicate on the issue of religion, brewing his coffee for him, but staunchly abstaining herself. In recent months he suddenly stopped chewing tobacco, unannounced. *What was the meaning of this?* Harriet queried. *It was a great relief. But does it have any further meaning?* She assumed that there would be a blessing at each meal and that Hank would take his normal turn. Fortunately he had learned a convenient wording from Carmen. He didn't balk about that.

It appeared that Hank was doing some thinking also. Everyone nearby saw that Harriet filled in the gaps in his life. Surely he realized that. Also he couldn't miss that Harriet had a keen wit and was so lively. She sometimes bounced and sparkled and Hank returned the smiles. But what people and especially Grandpa noticed most was that Harriet was not intimidated by Hank despite his decade plus of seniority. Yes, all this was giving Hank pause. *I could see from the first day that she wasn't going to let me boss her and I can live with that as long as she doesn't preach or nag.*

There hadn't been any formal negotiations prior to the wedding. Both assumed that life would go on much as it had been going for eight months. Naturally Hank would join Harriet in her bed. Both of them looked forward to that. But the rest would be the same. Harriet would care for Grandpa and the two boys, manage the kitchen and the money. Hank would farm and ranch and ask for help when necessary with watering turns and milking. He would prepare the ground for a garden; she and the boys would weed it, raise a substantial portion of their food—melons, squash, peas, corn, apples, berries—while tending chickens and pigs. With all that activity they could avoid the larger issues.

It was understood that Harriet would try to stimulate Hank's interest in religion and Hank would enjoy sidestepping the net.

Each had reasons to keep some private latitude. Hank didn't ask Harriet about what it meant to be sealed to Everett. She had a hunch he already knew but since he hadn't thought much about eternity, it was comfortable to settle for "until death do you part." On the other hand, Harriet tried to make a generous inquiry into his feelings about Carmen: "Don't you think there ought to be a picture of Carmen hanging in the house?"

"That would confuse the boys as much as posting one of Everett," he replied.

She could tell he didn't want to talk about Carmen, even though Harriet would like to have told Hank about Everett. She wondered why. What had caused Carmen's death? Had she gone into premature labor? Or was it something else? They had come to an uneasy truce on those subjects. Nearing the farm after church, Harriet realized they hadn't exchanged a word. They had both been alone in their private worlds. The boys were somehow subdued too. She chose not to ask Hank's reaction to the meeting. It was his first since his marriage to Carmen. She had her own hunches about how he felt. But she didn't want to box him in. She suspected he really feared becoming absorbed into the ward more than anything else.

Hank had run away from home and school after the eighth grade. That had been possible in wide-open Wyoming. He drifted—riding freight trains, catching farmhand jobs and eventually becoming a cattle driver. His own family disintegrated with the joblessness of the 1930s Depression. He never contacted them. When he settled into the Ridges family, he brought the bravado of the range and the decisiveness of a survivor. But underneath he felt the absence of education and heritage. As he sat in that Laketown Ward, he may have seen that he was not tied by blood to anyone but his son, a son who already linked himself primarily to Harriet who had been like a mother to him for nearly a year now.

Hank was obviously unaccustomed to lay religion. What little he knew of churches was that its business had been a matter for pastors and priests. But in Laketown and all of Bear Lake Valley and even the whole Great Basin, Mormons did their own preaching, their own praying, their own teaching, their own blessing. It didn't take two minutes for Hank to figure out that if he let Bishop Jaggi baptize him, he would be expected to tithe, to abandon tobacco and alcohol, to teach, to preach—to become a Saint!

Harriet surmised that the real issue was not tobacco, maybe not even tithing, but the preaching. She recognized a long habit of running from feelings of inadequacy, a feeling that others were smarter, or more glib, or more given to faith. After all, they were descendants of pioneers. Hank was just one step away from hobos and horse thieves. It was a lot easier to stay an outsider.

Chapter 5
Winter

Grandpa Ridges was often hard to live with. He could barely talk, his throat damaged by an illness which nearly destroyed his vocal chords. That, along with his general weakness, was intensely frustrating to him, but it did not change his mindset that he must work. Now, five years since his stroke, he had continued to deteriorate instead of recover, yet he still clung to life tenaciously, rising early as if the milking and irrigating still depended upon him. Though he could barely make it to the kitchen rocking chair, he was usually there by the time Harriet started the water boiling each morning. He would doze off, sometimes not saying a word for the entire day, unless it was his turn to bless the food. Then he insisted on attempting to pray, though no one could understand a word except "amen." On other days he strained his voice to squeak partial words of direction, hovering over Harriet, as if he had to approve each of her actions in the kitchen or with the children.

The main reason for Harriet's initial employment was to free Hank so he could work away from the house, in the adjacent fields. The boys were too young to be out on the land so she needed to divert them to other activities, to restrain them from the natural desire to roam. There was too much danger, or at least too much possible mischief, out in the fields. They could upset the irrigation system or get tangled up with porcupines. So Harriet needed to be more clever than they were to help them think they were enjoying the tasks she set them by the house—stacking wood, weeding the garden, playing with wood blocks and sticks, building forts. All this she had to engineer while she was cooking and cleaning. Having to make an accounting of these activities to Grandpa was most disconcerting, especially because his only communication was through gestures and squeaks.

Harriet understood that Lyman Ridges was still having a tough time letting go of his land. Three generations of Ridges wrested it so laboriously from the sagebrush and serviceberry. Grandpa personally knew every resident who had lived here since the Indians made way for them. He even remembered some of the colorful natives who included the valley in their annual nomadic wanderings. It was obviously hard for Grandpa to be transferring his land to Hank, a man he hardly knew, a man with no gospel conviction in his heart. But it was the only way he could figure to get the land into the hands of Carmen's son.

As time passed, his familial ties to his grandson became so strong that he grew determined to leave Peter not only with the land, but every shred of his knowledge, every detail of his past he could possibly recall.

These were trying times for Harriet. She felt obligated to listen to Grandpa's grunts and squeaks all during the years she cared for the two boys and then through her pregnancy and the birth of another son, Alan.

As all three boys grew, as Peter became six, then Everett four, and Alan two, Grandpa continued to look at the brood of boys surrounding him as though his charge to every one of them was to leave the only thing he had left to offer—his stories of the past. It was up to Harriet to help make sense of the stories, and to keep the boys quiet.

Today was going to be especially challenging. Grandpa clearly seemed to have something on his mind. More than usual, he seemed to be in his storytelling mood. It must have been because the snow had been keeping all three boys in the house this Christmas holiday.

Peter played with Lincoln Logs and an erector set around Grandpa's chair, gifts he had received many years ago from his mother Carmen. He placated his brothers, Everett Jr. and Alan, with cast-off pieces.

Grandpa signaled and wheezed at Harriet after breakfast. She was to forget her other priorities and sit by him to translate his raspy syllables into words and sentences the boys could understand.

Harriet was not happy with the timing. She never had been. Every week there were bread and cakes to bake, clothes to wash and mend, Relief Society lessons to prepare, ailing ward members to visit, eggs to be gathered, lunches to cook, floors to scrub. And today was to be their weekly trip into Laketown for Relief Society meeting and a long list of shopping and visits.

Every Wednesday Harriet bundled the boys in the Ford and drove to the meeting.

Abigail Allen often took them to her house for a couple of hours so Harriet could stay with the presidency, make visits to the sick or discouraged women, shop at the Merc and then come by to pick up the boys again. Abigail called it her "adopted Grandma program." She loved the boys as though they were three of her own. Hers had long ago grown into men.

Despite the pressure to be in Laketown by 10:00 a.m., Harriet knew she would only fuel a crisis with all of them cooped in the warm kitchen if she didn't take time to interrupt her scurrying for another retrospective look at what life used to be.

Hoping she could limit this one to half an hour, Harriet ordered the boys to sit on the kitchen floor near Grandpa's chair and "listen up."

Pointing to the Frigidaire, Grandpa moved his one good arm as if he were sawing. He rasped the word "ice." Harriet caught the drift and began an interpolation, enlarging at will.

"Grandpa is telling us that one day when he was your age, maybe a little older, he was home for Christmas vacation from school."

Grandpa nodded in agreement.

"His father, Peter's Great-grandpa Ridges, took him to gather ice."

Another nod.

"They didn't have refrigerators in those days. In fact we still have the old ice box in the barn that used to be in this kitchen," she explained.

The boys remembered the box with the funny door clamps. They had used the box as a prison for field mice. One time they had forgotten to let one out for two days and when they finally opened the door, it was dead.

Grandpa was saying "sleigh" and "horse."

"So they hitched the team to a sleigh," Harriet continued to translate. "Really it was just a haying flatbed with runners instead of wheels. The horses pulled them on the unbroken snow up the draw to the reservoir. It's covered up now by the new one we use today. In those days the reservoir was only half as big because the dam was not really strong. It was built by hand before the days of bulldozers. Sometimes it was washed out after a thunderstorm."

Following his cramped speech, she told the boys all she could understand. "So they reached the dam. Great-grandpa took ropes and tied one around this grandpa, who was just a boy. The other end was tied to his waist. Then he tied another rope from his waist to a bush. At first they broke the ice with a crowbar, and sometimes little Lyman would tiptoe to the edge and spike floating ice with an ice pick or break off thin pieces while his dad held the ropes.

"Never once did Lyman fall in, because Great-grandpa would tap on the ice first so he could tell how strong it was, whether or not it would hold a small boy.

"They gathered dozens of chunks of ice and broke them with a cement pick so they could hoist them onto the flatbed. Then they came back, carrying the ice into the old cellar on the north side of the bunkhouse. There they laid the chunks in a bay of sawdust and straw, covering them on all sides, top and bottom. Next came the tarp, which they wrapped over the whole mound. And guess what that was all for?"

The boys yelled: "To make ice cream". . . "To make ice suckers". . . "To slide on."

Grandpa laughed with glee. She had produced just the right effect, making his story come alive. Now he started again, pre-empting Harriet's intention to get on with her kitchen work. He rasped "ice" and "lake." Harriet paused, not sure, then Lyman signaled a digging action. Harriet still hesitated. He held his hands in a circle, then did the digging again and whispered "fi—fi—fi" but couldn't make "sh."

As a girl Harriet had seen the men cut the ice in the lake to fish, so she described it to the boys just as she remembered it from her experience at the lake's north end.

"The men bored holes in the ice and lowered small nets with bait and pulled out dozens of cisco, small fish about five inches long. The cisco made a run from the bottom of the lake to the ice every year for just a few days in mid-winter. There was no limit. They caught them by the hundreds."

Grandpa stammered and shook his head. "No." No, that was not what he meant. He held his hands parallel about two feet apart, indicating big fish. He wheezed, "Id—Id—Be—Be." Puzzled, Harriet listened closely to the swallowed whispers that followed his half syllables and grasped, "Ideal Beach."

"So boys," she continued, "Grandpa says they went to the lake at Ideal Beach when the resort was closed for the winter. Down by the marina, where you went swimming last summer, they could walk out on the ice."

Grandpa's eyes twinkled; he clearly liked Harriet's improvisations.

"There they had to walk out to get to the deep part where the big fish were swimming under the ice. If it was their first trip on the surface, they would tap on the ice after each step. They kept close watch for any cracks. Grandpa had learned to recognize the colors of the thick ice and thin ice and cracks. But they had big problems if the ice was covered with snow."

Grandpa laughed, coughing. He could tell Harriet was distorting his story to caution the boys, who might venture on the lake's ice someday for themselves. *Actually*, Grandpa thought, *Bear Lakers rode on the ice with impunity*. They drove sleighs and even autos callously on the frozen surface. He started the shoveling action again.

"So when they got way out from shore," Harriet continued, "where the lake would be about fifty feet deep, they chose a likely spot and chipped a hole in the ice. That was quite a job. They didn't want to cause a big crack, so they had to break little pieces with a hatchet. Eventually they bored several holes through which they could lower a fishing line. Grandpa says that some days he caught ten-pound brown trout as big as his arm from his elbow to his finger tip. He says they are easier to catch from the ice than from a boat in the summer. Maybe they are hungrier and go for the bait."

Grandpa seemed satisfied.

Harriet jumped with a sudden shock.

It was nine o'clock and Hank had not come in for breakfast. She paled. He had always been back by 8:00, at the latest, 8:30.

Not wanting to alarm the family, Harriet put on her heavy parka, fashioned from two sheepskins with the thick wool turned inside.

"I'm going to the barn to check on Dad, boys. You can play for another fifteen minutes. Then we'd better be abundling to get to Laketown," she urged.

Once outside, she closed the kitchen door tightly, looking around the screened-in back porch. Her fur-lined boots were in their place beside the entry. She had rarely gone to the outbuildings since Peter turned five. He had made most of the egg-gathering trips. That's how he filled his piggy bank— a nickel per dozen. She kept looking. The boots might not do if she had to tramp into the snow. Then she spied Hank's fishing waders. They were a mite big, but would be better if she had to make new trails between the buildings.

She headed right for the barn.

The tractor and the car were there.

That's funny. He's not gone anywhere. Yet he's not come in.

"Dad, Dad!" she called. Somehow she had fallen into the easy word which bound all the children together.

No answer.

She peered along the horizon, a full circle.

She walked, slipping the tall boots into the narrow path worn in the two-foot snowfall. The air was sharp. Her nostrils stuck together with each inhale, separating with exhales.

She reached the pigpen.

"Dad, Dad!"

The pigs snorted.

Shaking her head, she turned toward the sheep stall. The trail was so beaten in this old snow that she could not tell if he had been this way.

No sign of him there.

Standing in the trail she looked again in all directions. A mist rose from the snow as the sun began to warm the freezing air. The clear sky and the snow's white sheen glared in her eyes. It was hard to look into that brilliance. But by squinting she believed she could see a human form if it broke the surface where the air and snow met.

But there was no movement anywhere.

Picking up her pace, she trudged on to the baled haystack.

"Dad. Hank, where are you?"

The snow absorbed her shouts, muffling their contact with the outbuildings. Her heart began to pound.

Maybe I should call someone, she thought.

He wouldn't have walked over to Kane's. He would have driven.

Woodruff Kane, he would come in a minute, if I sent Peter for him.

She backtracked to the chicken coop. Swinging the gate inward, she hollered, "Dad, Dad, Hank."

The hens scattered, wings fluttering, feet scratching, dust stirring.

No Hank.

Harriet was really distressed now. She started to tremble. She looked north toward the reservoir. *Could he have hiked out to the dam?* she wondered. *What in the world for?* She thought of turning toward the reservoir, but it would take a half hour to get there. *What if he weren't there and I wasted the time instead of finding where he really is? What if he is hurt, and freezing?*

She pushed more ultimate questions from her mind.

Then it clicked. *If he went to the dam, I could see his trail. Why didn't I think of that first? I'm not being sensible.*

She scurried to the back fence and peered beyond.

But there was no trail of footsteps. She whirled about, folded her arms and lectured herself. *He's got to be here. He's not answering. So he's not hearing me. Something is clearly wrong. He didn't just forget to tell me where he went. Stay calm. You're the only one who can make the difference. I've looked in the barn, the coop, the pen. Where else?*

"The cellars," she called out.

She stomped back toward the bunkhouse, cutting through the crusted snow instead of taking the long way on the trails. As she reached the adjacent root cellar and ice cellar, she could see that the snow covering both doors was unbroken. It had been a week since the last storm. The snow indicated that no one had lifted the inclined covers. *Then the only other place is the bunkhouse.* "Dad," she yelled again, raising her voice to a scream.

She swung the door open.

The dark, damp interior swallowed the chamber against the snow's glare but there on the floor she could see the bottoms of two boots. On the floor was snow, tracks before the door, evidence that he had dragged himself into the shack.

She gasped a short, tense gulp.

She crossed into the darkness cautiously. He was lying face down on the wooden floor. Hesitating to touch his body, she yelled, "Hank!"

No motion.

She knelt slowly, touching his back lightly. He groaned, a grunting groan. She felt his hand, then his head. The skin was warm. She exhaled, blowing air between her lips, relieved.

Now she must think. Stop. Think.

How do I move him? Should I move him? He can't stay here. Another half-hour and he will start freezing. Maybe he has frostbite already. What has happened? I can't feel any blood. Maybe he is bleeding internally. I've got to get him to the house. Maybe I could drag him. But it's two hundred yards. I'd injure him. How about the car? I could get him to the house in the car if I could get him in the vehicle.

Hank's machines usually worked. The car started. She edged it to within one foot of the bunkhouse, having pushed the door of the shack open flush to the building, piling snow in its track. She crawled over to the right car door, reached over the seat and opened the back door into the opening. She then swung back to her own door, climbed out, ran around the front of the car and sidestepped between the car and the bunkhouse, inhaling and tiptoeing to squeeze between them.

Propping Hank's shoulders onto her lap, she hefted him teeter-totter-like, onto his knees. He began to moan, then to speak in half-words. She pivoted him on his knees, putting his arm around her shoulder and then inched him the four feet toward the car, balancing him like a heavy box, from one corner to the other. She put his arms on the back seat, then lifted one knee onto the car floor.

He sensed her actions and half crawled onto the back seat. She stuffed his boots in and pressed the back door shut. Squeezing back through the opening, she ran around the hood, jumped in the car and drove right to the back porch steps.

The boys helped her get him into the bedroom. Now he lay there, eyes opening and closing. He had coughed up some brownish chunks of blood.

The doctor could not get there until afternoon, he told her on the phone at Kane Ranch. He'd have to come from Paris and then only following a trip in the opposite direction to the hospital in Montpelier to deliver a baby. He didn't want Hank moved. He promised to get there today. He was confident from Harriet's description of what must have been a fall that it was a concussion. What Hank likely needed was absolute rest, not even moving his head, if possible.

Woodruff was on his way too, but as she suspected, he was in Laketown. It might take an hour, his wife said. He would bring Bishop Jaggi and consecrated oil for a blessing.

She knelt beside the bed, holding his hand. He seemed not aware, breathing steadily, restfully.

She talked to him tenderly.

She talked to God more firmly.

Chapter 6
Spring

By May, Hank's vigor returned in full force, having eluded him a full month following his January slip on the ice. His slight skull fracture from the fall had not brought on unconsciousness immediately so he had crawled into the bunkhouse to recover, ignoring the possibility that he might freeze. He had only intended to lie down for a few minutes to halt the dizziness, but it had been a near fatal choice. Harriet had earned parity that day; they were full partners now. He could have felt uneasy about becoming dependent on Harriet but realized that would have been silly. He felt fortunate to be alive and told her so.

"You realize that I would have died had you and the boys left for Laketown without checking on me."

"It's funny how it hit me all of a sudden. It was just as though a bolt of lightning struck me. Of course your breakfast was still on the stove so I wouldn't have left—unless I thought you were in town. At any rate, I'm as grateful as you are. We've got too much that is good ahead of us. These boys are priceless. They need a dad. I learned that once before."

With his recovery almost complete, Hank returned to his farm routine. The Herefords were to be driven up to the range today and Hank announced that Peter was old enough to make the run. This would be his first venture into manhood and perhaps insurance, should Hank become weary. His son would ride in the same saddle with his dad and would leave his brothers behind, sorely disappointed, impressed that a year or two in age made a huge difference.

Harriet was not all that pleased with Hank's idea of taking Peter along. *There could be a late frost, perhaps even snow, but even worse will be the rough company.* She couldn't read Hank's intentions. *Is he taking Peter to moderate the Thompsons' language, drinking and gambling? That could give Hank an excuse to distance himself from their debauchery. Or is he taking Peter to pull him into the so-called man's world? Is he trying to minimize my impact on his son? Or does he really need Peter's help, considering the effects of Hank's concussion?*

Though Harriet felt anxious, she did not want to accuse Hank, to insinuate, to imply her possessiveness of his son. She felt boxed in.

There was no stopping Peter now that he had reached age seven. From the moment Hank hinted of the possibility, Peter was totally motivated. Strong-willed to the core, the boy lived for independence. His egg-gathering began to have one purpose—to accumulate money that would transform itself into a .22 caliber rifle. It had never occurred to him that he had an obligation to help with the family. Harriet's chores seemed unimportant now. He resisted any of her attempts to civilize him. He was totally focused on the jack rabbits and sage hens he felt were awaiting his new skills. When his dad mentioned the cattle drive this spring, he forgot the jack rabbits and decided he could start with coyotes. Why not even take on a bear? He could just bound over adolescence right into manhood.

There was no talking to Peter. It didn't matter that he was only in the second grade. His talk was that of a man. He was going to spring camp, to eat grub from an open fire, to sleep in a bed roll, to watch out for rattlers, to shout commands at cattle and to conquer the mountains.

Peter Grossberg was his dad's boy.

The morning was thick with dew as Harriet said a hesitant good-bye to them. Heading out, they beat the sun by two hours. Peter held the reins but he learned the hard way to keep the steed on the trail, away from the bushes. When he forgot, the leaves of the underbrush obligingly drenched both riders' legs with heavy dew.

The route was south to the Laketown-Meadowville Junction. But instead of following the road toward Laketown, they turned right on the gravel extension that cut the foothills into two spheres of influence. The south part was the Kane domain, the north supported the rest of the Meadowville families. They would observe these boundaries and head the cattle northwest once the road got them into the high country.

As long as there was road to lead the herd, they could drive the animals easily. There was time for grazing, for roaming. Hank gave Peter free rein; he could shout and kick and lash a bit of whip as though he were setting the direction. The road would keep them together. All that was needed was a little energy from the rear.

It was mid-May. The cattle had been restless for a month, pawing at the confinement of their slushy, stinky corrals. They knew that the sun was warm, beckoning them from the boring menu of hay and alfalfa to the lush aroma of distant sweetgrass. Hank felt it too; his head reeled from the smell of pine. He left his mount, letting Peter herd while he hiked parallel to the road. He could keep an overview and feel the quaking asp in his face. Their buds had just broken; the starts were still but dwarfs of the round leaves they would become. Patches of snow snuggled in the undergrowth, melting and trickling like hillside springlets.

It would be the long drive today—at least ten miles. He chuckled that Peter had pretended to be so tough. They should make at least eight or so tomorrow to the top of Temple Fork Canyon. There the fifty head with the Ridges/Grossberg brand would meet two other herds at the rendezvous point. This year they had agreed on the spot, Old Ephraim's grave, a landmark for the last two decades.

From there they would range southwest until they found Jake, the Shoshone. No one had an idea exactly where that would be. He would just materialize somewhere along the drive. He always had.

Jake was a mystery. For some reason he latched on to the Thompson brothers. As a ranch hand for their father, Jake had seen the brothers grow from birth. Now he was attached to them as a sort of seasonal protector. In the fall he would disappear, return to his people, driving three or four steers with him. In the spring he would find the Thompson herd on the range without instructions.

It wasn't really necessary to have someone stay with the cattle. Most ranchers didn't. Cattle aren't sheep. The cattle could drive off the coyote themselves. The bears were gone. Rattlers didn't faze them—only the horses got skittered by rattlesnakes. The cattle could take care of themselves. Even the calves were usually ready to graze by early June. Nonetheless it was a luxury to have the Indian up there. Jake would move the herd on up to the higher ground once the snows had completely melted on the mountain peaks. That meant none of the three ranchers had to ride up and check on the herd. Hank did it anyway, as a reward for each month of tedium down below. The ranchers talked themselves into believing that they saved as many head as they paid to Jake. And humanely they couldn't stop him from doing what he had done for forty summers. His long, braided hair, his spotted pony, his U.S. Army rifle, his face like the Indian on the nickel—they all seemed to give him permission to use the range—permission that had a legacy much older than the BLM. If he hadn't appeared, they would have continued without him. But when he did, they followed his lead.

Hank's land was the closest to the meeting spot; he could make the drive in two days. The others had been on the trail for a week. Nonetheless he would likely arrive first. So he took his time. He dismounted when they reached the meadows and sent Peter to bring in the stragglers. The animals deserved a few grazing breaks.

The boy hardly needed instructions and the animals barely needed direction. It was a work of mutual consent.

Their steady pace brought ten miles by early evening. Then Peter built the fire, his dad explaining that it had to have plenty of air. The flame had to start low and catch the twigs above. Next came the larger branches, finally the logs. Fundamentals, yes, but new to each novice at a roundup.

They cooked potatoes in the coals, then scooped out the white insides from the charred skins. Hank showed Peter how to warm jerky on a stick like a shish ke-bab. Even raw carrots were sweet to their mountain taste. Then they sucked on taffy Harriet had hidden in their sack.

With the horses tethered and the herd settling near the brook, Hank taught Peter the nuances of a mountain bed. First, he packed loose boughs on the ground. Then over the boughs he put the tarp, followed by blankets folded in three turns. Then another tarp over it all.

The two snuggled in. Hank sensed that Peter wanted to talk about Wyoming cattle drives, but Dad sidestepped it and chose instead to focus on the stars—Orion, Big Dipper, Pegasus, Hercules. He told Peter that the Indians had different names for all of the constellations. Here they were out in Indian country and didn't even know the stars by the Indian description. Instead, the new white settlers used names created by Greek mythology three millennia in the past from lands they would never see. There was really very little communication between Anglos and Indians. Hank had heard that the Natives knew more about the stars than the Anglos did.

"Why don't we know more about the stars?" Peter asked his father. Hank glanced at Peter with pride and began another lengthy answer, when he discovered the boy had fallen asleep, no longer worried about the imponderables of the galaxies.

The next day they accomplished another ten miles by early evening, chose a site and set up camp before the others arrived. Hank laid out his bedroll for a snooze and told Peter to stay on the horse. "Let the herd graze," he advised. "Just keep them together."

He had slipped off to sleep when he was startled by the crash of lumbering hooves in the bushes. He jumped to his feet and grabbed his gun when he heard a bellowing laugh.

Razzle Thompson got a great kick out of that scare. His cattle were coming down the draw. It was good fortune that he was ahead of his stock or they might have trampled Hank.

Razzle was still laughing. "So you've retired have you—given the herd to the young 'un? I suspected you'd be the first of us to give out." Hank grabbed Razzle, wrapping him in a bear hug, squeezing tighter and tighter, his muscular arms checkmating Thompson.

"Okay, Uncle, damn it. I give," squealed Razzle.

They jumped and slapped each other on the back in boyish delight.

The Thompson herd was soon mingling with the Grossberg stock and young Peter came riding up in confusion about what to do.

"So look at who's running the herd nowadays," snorted Razzle.

Peter halted, questioning looks coming from under his oversized cowboy hat.

Looking at his son, Hank laughed proudly. "Well Razzle, I thought I'd get me a right proper cowhand and bring him to straighten up this heathen camp," he grinned.

"Ho—so you want him to learn about the ways of the world do ya? Well you know that I can make a master out of the boy, if you want that I should take him on as an apprentice."

"Nah, that warn't what I had in mind. I jest thought he ought to come up here and smell out the range. I'll do the teachin'."

"Ya mean we're not goin' to initiate this here stripling into the Gentile club?"

"He's a bit too young for that, Razzle."

Peter wasn't sure whether he liked the infamous Razzle Thompson yet, but he could tell the cowboy was trying to have fun at his expense.

"Hey Dad, looks like there's another herd on the way in," Peter responded, pointing to the east ridge about a mile away.

"Okay, son. Let's ride up there and help Zeke bring 'em down," Hank responded. Zeke Thompson was the younger of the two Thompson wildcats. It was he who included Hank in this circle. The two of them had ridden for the same rancher in Wyoming for two years. Zeke enticed Hank to move to the Wasatch, closer to the Thompson habitat.

By dusk all three herds had assembled. The "greetin' and hollerin'" of old time buddies had settled down and they turned to making a first class dutch oven stew.

The supper aside, Razzle built up the fire with large logs intended to burn slowly throughout the night. Then he turned to Peter. "Son, I guess we'd better give you your instructions about how to catch your first bear. You see, it was right here in this clearing that Frank Clark faced down Old Ephraim."

Hank knew that Razzle was the recognized master in telling the Old Ephraim story. When he heard that the gravesite would be this year's rendezvous, the storytelling alone had been almost enough to convince him he should bring Peter along.

"Yes, Razzle, I think Peter's a good candidate to carry on the tradition of this spot," Hank replied. "He's already saving for his first rifle. He just might track down a bear someday. I think he better be initiated in the Frank Clark club." Peter's eyes were widening. He didn't even know what the word "initiation" meant. He could tell though, that the two men, Razzle and Zeke Thompson, were intending to have some fun. He wasn't sure whose side his dad was on. So he refused to retreat to his father's pant leg. He was going to stare them down, to pass this test, whatever it was. The other two men took their cue and settled by the fire.

Razzle crouched on a boulder next to the flickering flames and, holding a long stick for poking in the coals, he began the tale:

"It was in late August of 1923 when Frank Clark, his brother Jared and Bud Shields brought their sheep herds from Malad and made their camp next to the meadow at the foot of this hill."

Looking downhill, Peter could see the last evening sun rays bounce at the lowest possible angle from the marshy puddles onto the luxuriant grasses.

"Frank had driven sheep on the backside of the Wasatch for two decades and much of that time he had seen Old Ephraim's handiwork—the carcasses of sheep the grizzly had killed. He had tracked him, as had others, because the giant bear's trail was easily recognizable, a misshapen front paw, probably from birth. Frank had laid traps at least four times before and had come back to see them lifted out of the wallow. Mind you, Frank had never got a shot close to Old Ephraim, even though he had fired several times."

Peter was fascinated, forgetting to be threatened.

Razzle continued, "Old Ephraim had long been a fair dealer. He had usually lingered on the edge of a herd, then ventured in at night to take only one animal, just for his sustenance. But in the last four years, for some reason, he had changed. Now he was lusting and slashing. He would charge a herd of sheep, sometimes in the daylight, and leave a dozen ewes torn open, not a bite taken from their hides. He had become a killer, just for the lust of killing.

"The gory tale had passed among the whole herding fraternity in southeastern Idaho and northern Utah. Old Ephraim was tried without appearing in court. The jury didn't even deliberate; he had to be taken. It was just a matter of who had the genius to lay a successful trap. Everyone knew Ephraim was a giant; his tracks told that.

"None of the sheepmen were happy with the plan. They had lived comfortably with the grizzly, admitting they were only guests in his territory. They knew the white man was the encroacher, and they respected Ephraim's seniority. After all, this valley wasn't idly called Bear Lake. Old Ephraim's ancestors had long presided in these valleys. Bear Lake Valley was a rich hunting preserve. Both Indians and bears knew it as their favorite summer domain. Now the Mormons had invaded, built fences, turned land into farms, claimed the range for cattle, and even worse, sheep. They transferred its wildness into civilization.

"Some of the hunters could even respect the bear's logic. He had probably felt the sheep and cattle had invaded his preserve unfairly. They came in numbers far too numerous. They had protectors: man. They were overgrazing, destroying the balance. So the rent needed to be hiked; maybe they would go elsewhere. The sheepmen knew Ephraim was right. Nonetheless they reached their verdict: Old Ephraim had to meet his doom."

The campfire was developing a bed of coals and the flames were dying down. Peter felt more comfortable with the storyteller, deciding that Razzle wasn't aiming any danger toward him.

Razzle picked up on the tale. "Frank could tell there was danger when he stopped at Temple Fork, that year of 1923. His horse skittered. The sheep refused to range. Even the dogs whined. They would not settle for the night. It lasted for two days and two nights.

"For some reason Old Ephraim would not take sheep from Frank's herd. But on each of the two nights, he ravaged the other two packs ranging on adjacent hills.

"Knowing Ephraim was there, the three herdsmen began the search. Frank saddled early on the third morning. He rode uphill, due east of the meadow, through a stand of aspen. He straddled a drain of spring water and watched it settle in a patch of willows. Then further down from the trees he saw a massive wallow in the reeds near a huge pine.

"He dismounted, knowing immediately that he must leave no human scent. Pulling a jar from his saddlepack, he rubbed fresh sheep grease on his boots, even the soles. Stepping lightly, he surveyed the setting. The wallow was larger than he had seen for any other bear, which confirmed to him that it was Old Ephraim's. For just a moment he shuddered; he'd discounted the exaggerations he had heard about this grizzly. But he could discount them no more. There was enough water in that wallow to drown a grown man.

"Remounting, Frank rode quietly from the spot, hoping to minimize the harsh evidence. Back at camp he unpacked his trap and gathered other essentials, sheep's blood, gloves, chain.

"It was noon by the time he had laid his trap under the water at the willows. He had been extremely patient with the procedure—re-greasing the boots and the gloves, screwing and setting the clamps cautiously, then pulling the trigger to hair sensitivity and gently unscrewing the clamps. His hands numbed in the cold water as he wound the clamps. Then he gently laid leaves in the water over the trap. Next he dug a trench for the chain and tied it to a fourteen-foot log half submerged in the mud. He buried the chain and replaced the soil, smoothing over the dirt and mixing it with matted leaves. Then came drops of sheep's blood over it all to drive away the human scent. Gentle steps took him away.

"It was his masterpiece.

"That night the animals were nervous again. The sheep sought their shepherd; the dogs slept with their backs against the tent. Clark hugged his rifle.

"The animals slept, though Clark did not," continued Razzle.

"When the sky finally began to grow light, Frank knew Old Ephraim had eluded him. But he waited. Let it be noon again and then he would inspect the trap.

"He took the horse with him so that he would have a quick getaway should he find himself in a dangerous situation. However, he knew he must walk in there, as difficult as it might be. His honor was at stake. He had trapped bear before. He was not going to turn his operation over to anyone else. What he saw sent shivers up his spine. There beside the wallow was the trap. Unsprung!

"Frank Clark stared. It was beyond imagination. No one would believe him. That bear not only scented him out, he had found the trap and had lifted it out without springing the trigger. Had he intended to reverse its bite on his would-be captor? Ephraim was a genius. No doubt about it.

"Half-tempted to ride to the other camps to invite them to come see this sight, Frank decided to go for the bear instead of the legend. Surveying the scene, he realized that Ephraim had abandoned the wallow. About ten feet downstream, the bear had created a smaller resting place. This one would be a greater challenge. It was still in the spring's runoff, but the water was shallow.

"Frank decided not to take the horse back to camp. He felt safety in its high-strung nerves. The horse's keen sense of smell would forewarn him if Ephraim returned.

"He repeated the laborious process, doing nothing different, just more patiently. Then he returned to camp.

"The night seemed long. The animals told him that Old Ephraim was back. They all fought sleep."

Listening, Peter inched along the log he had chosen for a seat. His fierce independence still seemed intact, but he glanced toward his dad.

Razzle resumed. "The stars were brilliant as they were about to surrender to sleep when . . ." Razzle slammed a log against the ground.

Everyone jumped. An actual roar boomed from above Ephraim's grave. It moaned, grunted and then burst into fury.

Peter leaped, rushed for his dad, who grabbed him, pulling him into his chest. The boy shook and stuttered, though he did not cry.

Undeterred, Razzle continued. "Frank rose, grabbed his gun." Razzle began an enactment, butting his rifle into the ground like a cane.

"Clark started up the creek, magnetized by the roars. His World War I rifle had six bullets, his side arm had but one, and he had a knife. He groped in the dark, confused with the roars of the wounded bear, with the sounds which seemed to keep changing direction."

Razzle was almost dancing as he portrayed Frank Clark's plight. The moans and roars from the darkness behind the grave continued their churning tones. Peter's arms and legs were shaking. Even Hank stared with wonder into the darkness of the trees.

"Then Clark realized that he had overshot his mark," Razzle said. "He had allowed the frantic animal to cut him off from his camp. Ephraim was between Clark and the camp. Clark could hear trees cracking, bushes folding.

"The darkness was retreating. Then the bear spied Frank Clark."

Just at that moment a figure lunged from the darkness. Both Peter and his father clung to each other at this surprise. Finally the source of the eerie sounds was unveiled. With a fur-capped head and weathered mountain attire, the old Indian immediately took the part of the bear. Razzle and the aging brave swung their bodies into the act as Razzle continued the tale.

"The hunter was calm, the bear confident. Each stepped forward, one slow step after the other. Frank was so awed that his arm froze. He could not raise his rifle."

Razzle and the Indian eyed each other.

"Finally Frank raised his rifle and shot, one bullet directly at the heart. Old Ephraim did not wince nor whine. He continued forward, looming ten feet high, blanking out the horizon."

The Indian rose to a stately height, raising both arms.

"He was the most awesome animal Clark had ever seen. But Frank was calm. He fired two more rounds directly at the heart.

"No result.

"Now Frank was nervous. He fired his last round from the rifle.

"The bear was not fazed."

The Indian continued his dance, slowly, tauntingly, stepping half steps toward Razzle.

"Frank decided to turn and run, even though the bear was bleeding from the nose and mouth.

"Frank's dog, Jenny, sensed the crisis. She had made her way around to Old Ephraim's hindquarters. She snapped, distracting the bear. Ephraim turned, lifting his left arm to strike at Jenny."

The Indian carried the pantomime to its dramatic height.

"Clark took the advantage, firing his sidearm with split-second timing into the opening behind the bear's ear. The bear whirled back like a spring, stared at Clark, and then sank to its knees as if to strike. Halting for a solid minute, Old Ephraim fell, face down, to the ground."

The Indian sank to the ground, writhing, and then exhaling as if it were his last.

For a long moment there was solemn silence. Then the men leaped to their feet and cheered.

Peter clung to his father. He had not cried.

The old Indian rose, then sat on a log by the fire. He had surprised them all, even Razzle.

It was Razzle's consummate performance. He had not let his friends know that the Indian's eyes had met his from the darkness of the trees. He had just improvised the communications with the old Indian's spirit. Razzle was as surprised as the others, because Jake had never been expressive before. Razzle felt a lump in his throat.

The old man sat on a log and began to stir the fire.

Hank whispered in Peter's ear: "If you get in your bedroll and go to sleep now, I'll let you round up the herd before breakfast."

Peter took the bait, but he dragged his bedding close to the fire, wanting to distance himself from the grave. He intended to keep listening to the bragging and the daring and the tall tales.

In his drowsiness he could see the bottles of whisky making the rounds, one occasionally ending up in the fire. The boisterous laughter kept on its crescendo.

His dad was taking his turn at the drinks.

Chapter 7
Ancestors

Peter, it seemed, was born for adventure. Sometimes it came without warning. More often it had to be created. This morning, back in Laketown, he planned a treasure hunt.

The treasure had not been buried; it had been stashed. Only three people seemed to know about it—Peter, Everett Junior, and obviously, their mom, Harriet.

The route to the hiding place was devious. First of all, they had to get the youngest, Alan, to cooperate involuntarily. At ages ten and twelve, Peter and Everett were experienced in their mother's manners. They knew that to execute their plan, Harriet must be totally preoccupied if they were to fool her. Eight-year-old Alan must mess up the kitchen floor with Lincoln Logs and the bottle caps they outlined the streets with as they built their cities. He must occupy Harriet to the point of total distraction with his humming noises and scooting about the floor, building his forts and railroads. She was always watching out for her brood with her second senses while her hands whirled away at household duties—banging the dough, slapping against the breadboard, rolling it again and then fluffing it into round loaves.

At the moment she was preparing a wedding reception for Mac Adams' daughter Amelia, whose mother had been buried last winter, knowing that if the Relief Society didn't help Mac, the girl would not be sent off properly at all. There was little Harriet could do about the trousseau. That was a matter of years. But a wedding could be pulled off in a month. All of the sisters in the ward would pitch in on the actual wedding day, but in the meantime there were fruitcakes to make for two hundred guests, and fruit dips, and so much more.

The boys' plan was that Harriet must be totally preoccupied. Alan would have to pile strawberry cartons to make the barracks; the lead soldiers would have to guard the gate. The sent-away-for cars, tankers and buses would have to be placed under the reverse-arched legs that so conveniently held up the kitchen table, the table feet elevating the broad-spanned legs just enough to allow the cars to park under their weight. Yes, Alan would have to build his compound all over the kitchen floor, gradually encroaching on Harriet's domain, so she would not miss Peter and Everett, Jr.

And they also knew that as long as Alan thought he was pre-empting the two gunny sacks of cars and bottle caps and strawberry cartons and soldiers without his brothers' permission, his creativity would flow. His designs would become more and more elaborate; he would forget to tag along with them as they got away.

Harriet expected the boys would argue and waste their effort at doing their chores, counting and recounting their chopped wood to determine what the pile was worth or chasing off after squirrels or wrestling with each other until they were hungry. Even if they roamed, they knew enough to be back at their chore when she would announce lunch by striking the sawmill blade that hung from the eaves of the back porch. She would bang with vigor, her forearm extended, her hand grasping the crowbar. She would want to hear their responding yell: "Okay, coming." It would need to sound from the right direction or she would hike to the wood stack and fetch them in with an eye well focused on Hank's expectation. So they had to be back and stacking before the summer sun reached its apex.

Yes, the pursuit of the treasure was like a hair trigger. If Harriet was duly diverted, they could steal away, not into the fields after porcupines but doubling back to the north side of the house, hoisting the ladder Hank had nailed together in ten minutes one day from siding scraps gleaned at Brother Glauser's barnraising. It had to reach just right, under the attic door, leaning level on the trim, soundlessly. It must meet the wall evenly and rest without the slightest wobble on the rocks below.

Peter had to climb first because only he could reach the knob, twist it and, as he ducked, swing the panel open. But Everett Junior refused to wait at the bottom, to hold the ladder as commanded. It was too mysterious to be down there alone. If the door blew shut he might be caught by an all-seeing eye. So he was just far enough below Pete's shoes that he could avoid those swinging legs as his brother's knees levered his torso into the gaping cavern of the attic. Junior needed to see Peter's welcoming hand reach to hoist him through the door and swing it shut behind them.

Then to the ritual.

The morning sun rays pierced the east dormer window, spotlighting the chest with its stickers from the Cunard Line. Fully three feet high and about half as long as a coffin, the huge case seemed to have come from the deep.

Harriet's father, Olie Nielsen, had used it on his mission to Scandinavia. Though it contained no bones of the dead, it held the treasures of their lives.

First they unbound the leather straps, slipping the belt-like binders through the buckles, each hole bouncing the tongue, until they freed the lid of the steamer trunk. The lid squeaked, moan-like, softly to their lift, then sustained itself, tilted backwards in midair when the hinges reached their limit. The wedding dress they expected to see was there, on top, just as they had last replaced it months ago. Prying their hands beneath its folds and raising it as if the bride were still reclining there, they set it beside them on the crossboards that tied the rafters together every foot or so. They turned quickly to the framed picture awaiting them.

There he was. Standing beside Harriet, holding her in his arms, the solemn figure stared at them soberly. The boys were captivated.

Both boys knew full well that this Sunday-suited ramrod man was Everett Proctor Senior. They knew that he lay under the soil of the St. Charles cemetery. Both were there on Decoration Day when Harriet haltingly held Junior tight, grasping his little hand, extending his index finger while tracing the letters E-V-E-R-E-T-T on the gravestone. They knew he was Junior's father, but not Peter's. Yet Junior called Hank father, just as Peter did. It was a puzzle. The question was: Why was the evidence up here in the trunk? Why didn't Harriet and Hank talk about it?

The white-framed picture was of Everett Sr. and Harriet standing in their wedding finery before a stone wall that seemed to be part of a castle. The picture had never hung downstairs in the living room. Instead, there was another picture on the mantle, of Harriet and Hank cutting their wedding cake. It was no mystery that the boys had different fathers. Somehow they both knew that.

There was much more to the treasure. Under the picture was a box they had opened before with big letters spelling "Paris." Of course it referred to Paris, Idaho. The high school was still there; Harriet would break out in the school song whenever the family parked the Ford by the school for Stake Conference at the Paris Tabernacle. The melody seemed somehow disloyal to the boys because they knew they would one day be rivals by attending North Rich High School in Laketown. So they would yell "boo" and Harriet would laugh her belly laugh, her bosom bouncing, and she would shake her fist as if she were offended.

The Paris box contained some papers in Harriet's handwriting and pictures of classmates. Down in the bottom of the box they found her elementary school report cards. How they had enjoyed that discovery the first time. Somehow it just seemed natural to read the teachers' comments: *a good citizen, teacher's best helper.* Teachers surely didn't write things like that about Peter. But then Harriet was a girl. Everett Junior still pleased his teachers, but he was only in the fourth grade. Peter anxiously took out the familiar files, starting a new pile on the closest crossboard. He was mining for new ore.

Junior was the first to see the elongated book they had found last time. He grasped it at each end. Last time he had tried to figure out its meaning—the charts with lines on them. Old handwriting filled each line. The names and ancient dates mystified him: Sylvester Allen, Lancaster, Middlesex, England, June 14, 1714. There were hundreds of such names, thousands. It was another mystery but not very interesting. So he passed it up to Peter, who placed it squarely on top of the Paris school box.

Today they wanted to explore further into the trunk. For example, they wanted to get beyond the pictures that had so often halted their pursuit. These were obviously the "pioneers" that Sister Johnson had told Peter about in Sunday School—when he was listening. They had to be pioneers, even though there were no covered wagons in the pictures. No Indians either. But the men had beards. That meant they were pioneers. Peter informed Junior: "These are the pioneers. I know. Sister Johnson told us the whole story. This one here is probably Brigham Young."

The people looked so funny, men in suits, their beards flowing down to their neckties. The women had braided hair wound in bobs on the backs of their heads. Their long dresses looked all the same. Most of the portraits were neatly mounted on grey cardboard, encased in an oval trimline, and the photographer's name was embossed near the bottom. The boys' favorite pictures were the perplexing ones: one bearded man sat in the center with several adult women and dozens of children around them. There were sometimes fifty people in a photograph. Surely it was some kind of family reunion, they thought. This was part of the mystery—who belonged to who? Were these Junior's ancestors or Peter's, or both?

Next to the box of pictures was Harriet's white-covered "Treasures of Truth" book, a binder at least three inches thick. Everett thought it must be about the size of Joseph Smith's gold plates. Peter hefted it out, dumping it in Junior's lap as though it bored him. It would occupy Junior while Peter continued to dig.

Junior leafed through the familiar pages, past the certificates and the pictures of Grandma Proctor holding a baby. Soon he came to a scene of Harriet as a child at her baptism. Dressed in white, she and Grandpa Proctor were standing somewhere on the shore of Bear Lake. He couldn't tell where, but he recognized the low, dry mountains in the background. It had to be Bear Lake.

Peter had found something new—a thin notebook of lined pages with only the first third used. The meticulously inked words were old but as clear as if they had been printed in a hand-cranked press, he thought. The first page got his attention:

> *The Diary of Justin Nielsen*
> *Written while in the Penitentiary*

Though Peter's reading was not his best school subject, he was more than motivated to find out who Justin Nielsen had killed or what bank he had robbed. And why the evidence was here in the attic? It began:

> *June 10 I was arrested by Captain Greeman on a warrant sworn by a man named Rench by which I was charged with breaking the Edmunds Law, living with more than one wife.*

"What was the Edmunds Law?" Peter wondered.

> *July 20. I was called to plead to my indictment with fifteen others all for cohabitation.*
> *The clerk: Mr. Nielsen what is your plea?*
> *Mr. Nielsen: Guilty.*
> *Judge Zane: Do you want any time or are you ready to receive sentence?*
> *Mr. Nielsen: I am ready.*
> *Judge Zane: Have you any promise to make as to the future?*
> *Mr. Nielsen: None. I have a family of eighteen which depend upon me for support. I could not conscientiously make any promise.*
> *Judge Zane: You are to be imprisoned in the Penitentiary for six months and pay a fine of $300 and cost, and rest committed until cost and fine are paid.*

That didn't sound like a bank robbery. And there was no blood. Peter turned the page.

> *September 1. Took my first lesson in bookkeeping and arithmetic. The cost is one dollar per month per scholar. The teacher is*

our fellow inmate Brother Rudger Clawson. This lesson comes at 10:30 a.m. every weekday morning.

September 7 Sunday. The day is spent in reading. No card playing or other plays are indulged in by the Brethren on this day. At 2:30 p.m. three bells was the calling of all prisoners to assemble in the dining hall for religious service. Andrew Jensen of the Fourteenth Ward did the preaching. He took the theme, 'Judge ye not, that ye be not judged.' Singing by the Penitentiary Choir. At 6 p.m. an entertainment was given in hall no. 3 which was very fine considering the place.

September 8. News arrived that President Cleveland said that no extreme measures should be taken in the enforcement of the Edmunds-Tucker Bill. Also news arrived that on election today in Brigham City the test oath was already administered to all voters, and Latter Day Saints as a general rule are ready to take it.

Perplexed, Peter closed the notebook, wanting to ask Harriet what it was all about, but knowing that the question would "blow their cover."

Junior pulled at Peter's sleeve. "What's this?" he demanded, pressing the big white book into Peter's lap. Junior was pointing to several pages of his mother's handwriting. He was openly jealous of Peter's reading skill. He could make it out himself but the handwriting discouraged him. The title was straightforward: "Faith-Promoting Stories in our Family." Down at the bottom of the page were the words: "Golden Gleaner Award Entry 1930."

In a low whisper Peter read: "My grandmother told me this story during one of the many times I sat with her and asked her to tell me stories. She said the grasshoppers came to Salt Lake Valley shortly after the arrival of the pioneers. They were eating all of their crops. Then seagulls flew in and ate the grasshoppers.

"One summer shortly after the arrival of my grandmother's family to Laketown, the surrounding area was plagued with hordes of grasshoppers that were ruining all of their crops. Times were very bad and about all they had to survive on was what they could grow. A crop failure would have meant starvation for many of the residents of Laketown. After much prayer and fasting a miracle happened. As they were about to give up, a strong north wind started to blow, and in just a short time all of the grasshoppers had been blown into the lake.

"My grandmother went on to relate that after the grasshoppers had all drowned, the wind changed directions and blew the dead grasshoppers back to the south shore of the lake. She said they were piled several feet deep all along the shore line."

"Gosh Peter, do you think that really happened right here at the south end?" Everett Jr. asked.

"'Course it did. I seen grasshoppers as thick as flies at the dump sometimes," Peter answered him. "But I don't know about the wind. It's comin' up and down all the time. That's not a miracle. That's just wind. Bear Lake is windy. All the time."

"Keep reading Peter. These stories are better than Grandpa's."

Peter leafed to another selection: "While living in Round Valley, Uncle John herded cattle up south of the valley. He had a small cabin that he and his family lived in during the summer months. The cabin was located on a spot known as Jacob's Meadow, which is about three miles south of Round Valley. This incident took place in the fall of the year after the cattle had been brought down from the higher pastures. It seems that he had to move the family cook stove from their home in the valley up to their summer cabin each spring and back to their home in the fall. Well, the day he wanted to bring the stove back to the valley there was no one around to assist him so he hooked the team up to the wagon and headed out to do the job himself.

"As he was attempting to load the heavy stove himself with little success, an old man appeared out of nowhere—a man he had never seen before—who offered to assist him in loading the stove. Uncle John accepted the offer, and soon the stove was successfully loaded on the wagon. As he turned to thank the man for his much needed help, he was nowhere to be found. He had disappeared as fast as he had appeared. Uncle John swears it was one of the Three Nephites who had helped him."

"Peter, what does he mean, one of the three Nephites?"

"Sister Johnson believes in them. She tell us all kinds of miracle stories. She loves them. And she usually cries. I can't stand 'em."

"But Peter, this really happened. Ma's Uncle John said he saw the man."

"Humpf."

"Peter, here's a new one. Look, it is written on different paper and it's about your dad."

Peter took the paper out and read it almost against his will:

"After dinner Hank had gone up to the combine to grease his machine and tractor. I stayed down to the house with the three little boys and canned peaches. After I got the peaches in the boiler I was supposed to fill the truck with gas and go up to the field. I was filling the tank but had only put in three or four gallons when I got this feeling that I mustn't finish filling that gas tank. I felt that up there something was wrong. So I let another gallon or so go in, but I kept feeling, *'No, I've got to go. I have to get up there. There's something wrong.'*

"The closer I got up into the field, the more urgent this feeling became. I got up there and pulled alongside the combine, jumped out and ran around to the back of the truck. I called his name. Then I called 'Dad.' I could hear him respond, kind of choked. He said softly, 'Now don't get excited. I'm caught under this platform below the combine. I can hardly breathe. I want you to get up onto the tractor and do exactly what I tell you. Don't—whatever you do—don't touch that lever. (It was the hydraulic lift on this platform that raised and lowered it.) If you do, it will release the pressure and it will come right down.'

"I got up on the combine and he told me what to do, step by step. He cautioned me again, 'Whatever you do, don't touch that little lever.' I put the clutch in, put it into gear. I turned the key on, and that thing would not start. I tried and tried. I didn't know what to do. I was saying a silent prayer all the time. He said, 'Well, we'll have to move it by the power of the battery.' He told me what to do. I put it in gear and let the clutch out. When everything was set he said, 'Turn the key.' I did and by the power of the battery it would go 'uh-uh-uh.' And it moved. He got out and burst into tears and said, 'Now I know that prayers are answered.'

"Now, you know what that taught me? It taught me that when people pray and somebody else is involved, the other person has got to be in tune so that when you have that prompting like I had, to get up there, you have to be in tune to receive that message. Otherwise he could have been gone. He would have gradually choked to death, because the platform was slowly slipping."

Peter was already at the bottom of the trunk. He had removed everything and still there was nothing about Carmen Hodges Grossberg. Why? There were two dead people in their lives, two graves to visit on Decoration Day— Junior's father and Peter's mother. But up here in the attic only Harriet and Everett Senior were in evidence. Where were the treasures about his mother? In Peter's memory there were some faint glimpses—of times when they rolled on the floor together, of playing tag and running through the house after each other. But the big memory was of his mom lying in bed sick for week after week. And then she was gone. He wished so much for a trunk with her artifacts, with her as the main character. Everett was lucky to have a treasure box, even if his dad was gone.

Chapter 8
Peter

Sometimes Harriet felt that Peter was just irreverent by nature.

For Harriet, Hank simply seemed to be a challenge—his living on the edge of civilization occasionally. But she knew his soul was growing. Peter on the other hand was basically a schemer. His boyhood was an increasing test of wills with Harriet, escalating each season as he became ever more creative in testing the limits of the whole community. Peter reveled in the Bear Lake tradition of pranks, like the day when he and the Kane boys spread Limburger cheese on the church door handle. Not that Peter was the instigator, but he knowingly tittered in the chapel as their elders sniffed, looking for the source of the smell while finding nothing.

Round Valley folks were accustomed to a good time, even to such occasional pranks. So the next time at the ward dance when Bishop Jaggi caught Peter and brought him by the ear to the recreation hall from the outside darkness, Harriet was not really alarmed. Neither was the bishop. After all, she had been caught by the same trick when she was a ten-year-old giggly girl walking along the sidewalk near her hometown ward house.

Those evening parties, for a missionary farewell or a Relief Society bazaar or a holiday dance, were a town highlight. Everyone came, active or inactive, religious or skeptical. It was rare for anyone to stay away. But it was boring sometimes—especially for the kids who were too young to dance, too active for old folks' talk, too anxious to eat but too early to get served. So they spilled out onto the town square surrounding the ward house, chased each other, threw rocks in the irrigation ditches, even fished for toads and frogs.

The old rhubarb leaf trick had caught her once too; she fell for the scare. It looked like a demon or at least a crawly creature, sliming across her path in the shadows as she and her girlfriends strolled around the square. They had screamed and run, only to turn back and see the boys hooting and whooping as they replaced their huge rhubarb leaf, snatching back its string toward their hiding place. That Peter was continuing the tradition was no surprise. Ordained deacon or not, it was clear that his thirteen years had absorbed all the tricks the valley had to offer.

The parents' usual method of containment was simply to keep their offspring working long hours. This preventative generally kept the youngsters in tow except on holidays. Hank was agreeable to this prescription too, but their boys were still too young to hire out for full ranch-hand status. Peter was simply early in his independence. His dad couldn't help but snicker when Peter outwitted the system at church or at home. After all, Hank was once a bucking colt himself. But the least snicker is probably what kept Peter going.

Most of Peter's escapades were innocent enough, so Hank didn't share Harriet's next concern when she discovered that Peter had led his brothers in the ice pick conspiracy. It was mid-July when she found the instrument, quite by accident. She'd gone to the tool shed on a normal errand, to sharpen knives. And there, above the door joist, on a ledge in the shadows where she always hid the key to the tool box (so the boys wouldn't cart the tools out to their haunts), her probing hand knocked off the ice pick. She jumped, half out of fright, half out of danger as the falling prong stuck in the floorboard, the handle vibrating with a twang, an inch from her foot.

Yanking the pick out of the wood, she wondered why Hank would be so foolish as to misplace the instrument. Then, as she ground each of the three blades on the whetstone, circling rhythmically, pressing lightly, she let her mind wander. Like a daydream, it started just naturally with the ice pick. Then the reality came to her. She halted, making the connection. The ice! It had been shrinking faster this summer than last.

Setting the knife down abruptly, Harriet marched outside to the cellar lid. Grabbing the leather tongue Hank had nailed to the door where the knob used to be, she hoisted the cover, opening it like a coffin, revealing the descending step ladder into the vegetable pit. As she stepped down into the dampness, Harriet placed the bracing board that lay in its place just beside the opening, almost by habit. Satisfied that it would hold the lid at a safe tilting angle, she surveyed the pit, its six-by-six-by-six cavern.

Harriet lifted the moist gunny sacks which covered each crate. The last of the carrots, the potatoes, the rutabagas were still there. She was proud of both the yield from last year and how carefully she had paced their use. They would last just right until the garden furnished the next crop in a few weeks. Then she stooped to the floor and brushed the straw aside, revealing the tightly placed blocks. There was the evidence she suspected: sharp edges where ice had been chipped within the hour. And lots of such edges. How fortuitous. Another hour and the evidence would have melted conveniently into oblivion.

So the boys had been regularly enjoying a summer refreshment, especially delightsome because it was surreptitious. She could imagine their secretiveness, stationing Alan at the shed to watch the back porch, even to survey the fields and warn of any oncoming adult. Everett would likely be holding the pit's door open with one hand and extending the other for ice splinters while Peter chipped away with their secreted tool. How delectable it must have been, especially to Peter who made the trio into an effective band of conspirators. Not a hint had crossed their lips. Harriet had been fooled.

That night, at the dinner table, just as her four males were about to get up from the meal, satisfied as usual, she pulled the ice pick from her apron pocket where it had escaped notice in the folds of her lap. She extended it, full length, above the table.

Wordlessly she watched the eyes of the boys. Alan gulped and looked desperately at his brothers. He gave them away. Junior jerked and poked Alan with his elbow. Peter's eyes just rolled incredulously; a thin whistle of air escaping from his lips as he pretended to be unaware of the proceedings.

Then Harriet explained to Hank what the incriminating evidence meant: not only were these three accomplices apprehended, not only was there a danger that the ice, so tediously sawed from the lake's winter surface and hauled and placed into the pit by numbed fingers, would fail to last until its usual deadline, but most of all, this threesome had perpetrated their deception, intentionally behind the back of the very woman who labored to lighten their life.

What should be done about it?

Well, the accusation was so clear that the boys, even Peter, denied nothing.

All awaited Hank's authority.

Trying his best to avoid bursting into laughter, but belying his sympathy, he responded: "This is clearly a capital offense. I shall go now and prepare the gallows." He got up, still barely suppressing a guffaw, and all the males sprang out the back door chortling.

Though she wanted Hank to join her police squad, she had to admit this was normal boyhood. Yet there was an edge of worry. Peter's pranks were his glory. She knew his mindset had already produced a multitude of such minor infractions and generally they implicated the younger siblings. Even though their temperament was much more malleable, much more loyal to her values, Junior and Alan were still influenced by Peter's charisma. They were dazzled by his daring, converted to his ethic: they never ratted on their pal.

Pranks at home might have been somewhat acceptable, but there was more public mischief. Harriet was still mulling in her mind what to do about Sister Gruble's report on Peter.

Last week after Relief Society meeting, as Harriet and Gertrude Gruble were driving the Laketown road back into Round Valley, Gertrude confided to Harriet that Alfred, her husband, had solved a two-year puzzle. He caught their son Norman and three other boys, including Peter, red-handed. They were smoking homemade cigars out in the west draw. Alfred had wondered why the chinking in the log cabin had kept disappearing. Now he knew: the boys had been chipping the manure caulking out from between the logs of the old homesteader's cabin that Alfred had converted into an animal pen. They had rolled the dried manure into rhubarb leaves which they had hung up to dry as professionally as Kentucky tobacco farmers. The combination of the two dried substances produced a cigar that would rival a box of Cubans in appearance. The taste, however, was something less.

Confiding in Hank would backfire, she concluded. He'd often propounded his philosophy: "Give the boys some rope. Don't hold it so tight. Why, at their age I was leaving home with my pony and staying away for a week at a time. My ma went near crazy with worry that I'd been kidnapped by Indians. These escapades of Peter's are innocently filling his need to rebel. Be grateful he can get it out of his system so harmlessly. He'll come around to the gospel you are so determined to get inside his gizzard. Don't push too hard or you'll force him into a real break. I'm not opposing you. I'm on your side but I'm in favor of his becoming a free man while he is at it."

There was wisdom in Hank's view, Harriet agreed. And his surrender to her values, ever so tenuously, was a delicate victory she did not want to disturb. But she also sensed in Everett Junior and Alan a collaboration with Peter, a desire to chart their own paths.

One summer at lunchtime Junior and Alan came into the house bursting with a report. "You gotta come with us to our new hideout. You must try our new game. You can discover what we have if you can really master the rules." The rules consisted of what they called the "silent treatment."

They had discovered nature at Bear Lake. She let them explain everything to her as though she had never been in the valley before. Their effervescence was so genuine that she recognized her obligation. She agreed to go with them the very next day. Mornings were best because the sun's rays were still cool, they said. Harriet knew the dew would be enticing at that time. Besides, the natural life responded to daybreak with the same awe as humans.

The four of them hiked single file, Peter in the lead, past the outbuildings, past the corral, into the wheat field and beyond, then down the ravine and into a natural blind. There Alan instructed Harriet that she had to become a log, to lie absolutely still for at least an hour. Yes, an hour. So silent that her breathing would not even raise her clothes. There could be no whispering, no wiggles. None of them could budge. Peter added that they could not even wave insects away. Here they must accept the surroundings, fade into them, for they were the guests of the forms of life that owned this turf. They must choose a position which elevated their heads, providing a broad view beyond the blind of fallen trees and entwined brush. When the hour had passed they could open their eyes, but that was all the motion allowed, the blinking of their eyelids. Then the pageant would begin.

Harriet smiled, inside and out, nodded in understanding and chose a spot, kneeling down, instinctively smoothing out a bed, brushing away twigs and pebbles hidden beneath the bunchgrass. Stretching out on her back and shifting her hips into the contours of the earth, she settled her head on a large stand of grasses which she had bent into a pillow-like pad.

As she exhaled long breaths to indicate her settling in, she felt Alan snuggle next to her shoulder. She naturally slipped her ample arm under his head to give him an elevated view.

At first the closed eyes invited a nap, but she caught herself, promising to give their adventure a full shot, savoring the breeze that caressed her cheeks. The many degrees of winds had been her companions in Bear Lake Valley, winds drawn to the breadth of the low open valley and the glazed surface of Bear Lake's oblong body of water. The breezes created new textures every hour and now brought a restful, cool stroking—an ebbing and pressing. It was as if the air cradled her in this moment of solitude.

With their eyes closed, they began to hear. They heard the sounds they had never heard before—sounds that began to fill the void. At least twenty different bird calls. As she listened, she made a mental search for names to match the rhythms, the tones, the timbres. A fly interrupted her concentration, its buzzing and skittering clattering about her head. But then it retreated beyond her hearing. The mental pictures of birds returned as Miss Ross had posted them on the fourth grade blackboard. A lifetime of living on the west shore of the lake had inspired a love for bird lore, but she had not carried on with her teacher's introduction.

Everyone knew there were woodpeckers here, but now Harriet realized that she did not know their call. She had only concerned herself with their destruction to farm buildings—first creating holes in the outside walls that became early spring nests, then abandoning them to a series of smaller birds which took over, invading the eaves and attics if one did not plug the holes.

The melodic clatter of robins was easy to recognize. She picked out hummingbirds that seemed to infest the valley. Usually she recognized their sound by the buzz of their wings, sometimes ducking as they fearlessly flew in most anyone's path. Their throaty hum reminded her of the slow gurgling of water in a garden hose. She could hear them now, but she could also hear other elegant soprano sounds. Which birds were saying what? Yes, she had lived right in the midst of them for thirty years and missed the nuances of the endless variety. The mooing of a cow interrupted the birds, its nasal bass carrying several miles. It was easily heard during the "silent treatment." Harriet sensed the direction of the moos and reckoned the distance. It had to be coming from the Kane ranch, at least a mile away. She could tell the Hereford moan; it bounced off the west hill before it landed in the ravine.

So she waited for Peter's signal. She missed it. His agreed-upon three tongue clicks did not awaken her. Alan could tell she had dozed. Her breathing betrayed her, so he squeezed her arm, a pressing squeeze without outward movement, just enough that she roused from her light slumber slowly, remembering her duty not to move a muscle.

With eyelids open she began to see like an artist, like a taxonomist, like a babe facing new life. The myriads of nature's creations had all been there before, always there, busily there, even on this low, windswept hillside. And she had paused often to enjoy a specific sight. But never before had she prepared for a full hour to enhance her perception. Never before had she witnessed her fellow earth creatures through the lens of such silence.

The rules of this game were 1) that everyone must remember what they saw, 2) list it all without a pencil, and 3) observe without binoculars.

So she began.

She found herself involuntarily imposed upon by her schooling, listing the perceptions into categories: mammals, birds, insects, leaves, grasses, flowers, bushes, trees. The moving things had all noticed the human intrusion. But now that the people had been inert for a whole hour, they returned to normalcy. Harriet soon realized that this pageant featured hundreds of players. Satisfaction would come to those in the audience who developed the most rigorous perception. In groundcover she counted fifteen varieties within a twenty-foot radius of her berth: single-stemmed, foot-long strands with tassles like wheat, sage green stems with a three-inch ball of delicate seeds resembling an overgrown dandelion ready to fly into the breeze, deep green grasses with broad flat blades folded in the middle, rounded straw-stemmed plants with fern-like leaves that burst into tiny balls of white at the top, reminding her of onions gone to seed.

Grasses were the most numerous but the least spectacular. Even the sagebrush seemed to outreach them, but only for a season. After a year or two the pungent leaves of the ever-present brush became sparse, revealing the gnarled strands of the branches, twisting as if beaten into slavery. The stolid serviceberry towered above the sage, immobile even to the wind's breeze. It made no statement at all, just occupied space. Harriet remembered the chokecherry's grandeur in the spring when its countless white blossoms showered the bees with options. The quaking asp were just the opposite, lacy, extended, frail. The branches sustained delicate leaves which pulsed with the slightest airflow, fragmenting the light and refracting differing tones of green.

The hour of surveillance rushed past, rewarding them with a visit of three deer which grazed deftly around them within a rod's distance. Chipmunks darted busily everywhere, pausing to hop back on their haunches, sitting erect, holding their retrieved food in their strong paws to nibble and then glancing in quick, angular movements, darting again on all fours.

The most memorable, most awesome, most graceful creature of all was the hawk. As if presiding over this acre, it glided with the wind currents, often hovering in the updrafts above ridges. It pumped those magnificently-spanned wings only two or three times and then, holding the extended pose, it flew with the breeze, wing tips cocked upward to control the airstream. Always the head and eyes were peering down at all earthlings as if to keep vigil. Then it would dive toward the planet, toward some unsuspecting prey, usually coming back up like a swimmer returning from the deep. Once it succeeded, clasping a squealing field mouse in its claws, fiercely commanding the sky with its wings despite the writhing of the varmint. Harriet shuddered.

Even Peter was stunned. He clicked his lips and the foursome stirred.

They arose from their nests, stretching strained muscles, but still keeping their silence. They began their trek homeward, past the Indian paintbrush, the purple thistle, the rare sego lily, the sunflowers. Once erect, they again gazed at the massive expanse of the sky—a sky that had been azure and almost cloudless two hours ago but now filled with billows of rain clouds rumbling over the west ridge. By midafternoon there would be a welcome downpour from a short thunderstorm that would sustain these desert hills.

Harriet reflected. It took a rugged individual to see beauty in these rather bleak, parched hills. There was none of the grandeur of the pines in the Tetons, none of the red colors of the Colorado Plateau. All appeared dry, uninteresting—until one resolved to play the silent game, to gaze over the expanse of the lake, until it was possible to absorb the movements in the sky and study the dynamics of the wind.

Harriet admitted that Peter was a positive influence for his brothers at times. *Yes*, Harriet thought, *that rascal Peter is good inside.*

Chapter 9
Bear Lake

When Peter had finally saved the last nickel of his nine dollars and delivered it to his dad, Hank matched it as promised and drove Peter to Laketown where he purchased the blue Zephyr—a full-sized, balloon-tire, two-wheeler from Clint Decker, who was selling off all his kid stuff to raise cash for his mission. Yes, it was a used bike but still a great birthday present.

Hank didn't believe in spoiling kids. When Peter, who had a $48 Schwinn racer in mind, kept hounding for a new bike for his birthday, Hank said he would give him half of the money for any bike Peter could afford. That pulled in Peter's sights quickly. He scrounged about until he heard that Clint needed cash right bad for three new blue serge suits to transform him into a door-to-door Mormon elder by July 1. The time was right and so was the price.

But he needed nine dollars. Jim Kane came up with the idea for the nine dollars. It was Peter's first real paying job—sawing logs at the Kane ranch. He and Jim were a real team, equally matched, their young, unshirted torsos gleaming with sweat in the sunshine. They pulled and pushed with even strokes, each on an end of the five-foot lumber saw.

Their growing friendship was what sealed the deal for the Zephyr.

Both Jim and Peter, now fourteen, would not be contained at the south end of Bear Lake—in Round Valley, Laketown and Ideal Beach. So while they hee'd and haw'd with the saw, they planned their conquest. They were going to circumnavigate the lake on their bicycles—the entire sixty miles. In mid-June he and Jim Kane planned for some action. One morning they simply slipped away from their early morning chores.

They hadn't told anybody because they knew permission wasn't possible. Harriet might object on grounds of the scenes of debauchery they would have to pass, Hank on grounds of work to be done before the Fourth of July. The Kanes would think similarly. So the boys would just do it and come back clean. Who could object after they had proven their point?

Getting away might be a problem, but Peter even had a plan for that. All of that first summer month Peter had been so proud of his sawing skill that he initiated his brothers into the craft. Hank had caught on quickly and commissioned the trio to take over his chore. Ten cents a tree-length log was his going price, more money than the two little boys had ever seen. Peter buttered up Alan into thinking that at ten years of age, he could pull the draw saw and keep up with Junior as Peter had done.

They were to cut up the fifty logs their dad and the neighbors had dragged down from Temple Fork Canyon, a winter tradition that bound the Round Valley families in camaraderie, even beyond church ties. The seven or eight men rode the upper Wasatch Range for a full week, marking and cutting and dragging the logs back into the valley's farms, providing all the homes with a year's supply.

The three sons were to cut the logs into two-foot lengths, slashing cross grain in the fresh, wet wood. It was a challenge. The blade could stick if the slice were not straight. But Hank bet the boys they could do it. The bet, besides ten cents per log pay, was for a trip to the Minnetonka Cave on the Fourth of July, complete with swimming in Bloomington Lake, and hiking. But they had to cut the logs by July first so Hank could ax them in quarters while the boys stacked them as tight as a stone hedge and have it complete by the evening of the third.

Hank's strategy of complimenting them had been taken up by his eldest. Peter enthusiastically coached Alan and Junior right into an acceptable push-and-pull saw team, the gaping teeth of the blade churning into the wood with ripping motions, a bit unsteady, improving each day. He had no need to coerce them. Hank smiled as Alan coaxed his brother to let him do the work. Peter was doing them a favor to let the boys try, just like the Tom Sawyer story he read at school.

At first Junior was against the idea of being teamed with his little kid brother: "He won't hold the blade straight. It'll get stuck, might even break, and he'll slow us down."

But Peter coached Alan in the rhythmic sway of his body, keeping the blade angle consistent, the pressure light, constant. He let him try for ten draws, later for twenty.

Finally he gave in to Alan's pleading to do a whole log, even though getting the blade started was wobbly. He praised Junior on how strong he was, how he was taking over Peter's job of being Alan's model. Peter would leave for a ten-minute excuse, then twenty.

So on the agreed upon morning when he and Jim planned to get away,

Peter helped the boys begin cutting in the crisp, early air. They had to work early, he argued, to meet Hank's deadline. Then he slipped away, this time not to return. With a fury he pedaled his Zephyr to Jim's and they were off. Down at the highway they turned left into the sun's first rays, then on their way to Laketown at full speed, not even looking back, driven by the fear that they might be apprehended in their flight.

Who would know what was in their minds as they cycled through Laketown, past the homes set back thirty feet from the poplar trees that grew beside the irrigation ditches, past the mercantile store and on to the highway gas station? Who would know they were conspirators? Folks would have no idea. Only Harriet seemed to read guilt from the clicking of their brains. And they were afraid some other adults might do it.

So they didn't look back.

"Should we take the paved road on the west side first or the dirt one on the east?" Jim questioned. Peter was not about to hesitate, nor to let Jim decide. With a head nod to his right shoulder, Peter pedaled off to the ruts of the east road. He may have realized they would be tired on the home stretch and need the smooth road, or maybe he was looking for the privacy of the barren east side.

Although Peter was initially disappointed that the eighteen dollars he and his dad managed to put together for his bike was insufficient to buy a narrow-tire model, he was suddenly pleased with the Zephyr. The balloon tires took the dirt much better than a racer. Jim's were thick too, fortunately, or they would have been defeated by their encounter with gravel.

"Hey, I'm ready for a stop," Jim yelled.

"Not till we get past the Rayburn ranch," Peter responded. "They've got a telephone. Ma could have got your Ma to call ahead and ask someone to set a barricade for us." Peter knew that his brothers would only last a few logs before reporting his absence. The family would be on the lookout for him.

They reached the ranch while the sun was still fairly low in the eastern sky. It was their first close up look at the legendary layout at the mouth of South Eden Canyon. Everyone on the west side peered at the Rayburn's place whenever they took in the expanse of the lake. It was the only green spot on the east side, occupying a delta that broke the sharp rise of the barren east hills just before they plunged abruptly into the deep part of Bear Lake.

"Can you imagine any man being that rich?" Jim shouted as they approached the gate.

Appraising the two homes and the dozen outbuildings, Peter responded, "Kanes are the richest ones I ever 'spect to know."

"Come on now Pete. I heard tell that Rayburn has two thousand head back up there in those hills beyond his alfalfa fields."

"Fetch, it looks to me like your dad and uncle got that many between them."

"Golly gads no. Don't you know nothin' 'bout what's going on in Rich County?" Jim exclaimed. "All the farmers in Round Valley together don't drive a thousand to the range in the spring. And they have to graze on government lands. Rayburn never has to drive 'em beyond his own land.

"Ol' Rayburn's kind of the county lord ya know."

"You mean President Rayburn, don't you?"

"Well, okay, if you like it that way."

Peter snickered. Imagine him being the one to call for reverence, suggesting that they conform and call Brother Rayburn by his church title since he was one of the three in the stake presidency. He realized that the Kanes and Rayburns were keen competitors. He could sense it by how they talked at the ward house in Laketown—so formal with each other.

"Well, all I know is there's only two places called 'ranch' and yours is one of them," Peter replied. "The rest of us is farms."

They rode past the Rayburn place, enjoying the chance to see it close, to see a layout where there were hired people, both men and women.

"Ya know, that house on the right is where the Allens were the hired hands for several years," Jim pointed out. "The Rayburns even have help with their housework. That's something you'll never see at the Kanes. We kids do all that kind of stuff."

"Well we do too, so don't call yourself persecuted."

About two miles north of Rayburns they came to a clean, sandy beach, vacant but with evidence of a previous visitor—a firepit with gray, caked ashes. It took no cue nor conversation. They stripped naked and ran into the water, jumping in to their shoulders. Shivering, they chopped the water like windmills until they got warm.

"I've heard there are tiny crabfish on the bottom over here," Peter said.

"Do you have any idea how deep the bottom is?" Jim protested. "This isn't Ideal Beach, you know."

"I don't know but let's try for it."

"Nah. I don't like crabfish. I only eat fish with fins," answered Jim.

"Where'd you get that idea?" Peter asked.

"Haven't you read the Old Testament?"

"No, and neither have you."

"Like so much malarky I haven't," Jim countered. "I got clear up to the flood once. Anyways Sister Johnson gave us a lesson on it about how the children of Israel didn't eat pork and only ate fish with fins. Weren't you there?"

"So do you eat pork?" Peter grinned.

"Don't even know what it is."

"Thought so, dummy. It's pig and you Kanes eats lots of pig, 'cuz I seen you slaughter 'em."

"Sure. Well I still don't eat crabfish."

"Have you ever read that crab is against the Word of Wisdom?" queried Peter.

"Nope, just beer and cigarettes."

"Okay. So let's dive for crabfish. I don't want to eat them. I just want to see them."

"Hey, look," Jim said, signaling to shore.

"What?"

"There's somebody in our camp."

"You're right and he's got a fire going."

"What about our clothes? They're just lying there on the beach. How're we going to get out without bathing suits?"

"We're pickled," Peter said.

"Guess it's not our camp."

"I think he seen us. He's motioning. There ain't no one else around here he could be motioning at."

"I'll bet it's someone my dad has sent to catch us."

"The Kanes might have a wide swath in this county but that guy ain't no one from around here, least no one I've seen before."

"You know, we haven't really got much choice but to get out." Jim gave up.

"We could swim across the lake to Ideal Beach," Peter offered.

"'T'ain't never been done and you know it," Jim said

"How 'bout swimmin' over to the Laketown launch?"

"You crazy? I can't even see it from here. And then where would we go with no clothes and no bikes?"

"Okay," Peter finally gave in. "Swallow your pride. He's still signaling at us. The least that will happen is that we'll get our bottoms branded."

"Here goes. Beat you to the beach."

The man on the beach, a lone fisherman from Ogden, was delighted, remembering his boyhood. He had six large trout already fried to share with the novice rebels, not even kidding them about skinny-dipping. Peter and Jim were greatly relieved to discover he was not searching for them. In fact he had no idea they were AWOL from their families. So they accepted his hospitality, his lunch, and before noon they were back on their bikes, relieved, refreshed and behind schedule.

The repast gave them renewed stamina to combat the high sun which was taking its toll. Not only were they sweating from pumping their bikes as well as the 75 degrees at 6200 feet above sea level, but they were still fighting the dirt of the east road.

This side of the lake was nothing like the west where farms and trees filled the gradual foothills that rose from the lake bed. Here the hills were abrupt and parched; only cedar trees broke the grayness with some dark green. They pedaled on and passed the "Welcome to Idaho" sign, cheering to have reached that far. They renewed their efforts so they would have time to spend at their main destination—Fish Haven—the resort on the Idaho west side. Dancing, roller skating, bathing, boating—they were all available at the lake's major resort. There one could find strangers from Wyoming, from Cache Valley, from as far away as Salt Lake City. Those city folk were funny to see in swimming suits, so white-skinned that they looked as though they had been bleached; the farmer types were two-toned: wind-chapped brown on head and arms, white on their spindly torsos. The boys just had to make Fish Haven by mid-afternoon.

They were nearing the north end where the cliff-like hills would soon terminate and open on to the Montpelier plain. A group of six houses, cabins really, caught their attention. Not a soul was in sight. The buildings stood there like a ghost town, their windows and doors barred with wood panels, a covering against intruders, both of nature and of man. Clearly the summer tourist invasion had not begun.

Peter was fascinated. "Gosh Jim, can you imagine people having two houses? And they hardly ever use the one here."

"What a waste," Jim agreed. "They probably live in one of those mansions down in Salt Lake that I seen last year when Dad took me to General Conference. You know there is a street down there with three and four-story tall houses on both sides of the street. They look like castles."

Peter was quiet, thinking.

"Or maybe they are from Ogden," Jim continued. "Dad says those railroad people make all the money and they come out of Ogden."

Peter couldn't figure it out. "Well I don't see why rich people would come to this spot with no trees. It's lots prettier in Round Valley and no travelers come there."

"No wonder they don't come here very often," Jim added. "It is so boring, nothing to do."

Peter imagined. "It looks like a robber's hideout," he said.

"Gee, do you think robbers break in and stay here?" Jim caught on to the idea.

"Hey that's not a bad idea," Peter's eyes danced. "Shall we try that next time? I bet we could stay here a week and no one would know."

"Just so long as we come in the spring before the owners get here."

"What would we do for eats?" Peter asked, excited now.

"I'll bet they've got canned food stored in cupboards."

"We could fry fish. We would probably find a rowboat locked up somewhere."

They pedaled on, minds awhirl at their own inventions. "How about stopping at the Hot Springs? I'm really dirty," Jim suggested.

"Well, look at the sun. The day is more than half gone and we're not even half way. Fish Haven will be more fun than a hot bath."

Jim acquiesced. They took the left fork that soon led to the asphalt highway. In a spontaneous cheer they congratulated themselves on their victory. No more gravel.

Pedaling with ease and doubling their speed, they passed the Utah Power and Light plant and watched water flow out of the lake to drive the electric generators there. In no time they reached the west highway and the St. Charles Junction, cheering again and turning left, heading south. Now they were on the main stretch toward the populated area of the lakeshore.

Past the ward house, past the store, past the gas station, past the cemetery turnoff. It was not possible to avoid people any more. They began to recognize faces: Pugmires, Mechams, Wallentines.

In order not to be diverted, they tried looking official, as if on an errand, sure of where they were going. They waved the community wave at the oncoming traffic. Everyone who was native in the valley always waved to everyone else who passed by. Only the tourists didn't respond; they seemed to be escaping familiarity. The boys needed to look unafraid of being recognized.

It worked. No one hailed them down, even when they passed a hay wagon, heavily laden, with a boy riding the load at the back and his straw-hatted and overalled dad driving the team at the front. They just waved and passed. The boy, near their age, probably a year or two older, undoubtedly went to Paris to school. They had never seen him before. They pedaled on; four miles and Fish Haven was coming up. They picked up speed as vigor came, vigor for excitement, relief from the tedium of pumping.

In a grove of massive trees—cottonwoods and box elders at least five decades into their growth—was Fish Haven resort, its huge square roof encompassing the roller rink, the cafe, the shop and the bowery. There were adjacent bath houses for changing into swimming suits. And there was the launch house where the paddle boat used to dock before it burned and sank.

There was plenty for boys to do at Fish Haven. Peter heard how the Budge kids crawled along the bath house roofs and watched people dress, and especially undress. There was row boating but it was silly to pay for it since they could do that at Laketown for free. And besides, he had heard of the tragedy when three people, rowboaters, not knowing the danger when thunderclouds rolled across Swan Peak, were caught in the sudden transformation of the lake into waves. They capsized, panicked, tried to swim to shore and drowned. Of course Jim and Peter knew about the clouds and watched every afternoon to adjust their activity to the possible cloudburst. So far today the clouds were high, white and scattered. That meant safe weather for boating, but somehow boating was for tourists. Locals could find better things to do.

Their most important goal was to spend their well-secreted quarter for a hamburger and a root beer. At the soda fountain they watched as the meat sizzled and the plump waitress, likely one of the Budges, took the jugs out of the ice cream cooler and flipped the spigot, letting the cold liquid flow into the frosted glass. The foam spilled over the top as she set them before Peter and Jim. The boys immediately sipped the tan bubbles into their puckered lips but waited to lift the glasses to their mouths until the burgers were served up. Plunking their quarters on the counter with a firm plink, they walked through the cafe aisle, through the door into the elevated bowery, past glancing eyes, acting as though this was a daily occurrence.

The bowery was busy with picnicking families, roller skaters, boat watchers, cafe regulars, drowsing oldsters and beer-bellied rowdies. The duo settled at a far table near the edge, where they would be safe, even semi-private. Jim looked southeast toward the lake, Peter opposite.

"Make it last, Peter. We ain't in no hurry."

"Let's kill two hours and head home when the sun gets behind the peaks."

But Jim wasn't sure. "Can we make it before dark?"

"The way I figure, it'll take three hours at the most. We'll make it by nine thirty."

Jim was leery. "It'd be better if they don't see us coming up the road."

"Yeah, but I don't want the sheriff after us either," Peter said.

"Your Ma will be beside herself if it's dark. She'll call the bishop, maybe up here to Fish Haven," Jim responded.

"Well, if we're lucky, our dads won't be in until dark either."

"Yeah, but after that it will get tense."

"Okay, let's aim for nine," Peter concluded. But then suddenly he jerked, grabbed across the table for Jim's hand. "Don't move," he whispered.

"What's up?" Jim questioned.

"We're had."

"Why's that?"

"My dad just walked out the cafe door," Peter said through his tight throat.

"Hank?" Jim's mouth flew open. "Onto the bowery?"

"Yeah."

"Oh hell."

"Hey, watch your language, Jim Kane. You're supposed to be reforming me."

"I ain't no saint. Not yet, anyhows."

"That's funny."

"What?" Jim asked again.

"They don't seem to be looking for us."

"They?"

"Yeah. Dad is with two other guys. Oh hell. It's probably the Thompson brothers. They usually head for beer."

"Who's just corrected my language?"

"It's catching."

"What does it mean, three of them together? Is it a posse?" Jim asked.

"It can mean that they just accidentally bumped into each other. Or it can mean Dad doesn't even know we've gone."

"You underestimate your ma. I'll bet she's sent a posse."

"Well, we sure don't know. Either he is sent to look for us, or he come here to meet the Thompsons," Peter decided out loud.

"What they doin'? I can't stand not lookin'."

"Don't move. Just keep eating, Jim. Slowly. No one should notice us."

"Well, tell me what they're doin'," Jim insisted.

"They've sat at a table beside the bandstand, sort of hidden."

"They picked that on purpose. From what I've heard of the Thompsons, there'll be lots of boozin'."

"They've got brown paper bags with them. You know what's in 'em."

"Do the Budges allow liquor here?"

"I'll bet they don't drive no one away," Peter claimed.

"How about us just quietly slipping over the edge here and going down by the boats? They'll not see us go, if they're not spying out for us," Jim suggested.

"Well, I'd sort of like to know what they're up to."

"Hey, they're supposed to be after us."

"Maybe, but just the same, I know them Thompsons. Wherever they's at, there's liveliness."

"Let's not put the noose around our own necks."

"C'mon, we're out for fun," Peter insisted.

"What do you propose?"

"I want to spy on them. Wouldn't that turn the tables?" Peter leaned over the table.

"Well, we got to get a lot closer and we got to be out of sight."

"I've got an idea," Peter said.

"What?"

"The slats between the bowery floor and the ground are old and rickety. We could just jump over the edge beside our table here, wait for a time when no one is looking and pull a couple off. Then we could crawl in and we'd be under the floor. It'll be no trick to wiggle over to the spot directly underneath them."

One at a time, the boys slid along their benches and dropped on their rumps to the floor. For a while they dangled their feet over the edge, then pushed off with their wrists and jumped noiselessly four feet to the ground. Sitting there on their heels, they peered along the latticed enclosure. To their right about twenty feet, there was a break already made in the fence laths. Crouching, they scurried to the opening, and looking left and right for possible witnesses, they crawled through the opening wordlessly, partners in crime. The crossbeam supports, which diagonally sustained the bowery floor, made a real obstacle course. Climbing over and between posts seemed to enhance the secretiveness.

They dodged pipes and passed a dead porcupine, its stink driving them away with haste. Jim was in the lead. He had counted the major beams that held up the bowery roof—seven on each of the four sides. The same seven beams divided the light coming in from the lakeshore side. Obviously the Thompsons and Hank were sitting between beams one and two in the northeast corner. He headed in that direction, calculating their location in his mind. Peter was not far behind.

Holding his hand up in a halt signal, Jim cocked his ear to sort out the confusion of sounds from above—scraping feet, jukebox music, bench dragging, wind whistles between the lattice openings. He moved to the left and signaled Peter to crawl nearer. Jim figured out where the bandstand support beams came through the floor to the ground, resting on cement pilings. Picturing the bowery's floor plan in his mind, he deduced the trio's location and halting to cup his ear again, he nodded his head with assurance.

"This is them; I can hear your dad."

Peter crawled up beside Jim. "Yeah, you're right. I can make out the Thompsons too. It's them for sure."

They settled in. Each choosing a beam to lean against and squatting their rumps into the dirt, they stretched out their legs.

"Have another snort, Hank? It'll do you good after all that married livin'."

The boys' eyes opened wider.

"I tell ya, I saw it myself. Them elk swum across the whole dern lake. They was skeared somehow; I dunno why."

Peter nodded, "That's got to be Zeke. He's the younger brother."

"It was right near here. They was obviously headin' south to winter in Blacksmith Fork as usual or somewhere they could raid haystacks in the winter. There was a dozen of 'em in a herd. They had nested the night here below the highway, 'bout a hundred yards from the lake in the high marsh grasses. And sumpthin' skeared 'em. Not all of a sudden. But they started sort of gradually backin' toward the lake. Either it was cars or people—not anything of animal life. But they musta' felt trapped. The resort kept them from movin' south. The lake penned them in on the east and north and the cars or whatever it was pressed from the west. Then one of them stepped in the lake. The others followed.

"They'll do that, ya know—herd instinct. People on the bowery was standin' up and shoutin' to look. That prob'ly drove the elk on. The animals just swam out into the lake directly east. We watched as long as we could see them. I didn't know them massive hulks could swim."

"And how much had you been drinkin'?" Hank's voice.

"No more 'n now."

"That's quite a lot. Look what's left." It sounded like Razzle. "Have some more. You make up great stories when your belly has juice in it."

"You don't have to believe me. Any of the Budges will tell the same story. It was the biggest event in ages around here, was even in the newspaper. What's more, them elk must have got to the other side and spent the night because the next evening they swam right back to the same spot here. Old William Budge tells that they were so exhausted that he walked right up to them. But they was up and gone by the next morning."

"Ya know, Zeke, I'll bet you believe in the Bear Lake monster too." It sounded like Razzle.

"Well, don't you?"

"Nah, you just explained it. The monster was most likely an elk."

Zeke replied, "C'mon Razzle, you're goin' to ruin all the fun of this valley. Without the Bear Lake monster we won't have nothin' left fer color."

"Oh you'll still have Brig's polygs and their illegal sex that borned most folks."

"That's enough, Razzle," Hank said. "You'll get yourself beat up, chewed on and spit out in bits if you insult the birthin' of these saintly souls."

"It ain't the birthin' that interests me, Hank," Razzle argued. "It's plantin' the seed that twarn't so saintly. That Charles C. Rich had him a reg'lar harem. His nights was mighty fruitful, visitin' first one wife, then another."

"That's what they mean by 'an active Latter-day Saint,' ain't it?" Zeke chimed in.

There were guffaws, clink of bottles, gurgling, and more laughter.

The boys looked at each other, shook their shoulders, squirmed and perked their ears again, like listening to a radio station amid the static. Peter was playing along with Jim, acting like he enjoyed this spying. But he was trying to cover up how mortified he felt to have Jim discover, first hand, the seamy side of Hank. Jim's dad would never be involved with such sleazy friends. Jim probably knew that boozing happened at several spots in their county but it was not something to be proud of.

"Well, I ain't going to give up my Bear Lake monster either," said Hank. "I like him. Give us Bear Lake fans another century and we'll oust the Loch

Ness Monster from its perch of fame."

"The what?"

"The Loch Ness Monster," Hank said. "That's some story in Scotland. Them Scots, they swear by it. There's a monster the size of a pirate ship in the bottom of a lake there."

"Well ain't you gettin' culture down there in Round Valley. I suppose you'll make the grand tour some year now. Where'd you hear all this?" Razzle asked.

"Oh, I got me an educated wife you know. She reads books with the ladies."

"Uh huh. I bet she learned it in church. Monsters, angels and Joe Smith's gold plates. They go together."

Laughter, glasses clinked, gurgles, laughter again. A whiskey bottle fell on the ground just outside the lattice slots where the boys could see it.

Peter stared at Jim, not because of the laughter above but because Jim had just put a cigarette in his mouth. "Where'd ya get them cigarettes, Jim?"

"They was just sittin' right on the bench when I set down," Jim replied.

"A whole pack?"

"Well, there's only three left. But whoever left 'em had us in mind. He stuck a book of matches inside."

"Why didn't you say somethin'?" Peter asked.

"Wanted to wait 'til we were alone. And we're sure alone. Here, have one."

Jim passed the pack to Peter, taking one for himself, lighting it and taking a short puff.

"I ain't a smoker," Peter said.

"Oh you ain't, eh. What about cigars?"

"Well, that was homemade. This is real stuff."

"Try it—they're mild compared to our cigars. I don't even cough."

Peter didn't hesitate. He reached for the book of matches and lit up.

"Remind me to get that whiskey bottle when we get out," said Jim. "Old Erwin at the merc really gets excited about a new empty, 'specially if it's not a beer bottle. Ain't it funny. Ya can't buy a genuine bottle in any town around here except in Montpelier, but we can take empties right into the Laketown Merc and ol' Erwin'll refill 'em."

"Hank says he mixes it with water," Peter responded.

"Well that's how one lie begets another, my ma says."

"Who gets the last cigarette?"

"You can have it."

"Split it with you," said Peter, turning his ear again to the voices above them.

It sounded like Zeke talking now. "You're a doubter of everything, Razzle, but you just try out the question on the old Indian. Jake'll tell you that his tribesmen have lost some of their members to the monster. That's why you'll not catch any of them swimming in the lake—not a one will do it. And old Charles C. Rich—he put an article in the paper telling people the stories was true. I myself heard old timers tell of a sighting between here and St. Charles years ago. The best explanation I've heard is that it's a descendant of huge animals like dinosaurs that lived in Lake Bonneville ten thousand years ago and covered the whole Great Basin."

"You're spinnin', Zeke. You're just spinnin'," Hank said. "Maybe it was a buffalo."

"Them's that sighted it said it can swim as fast as a locomotive on the surface."

"Have you seen it?"

"Nope."

"No jury would buy that."

"Let's have another round," said Zeke.

Below the floor Jim held out his hand, "Here's your half cigarette, Pete."

"No thanks. The first thing Harriet is likely to do is check my breath."

"Ever heard of Sen-Sen?"

"You got that stuff with you again?" Peter asked.

"Sure, always have one in my pocket."

"I thought you gave up the habit."

"Did, but we're on vacation." Jim grinned. Peter could barely see his face in the darkness under the floor.

"Well, you go ahead then. Besides I've got to concentrate on my spying." Peter perked his ear again.

Razzle was talking now. "Hank, I gotta congratulate you on havin' a son who's got yer same gumption—running away from home at fourteen."

Jim looked at Peter wide-eyed. Whispering, he said, "See, they know all about us."

Peter could think of nothing to say but he pointed upwards to hush Jim.

"Nah, they's not runnin' away," Hank was saying. "I ain't even worried." There was a pause. "But Harriet sure is."

Zeke gave a slight laugh. "There, you see. Hank you have to follow orders—women's orders. Why don't you hang it up and come back to the range? We could get ya a start."

Razzle followed Zeke. "It ain't natural fer a stud like you to be kept in a corral."

Hank seemed to push his chair back in the floor above them. "I'll keep it in mind, boys," he said. "But for now I best be headin' for North Beach. That's where them kids is likely at."

"Here's one for the road," Razzle cheered.

"You'll need it if them boys're not at North Beach," Zeke added.

"Better try Hot Springs, too," Razzle advised.

"What if they're at the bars in Montpelier? Then you'll have to carry 'em home," Zeke had a grin in his voice now.

"Yeah, one under each arm. Better have two for the road," Razzle chuckled.

Peter said nothing, but inside his head his thoughts were reeling. Jim looked away, his cigarette butt losing its last glow.

"C'mon Pete. They've gone. I can hear their steps. They's likely goin' back through the cafe and out into the parkin' lot."

"We'd better stay put 'til we know they're gone." Peter did not move at all.

"If we're going to get home, we'd better head out. We've been here longer than we planned. It's already dusk."

Peter began to move when he determined that the men were gone. "Well let's take a wide swath around the building. We can pick up a couple more bottles," he added as an incentive to Jim.

The boys, taking the reverse obstacle course, were soon through the lattice opening and secreting their way through the trees toward their bikes at the cafe door. Eyes darting carefully about, they walked slowly but unsuspiciously. They reached the bikes, mounted and started to ride toward the stone-pillared gate.

There at the gate was Hank, his back to them, unsteady in his walk, a whiskey bottle in his hand.

Peter's knuckles turned white as he pressed the handlebars.

A car was coming behind them.

Jim sped up and passed Hank without hesitation. The car pressed nearer to Peter. Jim didn't look back but kept pedaling. As he got into his car, Hank took no notice.

Peter drew a deep breath, lunged and rode past Hank's vehicle. He kept pedaling but his thoughts were churning. *Why isn't Hank turning toward North Beach like he said he would? Is he so drunk that he forgot or does he know that Jim and I are heading south?*

They both turned south at the gate, continuing at a steady pace. Peter caught up with Jim, looked at him breathlessly. "Did he see us?"

"He was too soused," Jim said.

Peter was silent.

They pressed the pedals, a plodding press. It was not fun. It hurt inside.

They reached Camp Hunt, the boy scout camp on the shore. It was deserted and inviting but they felt empty inside now. The fun was over, replaced by fatigue, empty fatigue. Just past the Garden City Junction, the Ford passed them, headlights beaming. It was correct for him to have the headlights on. As he edged up to pass them, Hank did not turn his head. Nor did Peter.

Chapter 10
Uncle Golden

At breakfast Saturday morning Hank said nothing to Peter. Peter looked past Hank. The oatmeal mush seemed to stick in Peter's throat. Hank refused his. Everett and Alan were wide-eyed, waiting for action. They had questions ready: "Did Dad catch you? Where? Where else did you go? How did you keep it secret? Did you go alone? Why did you stick us with the sawing? How are we going to meet the deadline? Will we miss the trip to Minnetonka Cave?"

Somehow neither Junior nor Alan had the gumption to venture the first blaming comment. They had been outwitted by Peter so often that they were hesitant to take him on, even though he seemed such a likely target right now. The uneasy silence at the table restrained them.

Hank looked at Peter several times. Peter looked at Hank. Each seemed to have a different message, perhaps of anger, perhaps understanding. Peter had certainly pushed the boundaries. He tried to dodge Hank's eyes, not knowing their future. Even Harriet's eyes expressed an unwillingness to initiate the blame. Her strategy had long been to bring Peter into the fold before he set out on his own. But she wanted to avoid pressing him. These last years between his fifteenth and twentieth birthday were to be the capstone, the time Peter could gain his own convictions about faith and virtue.

Harriet had done all her talking the night before. Too much. It was all about Peter and Jim—that they were old enough to realize how much hurt they had caused. What had they been thinking to embarrass their parents so? The whole of Round Valley was concerned. And for Peter to let his brothers down on the bet that they could finish the work. "Surely you didn't think Alan and Everett would stick with the job. The logs will not get done now. If you had asked for permission, I would have agreed, but for next week. This week is log cutting and Stake Conference. That means Saturday and Sunday are taken. I don't mind boys being boys. It was a fun idea to go around the lake. I can understand that. But being deceitful about it. That's where it hurts."

Harriet continued on and on, counterproductively.

Why no mention of Hank? Of his alcoholic breath, of his not finding the boys? Harriet was teary-eyed last night.

The boys thought they had better just avoid the subject today.

All three of them finished what they could eat and escaped out the back porch to the welcome routine of work. They would do a double dose to make up for yesterday. Alan and Everett trailed Peter to the woodstack. For Peter the sawing was to drown out the forbidden questions. For the boys it was to hope the trip to Minnetonka Cave could be salvaged.

For Hank the day was a return to his old feelings of defeat. During his years in Round Valley with Carmen he had been haunted about the land—this farm that was not really his. He felt that the town didn't seem to want him. Yet he was crucial for the farm, though he felt estranged. Could he live with it or should he escape?

Escape hadn't seemed necessary. Grandpa Ridges was reconciled that the land would belong to Hank, reconciled partly because Hank married Harriet. She was a good replacement for Carmen. The town folks had warmed up to Hank a bit, especially with the presence of three sons in the Ridges homestead.

But there were concerns. Harriet seemed as much in love with the people in the ward as she was with him. Often her priorities were at the chapel instead of at the farm. She was constantly helping the sick, teaching classes, preparing dinners, attending book groups or quilting bees. *She seems to lust for heaven more than for me. She is a super Christian to everyone but me.*

Hank loved the earth, the here and now. But he felt the priority of Harriet's first husband in her heart. When the Round Valley couple married he gave no credence to the weird idea of being married after death. Carmen had mentioned it but he had dismissed it as a screwball fantasy. It was clear Harriet believed it and, in her mind, Everett would be her companion eternally. Why should he worry? But he did. That showed a change. At first, their marriage had been a union of convenience, but now Hank wanted her and wanted to be her major focus.

Harriet was also pondering her situation. She wasn't sure she really knew this Hank Grossberg. He would move in the direction of decency for months and then he would slip back like last night. She knew he felt guilty and that heartened her. So she tried not to place too much blame his way. Whenever she said anything, he clammed up. She could never feel as though she really knew him inside. Why? Was he hiding something, or did he just feel inferior? Maybe she would never know.

Today was not a good time to talk about it. Yesterday's relapse seemed to defeat his efforts to win her approval.

At supper that night Harriet spoke only of the forthcoming conference. J. Golden Kimball was coming, Round Valley's own hero. Imagine a church with a half million members and one of the top leaders at church headquarters was from right here in this tiny vale. Well, almost from here. He had actually lived in Salt Lake City until he was fifteen when his famous father, Heber C. Kimball, died. Then many of the Kimball polygamous wives had scattered with their broods. Christeen Golden Kimball had brought her two sons to Bear Lake Valley to begin a farm.

Hank had heard J. Golden wasn't perfect and he was anxious to let Harriet know that. "Harriet, you'd be surprised about J. Golden Kimball. Twenty years ago when I was on a ranch in Wyoming, I heard miners in bars up there talkin' about him," he announced.

"There's not much that would surprise me about J. Golden Kimball. But you know, Hank, all the stories about him are mostly made up. He doesn't really swear that much." Harriet always seemed to be one up on him.

"That's not what I heard. He was really a muleskinner from the time he was livin' here. And muleskinners have the most colorful language in all the world. Mules don't understand anything but curses."

Curious, Peter joined in. "Is this the guy Grandpa told us about who always said 'hell' and 'damn'?"

"Yes, that is the man, not the 'guy'," Harriet responded.

Peter had heard his grandfather tell tall tales about J. Golden. "Remember how Grandpa told of the time when he visited right here in Laketown and the bishop told Elder Kimball that some of the boys here in town were gettin' wild, drinking beer, smoking cigarettes, knocking over crannies and just raising a ruckus, even carrying revolvers. Grandpa said Mr. Kimball told 'em to 'go to hell.'"

Harriet grinned. She too had heard the story, and what's more, memorized the speech. "What he said was 'Go to hell. That's where you're going anyhow. And if you don't quit carrying six shooters around, the damn things will go off and blow your brains out.'"

Hank began to relax now. He could remember a few stories himself. "Up in the Wyoming bars they tell of the time he was asked to speak at a funeral of a man he barely knew. While he was listing the virtues of the deceased, he saw the man he thought was dead walk in the chapel door, calmly stroll to the front and take a seat. No one else seemed surprised to see him enter.

Golden stopped, turned to the bishop and asked: 'Who the hell's dead here?'"

Harriet and the boys laughed, but she still wished to issue a caution. "You know not everyone gets the same kick out of those hells and damns as you might think. I heard that a refined lady stopped him on the streets of Salt Lake one day and said, 'Brother Kimball, I wish you wouldn't swear in your sermons. I'm afraid if you keep doing it, you'll be excommunicated from the church.'" Hank lowered his voice as though he was trying to get by with something new. "They say he responded, 'Hell, sister, they can't do that. I repent too damn fast'."

Harriet was forgetting that she was supposed to be upset. "I've heard Bishop Jaggi tell about the time right here in our meetinghouse that the brethren were waiting for Brother Kimball to arrive at the meeting. Pretty soon they heard yelling down the road. The closer it got, the more cursing they could hear. It was Elder Kimball trying to get his mules to go faster."

"Was he late?" Junior asked.

Harriet was laughing now. "Late enough, I'd guess."

"The Thompson brothers can tell fifty 'Uncle Golden' stories," Hank commented. "It's the only religion they know. I'd bet they'll come to the conference just to see him."

"If they're sober," said Harriet, still giggling. But at that comment she suddenly sat up and looked around at her boys. Her voice changed. None of them could tell how she really felt at that moment. "Well that's the man we'll have at the Paris Tabernacle tomorrow," she said. "So straighten up your act and hope he hasn't heard about your Fish Haven antics, any of you." Harriet didn't have to urge Hank to come to conference this Sunday. Baptized or not, he wouldn't miss the muleskinner.

The boys usually complained about sitting on hard benches for two hours, but at least Peter was not in a good bargaining position this weekend. So they were all in the Ford and driving up the west shore in the morning fragrances of lilacs and chokecherry blossoms.

Thirty miles to Paris was not long enough to put the boys to sleep. Peter's memory actively retraced his adventure with Jim Kane in reverse direction.

Even from a distance they could see the roof of the Tabernacle, its majestic central tower piercing the cloudless sky. The town square of Paris was crowded with mingling folks, cars crammed in for blocks, everyone strolling toward the three Romanesque entrances of the building which dominated the landscaped green. The Saints were shaking hands, embracing friends and relatives they had not seen since the last conference. Children tugged at their parents' hands, some breaking loose to run across the expanse of the ten-acre town square.

This was an event—probably the largest assembly in five years. There were men coming who hadn't been in church since the last time J. Golden was in Bear Lake. They were easy to recognize because they hadn't dressed in Sunday suits. They had come in from the range as they were, tobacco-stained teeth and sun-baked faces. Some had shined their cowboy boots and put on fresh work clothes.

As Harriet guided her brood through the entrance, the boys tugged for her to lead them up the balcony stairs. She was determined, though, to carry out her planned strategy. They would sit near the front where J. Golden could look them in the eye. Reluctantly, inside the vestibule, they went down the left main floor aisle; the boys peered up to the vaulted ceiling with its intricate wood patterns.

Harriet led her troops to the north side, about four rows from the front, beside the pillars that held up the balcony. It was the traditional place where the Proctors from St. Charles sat, where Everett Senior's clan proudly showed off the latest offspring, whispering and greeting until the pipe organ sounded the last note of the prelude.

"Where's J. Golden?" Peter whispered.

Harriet craned her neck, surveying the men in dark suits congregating on the stand. There were at least twenty of them. She could usually distinguish the visiting dignitaries from the local high council members. The local leaders wore a weather-beaten dignity; Bear Lake geography had baked it into all of them. Hopefully J. Golden would not have the white skin and fine clothes of the Salt Lake brethren. She believed that somehow he wouldn't have become 'citified.'

Finally she saw him. There he was, taller than the rest, and boney thin, his balding head encased by spectacles part way down his nose. The three men of the stake presidency guided the official Salt Lake party up the stairs to the leather-covered bench of the presiding dais. Peter identified Brother Rayburn among them. Harriet poked Hank, pointing at J. Golden. He nodded. This was the first time Hank had actually seen "Uncle Golden."

It was also the first time he had been in the Paris Tabernacle. He agreed that the building was a masterpiece. He admitted to himself that it was amazing that the local folks had built it with their own hands over fifty years ago. They had no trucks to haul stone or electricity to drive a sawmill, he realized. He knew that building the stone walls and roof beams was beyond his ability yet it was just plain people like himself who built them. Hank was impressed.

President Budge beamed delightedly. With the choir elevated just behind them and the twelve members of the high council (including their neighbor Brother Kane) in the descending rank just in front of them, the brethren on the Tabernacle presidium presented an imposing array of authority. White doweled banisters separated each group, the choir, the presiding presidency, and the high council, a framed-like encasing for the authorities.

The tall, gold-leafed organ pipes backed them all up, their tones now reaching a crescendo that signaled the time for beginning as the stake president arose.

The organ stopped. President Budge stepped to the pulpit. He surveyed the crowded benches, row upon row clear to the back and encircling the U-shaped balcony. From all directions faces peered at him, anticipating wisdom. He cleared his throat. Quiet had won over the audience. He announced the preliminaries. The choir then sang "Holy, Holy, Holy," with Emma Wallentine as soloist. Alan and Junior giggled at her vibrato. Harriet poked Everett Jr. with her elbow. Peter sank down in his seat, his eyes raised, his head nodding left and right in response to her warble. The meeting was obviously an endurance test for Peter.

For the Grossberg family, the preliminaries occupied the whole first hour. They had come to hear J. Golden Kimball but there were other speakers and musical numbers that had to be completed first. The boys became fidgety. Finally came a "rest song." The people stood and stretched. The children welcomed relief. The organ soon engulfed the rustling with a measure of "High On The Mountain Top," reminding all of the familiar tune. Alan whispered, "I need a drink." Harriet shook her head a firm "No." Peter refused to stand up. Instead he turned the pages of the hymnbook that some compatriot teenager had defaced by penciling witticisms to the titles of the hymns. He poked Everett, inducing him to laugh along as they read: "High on a Mountain Top" (That's where I'd like to be right now); "Have I Done Any Good?" (My mom doesn't think so); "Come Ye Thankful People Come" (Let's go on a hike); "Do What is Right" (or you will get it from Dad); "Now the Day is Over" (Finally); "Rise Up Ye Men of God" (Ladies stay seated).

Harriet was embarrassed. Hank refused to take notice.

The congregation sang with varying degrees of gusto, all relieved to stand, some familiar with all four verses, some accustomed to wait out the songs, sparing their neighbors a monotone. J. Golden Kimball strode to the podium and looked them all over intently.

He began with a moment for relief, "I see lads here whose minds drift in this room, whose eyes scan the patterns on the ceiling while old men drone on here at the pulpit. Well, young people, that is all right. Just look up there and figure out what the ship builder James Collins, did when he built that ceiling with all those wood patterns. Can you figure out how the squares match, how the diagonal lines run in pairs? You study it up there and imagine that the ceiling is a huge sailing vessel turned upside down; for that is what it is. Then come up and show me your drawing."

Junior looked at the ceiling intently, seeing how to match the patterns. Peter sighed and sank down on the bench, his feet reaching clear through to the next row. Harriet pulled at him to prevent his feet from hitting the folks in front of them.

He continued, "One of my old friends, a friend from the time when this building had not yet reached the square, grabbed my arm as I came in today and took a long look at me and said, 'Hell, Golden, I thought you were dead.' Well I may look like I'm dead, but I'm still kickin'. Another friend stopped me a short while ago (everyone thinks I am about to die) and said, 'Uncle Golden, you must be very desirous of checking out and going to the other side and finding out how much of what you've told us is true.' I am here to tell you good people that I don't resent that kind of humor because I have the same testimony that I had fifty years ago when I left these valleys for the full-time ministry. I may not live up to all the principles of the Gospel, but I can testify in all humility that I believe even more strongly in the Gospel of Jesus Christ and in the divinity of this His Church.

"The Lord knows if there is anyone I sympathize with it is a man who is not doing his duty and who is a member of this Church, because I know how he feels. I am going to tell you how he feels, because I know whereof I speak. I have been in that place, in the history of my life.

"I remember a young man, highly cultured and educated at the University of Utah. I will never forget that young man, no matter how long I live. It was the time of the World War and he had been unfortunate. I did not know him; I never saw him before. He came to me in great distress. As I went to the Presidency, that young man repented, and he was baptized and confirmed. He went into the war, became a lieutenant and the last I heard of him—he wrote me several times—his letter stated: 'I know God forgave me, for I have felt the influence of the Holy Spirit in the army. That has brought me joy and happiness.'"

Glancing at Hank, Harriet could see that he had not tuned out J. Golden.

"A man who considers his religion a slavery has not begun to comprehend the real nature of religion. To such men, religion is a life of crosses and mortifications. They find their duty unpleasant and onerous. They feel themselves enchained within the bounds of a religious system. To such men religion is oppressive. They can't be happy in the Church not doing their duty and they are even more unhappy out of the Church. They are only happy doing their duty. The question is, do we really love Christ? It is not a burden to serve Christ. We as Latter-day Saints, holding the priesthood as we do, should become more intimately acquainted with Jesus Christ who is the way, the truth, and the light. It is not a burden to sacrifice, it is no burden to repent. It is pure joy to be a free man. I know."

Though this kind of talk might have been too heavy for Hank, he remained calm, not wanting to let anyone know he was drifting. Then Brother Golden caught his attention again. "Now I talk to lots of people who feel they are not worthy. I sort of specialize in people who feel they are as weak as I am. I guess they think if the Lord can make a General Authority out of a muleskinner from Round Valley, then the Lord might be interested in them. Just last week a lad from St. George walked into my office. I'm sure one of the brethren sent him to me when he heard his story. The boy wanted to become a missionary. He had lived a rather wild life. Now I can understand that kind of boy. His Bishop told him he would have to put off all his sins. The Bishop labored with the lad and the boy genuinely repented. He mastered all his problems but one—he could not stop his swearing. So the frustrated bishop sent him to Salt Lake to have the brethren decide if he could go on a mission.

"Well, when that young man explained the situation I told him, 'Of course you can stop swearing. Hell, I did.' Now some of you may think I'm still swearing but I can tell you that my present vocabulary has been trimmed down from a far more colorful one. That young man went on a mission to the southern states. That's right where they need some colorful language."

Harriet began to squirm now.

"That reminds me that the last time I was in Laketown I had to use some colorful language with the younger generation who were getting a little wild. One of the reasons I love to come to Bear Lake is because I feel perfectly free to say things that the people need to hear. I'm not going to close my mouth. I cannot talk if I have not freedom. If I cannot be frank and honest then I will feel that my usefulness has come to an end. But for me to be my natural self is somewhat dangerous.

"Now those young men needed to hear what I said. In fact I am frankly worried about our younger generation. For forty years I've been on the Young Men's Mutual Improvement board and I love working with the young men, but I fear that this generation has had too much ease, too much money, too much pleasure. They have lived on milk and honey when they should have been fed on brown bread and slept in the mountains. Some have come to think that their personal success, their ease, their income is of prime importance. I am sorry that my children have not lived on the kind of food I was brought up on in Round Valley. This world was not made for people with no more ambition beyond eating, sleeping and begetting. We ought to have some divine purpose. That is truly living."

Peter seemed to be turned off now, probably not knowing what it meant to be living on milk and honey. Instead he thought that Kimball was too skinny to throw bales with them, not being able to lift one above his waist.

Uncle Golden continued, "Now I don't mind people being independent; it takes intelligent people to understand what I am trying to get at. I don't like to skate around on thin ice. I like to be direct but I do not do your thinking for you. You have to do your own thinking. I sometimes have to give you a little chaff to get you to take a little wheat. My trouble is that too many people choose the chaff instead of the wheat. They don't watch the signals."

Peter's impressions seemed to be challenging the revered speaker. *Well I plan to do my own thinking, thank you*, thought Peter.

"Whenever I get up to speak in the Salt Lake Tabernacle, I'm always in danger. I always think of the danger signal: 'Safety first.' With that sign in my mind, the clock in front of me and President Grant behind me, I have a damn hard time gettin' inspired. Now I can't see that clock over there on the wall any more. My eyes aren't so good. I take it we will all be relieved now that I am through.

"I love God and I love God because He is a God of love, because He is a God of kindness, a God of forgiveness, for He has provided an opportunity that, with all our weaknesses, we can repent. And if you take from me the joy, the happiness, the peace of forgiveness, for heaven's sake what have I left? I would not give you a nickel for the whole thing."

Harriet thought, *Now that's the point. He is right on target.*

"I love this work. My brethren have been wonderfully good to me. They have been patient. God knows that, or they never would have endured me because I have said things that I was sorry I said, but I could not take them back. I sustain and uphold the hands of the priesthood and I desire, as you do, to be saved and exalted in the presence of God, which if I know anything, I know must be the greatest gift of God to his children. God bless you. Amen."

As the choir sang the concluding song, the family got ready to go. Alan had slept through most of Uncle Golden. Junior was still fascinated with the ceiling but he liked the stories about being a missionary in the South with B. H. Roberts. Peter masked his interest in J. Golden by squirming and preparing to jump into the aisles and make for the door. Harriet had to chuckle about Brother Kimball's tales, even though they emphasized the swearing. Mainly she was excited that Hank seemed to take some of it in. Hank kept his own counsel, but he would really have liked to shake J. Golden's hand.

So it was fortuitous when Hank noticed that Everett Junior had escaped. As Harriet looked around she was taken aback to see Junior right next to Elder Kimball. There he was, paper in hand. She realized that Junior intended to take him up on the challenge to decipher the ceiling pattern. Thinking quickly, she asked Hank to go up and retrieve Junior. That's all it took. Hank walked to the stand, ostensibly to retrieve Junior. He placed himself next to the stair where J. Golden would have to come down. It worked. Golden took his hand and Hank said: "We're keepin' the fields growin' in Round Valley for you."

"You are? Which farm?" Golden inquired.

Hank answered, "You know the Lyman Ridges place?"

"You bet I know it, right by the reservoir. Do you want to trade me places? I'd be a lot better off if I were driving your tractor instead of driving all over the church. How about a trade? You do the preachin'."

Hank replied, "Well, I've still got to get rid of some hells and damns."

Golden laughed a gusty laugh and gave Hank a hug.

On the way home Harriet did not press for a reaction from each. The comments came easily though and were rather upbeat. Even Peter got something: "I always wondered why that ceiling was so mixed up."

Chapter 11
The Trophy

Harriet took special care of Grandpa Ridges during the final painful days of his life. The last month he was completely bedridden, and had to depend on Harriet totally.

He always tried to express his gratitude in his raspy whispers. His last breath was labored and painful but he took it in his beloved Round Valley. Harriet felt fulfilled that she had played a part in assuring his comfort during his concluding years.

Such satisfaction eluded her in dealing with Peter. She had been careful not to pre-empt Hank, not to nag or dominate Peter. It was going well until Peter entered high school.

Her strategy was to win with love, but from the first day of high school Peter began to talk down Bear Lake and Round Valley. He refused to tell Harriet where he had been upon returning late in the evenings, insisting on "Independence above all else."

It was a confrontation that lasted two years. Harriet hoped Hank's assessment was right: "Hold on to the reins but not too tight. It will pass."

Finally, after one of Peter's suspended absences, they received a letter from him—postmarked Fort Ord, California. They were stunned. It crushed them. It capped two weeks of anxiety.

During that painful fortnight Hank had tried to maintain that Peter was just going through a normal stage of adolescence. He restrained himself from repeating that in Wyoming he had run away regularly in his early teens and permanently by sixteen. That would almost suggest Peter was overdue at seventeen. Obviously such talk would be counterproductive for the other boys. Hank knew that. He was churning inside more than he admitted. He knew of Harriet's dogged resolution to contain Peter's aggressive personality within the bonds of gospel living. And he knew times were different. This was not the Great Depression; Peter had no need to escape a deficient family. He wasn't Razzle Thompson, wandering on the edge of society.

Peter was a dynamo, elected to be student body president of North Rich

High next year. Sure it was the state's smallest high school, but he was an electric personality, a born leader, a dashing figure who drew people to him everywhere. He was Hank's son in that he ranged free, but he was not like him in feelings of inadequacy. Just the opposite. No, he had no need to run. For that matter, neither did Hank. Maybe Hank was more like Peter than even he admitted.

Damn those Army recruiters, Hank murmured, forgetting his language. *They feed on the vulnerabilities of Bear Lake kids. They fly around like magpies waiting for the mothers to leave the nest. They seem to know which ones are disgusted with the obscurity of our valley.*

For a year in talking down his birthplace, Peter had threatened to go into the Army to get away. Hank had supported Harriet in her firm denial. She would not even discuss Peter's plea. The Army was an unworthy place for Peter's abilities, she told him. At least there would be no considering it until he graduated from high school. Peter had no need to get the Army in his head yet.

Everyone in the family knew the track Harriet held out for all three boys: first high school graduation, then either full-time work in the valley or a year of college. The big step followed—a two-and-a-half-year church mission—somewhere in the wide unknown. It was the grand adventure, but vague because the destination was in the hands of the Prophet, President of the Church David O. McKay. It could be Samoa; it could be Nashville. Maybe one would be sent to the Navajos or the Norwegians. The faithful response was simple, "I'll Go Where You Want Me To Go, Dear Lord." After their mission the boys would be free, but Harriet's hope even extended beyond that time—more college, and marriage in the temple. Harriet's plan was the high road. Each of the three boys had a mission savings account under Harriet's sponsorship. They had put their quarters and occasional dollars in, and she had given the total a boost on birthdays and Christmas.

But Peter had always fought against lock-step plans. Even at six he had questioned, refusing to follow directions, asserting his own will. It never dawned on him that age brought wisdom and deserved respect. He savored dodging pre-set benchmarks. When he had disappeared this time, Hank had attempted to calm Harriet, pointing out that it was the natural summer reaction. Two summers ago Peter and Jim escaped for the well-known one-day circumnavigation on bicycles. The next they were gone for a full week. Only later did the parents find out that the boys had holed up in a cabin on the northeast lakeshore.

So this two-week absence was just a normal escalation, Hank argued. But he wasn't sure. Peter had not taken Jim with him this time, nor had he confided his plans to Jim—if Jim's report could be trusted. A recruiter had visited the area but that business had been settled, Hank thought. And surely Peter would not desert his coming student body presidency. Hank tried to portray confidence; this was a temporary and understandable escapade.

The letter from Fort Ord shattered Hank and ruined Harriet's hopes and plans for Peter. It wasn't hard to imagine how the seventeen-year-old could fool a distant enlistment officer about his age. Peter's stature, his confidence, his scheming could easily knock them over. And in hindsight, it was understandable that this would be the capstone of the ever-escalating confrontations between Peter and Harriet, Peter and Bear Lake, even Peter and Hank.

Looking back, Harriet suffered, remembering their clashes—clashes about doing homework, about occasional cigarette smoking, about saving his money for a mission, about refusing to give details after staying out until 2:00 a.m. on ball game nights. There was nothing terribly unusual about such teenage confrontations, except that Peter knew he had the upper hand. He knew Hank would not engage in the discipline. Peter had an ultimate trump card. He never let the words pass his lips, but his eyes often sneered the veto message: "You're not my real mother."

So Harriet had reined in her temper, intending to outfox Peter. Her plan was to win him by endurance, loving but firm. She would never give up, even if she had to win alone. She knew from the start that Peter was both smarter and more talented than she, but that didn't make him right. She knew the gospel values were superior to any dashing enticements Peter could find. She had no apologies for attempting to divert his choices in that direction. The challenge was how to get those choices to be his own—freely made, made from his own heart, his own personal convictions. How could she help him stumble into his own victories with virtue?

One thing was clear to Harriet: the Army was the wrong setting for Peter. So the letter was a disaster instead of the solace Peter hoped to offer:

Hi folks—

I'm at Fort Ord. I've signed up for four years to become a helicopter crewman. I don't expect you to understand. I've got twenty reasons that have been buzzing about in my head but I won't bother you with them. Some day you'll feel okay about it. I just had to get away. The recruiter promised me I can get my high school diploma in the Army. I promise you I will. I'm not a dunce. I'll have to have a certificate to go anywhere in the Army.

Bear Lake was driving me mad. I was so boxed in. I just don't want to get stuck there all my life. I know that insults you but please don't hate me. I've got to live my own life. I feel bad about the student body thing but I would have exploded if I had stayed and they would probably have unelected me for being drunk or something. So please tell the principal he can have the other officers replace me before school starts.

Basic Training is hell. The physical part is a snap even though the sergeants think it is so tough. I guess that is one thing Round Valley gave me—muscles. But the pain is that we are forced into rules. Funny isn't it—just what I was trying to avoid. They confine us, yell at us, police us. But at least this will end in six more weeks. Then I will move over to the helicopter school.

Mom, you will be surprised what I did in Salt Lake City. Oh yes, I thumbed through Logan Canyon. The first guy to pick me up was going clear to Salt Lake, otherwise I would have stopped in Logan. Lucky for me I went to Salt Lake because they had a group being inducted at Fort Douglas in two days. By the way, I took some of my bank money with me. So I had to kill some time. I wandered all over, stayed in a little hotel by the bus station. Finally I ran out of things to do so I went to Temple Square. I was there for a half day! I took a tour, listened to the noon organ recital and then roamed through the museum. One of the old men there must have thought I was loitering so he started talking to me. When he found out I was going in the service and had not been interviewed by my bishop, he really took on the job. Anyway I came away with a servicemen's packet—you know, the little pocket *Book of Mormon* and *Gospel Principles* book. It even has hymns. So I'm equipped. Tell the Bishop.

I'm writing this in the can after lights out so I guess I'd better quit before the sarg discovers I'm not in the sack.

I don't mind telling you that I really miss you and that I have a hard time at mail call. So WRITE PLEASE. Even though I pulled a dirty trick on you, I hope you will forgive me.

Love,
Pete

(The army can't hack the name Peter)

Peter couldn't have chosen a worse environment, as far as Harriet was concerned. She had watched it over and over again, rebellious teenagers fleeing some Bear Lake town. Soon they came home to show off a uniform, but their hands were stained with tobacco and their tongues with vulgarity. Thereafter they came back seldom, finally only to family funerals. Then it was clear they were no longer of the faith. Many of them went through several marriage partners and seemed to be so terribly unhappy, pursuing adventure, finding only carnality.

When there was a real war it was a different matter, but when the military was an avenue for escape, it was tragic to see the results. She had watched Abigail Allen go gray prematurely over Alma's enlistment. He had clearly avoided going on a mission, signing up even after his interview with Bishop Jaggi. It was not only humiliating for the Allens, but it was demeaning for Alma to choose the lower road just when he was on the edge of his potential.

And now Peter, Harriet thought. *Peter is too zestful, too sharp, too witty for the Army. He could go anywhere, become anything. Why waste it on helicopters? Oh how stupid smart kids are. They are seduced by adventure and end up in blandness. Then they have to defend it—even from themselves. Well it is not over yet*, Harriet told herself.

Miles from Bear Lake, Peter Grossberg sneaked back into his bunk on tiptoes, slipping in between the sheets and pulling up the blanket over his shoulders. He had been accustomed to blankets clear up to his chin in the cold of Bear Lake. Now, even in the humidity of a Monterey Bay summer, he still couldn't sleep without something over his shoulders. His bunk mate in the bed next to him seemed to be asleep but in a moment he shifted under his bedding. "Thought I was asleep didn't you, you little bastard."

Pete flinched. "Yah, you're a good 'possum," he admitted quietly.

"What's a 'possum?"

"Gads, Alex, you've really had a deprived childhood, living on the asphalt of Los Angeles," Pete said.

Alex laughed heartily, "Crazy country boy."

Peter and Alex shared a squad leader room. They were picked out from the group of recruits in their platoon on the first day, Pete as platoon leader and Alex as one of the four squad leaders. The captain just walked around the fifty-man platoon and picked out five men, arbitrarily. No one knew what he was doing as he walked up and down each of the four rows and eyed them over silently. Then he pointed out, "You and you, and you."

Four of them were placed at the right end, first position, of each row. Pete was told to come out in front of the group.

"These will be your leaders," the captain announced. "They will serve as long as they are effective and as long as you men respond to their leadership. Sergeant Jackson will show them what to do. But mainly these five will be your leaders—until I replace them." Then the captain did the same for each of the other three platoons—two hundred men making up Company A, First Brigade.

Jackson, a huge black man with service stripes all up his left sleeve, watched with detachment. He was obviously a seasoned soldier, old enough to be the captain's father.

Pete guessed that Jackson had likely not gone beyond the fourth grade. When the captain appeared, the Sergeant yelled "On yo' foots." The men scrambled to their place in the formation. Jackson got respect just by looking at you.

So it was. Pete had fled his student body presidency and here he was platoon leader in a class of the same size. Ironic. And Jackson made the North Rich principal seem like a gentle grandma.

Their appointment leaders gave Alex and Pete a room together. The three other squad leaders were next door and the rest of the platoon were in the big barracks room, packed in, bunk after bunk, two high, so close and so high that every snore stirred the rest.

Pete determined to educate Alex in some country jargon. "A 'possum, you dunce, is an animal that can act asleep to stalk and fool its prey," he said.

"I s'pose you have them at Bear Lake."

"Nope, never seen one."

"But I thought you farmin' folk was country cousins wherever you live."

"Probably. 'Possums are in the south, I think, but somehow our people talk of them."

"Well, I wasn't exactly stalkin' you."

"If you weren't, you were still doing a good job of lyin' in wait," Pete countered.

"I learned it when I became streetwise."

From the first, Pete had a feeling that he wasn't country-wise. Alex had some kinds of experience Pete had never dreamed of. "I just don't get it, Alex. You had all I'd ever want, the excitement of the big city, money, women. And yet you join the Army. It doesn't make sense. I had to sign up to find life; you sign up to lose it."

Alex snickered, "You know, Pete, you are so naive that I find you're the best entertainment available." There was a pause. Pete thought he felt an oppressive darkness. Alex went on and Pete froze. "I was about to be sent up for dealing. I had the choice of two years in the pen or two years in the Army."

Pete tried to keep a normal tone to his voice. "For dealing? What were you dealing?"

Alex's tone deepened. "I wasn't dealing cards, you naive jerk. They thought I was pushing drugs." He paused. "Actually that was just the cover for more serious business. I'd been dealing since I was thirteen, but I've long since graduated."

Pete did not know whether he ought to pursue the conversation. "Alex," a rasp was in his throat. "What the hell are you telling me? And why? I had no idea. Why are you unloading on me? Maybe I'm a plant."

"Ha." Alex rocked the bed when he moved. "Look punk. I like you. You're so clean I can't believe it. People like you aren't made any more. Damn it to hell. I like you more than anyone I've ever known—and we've only been together two weeks. I'm five years older than you, I think, but I don't mind having you for a leader, though you know I don't give a damn for any of this platoon business. I'm sick as hell that we only have six more weeks. How's that for wild? I'm enjoying this mess. I'd go for helicopters if we could be together, but I don't suppose I'll have anything to say about it. But I want you to know the real me."

Pete was stunned. He was most surprised that Alex's comments warmed him so much. There was no doubt that he had a friend. "Alex, you know I feel the same way. The other night when we were talking about our families, even though you didn't say much, my guts just made me want to let you know that you were pulling me through. I was so homesick for my family I wanted to bawl. But I have hurt them so much that I don't even deserve to be homesick. And I am not about to let on to anyone anyhow. You helped me live without them, even helped me decide that I had to write them. So you've got to know that I love you like a brother. I've said it and I'm glad. How did this happen in two weeks?"

Alex had turned his head. His words softened in the darkness. "Well it's an illusion because you didn't know that I'm a con man."

"Oh get off it. Quit knocking yourself."

"Peter, you're nuts. I'm part of the Mafia."

"So what?"

"Do you know what the Mafia is?"

"Well, no."

"That's fine. I hope you never learn. Anyway it is not exactly the Lion's Club. I'm in the Army because it's a lot better than the clink."

Peter felt the bonds of friendship. He wasn't going to let his friend talk himself down. Alex had told him earlier about two widows he had been generous with. "What about those two young widows that you help out?"

"Well they're the salve to my conscience. Anyway, the money I give them is laundered."

"I suppose that means it's not yours."

"You could say that." Alex was coolly silent. "'Nuf about me. You've never really leveled with me about why you're in Uncle Sam's Army. You are the brightest, handsomest, best kid I've ever seen. There ain't no sense in your being here with us rejects."

Pete didn't like Alex to refer to himself as a reject.

"There you go again, cuttin' yourself. I'm going to start socking you every time you say that about yourself."

"Pete, that's one thing you're not ever going to do. You know I groove on you. I feel like I've got to protect you from becoming like me—but if you ever hit me, my instincts will take over—and street people play dirty. So don't find out how rotten I am."

"Damn it, Alex, there you go again."

"Okay. I'll give it a try; be kind to myself a week. So now we're down to your turn at confession. Why are you here?"

"To fly helicopters."

That wasn't enough for Alex. "Oh rats. How dumb do you think I am? What are you running from? We're all running from something. I'm running from the law. What are you running from?"

Pete hesitated. But he knew what he wanted to say. "You'd have to know my mom, my stepmother."

Alex laughed briefly. "So that's it. She hates you and loves her child. Sounds like a soap opera."

"No she loves me as much as the other two. In fact she suffocates me with it. She had my whole life planned and she is so clever at sneaking her design into my head. It is always there. There's no escaping it. I am supposed to be a saint."

Alex laughed again. "I guess that's why you are. She has been mighty effective. How about your dad?"

Pete felt the words come more easily now. "He's a free man—but he doesn't want me to be like him. He agrees that ma's plans are better. How's that for copping out? He doesn't have to be a saint, but I do. He just walks out if there is ever a contest and lets Ma's message consume me."

"So you are running."

"Of course. Why do you think I wouldn't write them? Ma's the kind that would write a congressman and get me out."

Alex snickered. "You don't know the Army, buddy. The Army is hungry for fodder. They won't give you up."

But Pete wasn't ready to give in. "You don't know my ma. She's got access to information that could get me out if she wanted to. I'm gambling that my enlisting is a clear signal that I can't stand it in Bear Lake and that if she forces me home, all hell will break loose."

Alex's voice changed. "Don't you sound tough," he sneered. "Sounds more like idle threats to me. Your dad might just change his colors and sit down hard on you for the first time."

"He'd be a hypocrite if he did. Just this once I hope he won't support her."

Alex turned his face to Peter. He raised himself up on the bed. "Damn it Pete, you make me feel old. Because . . . because I'm afraid. I wish they would get you out. You don't belong here. It's going to ruin you."

For a moment Peter was taken aback. Alex sounded so sincere. "Alex you don't know Bear Lake. There's no bar, you can't buy a car, it's so far away from everything, not enough people, always the same ones. I knew too much about everybody. They had me branded. It was boredom. There was fifty kids in my whole high school. I faced the same six teachers for three years. Two of them were idiots."

Alex laid his head back down on the pillow. He sighed. "Our teachers didn't last a semester. They couldn't dodge the switchblades."

But Peter didn't hear him. "In Bear Lake it's a mortal sin to smoke a cigarette. You've got to go to church three times a week and sit in Sunday School classes taught by numbskulls. We've never heard of drugs—don't even know their names."

Alex was still trying to get through. "In our school every third locker was a drug store. You could buy what you wanted, even pass it in class. And we had a funeral every month—overdose, suicide, knifing."

Pete continued, as though Alex hadn't spoken. "If we did anything, even smoke, the bishop knew the next day. People are so petty they can tell who sings off key before they walk in church."

Alex muttered. "The man next door to us died in his bathtub and no one found him for two weeks. We didn't even know his name when the cops came to ask us questions."

"My folks make a virtue out of poverty. They are working land that thaws out only for three months. It will never yield enough to get one month's income in the bank. They think sacrifice makes a person holy. Being rich is sinful."

"I've carried a million dollars of greenbacks in my briefcase and wondered how many funerals it took to bring them together—and how many more were coming—including mine—each time the bundle changed hands."

A light from the road flashed across the windows. For a moment they were silent.

"Oh damn it, go to sleep, 'Lex," Peter finally said, "You're worse than ma."

Peter could hear the grin in Alex's voice. "Sweet dreams, Peter, my lad. Just know that your elders want the best for you."

The next day Peter drew the duty roster turn to guard the barracks—a whole day sitting in the big hall to prevent wholesale thievery that would otherwise occur. Every man in the fifty drew the duties—KP, GI party cleanups and barracks guard. By rights he should be with the company, calling the march as they moved from class to class. But he wanted to make a point: everyone should pull every duty—no bugging out. Bug-out-ism was the bane of the Army. Peter was going to beat it somehow—at least for his one platoon. So he determined to take his turn at all duties. Alex could march the men.

For a while he inspected each bunk, each footlocker, each wall locker. He straightened. He shined. He hoped the men would notice. Then he amused himself by examining what the troops had hidden in their trunks, under the display tray.

After mess he went back and sat. He pulled out the pocket Book of Mormon and started to read. He shifted restlessly, replaced the book in his breast pocket. Realizing he had not inspected the squad leader's rooms, he went upstairs and began the process, first the lockers, then the bunks, then the footlockers. That killed a half hour. So he went to the next room, his own. *This will be fun*, he thought. He looked at the room which he knew inch by inch—this time with detachment.

Admittedly his own locker and trunk were not models. He straightened, cleaned, reshaped, until they were spotless. Impressive. Then he turned to

Alex's. He must not do that handsome lummox's work for him. So Pete just looked closely. The gym bag in the locker was obviously covering something up. So Pete lifted it up to see. No problem, but the bag was unduly heavy. Why? He set it back down, then wondered. He picked it back up. Paused. Then he unzipped the bag, apologetically.

Inside was not the basketball uniform the bag was meant to contain. There were some dozen magazines. Pete took one out, turned the pages.

Wow!

Pete had never seen such a thing: women and men partly clothed. Peter looked around. He looked at his watch. He slipped the magazine under his T-shirt, zipped up the bag and returned it to the wall locker.

Walking casually, Pete went back to the platoon bunk room. He walked slowly through the room, did a smart about face and walked back to the door, pushed it open and walked toward the latrine. He heard the clerk clicking away at the typewriter two offices away and saw light coming into the hallway from the CO's suite. Calmly he pushed the latrine door open and went into one of the six stalls. Inside he closed and locked the door and sat on the john. The magazine fell into his waiting palm. He looked at the pictures, turning the pages slowly. His face flushed. Then came a section of short stories and articles and letters. Reading, he looked at his watch and read more.

The magazine had its effect.

For the first four weeks they could not leave the company area except in formation and with a cadre leader. They had heard of a USO on post complete with soda fountain, library and night club. But they didn't even know its location, should they slip away.

Alex could have swung some kind of deal to get them a break but he abandoned the try when Pete made it clear that he would not rink out on the platoon. Alex concluded that Pete was really a patriarch at heart.

So there was lots of togetherness for a month.

There was one exception though, one escape—church.

The army had to let men go to church each Sunday. Some of the guys got up for mass. Several went to Protestant services at the post chapel. Alex did not mention it. Neither did Pete.

Alex had placed his transistor radio on the window sill. It was expensive, the first one Pete had ever seen. At night they listened to California and Mexican stations, sometimes picking up KSL. Pete was amazed that the "clear channel" station in Salt Lake came over the Rockies, as strong as they had ever received it in Round Valley.

The third Sunday morning Pete could not sleep in despite how much he had longed for the week's only respite from marching, cadre stares and the ever-present responsibility. So he turned on the radio, ever so softly. He held it to his ear and turned the finder aimlessly, one eye on Alex to assure he did not stir.

Preachers and gospel singers were having their one chance in the week. They didn't interest him. He kept turning. Then came the recognizable tones of the Tabernacle organ at the "Crossroads of the West." Tempted to turn on by, he overcame his desire to disguise his affiliation. Perhaps it was his recent visit to the Tabernacle that caused him to halt. He settled back on his bunk, turned the instrument even softer, placing it on the pillow beside his head.

He closed his eyes and admitted he was homesick. The familiar songs vibrated in his chest. The "Spoken Word" by Richard L. Evans didn't seem like a sermon. It seemed so sensible, so sound, so wholesome. His pride was stirred that the Mormons were heard here in California—that their message was of such quality. The choir seemed like the American flag to Peter—what they were to fight for.

He lay there comfortably for fifteen minutes, wanting to sing. Then Alex shifted in his sleep. Peter jerked the nob, turning the radio off. He put it back on the window sill. Alex went back to sleep. Pete got up. He decided to go down and survey the bunk hall.

On the fourth weekend of basic it was customary for Fort Ord companies to put on a "do." That's what the CO called it. He made it very clear to Pete that this event must be a premier performance and it must be put on by the trainees. They were welcome to invite their parents, wives, whomever. He, the CO, would see that the cooks did up an impressive feast. He, Pete, was to see that the trainees were impressive to the visitors, which incidentally would include the Brigade Commander, maybe even the Post CO, should he choose to come. Preferably there should be a display of everything they had learned: physical training, marksmanship, marching, bivouac preparation, map reading and so forth. And of course, the barracks were to be spotless, open for inspection. If this went off well, the men would receive their first weekend pass.

Why Peter? There were four platoon leaders. *Why did he choose me?* Peter thought, but he dared not vocalize his protest. "Yes, Sir." *Damn, this is just like being student body president.*

The CO, a pint-sized Ranger and all muscle, announced this new project at the end of the first week, then looked squarely at Pete. Both he and Alex had survived the leadership cut that day. Two of the other three squad leaders had been replaced. Pete was determined to survive any further purges. And evidently the price would be to do the CO's bidding on the fourth weekend affair. Unlike Peter, Alex didn't seem to care about being cut. But Pete needed him. His presence was simply commanding. Not only was he the oldest of the men—about 23, Pete estimated—but he intimidated anyone, even the cadre. Tall and dark, his hairy torso, receding hairline and darting eyes were impressive. Unless Alex really screwed up, he would stay a squad leader until the end. Since it seemed he liked the semi-private room and kid brother roommate, he would likely give it just enough effort to last it out. So the two of them were semi-secure in their posts. In return they had to see that the fourth weekend came off with some pizzazz.

Pete knew immediately what they would do. It would be a roadshow—just like the Bear Lake Wards did every other fall. Instead of wards, there would be platoons. Each of the four platoons was to prepare a skit. It was to be full of wit but had to actually show one of the skills the CO wanted. The overall theme would be "You can sleep well—your Army is on watch." That would give the audience a laugh and the men an excuse for some goofing. They could dance or do slapstick or sing, but there would be no vulgarity, no suggestiveness, no demeaning the Army. After all, the Army had "church" standards too. And there would be a winning prize—a weekend pass right after the show, a chance to be with the families who traveled to see the presentation. *The CO won't be able to turn me down if I save his ass in front of all that brass!* Peter thought. At least that was how he explained it to Alex.

The con man stood in amazement. "Where does this kid come up with such ideas?"

"So now our next problem is to select a director in each platoon. We know only our platoon, and I don't think the platoon leaders should be the skit leaders. We've got to find guys with song and dance skills, guys who have put on assemblies in school or who are great jokesters."

The weekend special was a blast. The men took to Pete's format with alacrity. The incentive was there and some half of the men had a guest to impress. It had all the makings of a happening. Pete and Alex sat back and watched it work.

Squad A did a demonstration on bivouacking. They raced to get twenty pup tents set up, taut as a sheet of metal, hamming it up, rolling out sleeping bags and snoring in them. The B squad did physical training. Stripped down to shorts and tee shirts, they went through the whole routine—pushups, running in place, stretches. Almost like a dance company they synchronized bug-outs, skipping a beat, missing a pushup, each in turn. It took some good timing and the audience clapped with delight. The third squad demonstrated first aid, making tourniquets, tying arms in slings, binding knees, even making a neck brace. Of course the guys hammed it up to act, as though they were suffering. The fourth squad conducted a race at disassembling rifles, cleaning them and putting them back together. The operation wasn't quite as flashy as the other three, but it had the element of a race.

The CO was undone with pride.

Pete and Alex were sufficiently repaid with the idea of a real weekend. Pete just assumed that he and Alex would do the town together. At least he didn't see Alex planning anything else. After the feast was over and the CO shook Pete's hand well beyond the necessary civility, Pete and Alex met back in their room. Pete felt pretty good about himself—as though he deserved a chance at riding high.

"Well, let's go," Peter said.

Alex looked up at him from slicking his hair in the mirror. He was surprised. "Go? Where?"

"Aren't you going to show me the sights of Monterey?" Pete was like a kid with his hands in his pockets.

Alex seemed taken aback. "What if I don't know them?"

But Pete wasn't to be discouraged. "Look, if you don't know them, you'll figure them out on the spot. You could smoke out any city in the U.S."

"You overdo it, Pete."

"I know experience when I see it. C'mon. It's not every week you get to initiate an innocent."

Alex stood back from Pete, hesitant. "Haven't you got a better offer?"

"Watch it or I'll have to start with fists."

"You know better." Alex grinned.

Pete was practically dancing on the balls of his feet. "C'mon, let's get out of this hole. I want to see a movie, a woman in a dress, an overstuffed chair, and get a malt," he was griping. "Let's play like we're humans."

"In uniform—that will ruin it."

"Well, we don't have to look at our uniforms. And the people around here seldom see anything else. So let's be off."

For a moment there was a pause. Alex looked askance at Pete as though he hoped this wasn't happening. "Well, where do you want to head?"

"I haven't the faintest. I'm following you."

"Well that means Pebble Beach. You know they don't do it less than $100 a plate and a thousand dollars a night."

Pete didn't get that one but he saw he'd been had. Alex headed out the door; Pete followed heel.

They bussed downtown to the Customs House and strolled along the waterfront. Pete had never even seen the ocean, much less a fishing fleet. He was bedazzled with excitement. They found the fish restaurant Alex had written down. Pete was lost in the menu. After searching vainly for trout, he settled for halibut. They took in a movie and then wandered back toward the Customs House. There on a side street was an upstairs hotel. They went in. Alex gave Pete's full name. The desk clerk looked on his list and found it. He gave Alex a registration card and then two keys. They climbed a flight and found room 12.

When they went into the room, Pete turned and slammed the door. "You con man! You cursed con man! You had this all set up."

Alex grinned, "Do you think I was going to waste my chance to be civilized for a weekend?"

"No, but you didn't even ask me."

"Did I need to? Seems like a few hours ago you were asking me."

Settling in, they each took a hot shower, looked at the harbor lights at night, and watched late night TV—two wrestlers no longer in their prime—Gorgeous George and Red Berry. Finally they dozed off. They didn't wake until noon Sunday morning. That left them only five hours to be back to base.

But Peter wasn't ready to go. "Hey Alex, you know what I want?"

Alex had his own idea. "Nope and I don't care, 'cuz I want Sunday dinner, one with a tablecloth. Is that what you want? I hope."

"Well . . . ," Peter looked sheepish, "that too." But he had something else in mind. "You know last night we passed a tattoo shop. That's what I'd like—a tattoo."

Alex did a double take. "Oh, you're nuts," he scowled.

"Look who's talking," Pete shot back. He'd discovered a few things on his own. "You've got three of them and one is in a rather delicate spot."

"Yes, but I'm dirt," Alex said in his own self-demeaning way. "You're a blond. You are beautiful as you are. Some woman's going to go crazy seeing you in the nude."

"I gather you have them lining up. Your tattoos don't drive them away."

Alex teased, "Oh, it's my money."

"Oh no it's not. I've seen what you've got to offer."

Alex shook his head. "Kid, you'll be sorry if you do it. I'm sick of mine and I can't get rid of them without making it look really bad."

"Well I'm gettin' one whether you come with me or not."

Alex had a couple more cards up his sleeve. "It's Sunday. They won't be open."

But Pete wouldn't listen. "Let's just go by and see."

"Not until after dinner," Alex hedged again.

Pete agreed, "Okay, it's a deal."

Alex did all he could to make it a leisurely dinner but the tactic did not work. The shop was open. Pete chose a pattern mainly because it took less time to apply. He flexed his right arm bicep and took the pin pricks, refusing to wince. They missed the 4:30 bus and had to take a taxi to the south gate, but at least they made it within the limit. How disillusioned they were when the guard didn't even look at their passes. They could have been hours later. And now they had at least five miles to walk up to Brigade A.

But it was a great evening. They walked along the coastal road. There were no sidewalks beside the road and the water cactus often covered the side hills right down to the edge, so they had to walk in the road. That was okay because they watched the sun setting into a fog that churned up and rolled in. Everything seemed right with the world.

Unabashedly they walked along with their arms on each other's shoulders. As they sauntered, virtually alone, they were silent, gazing, breathing, being immersed in Pacific smells. A car approached; they could hear it interrupting their interlude from behind.

They instinctively dropped their arms and stepped off the pavement to let it pass. It drove up to them and stopped. They saw the words "Military Police" on the door. A helmeted black MP got out of the car and looked at them.

"Let me see your ID cards."

Peter was stunned. What was up?

Alex, acting as calm as the evening, reached in his rear pants pocket and withdrew his wallet. Slowly, eyeing the MP, he took out his card. Then pausing to looked at him straight in the eyes, he handed it to him. The MP read Alex's full name and serial number to his colleague behind the wheel, then he returned the card to Alex. He turned to Pete and demanded his card. Pete masked his terror, took his time and handed over his card.

"Peter Grossberg," the MP read. "Okay what're you two doing?"

"Headin' toward the First Brigade," responded Alex calmly.

"Why don't you take the bus?"

"Missed the 4:30 in Monterey and took a taxi to the gate. Be damned if I'll pay for one to the barracks."

"You're not heading toward First Brigade."

"We're not in a hurry."

"Go on. But just watch out. We've got your name on our list." The MP got in his car and they drove off, slowly.

Alex seemed calm but Peter was anxious. "What the hell was that all about? Are those Mafia watchers?"

Alex began to laugh, first a chuckle, then a chortle, then a howl. Pete looked around to see if anyone would hear them. He looked at Alex, dumbfounded.

Pete guessed something was up. "Alex", he snarled. "How do they know who you are?"

"You're as stupid as I am. I thought the worst too. They had no idea who I was and they still don't. They thought they had found a pair of fairies." He roared again.

"There's a disguise I haven't tried before."

"Fairies?"

Alex stopped, pondered Pete's puzzled eyes. "Oh hell kid, forget it," he grinned. "Just forget it."

Bivouac occupied the next week and soon they were within days of completion. They had crawled under barbed wire with live bullets firing overhead, scaled bare walls and clung to rope bridges, made it through the obstacles almost with ease, except for trying to play poker in the dark.

Alex said nothing about the coming furlough, always holding his cards close to his chest. He never revealed much of importance about himself, never probing too far with Pete. He had never said whether he wanted to see his folks or whether they wanted to see him. But Pete always wondered and he wondered about those two young widows, whether or not Alex was going to play more Robin Hood.

It seemed inconceivable that Alex and Pete would just shake hands and walk out of each other's lives. Pete wanted more. He tried to hint. He thought about following Alex wherever he went. He had no plans to spend the week in Utah. He wasn't going to tell Alex that he could not be seen there until his class had graduated and dispersed. He was staying on at Ord for helicopter training, and needed no transit time. Finally Alex announced he was going up to Fort Lewis near Seattle, giving them plenty of time. He didn't have to report for fourteen days. Pete had wanted Alex to show him California, but he hesitated to say anything because he had no idea what Alex's legal restrictions were. What would the police let him do? What would the Mafia expect? He didn't dare ask. That would violate the veil of privacy Alex had drawn about him. Could Pete gamble again, gamble that Alex was already making reservations? There seemed to be no evidence and Pete was watching closely.

On the last day Pete took some liberty with his position. He wanted to pack alone and then be free to supervise his men's departure. He liked them, most of them, and he wanted to say good-bye as they each left. So he turned the platoon over to Alex and went up to pack. He was going to leave his footlocker and duffel bag in the basement of Company A. The mail clerk would hardly turn down that request after all Pete had done to make the CO look good.

So it didn't have to be fancy packing. But when he threw his things in the foot locker, it was smaller than he anticipated. He took off the display shelf to reshuffle the contents in the lower part of the chest. As he pushed his clothes and towels about, he felt something hard. He hadn't put anything hard in there. Brushing the clothes aside, he uncovered them—the twelve magazines.

So Alex knew. Pete had been secreting them out, one by one to read in the john. But he had replaced them secretly and in exact order.

"That damn Alex!"

He covered them up, transferring the towels to the duffel bag. He dragged them into the basement and rejoined the company.

The CO came out to the last formation. He brought three trophies and matching certificates, one for the outstanding trainee, one for the outstanding squad leader, one for the outstanding platoon leader. The man with the best PT and marksmanship combination score won the first. Well deserved. A squad leader in the first platoon won the second. It was good they didn't give it to Alex. He would have thrown the trophy in the bay. But as feared, Pete was the winner of the squad leader trophy. Considering the skit success, there was hardly any other choice, but Pete felt he didn't need it. Then again maybe he did. He would send it to Harriet as a consolation prize, a testimony that he wasn't going completely to pot.

Then it was over. The men ran for the barracks and headed out as fast as possible. Pete seemed like an old-time preacher as he stood by the barracks door shaking hands with the fellows who stopped in mid-flight to say goodbye.

He was getting antsy. What was happening up in his room? Was Alex sticking around? Certainly he wouldn't leave without a handshake. And like it or not, Pete was going to turn that into the hug he had longed to give Alex. But Pete wanted more than that farewell; he wanted one more week.

When he got back to the room Alex was gone. But his footlocker and duffel were there. So Pete decided to wait him out. Then he heard a horn. He looked out the window and saw a taxi. Alex ran up to the cab and spoke to the driver. Then he ran back up to their room.

"Hey, help me down to the cab with this stuff, will ya?" Alex yelled.

Pete was awestruck. "Then what?"

"Then I'm leaving."

"Just like that?"

Alex stopped for a moment to look Pete's way. "Well the CO wants us to vacate for the next batch of bastards."

Pete knew that. "I'm being evicted too," he said.

"So are you going?"

"I don't know."

Alex grimaced, gathering up his things. "Don't know? Sure the hell you know."

Pete continued trying. "You know I'm coming back to Ord for the next cycle."

But Alex didn't understand and it was obvious he couldn't stay. He pulled at his foot locker. "Hey, that taxi won't wait. Grab the handle."

They each hoisted one end of the footlocker. Alex tackled the duffel bag with his free arm and Pete grabbed the overnight bag with his, the trophy all boxed up and addressed to Harriet swinging on his index finger, which he'd slid under the binding string. At the taxi they put Alex's gear in the trunk. The driver got back into the front seat.

Alex extended his arm and hand. He looked at Pete briefly. "So this is it."

"Oh hell, Alex."

"Cut out your swearing, Saint."

"Alex, I wished you'd be more honest with me."

"Hey this is not time for me to start. I'm incurable."

"Yes this is. I want to go with you for this week, and you know it."

There was a quick silence. Alex's mind was calculating. Pete could tell that he was thinking of the security risks.

"Well I haven't called ahead this time," Alex grinned wryly but he nodded his head toward the taxi and they each jumped in a rear door.

This time it was all of Los Angeles—The Brown Derby, Wilshire Boulevard, Sunset Beach, LaBrea Tar Pits, I. Magnin's, Grauman's Chinese Theatre, 20th Century Fox Studios, Farmer's Market.

Peter was dazzled. The Pacific breeze was perfect, even more sensual than Monterey. He was blown away at I. Magnin's where he saw hundred dollar bills by the dozens and diamond necklaces. The car Alex owned met all expectations—it was an MG. Each night the impressive Mt. Palomar challenged his vision of what beauty really was. It was a whirlwind week.

They first stayed at Widow #1's house. Though she hadn't expected two, Alex smoothed it over. Pete slept on the front room couch, listening for the two children in the morning while Alex stayed in the bridal suite. That's how it went until the last night when they met Widow #2. She was young—almost innocent, it seemed. Her long red hair flowed over a transparent white chiffon dress with delicate white lingerie underlying it like lace curtains.

The four of them went to dinner, a restaurant with tablecloths and candles. Afterward they drove back to Palomar in the Widow #1's Chevy sedan. They parked to look at the city below. Extending to the horizon, the lights twinkled in to the stars that met them in the distance. Alex took Widow #1 in his arms. His hands were quickly busy. Pete soon found his date sliding to him, her one hand on his leg and other tickling the back of his neck. Pete already knew how to kiss, but he had only heard of French kisses. He learned fast.

Then suddenly Alex turned on the engine and drove back to the house. Alex and widow # 1 jumped out, and handed the keys to Pete.

"See you later," Alex grinned.

So Pete was to drive Widow #2 home. Of course. It surely would have looked funny for the three of them to drop her off. So Pete and the lace dress got in the front seat. She had to tell him where to drive, and she took liberties with the directions, sending her hands up and down his body. She tickled and teased while he drove. Pete had never dealt with such overt petting. The arousing was getting him, his resistance declining.

They finally drove into the driveway. She handed him the apartment key.

Looking back the next morning as he left her house, Pete was muddled in his mind. At least she didn't know it was his first time. The magazines had been good for something. But otherwise he felt a sickness. Was this what he had been saving himself for?

On the ride back to Ord he pulled down the bus window and threw the trophy in the bay.

Chapter 12
Junior

Returning to North Rich High School that fall was humiliating for Junior, staring at the void Peter left—the student body presidency he walked away from. The principal didn't seem to know what to do and took three weeks finally to appoint Jim Kane. Jim had been Peter's cohort in many escapades, but he hadn't seemed to be so critical of Bear Lake. His appointment underscored that point. Jim was a good athlete, but he didn't compare to Peter in social skills. Several of the students thought they were helping Junior by telling him that Jim was a poor second choice. It didn't help a bit. Junior felt they were really saying he was somehow responsible, that he should be a dynamo like Peter. Junior knew he could never meet that expectation.

The principal had expressed high hopes for Peter's leadership, confiding to his faculty that being president would help the Round Valley teenager understand the value of institutions and discover the way to bend them to his will. One teacher responded by saying that if Peter stayed and filled his office, he would be delivering a message to others who spouted negative ideas about hick towns. Like Harriet, the high school staff hoped to save Peter a decade of self-destruction. It was a choice between Harriet's path or Hank's. Not that they expected him to remain at Bear Lake for long. No, that was not the requirement. Instead the faculty hoped his departure after graduation would be certified, maybe linked to a credible job, a step toward mature productivity.

The North Rich students felt abandoned. Peter was their natural leader, a friend to the whole senior class, all twenty of them. The rest of the fifty-six students also saw Peter as their leader and clearly felt betrayed. Most had voted for him at his request. Now he had skipped.

Into this emotion walked Junior. His peers saw Peter and Junior as brothers, even if they had different last names. No one blamed Junior. They just thought about Peter whenever they were with Junior, sometimes saying something awkward like, "How's the runaway?" Junior felt two feet tall.

Even if some didn't say anything, it seemed to be in their eyes. He couldn't come up with a defense. The situation seemed worse than the occasional premarriage pregnancies. At least those kids usually stayed and faced the music. Somehow Junior felt he had to make up for Peter's betrayal.

Thankfully there was basketball. Even though he was just a sophomore, he was the tallest in the school. With such a small student body, all of the males were drafted for athletics; he was automatically a starter on the team. They barely had enough fellows to field a football team so that sport was not a high point. Basketball was the center of the school's identity and it was Junior's passion. He had a real talent for running, for dodging, for shooting. He was determined to bring honor to the school, to make amends. Star status was soon upon him.

The adults in the south end of the valley attended the games with a passion. They sensed the promise Junior brought, hoping for three full seasons of his success. They couldn't help but wonder if Junior would abandon them as Peter had done. But it became increasingly clear that Junior was cut from different cloth. If Peter was Hank Grossberg's offspring, Junior was the embodiment of Harriet and her deceased hero, even though Hank had partly raised him. The adults gained confidence in Junior; it was quiet, unspoken.

Harriet and Hank were the ones for whom Junior hurt the most. He saw the suffering in their eyes. Sometimes tears came to Harriet for no apparent reason. She obviously loved Peter. Junior didn't know if she feared for Peter's safety, but because of her increased instruction to Junior, he concluded that she feared mostly for his soul. She constantly talked to him about using "clean language" and avoiding "dirty jokes." She prayed that Peter could avert the "influences of Satan."

It was pretty clear that Peter had chosen mammon. No one said it out loud, but Junior knew all along that Peter had been resisting a mission. The oldest Grossberg son had sensed early on that Harriet's Bear Lake plan would send him out as a Mormon proselyter. If he wanted to avoid being the Lord's ambassador, he needed to disqualify himself. That is what he did.

Peter had chosen for himself a secular mission, one he had told himself would provide as much travel, as much opportunity to see the world but would not require conformity. At least so he thought. Junior sensed it coming and wondered how Peter would sidestep the Lord's mission. But just to walk out on his friends—that was a cheap shot. He could have waited one more year. Then he wouldn't have had to lie about his age.

Most of all Junior felt for Hank. He sensed that although Hank had sometimes interfered with Harriet's discipline of Peter, he mainly turned Peter over to Harriet because he felt her training would be superior to his. Peter's rejection of her plans for him had checkmated Hank. His son's rash action meant he would likely waste precious years as Hank had done. Hank found little outlet for his pain. He couldn't help feeling he had set the bad example.

In Peter's case, fleeing had not been necessary. It was simply rebellion—not well thought-out. He acted on impulse. His pride would not give an inch. Peter refused to communicate about the implications and causes of his actions. His letters home were brief, without a hint of contrition. Worst of all was his refusal to return for a visit. This seemed like an unnecessary slap. And it hurt deeply. Junior knew Peter would not come back. He refused to face his classmates.

Junior, on the other hand, set out to make up for the hurt. To soothe Harriet's pain, Junior achieved in academics. He didn't need to do that to win his peers' approval. In fact, high grades and athletic prowess seemed contradictory to some. But Junior determined to excel in both.

Harriet had urged books and homework on Junior from the start. In her mind he was bound for the State University, like his father, also for a mission between the college years. Everett Jr. didn't sense the need to resist as Peter had done. For some reason from the very first, Peter's mind had been on fire with independence. On the other hand Junior had kept depositing small amounts of his earnings in a bottle that Harriet took to the Logan bank a few times each year. He had more than $200 by now, his mission fund.

One reason Junior liked school was Mr. Bradley. The short, stocky teacher made math easy, sometimes by joking. Just for fun he would often write problems on the blackboard with both hands at once. That stirred lively talk in the halls.

By the time Junior took physics in his junior year, he knew all the stories students told about this teacher with the bow tie. It was clear that sometime in the year Mr. Bradley would literally electrify them. They didn't know when it would happen, but if the last years were a prediction, he would run electric wires down the cracks in the floor right to the metal legs on the desks. At the right time he would send a shock to whichever student he chose. Every class for a decade had been treated to the trick. Last year Mr. Bradley even wired the students' benches at graduation and surprised them right at the end. The audience thought it was a spontaneous ovation when all eighteen seniors leaped into the air with a yell. But the class members realized that had just been the last laugh at them for their infamous trick on him when he arrived in class one day to find his geometry room planted with trees and sod—yes, right on top of the wooden floor.

Mr. Bradley had a message—one that Peter refused to hear. Though he was born in Bear Lake Valley, he became an electrical engineer with a university degree from State College. He had been employed at Thiokol, making rockets over near Tremonton. His escape from ranching life had taken the high road, the respectable escape. His future was secure as long as America needed missiles to defend the world from the communists. He might even get rich by putting such applied science to commercial uses. Certainly he would have enough money to send his seven offspring through college.

So what was he doing at North Rich High School? He made no secret of it. He would wait until the right time, perhaps after one of his tricks. Then there would be a moment when their defenses were down and he would slip in his message. There was a good reason he had abandoned his career as an engineer and come home to teach at this small high school. He wanted to do something positive instead of making weapons. After searching the world for what it should be, he decided it was to come right home and teach math and physics to the Bear Lake kids. They were his inspiration. He could help them become competent and avoid obsolescence.

Junior was captivated by Mr. Bradley. In the next to his last year, Everett found excuses to linger and joke with him, listening to stories about being an engineer, about doing physics experiments at college, about designing model bridges that would hold great weights and win contests.

Mr. Bradley didn't limit his messages to math; he expected Junior to be a champion—in basketball, yes, but in manhood mostly, revealing that he had known Junior's father, not well, but he knew what he stood for. In unspoken ways, when the two of them were alone after class, Mr. Bradley transmitted a feeling of trust.

In Junior's senior year he took Mr. Bradley's pre-calculus class. There were only four students, all young men. It was clear that if you took that subject, you were going to college. There was no reason to choose calculus unless college was the goal. Junior had slipped into that mold without even questioning.

Junior's mind was fully engaged with the precise material. He realized that math was more than doing problems and getting correct answers. He and

Kurt Kane, Jim's younger brother, did their homework together. It was like pulling a log because Kurt could only memorize how to do each problem. That might have been enough to squeak by the tests but the magic in the procedures never "clicked" in Kurt's mind. Junior actually got excited when that "click" would come in his, when the process would be clear, not just the answers. Sometimes it happened when Mr. Bradley was at the blackboard pumping out numbers. At the right moment the teacher would hesitate and look at his four students. Just then the solution would appear in Junior's mind. He would know what Bradley would write next. Occasionally Mr. Bradley would pause, teasing Junior into saying the numbers out loud. Then the teacher would almost jump with delight, affirming Junior's perception. This was real excitement—every bit as powerful as making a score in basketball.

Woodruff Kane's visit was a surprise; he and Hank had been talking regularly in the field for years. In fact, Hank had come to consider Woodruff a friend, despite the gulf between their incomes. Hank had begun to call him "Wood" and felt the acceptance as a near equal. It had been partly because of their sons. Peter and Jim had been bosom buddies, often in their plots. Now the next set of boys, Junior and Kurt, had become inseparable; somehow it was goodness that bound them together.

The two younger boys linked the Kane and the Grossberg families more than the joint fence line had. Although the social distance had been somewhat overcome, there was still the matter of the church. The Kanes were elevated, not just because of acreage and herd size, but because Woodruff was a member of the Stake High Council—the twelve assistants to President Budge in leading the Bear Lake Stake of Zion. He was regularly received in every ward in the Bear Lake Stake—meaning all the towns on the west side from Ovid to Laketown. Everyone knew the Kanes. Hank, in contrast, was not only comfortably obscure, but he was a "gentile"—one of those rare folks who was not a church member but who doggedly stayed in the valley. Bear Lakers were used to some outsiders who came for a while, employees of the Forest Service or school district or power company. Not Mormons, they were welcome; no one expected them to sink roots and they seldom did.

Hank was betwixt and between. He had sunk roots, owned land, fathered offspring and married Harriet who was at the center of the ward. Hardly anything happened in Laketown Ward that hadn't included Harriet's help. But all of it had slipped by Hank. He came for the blessing of babies to make it clear that he approved of their being the next faithful generation, but he was not one for joining the flock himself.

That was what made Woodruff's visit such a surprise. First of all, he came to the front door. That had never happened before; the fence line or the merc was the likely encounter spot. He made it clear that the matter was to be between the two of them, so they sat on the front porch, just Hank and Woodruff. Hank was not uncomfortable at all because they had waterflow from the reservoir to talk about—and fence repairs. That had never required a visit at Grossberg's house, though. This could be unusual.

Unusual it was.

"Hank, you know I'm on the high council. You probably don't know that I am in charge of supervising the Sunday Schools in all of the wards. There is a Sunday School superintendent in each ward and he enlists the teachers and supervises them. I'm responsible to oversee the superintendents. We have a Stake Sunday School superintendent who goes with me and encourages those ward leaders and conducts an annual Sunday School conference. My responsibility is to appoint that Stake Sunday School superintendent and I'm here to ask you to take that job."

Woodruff stopped, letting it sink in.

Hank was silent, just as Woodruff hoped. It was clear that Hank was not seeking retreat by claiming inadequacy. He was just silent, appraising the situation.

Woodruff was playing a trump card—their friendship. He had waited for several years for this moment, waited until they had built real trust—an equal trust. This couldn't be manipulation. Too much hung on it.

Hank had never been a Sunday School teacher. He had sat in a class, maybe only three times. Listening to class members read and discuss excerpts from the scriptures did not engage him. Woodruff didn't need to be told that.

Hank was not a public speaker, but this job didn't really require that. Hank did own one suit, one white shirt and one tie which he had worn for the wedding and for Alan's baby blessing.

Woodruff knew all this, so negotiating was not the issue.

Hank skipped to the main point: "Does this Sunday School superintendent have to be a member of the church?"

"Well, I think so. Perhaps we could get away with it for a few weeks, but baptism is pretty well required."

Silence.

"So let's have you baptized this Saturday." Woodruff had not hesitated. "How do you feel about that?"

Hank was still silent. The request seemed to be churning in his thoughts. "Well, no one has asked me before." he said uneasily.

Woodruff marched ahead, "I'm asking you, Hank. Not just because we are friends. Your Heavenly Father wants it and I think you want it. I've watched you for nearly two decades and I can sense there is something powerful going on inside you. I don't know all that you are feeling, but you have a spiritual side that is important. You have let it grow naturally while others like you sometimes stamp it out. You haven't. Now's the time to open the door and let it blossom. So, next Saturday. Is that agreeable?"

Hank looked at Woodruff right in the eyes, and felt warmth. He nodded.

"I've made an appointment with Bishop Jaggi for tomorrow night. He will interview you for a recommend and set up the details. Then next week we can talk more about this Sunday School job."

There it was. Short, to the point. They parted with a long handshake.

There was the matter of who should baptize him. Immediately Hank thought that Peter was the appropriate one to do it. Certainly he would have asked his oldest son, were he available, spiritually or physically. The next question was whether to invite Junior. He was a priest in the Aaronic Priesthood and thereby had the authority to perform the baptism. Alan was too young; he would have been a good solution because, unlike Junior, Hank was his real father. The question was: "Should it be Junior or Woodruff?" Hank admired Woodruff. He believed it would be nice to show that respect by inviting him. But he could also accomplish that same thing by asking "Wood" to do the ordinance of confirmation that would follow the next day in sacrament meeting.

Then there was the matter of informing Harriet. Hank knew Harriet would be overjoyed. He wondered a bit if she would think he was sincere. But that did not deter him from having some fun breaking the news. So he decided to let it just fall together.

The next evening Junior came into Harriet's kitchen in the late evening and confided to her that Hank had just asked him to be the one to baptize him. Harriet lost her composure and let out a shout. Then she realized that Hank was listening. She rushed into the living room and kissed him and cried unashamedly in his arms. Junior was deeply moved and could sense Harriet's equal response as he gave his mother a great big hug, his long arms reaching all around her, so reminiscent of Everett senior.

The baptism was a solemn and quiet event. Both Woodruff and Harriet wanted it that way. Hank was too new at this point to quite realize what they were doing. They did not invite all of the ward members. Their hope was to allow Hank to ease into membership naturally, not as a celebrity.

Harriet didn't quite know how to feel about this sudden conversion. Did it mean that she had been the obstacle? Should she have "invited" him years ago? Or was her low-key strategy part of the reason that Hank could respond to a manly approach from Woodruff Kane? At the ceremony she touched his hand gently. It fit with the quiet baptism ceremony, transmitting her deep feeling, yet allowing Hank to slip into the fellowship without fanfare.

The Grossbergs made the transition to a united family quietly. Harriet mentioned the baptism in Peter's next letter, without a lengthy description or any hint of victory.

Junior and Kurt Kane's friendship was high adventure for them. It was not what Peter would have called adventure but it was an excitement of mind and spirit. Both boys had reasons to admire each other. Clearly Kurt's membership in the most prominent family impressed Everett Junior. The aura of Junior's athletic heroism caused Kurt to feel privileged to be with him. They felt a bond, just being together, but it was talk and dreams that also bound them.

Another boost to their convictions was seminary. Each of the Laketown teenagers had to decide whether to take seminary seriously or just endure it. The released-time religious instruction program allowed students to cross the lawn over to the church between their regular courses and have a class in the scriptures. Brother Allen, a handsome twenty-nine-year-old, had been their teacher for two years; he had made the choice attractive. But now his replacement was Brother Niederhauser, not nearly so flashy. Brother Allen was transferred to Logan, a step up. Somehow North Rich was a beginning assignment. One or two winters was enough to get teachers hankering for a warmer locale. No one expected the Niederhausers to stay long either, especially because they were in their fifties. Their children were all grown, and here they were in Laketown with no relatives nearby.

There was a reason the Niederhausers came, a most unusual one. Three years ago their life had taken a sudden turn. They had been presiding over the Mormon missionaries in Czechoslovakia when the communist coup happened. Not only was Eduard Benes ousted in Prague but the Mormon missionaries were kicked out of the country. Some even spent a few nights in jail before Niederhauser went to the American Embassy for help to extricate them. Within hours they all fled to Germany.

President Niederhauser was not released from his calling as the Czech Mission President. The church leaders merely put him on hold, hoping that diplomatic negotiations would allow him to return. They asked him to take seminary teaching positions in the meantime. Here the Niederhausers were now in the West, but they were still hoping to get back to Prague. The seminary department gave them this temporary post in Laketown. It could be a transition to another assignment in Europe.

The town folks were thrilled to have them. Their presence brought the world right into their living rooms. But for Junior and Kurt it was another matter. The young dynamo, Brother Allen, was gone. He had been their model for their freshman and sophomore years. They were deeply impressed with him, his handsome physique, his beautiful wife, his two small children. The Allens had been an example of where Junior and Kurt intended to be in a decade—not seminary teachers, but wholesome, vibrant and well-married. Brother Niederhauser was older than their dads. Wrinkled and paunchy, he was not nearly so impressive to boys.

It took only a week of walking across the lawn to the chapel at 10:10 a.m. to change their initial perceptions. It was clear that Brother Niederhauser was a real live hero—a man who had faced Red Guard machine guns and saved two score of young missionaries. To Junior and Kurt he seemed in the category with Stephen who was stoned at the time of the Apostle Paul.

Here was a man who had gone to Czechoslovakia right after World War II, soon after the Nazis were defeated. He sifted through the ruins of cities and towns, finding the survivors who had become Mormons in the 1920s and '30s when he was a young missionary there; he had learned the Czech language then and knew the 300 Latter-day Saints in that land.

In 1946 he had returned with a handful of new missionaries and helped them learn Czech. Then all of them searched for the survivors. They found about ninety. By 1948 they had baptized another one hundred. Then the communist coup had happened with lightning speed. The whole of Europe was shocked. It was so sudden, so ruthless. Hardly anyone noticed that a tiny by-product of that takeover was the expulsion of the Mormon missionaries. The Niederhausers waited in Germany for several months, hoping to negotiate a re-entry, but without success.

Brother Niederhauser was living evidence that there were great issues in the world. Some Bear Lake teens focused on finding a way to spring themselves into the bigger world, perhaps Ogden or Evanston. Junior and Kurt could see that life had greater challenges than escaping small town America.

These stories about Europe opened their ears, but it was Brother Niederhauser's teaching style that captivated them, involving their class in something others might consider boring. They would start off each session by turning to an assigned page in the Bible. One student would read about a column of verses and then the teacher would say, "What in the world does this mean?" waiting for answers. They knew he wouldn't let them off the hook. He could wait for five minutes if necessary.

He didn't want them just to adopt his ideas, so he waited for their halting suggestions. Then he congratulated the student attempts. He would say: "Do you get it? Do you see the strength of Joe's or Sally's point?" He would add layers of meaning to the suggestion and make it seem profound. Sometimes he would trick them by doing the same thing to an idea that was false. He kept going until one of them just had to say: "Hey, wait a minute. You're fooling us." He would respond: "How do you know?" Then everyone would jump in and try to tear him apart. It was as much fun as one can have in class. They soon realized they were actually thinking, not just repeating.

The by-product of Brother Niederhauser's class was that Junior and Kurt started talking on their own. They instituted their own ritual. On Sunday evenings after sacrament meeting they would gather up the five or six fellows in the priests' quorum and go to the Laketown Malt Shop on the highway turnoff into town, buy a double thick raspberry malt "to go" for thirty-five cents and drive up the highway toward Randolph. About a mile up the hill they would take the turnoff to the overlook, pull whatever vehicle they had borrowed out to the edge of the hill and take in the view—Laketown in front of them, Round Valley three miles further west and to their right a full-length view of the lake—twenty miles of water, clear into Idaho.

This was the traditional parking spot for courting couples, but the fellows spooned the thick malts and joked and waited for the stars. It wasn't too unusual for the sheriff to pull up, shine his flashlight into cars and harass hankypankers. One time he even shined his light into their car. They hooted and howled to see the sheriff's surprise when he saw six fellows, the priest's quorum, dressed in their Sunday best, a far cry from what he was looking for. They were holding their own kind of testimony session.

Many a Sunday night those six pondered the meanings of the galaxies. Their seminary studies came up, particularly God's conversation with

Moses: "Worlds without number have I created . . . I also created them for my own purpose; and by the Son I created them, which is mine Only Begotten." They would peer out into the millions of stars and worlds displayed before them and launch conversations that went on for an hour, sometimes two, about their place in God's plan, eternally expanding. They were hooked, enticed into God's Kingdom.

Do you think new worlds are really still coming into being? Are there any that have human beings on them? Will this go on eternally? Will we be able to participate in such creations after this life? Will living the gospel principles here enable us to be so involved hereafter? Junior pondered.

In Junior and Kurt's view, manhood was defined by self-mastery. That meant getting beyond the escapades of their older brothers. Perhaps it was beer and cigarettes that separated the men from the boys at North Rich High. The students had a choice—would they join the clique of rebels which slipped over to the merc to smoke between classes or not? Junior and Kurt easily could have joined in, but they didn't; it was an achievement to resist.

Their choices did not go unnoticed by the adults in the ward. For example, Woodruff Kane asked Junior to come over to his house for a visit. That seemed unusual. Though the Kane home was the closest dwelling to Hank and Harriet's in Round Valley—a mile away—Junior had been there almost every day because he and Kurt biked to school together. This was different; this was to see the dad, not the son. So Everett Jr. bicycled over to be there as requested.

Junior walked to the door feeling not only curious, but a little nervous. He waited for Woodruff Kane in the large, dark front room. Mrs Kane had tried to make him feel comfortable when she came to the front door. When Mr. Kane came down the stairs, he was still pulling on his tie. "Hello," he said in a cheery tone. He sat with Everett Jr. on the plush sofa. "Everett," he began, "I've asked you to come over because the stake presidency has a request of you." Everett didn't breathe for a moment. Woodruff didn't take long. "They would like you to organize an overnight hike and camp for the high school seniors in the stake."

"Wow! That's a great idea. I'll be glad to do it."

"They have reserved the cabin above Tony Grove in Logan Canyon. There will be seventeen- and eighteen-year-olds from the three high schools—Paris, Laketown and Randolph. That is a potential of forty-five to fifty youth."

"That will be terrific," responded Junior.

"We mean it to be fun but also sort of an end-of-the-year celebration. We want the group to be led by their own peers to signify that you are now adults. So you should prepare your own meals. The president asked me and Brother Hansen to come up later in the evening to chaperone but not to supervise. You are in charge. We also want it to have a pioneer theme, so we'd like everyone to do some hiking. What would you think if the group started from the highway and hiked in to the cabin above the lake? That would be about five miles."

"That sounds fine," Junior said. "The fellows can carry their sleeping bags in back packs but the girls might not be fit for that."

"We'll leave that solution up to you. Choose a couple of girls and two or more fellows to help you plan. Include some from other wards. I'll ask them to serve once you choose them," affirmed Brother Kane.

For the next month Junior and his committee went to work, and by the appointed Friday evening the group had hiked in, prepared a meal, enjoyed it and presented a zany program of songs and skits. Junior expected the chaperones by ten p.m. but they didn't arrive. So the young people decided to kill time with the game Twenty Questions. They divided into six teams and were quickly underway guessing, "Animal, Vegetable, Mineral." With teams that large, the action was quick. A half hour passed and they were ready for a change, so they shifted to Charades, using the same teams.

Eleven p.m. came and went. Junior's mind was racing. *What if there has been an accident? What could be holding up Brother Kane? Could he have forgotten?* Because the group hiked in, they did not have a vehicle to drive out and see if the men needed help.

What should we do? Junior asked himself.

It isn't really proper for the fellows and girls to sleep in the cabin together without supervision? I don't know if I can trust all the guys. There are two I'm rather suspicious of. They like to tell off-color jokes, and I'm not about to put the girls in any danger.

Junior pulled Kurt aside, though he was not on the committee. His opinion would help at this moment.

"What do you think we should do if your dad doesn't arrive? Can you imagine what has held him up?"

It was clear Kurt had been wondering the same thing. "He is often interrupted either with ranch emergencies or church ones. Perhaps he had to take someone to the hospital." He paused. "But he knows you will handle things. I think you are right to have an alternative. There would be many angry mothers if we slept in the same room together," Kurt responded.

With that support, Junior pulled each of the committee members aside as inconspicuously as possible. The fellows did not think there was a problem. The two girls were firm that it would not be proper to sleep in the same rooms. "Stick to your guns, Junior," one of them said. "You know what is right."

How easy that was to say, but Junior would have to pull off the decision.

As the twelve o'clock hour arrived Junior chose the moment when a charade finished. He stood up: "The midnight hour has just arrived. We are about to be turned into pumpkins. So it is time to hit the sack. There is just one problem. Brother Kane and Brother Hansen were supposed to be here at ten p.m. We don't know what's holding them up. I think we should assume an emergency has come up and that they will not be coming."

Two fellows hooted, others laughed.

"The committee members and I have discussed the situation and they support me in concluding that we fellows should leave the cabin to the girls and we will take our back packs down to the lake where we can bed down."

One of the hecklers shouted, "Not us. You be the hero."

Junior continued, "Gentlemen that we are, we know it is our job to protect the reputations of these fair damsels."

That got a chuckle from the guys.

"Besides we are pros at camping and would really rather be by the lake. Isn't that right guys?"

A couple more fellows pitched in: "Right, heroes we are."

Junior continued, "The fellows have backpacks. The girls don't—otherwise I'm sure they would insist on trekking down the trail!" Several girls responded, "Three cheers for women's rights."

He picked up on their response, "In return, you suffragettes, we'll be back at seven a.m. for the breakfast you will have prepared by then." The girls protested loudly. Junior retorted, "No sleeping in. This is no slumber party. The ravenous wolf pack will invade at 7 a.m. For your own protection, be ready." The fellows bellowed approval, all except the two protesters. "So guys, grab your packs. We leave in five minutes."

There was some grumbling, but the fellows gathered up their packs and were about to head out the door. Junior saw the two hecklers were not making a move. He realized that he could have a real crisis on his hands if the two stayed and all the rest left.

"Okay, guys. Our two brothers over there want a winning coach's ride off the field." Kurt led out, along with Junior. The whole bunch of fellows pounced on the two, lifted them up on their shoulders, laughing with full vigor, and carried them out the door and down the trail.

The two protesters saw that resistance would not work against such a majority. They fell in step and were soon at the lake shore putting their sleeping bags in place.

The diehards intended to have the last laugh. They settled down and waited for their chance. It took two full hours for the guys to stop talking. Once they were all breathing steady sleep rhythms, the two slipped from their bags, grabbed a flashlight and began their hike back to the cabin.

About half way to their goal their flashlight suddenly illuminated the faces of Brother Kane and Brother Hansen coming down the trail.

"Hello brethren. We're looking for your friends. We've checked on the girls and they are all sound asleep. But we don't really know where the fellows are."

One gathered his wits and said, "We're down at the lake. We've got them all bedded down and were just coming up to check on the girls."

"Very noble of you. We've just done that, so please lead us to your friends. We are very impressed with your leadership. Just wait 'til we report on your gallantry."

At breakfast the next morning, Junior called on one of the fellows on his committee to bless the food. Right after the blessing, Woodruff Kane stood up. "Brother Hansen and I want to tell you how proud we are of you. We were held up because of a minor emergency that took a lot of time. I won't go into that. During that wait I assured Brother Hansen he could trust you to be completely circumspect. When I met you two fellows on the trail and heard your explanation, I was most gratified." He pointed to the two hecklers. "I knew you would have the safety and reputation of the girls uppermost in your minds."

The room erupted in laughter and hooting.

Kurt stood up, intending to correct his father's implication of credit. Junior pulled him back down and whispered: "We don't need the credit. Let those two be reported as squares to their parents and the high council. They might even like it. We need more squares, don't we?"

Less spiritual was the matter of alfalfa. Junior's life was divided between three kingdoms: North Rich High, the church and the farm. On the latter, alfalfa was dominant. It was feed for the herd when they were brought down from the range in the late fall. By then the barn needed to be stacked to the highest beams with hundreds of bales of alfalfa. The Grossberg fields raised mainly alfalfa, some wheat, but mostly the leafy plant imported from France in the 1870s that made the cattle business possible in Utah.

Alfalfa needed water to grow. Summer cloudbursts were a great help when they churned over the western mountains about every third afternoon, dropping maybe a quarter inch of rain. There were irrigation pipes too, which brought water to each field about every fifth day. The irrigation water from the reservoir supplied a limited sufficiency to the ten farms in Round Valley. It came through the ditches which fed the field pipes. But those long metal tubes had to be moved by hand daily.

That is where Junior and Alan came in. It was much easier to move the pipes if there were two sets of hands. They could do the whole job in two hours, if they hustled. They performed the back-bending task late afternoons so the water could be turned on in the early mornings and run much of the day.

The boys were not daunted by the task itself as much as the boredom that sometimes overtook them. "Have you ever estimated how many pipe moves we do in a summer?" asked Alan.

"Nope, but once you give me the number then let's multiply it by ten for the years since we started until we graduate from State College," replied Junior.

Alan became creative. "So let's do something to prevent boredom."

"Like what?" queried Junior.

"How about trying to stump each other with a new word each time we pick up a pipe?"

"You are trying to make me into a philosophy major," Junior grinned.

"Okay, you propose something," he challenged.

"Let's do Twenty Questions. That way each one of us can pick a category we like, animal, vegetable or mineral. We can only ask one question each time we connect a pipe."

So they tried it for about an hour each of several days. They had to admit it was enjoyable mental banter. It wasn't just a game of wit but a time in which the brothers looked out for each other. Peter's absence made it easier for Junior and Alan to have some serious time.

The much bigger job was cutting and baling and hefting the bales onto the wagon bed, six rows high, and then delivering them to the barn and hoisting them onto the haystack in such a manner that it was as solid as a brick wall. Mornings proved to be the best time for lifting the bales, before the heat of the day arrived. They weren't able to play Twenty Questions then.

By the summer before his junior year in high school, Everett Jr. was strong and skilled in alfalfa harvesting. He was bringing Alan along, not just because he was the obvious successor but because it was a two-man job. For several summers Alan had driven the tractor at five miles an hour while Hank and Junior threw the bales on the wagon. At certain points they would have to stop and fit the bales in tightly together so they would not tumble on the drive to the barn. On rare occasions Harriet drove the tractor while Alan and Junior threw the bales up to Hank, who fit them into the criss-cross pattern. But Harriet was often on an errand of mercy or community action, so the threesome went at the job. They became efficient.

Having sons was a great advantage to Hank. In fact, that kind of a labor gang was the core of success. Those ten or fifteen years when boys could be the source of labor were the high point in the family business, the reward for the ten preceding childhood years. Realizing that now, Hank felt guilty for abandoning his parents when he could have been the best help. Peter had done the same—ducked out just when he was the most valuable, a painful reminder of Hank's youth. Tit for tat. So Hank was grateful for Junior and Alan and apprehensive about their inevitable departure.

This summer another transition occurred. Hank, who had thrown bales in the past years, drove the tractor. Was it to strengthen Alan's muscles for the possible departure of Junior? Or was Hank's strength diminishing? He certainly would not let on, and just to prove it he would trade around with them sometimes.

It was almost taken for granted that Hank would always have necessary help. But looming in all of their minds was the prospect of the boys' attendance at college which was no longer that far away. Harriet and Hank had reasoned that even college should not present much interference because most of the bales could be in the barn before late September. Even then they could expect Junior home on Saturdays until the job was done. The cutting could be achieved without the boys and even turning the hay, if there had been a thunderstorm. The baler was another matter; Hank insisted on driving the baler, his pride and joy. Once the cuttings were dry, the baling was just right for a dad's job.

Every year Hank hoped for three cuttings. The extra one would provide enough feed to sell some. With each rainstorm his hopes would soar. But he knew it was not so much the matter of water as it was temperature. They had no control over the frosts which could halt the growth in the fall. Similarly they could not prevent the relapse of winter as late as June. His greatest fear was being limited to one cutting. The growing season in Round Valley, the whole of Bear Lake for that matter, was ninety days, if they were lucky. So it was usually two cuttings. Of course they cut one field at a time in order that the hay would not lie about and get wet. That pretty well spread the baling and loading and stacking through many days.

The sons were tied to the job, and yet there was not really a way for them to earn any money by it. The product was consumed right on the site. Only when the cattle were butchered was there a payout, and that often depended on the market price over which they seemed to have not the slightest influence. Life in Round Valley was labor intensive, cash poor. It made for great physical bodies in fabulous clear air, but it got monotonous, making escape to State College look inviting.

Chapter 13
Aggieland and Beyond

Attendance at the State Agricultural College in Logan was an exciting prospect for two farm boys from Bear Lake and settling into an apartment on Darwin Avenue was a snap for Kurt and Junior. Kurt had been aware earlier that two beds on the south side basement of a duplex would be available so he put his name down for them. Junior was delighted to be the follower in such an arrangement, partly because the place was close to campus. Though the basement was somewhat dingy, by now it had hosted a generation of Bear Lake freshmen prior to their missions. So the duo decided they could hack it.

That first afternoon they unloaded their gear and began exploring, particularly in search of the famous Aggie ice cream. The pursuit took them to the Quad, the heart of the campus, where six buildings surrounded the huge quadrangle lawn, two on the north and two on the south, the library on the east end and Old Main on the west. It took only one quick look to discover where people were exiting with ice cream. Entering the animal science building they approached the lobby counter, received their double dip cones, paid their fifteen cents and went back out to the tree-shaded sidewalk. Sitting on the stone benches surrounding huge maple tree trunks, the two newcomers ate their delicacy for lunch and surveyed the formal quad.

On the east end was the library, built with a Renaissance-style facade that most students would not recognize as being European unless they took a Western Civilization course. It housed a huge reading room the full length of the second floor, reputed to be a great spot to survey the girls one might date. The south end of the Quad was the location of the castle-like Old Main. Its tower was reminiscent of St. Marks in Venice; that fact would also require historical knowledge to recognize it.

Oh yes, there was the chemistry building next to Old Main on the north and the landscape architecture lab on the south. All three of these stood at the top of the stately Old Main Hill, peering onto verdant trees and a broad grass area down the hill to Sixth East Street at the bottom. To the north and down the hill a bit was the forestry building. On the south side of the hill was an amphitheater, built by the CCC fellows in the 1930s, a great place for outdoor musicals.

Sitting on the top row of the amphitheater, the boys had a spectacular view of Cache Valley, encircled by mountains, the Wellsvilles in the distance, about twenty miles to the west. The expanse of the valley from north to south was approximately the same size as Bear Lake Valley but without a lake. Everyone knew that the farmland of the valley was rich, watered by Bear River on the north and several streams flowing from the towering mountains just behind the campus. The Logan River, which came out of Logan Canyon, was the lifeline between Bear Lake and Cache Valley. Close to the confluence of the rivers in the middle of the valley there were wetlands, home to thousands of waterfowl.

Gazing at the vista Junior observed: *This Cache Valley is a place of productive agriculture with a growing season a full month longer than our Bear Lake Valley.* Its name, "Cache," was derived from the fact that fur trappers cached their pelts in the valley in the winter to be available for the annual spring rendezvous in the 1820s. It was easy to conclude that Cache Valley had many advantages over Bear Lake.

Another feature of this outlook was the benchlands which demonstrated the levels of an ancient lake that had existed at least ten thousand years ago. Kurt and Junior's teacher, Mr. Bradley, had taught his students about Lake Bonneville that had once covered much of the state of Utah, including Cache Valley. From this top row amphitheater seat Kurt and Junior detected two levels of that ancient lake just off the hill to the south. For millennia alluvial fans of sediment off the mountains had been deposited, creating a delta which was now the level of the campus. Then the water broke out up in Idaho, and the lake dropped to the next level.

The boys could see exactly where the next alluvial fan built a new delta; on that level stood the Logan LDS Temple. *This is another advantage for this area*, Junior reflected. The temple sat on the edge of the hill, presiding in a stately manner, its two towers, one on the east and one on the west, beckoning for all to come. It could be seen from almost any location on the valley floor, the final level of the lake which then drained into the Great Salt Lake, its present remnant.

Junior and Kurt remembered the stories of their ancestors who worked the lumber mills at Temple Fork in Logan Canyon to prepare the huge beams for the floor joists and roof supports for the temple. The temporary scaffolding erected around the whole building supported the workers who hoisted the stone into place. That also required thousands of feet of posts and planks. The resulting monument inspired reverence, a realization that in a few months they would likely go there to make solemn commitments prior to their missions.

Surely this was one of the most impressive campuses anywhere. Where could a campus command such a view, boast links to a pre-historic lake and rich agriculture, be set up in such geometric splendor, enjoy a view of a sacred temple and be encircled by mountains?

That first night in the apartment, the two new students were occupied with getting their possessions appropriately placed in closets, making beds and arranging the apartment to seem liveable. It took some sweeping and washing in the kitchen to even meet their standard. Then it was time to try out their beds. That brought up an awkward moment: *What about prayers?* Their parents had taught them to kneel beside their beds at night and pray. They had both done it since childhood, but here they were together, two in the same bedroom. Junior looked at Kurt. Here was his buddy of two decades. They were real compatriots, had done some serious talking about all sorts of things, but had not shared this private moment. Kurt could sense Junior's feelings and quickly realized what the subject was. So he nodded to him and said, "Of course, who's turn is it?" Junior responded, "Okay, I'll go first." They knelt and Junior was the voice. Upon conclusion, as they stood up, they grabbed each other with a hug as intense as any they had ever shared on the football field. This was an even better adventure. It became their nightly ritual, increasingly binding them as brothers.

A change in their life came in the form of two roommates, not of their choosing, who arrived the next day to occupy the other bedroom in their basement digs. Bill and Ned were buddies from Bountiful High School, quite a contrast to the Bear Lakers. There had been more than a thousand students in their school. The football team played in the top category, against Davis and East and West and South high schools along Utah's populous Wasatch Front. Those contests had even been reported in the *Salt Lake Tribune*. And since girls were their chief occupation, they had already gathered the dorm room numbers of a dozen they had hoped to impress with their money, clothes and pizzazz. They were clean guys—no smoking or drinking—but they were definitely on the fast track. Bill was particularly glib. He always had a joke about to form on his tongue. Junior wondered if he ever had a serious moment, or a quiet one.

Bill was surprised the Bear Lakers were slow movers when it came to girls; he had thought farm boys could teach him a thing or two about sex. However these two just didn't seem aware of how the girls wanted to be wooed. So Bill took it upon himself to help educate them. Each morning one of the two Bountiful boys reported on their conquests of the night before. The first tale was an Aggie tradition. There should be a stroll in front of Old Main in which the girl sat on the block "A" monument to be kissed. It was part of the folklore that all the alumni knew and that fellows such as Bill delighted in perpetuating. Bill set it as a goal for Kurt and Junior, taunting them for a positive report.

One of the reasons the Bountiful duo liked the apartment on Darwin Avenue was that it backed onto the Delta Gamma and Kappa Kappa Gamma sorority houses which faced Eighth East Street. They could see into the back bay windows and knew when activities were underway. It was not at all unusual for the girls there to yell out for the two and bid them into the house on an excuse to fix something or lift something or any other flimsy plot. The fellows soon had a free admission ticket. They were smart enough not to abuse it, devising a strategy of making themselves wanted instead of being too available. The result was that any girl in the house was willing to date them. They were known as clean kids, but that was within a sorority definition. Clean meant safe but not lacking in testosterone.

So the boasting included ways to kiss every girl and to kiss at length and maybe even more. They reported on the different places one could "perform." Old Main Hill was one of the best. Ned tried to make it clear to Kurt and Junior that the women wanted this romanticized recreation, even if they protested. That was how one achieved manliness—by asserting his passion and by stimulating the girls. The women loved it, according to Bill, and it was the sign of adulthood for men and femininity for women.

Junior wasn't sure about such an extracurricular activity. "Gosh Kurt, do you think these guys go 'making out' every night?"

Kurt hesitated. "We saw that stuff happen occasionally at the Laketown lookout with kids going steady but Bill and Ned seem to be at it as a daily diet."

Junior knew he didn't like the idea. "I'm sure glad you and I are together. I'd feel out of touch with reality if I were alone with them," he confided to Kurt.

"Let's keep a united front," Kurt said. "If we are clever we can make them think they are the ones that are out of step."

Junior thought it was a good plan. "Okay, we'll outwit 'em, all the while being more and more their buddies."

That began the pattern of lingo in their apartment. Bill and Ned pushed for "making out" while Junior and Kurt dodged the ball, countering with the delights of restraint and innocence. They even tried to stir a bit of guilt in the Bountiful boys. They called them "talk commercials" from their parents. "Remember who you are," and "Treat the girls like you would want your sister to be treated." It was fun banter with the two sides pretty equally matched.

As much as the Bountiful Boys were the object of their commercials, the four fellows next door who inhabited the north half of the basement were not. Fortunately, they had their own entrance, even their own driveway. The separateness did not end there. Their lifestyle made the Bountiful Duo look square. Their garbage can was filled with beer bottles and their apartment often had females there all hours of the night. The two quartets had hardly a word to exchange with each other, each standing their ground rather judgmentally. Junior could not tell if the neighbors had Mormon backgrounds that they were defying or if they came completely from the outside. Either way the rowdies added to Kurt and Junior's determination to stay "straight."

Then came Allison. Junior had no intention of dating much his freshman year. Bringing in the alfalfa bales at home would keep him busy Friday afternoons and Saturdays. It was a convenient excuse to avoid women. He didn't complain. It was better that way. The times with Allison weren't really dates anyway, just study sessions.

Initially there were three girls from Mary Nelson's calculus class who met Junior at the library at two p.m. Monday through Thursday. The only three females who dared to take calculus, they were intimidated. Allison asked Junior to study with them. Why? First, because he obviously understood the fabled teacher, and second, because he was not "on the make." His confirmed innocence attracted them immediately.

The three girls had registered for Miss Nelson's unknowingly, believing a female teacher would be sympathetic. Once they saw Miss Nelson they were even more convinced. She wore a long dress with printed patterns, and her nicely curled hair gave her an aura of being a motherly type—certainly traditional and trustworthy. Little did they know that the faculty in engineering—all males—recognized her teaching as the best preparation for their aspiring engineers.

Once she hit the blackboard, it was clear that she expected them to be math lovers. The formulas flowed with a fury. She kept chalk in both hands, made the corrections and conclusions with the left while the derivations came from the right. Junior knew that trick from Mr. Bradley and it took only ten minutes for Mary Nelson to realize that he was a North Rich product. So she zeroed in on him, asking for his answer before she would write hers. Most often Junior was ready. That set him apart.

Why did he know the answers so soon? It was simple. Junior worked all the homework problems the night before class, all of them. Not only did he work them but his mind could derive them logically. It was his real excitement. He was matching his intelligence against the classic thinkers from distant centuries who had invented the calculus. If he felt he could comprehend the process clearly, he could do almost anything—physics, engineering, astronomy. Understanding calculus meant admission to the scientific elite. That was a dimension of manhood the Bountiful Duo had yet to uncover.

Once the three females saw the results of their first test, they latched onto Junior. The exercise began every afternoon at two p.m. Junior didn't mind it, claiming that he had to do the problems anyway. He would just do them with the girls, even if it took twice as long. He called it his "service to womankind," refusing to admit that he enjoyed the feminine attention.

Problems arose as the trio shrank. Without consulting any of them, one girl dropped the course. Junior felt bad, not only for her but for girls in general. Why did they flee science? In elementary school the girls seemed smarter than the boys, but by high school most shunned trigonometry, the course that opened the door to science. So by pre-calculus it became a male club. A female engineering major or physics major was rare. Had anyone seen a girl with a slide rule hanging from her belt?

Allison had still not told Junior why she was taking calculus. Was she intending to go to medical school? She didn't say, but even if she was, she didn't really need calculus to get in. Was she planning to get a Ph.D. in science? That would be amazing. To Junior she seemed to be the motherly type. He obviously had something to learn, and Allison was being coy.

The second girl just got lazy. She was understanding the problems all right and could get a "C" on the tests, but doing all the homework problems seemed like overkill to her. The study sessions cut into her campus activities in student government, which were higher on her priority list. So by midquarter she quit coming. That left the two of them.

It seemed just fine, the high point of his day. Allison was always there. She needed no reminding. And Junior was careful not to suggest that she did. He also learned something quickly once it was down to two. With three girls, he had been the center of attention. They had made a big fuss about him, even brought him cookies. Once the others departed, Junior realized that Allison didn't really need him. In the excuse of efficiency, he suggested they split the problems and then share the results with each other. Only rarely did he have to modify her solutions. She returned the compliment by correcting him a couple of times.

Junior was soon in love. This was not in the plan. They hadn't even held hands, but more and more he found himself wanting to. They hadn't been on a date and that would have to change. Kurt would have to be consulted on such matters. Why? Because Kurt's car brought them back to campus from their farm work on Saturdays. Junior wanted to be back Saturday afternoon to take Allison to the Homecoming Dance in mid-November. What's more, Kurt would have to get a date so Junior and Allison could occupy the back seat.

By the end of October the hay was in but there were other jobs on the farms—a minor obstacle. Usually Junior and Kurt had driven back to Logan Saturday night so they could attend the college ward at the Institute, almost next door to their apartment, on Sunday morning. It would just have to be earlier, Junior argued. The big challenge was convincing Kurt to get a date. He had no well-cultivated afternoon study group. He was not about to let Bill arrange a date with one of the Delta Gammas. None of that. Junior and Kurt decided not to even let on that they were going to the dance. Kurt had to survey the college ward and find a likely candidate there. It wasn't a tough job because Kurt was clearly a handsome catch. They had a month to do the sifting and he rose to the occasion, still mystified that Junior was obviously thinking beyond just a date with Allison.

The homecoming evening was first-class. Allison invited the foursome to her home in Amalga for dinner, the town where the Amalgamated Cheese plant was located. Junior and her father, a dairyman, hit it right off. Junior specialized in steers and her dad in cows; each was glad they weren't doing the other's job. Allison's father was tied to his milking barn every morning and evening. Junior's dad was tied to his land from sunrise to sunset.

Both were workaholics. Junior didn't mind working; he knew the growth in character it had brought him, but he did not intend to toil with animals or with farms after college. Like a farmer, he didn't feel right unless he was on task, some task. That is why he was doing so well in calculus and chemistry too. He saw a lot of Hank in Allison's dad and it gave him more respect for his adopted father. It also increased his interest in this farmer's daughter. Her cuisine capabilities were delightfully demonstrated that evening, making the whole event memorable.

It was the highlight of the quarter when Bill and Ned and their dates bumped into Junior and Allison, Kurt and Shirley on the dance floor. It was the comedown the Bear Lakers had long wanted to deliver. No, the Bear Lake farm boys hadn't needed Bill and Ned's coaching to do just fine at the posh event. The next day the Bountiful Duo demanded a full report. Did they get to the "A" on the hill and do their duty to manhood? Obviously not. What a disappointment. Didn't Kurt and Junior know their role? How disappointed the girls must have been. What could they say to their roommates?

One date led to another. By Christmas Junior was in a predicament he had never considered. He still had not taken Allison to the "A" on the hill for that ritual kiss—and not anywhere else, either. He was sure the daily study sessions in the library would not terminate just because the calculus class was over at the end of quarter. Those chairs in the library knew their permanent afternoon occupants by now. Where was all of this leading?

Bishop Cannon came to the rescue. He gave Junior a rationale for what was happening. One Sunday morning before Christmas vacation he gave the priesthood lesson to all the men in the student ward. It was pretty explicit. "I am concerned that young men who hold the priesthood often came to campus and adopt secular standards for dating. They use pressure to get their dates to 'deliver' and pick up on the next date where they left off on the previous one. Soon they press the girls beyond their comfort level, causing real guilt feelings. This 'conquest' approach is based on major flaws.

"Fellows who like to get their satisfaction with girls are training them to resist men. What kind of a marriage will they have if the girls resist them and feel guilty about them? Far wiser is it to master one's passions, protect the girls from the bestiality within us, discipline ourselves and wait for the girls to want our affection, then share it sparingly."

The bishop knew exactly what Junior needed to hear. Now he had an explanation of the difference between the Bear Lakers and the Bountiful Boys. Though Ned and Bill were active Mormons, they often slept in and missed priesthood meeting and that was the case today. Junior hoped they would hear of the bishop's talk through the grapevine. He was not about to tell them. It would be too self-serving, but he knew the direction he was going to continue with Allison.

Junior found himself plotting. It had never crossed his mind not to serve a mission. He had been saving his nickels and dimes since childhood for his mission fund. Peter's escape to the Army underlined Junior's intention to be a missionary, not to make up for Peter but to set his course in the direction of virtue. Now he was wondering how he could substitute marriage for mission. *Is this really possible? How could I ever justify this early marriage? I have no intention of using it as an escape. How could I ever finance a marriage?* This would not be a rushed marriage, because they would have to be engaged a long time, perhaps a year, to save money. This marriage could be disciplined and virtuous, but it would pre-empt a mission.

Why not go on a mission and then come back and marry Allison? Well frankly, he was worried he might lose Allison during the two-and-a-half-year absence. She was a top-rate catch. He was not the only one at her door, even now. Besides, he was throbbing with love he wanted to share. Wow, could this really be happening to him? If so, how would he ever negotiate past Harriet and everyone else?

Then a thought came: *How about Hank? Maybe I could find an ally in dad.* Junior's mission would certainly be a drain on Hank financially and in lost farm help also. Maybe Hank hoped to postpone the inevitable loss of sons. Junior knew in advance what Harriet's response would be, so he didn't think of starting with her. Of course Junior had mixed feelings himself. There was no question in his mind about the truthfulness of the gospel or the validity of spreading the word. He didn't have to go on a mission to develop his own convictions.

He was not trying to duck the mission. He agreed that missions are of prime importance and he had every reason to accept such a call. He knew he would be a solid missionary, a dutiful one. The problem was that he was in love. He wanted Allison; especially, he did not want to lose her. There was no question that they would live a life of complete devotion. *Then we could go on a mission as a couple after our children are raised. How about that?* It was a contest between two goods. Could he believe that?

During the first evening of the Christmas break Junior and Hank were in the backyard. Junior was splitting the cut logs and Hank was stacking them. Alan was on a debate trip with his school team overnight in Ogden. Hank was acting as Junior's sidekick in place of Alan. To make conversation, Hank asked for a summary of his first quarter at college. Junior sensed he could choose the topics and be safe. Hank intended it that way. So after talking about engineering and calculus, he moved on to social life. Before long he and Hank were right there in the library with Allison. Junior stopped. It was a poignant silence. Hank looked in his eyes, waiting for the dilemma that was clearly churning. When Junior couldn't quite find the words, Hank helped.

"Junior, if you don't go on a mission, who should?"

That was all that was said.

The next afternoon was Sunday. Kurt and Junior met at the malt shop and drove up to the overlook, just the two of them, for old time's sake. Kurt wanted to talk, talk about missions. He was getting hyped but he had something on his mind: "Everett Junior, of all the people in the world, you know the most damaging things about me. I want you to tell me straight what you think about my going on a mission."

"What do you mean, Kurt? Of course you are going on a mission. I have never had a moment's question that you would."

"Yes, but am I worthy?" Kurt asked. "You know the junky things I've done. They are not huge and glaring, but I need your forgiveness, your support."

"Forgiveness, for what?"

"Hey come on. You have a memory."

"Kurt, I will be there to vote the day you are proposed to be ordained an elder. My arm will be raised high. I am proud to be your closest friend. You inspire me and I hate to see our year end in June. Until then you keep me on the track."

"Track to what?" queried Kurt.

"The same track you've kept me on 'til now."

"You know what track that is," Kurt said.

"Sure," Junior hesitated.

"It's the track that leads to a mission."

Junior was surprised at Kurt's words. "Well yes, sure."

"C'mon Junior, you know what I'm telling you."

"What?"

"Junior, Allison will not marry anyone but a returned missionary. Obviously, you realize that."

"I do?"

"She told me that herself."

"She did? When did you propose to her?" Junior teased.

"Hey, she came to me as the source. She wanted to know if I thought you were firm in your intentions about a mission. I told her I was sure you were. How's that for being your agent?"

Gee thanks, Junior thought. "You are all heart."

"My going on a mission doesn't depend on your going, but your going is vitally important to me."

"Of course," replied Junior, his thoughts clearing.

"Well, I just want you to know I am in the repenting mode. I want to straighten anything out in my past. You are much of my past and my future too. So I am going to talk with the bishop tonight and just wanted you to know."

"Tonight?"

"Yes, and before I do I want you to hear me say that you are my inspiration."

Junior had just been caught off guard and felt he could have been blown over with a feather.

Late Sunday evening Bishop Jaggi drove up to the Grossberg home. He asked if Junior would take a ride with him. It wasn't a long conversation. In reality it was an interview to determine Junior's worthiness to be ordained an elder. He evidently felt Junior did not need a week's notice to get his "house in order."

"This is not a mission call," said the bishop. "That will come in about five months, so you have that time to prepare. I want to send yours and Kurt's recommendation to the stake president tonight so you can both be ordained to be elders next Sunday, prior to going back to campus. That way you can serve awhile as elders and prepare yourselves for the temple."

Junior could barely breathe.

"Wow. This is coming faster than I thought."

"Yes, you are almost middle-aged," the bishop joked. "But seriously Everett, I have great confidence in you so I want you to move forward. I advise you to go to the temple by April so you can have a couple of months to attend the sessions there before school ends. Being right in Logan, within sight of the temple, is a privilege you might not always have."

One week later Kurt and Junior were presented to the quarterly stake priesthood meeting to be sustained as elders. Five others from the various wards along the west side also stood to be voted on. Following the meeting all seven of the young men and their families gathered in the high council room. Kurt was ordained by his father, a member of the Stake High Council. Naturally Junior had asked his paternal grandfather, Grandpa Proctor from Ovid, to ordain him. It was a simple moment as Grandpa laid his hands on Everett Junior's head and spoke words of authority that gave him the power to act in the name of Christ. Hank and Harriet were there. Hank seemed comfortable, even proud. Of course, Harriet shed a few tears. Junior wondered if she was allowing herself to reflect on Everett Senior.

The next Sunday, in Logan, Junior was called into Bishop Cannon's office during Sunday School. The bishop gave him an assignment. He was to organize a monthly baptistry excursion at the temple, including about fourteen fellows and ten girls from the ward. Brother Cannon had reserved the fourth Thursday evening at 8:30 p.m. for their group. He said he would announce the plan in the sacrament meeting that day. Junior was delighted to take it from there.

The following week Junior passed around a sign-up sheet in the priesthood and Relief Society meetings. He noted a time for each of the volunteers to meet with Bishop Cannon on Wednesday evening to obtain a recommend, if they did not already have one. The next week he reminded them all to meet at the Institute at eight p.m. so they could ride together to the temple.

Thursday evening they met and arrived in plenty of time. The greeter, dressed in white, directed them to the baptistry in the temple's basement. A middle-aged couple, also in white, met them there. They instructed the returned missionaries how to perform the baptisms, how to act as witnesses, how to perform the recording and confirming. The other fellows and girls, all dressed in white, prepared to be proxies for deceased people for whom they would be baptized and confirmed. The whole process took two hours—time to sit there in the heart of the temple silently and contemplate, watching the baptisms occur. This was one of the most sacred places on the planet, Junior felt—sacred because of its construction, because of its dedication, because of the ordinances performed here. Being here helped him decide to go the next step.

That day came quickly and so did the solemnity that was appropriate to the event. The temple ceremonies brought Junior to the sudden realization that he was an adult. The move into adulthood had been so gradual and so comfortable for him that he was not quite prepared to realize that youth was over. The temple endowment brought that realization into clarity. His brother Peter had demanded adulthood and postured for two or three years to find a way to get his demands met, to find entrance into adult institutions.

Everett Jr. just slipped in quietly. As long as he worked at the farm he seemed to still be a youth because he was under Hank's supervision. And being a student also kept him in a subordinate status. Then came Allison and serious thoughts of marriage. That brought possibilities of having to be independent. Now that marriage had been put on hold, however, he seemed back in the youth category. The temple ended all that.

The ceremonies were clearly a manhood ritual. He thought of his baptism at eight years of age, bringing him into the Christian fold. The temple was like a graduate level baptism. Once the ceremonies were concluded, he had consecrated his life to that same purpose as he had at baptism, but it was so much more amplified, so clearly the commitment of an adult. He had set his directions in life by covenanting again, this time as an adult, to devote his life to serving God and His Son. He was a sober man when he left the temple that day.

The next and natural step was becoming a missionary. Right after spring quarter the interviews and farewells and one week of training in Salt Lake City came in swift order. Soon he found himself as the junior companion to Elder Bullock in Buffalo, New York. This was a culture shock. He had never lived in a metropolis among laboring class people, poverty, tenement housing. It was new, if not hostile. And the Mormons were totally insignificant. There were few of them in Buffalo and the rest of the people seemed to care less. He felt marginalized but full of purpose. Nothing he saw seemed to invalidate Laketown and what it stood for. In fact, quite the opposite. It was not that he felt people should live in rural settings. Not at all. It was that they should dedicate their lives and find meaning in the gospel. Those vows he made in the temple seemed even more valid as he wandered through the secularism of Buffalo, of urbanism, of industrialism, of people mostly concerned with themselves.

Harriet found Junior's letters home to ring almost like scripture. Naturally she hung on his every word, but she didn't need any convincing. So the letters became her propaganda avenue. Using the excuse that they all wanted to know of his mission, Harriet brought the letters to the dinner table and asked that they take turns reading. Alan saw through it immediately but did not object. He knew that parents had to get in their commercials. That was what parenting was about when one had older adolescents to guide. Alan did not consider himself in need of such direction. He was on track, even if it was a wider track.

So they read:

> Here I am in Upstate New York, not far from the famous sites of early church history—the Hill Cumorah, the Sacred Grove, the Peter Whitmer Farm—all places where Joseph Smith received revelations and translated the Book of Mormon. I haven't been to these places yet, but will get a chance during August when the pageant is performed.
>
> Obviously I have never lived in a big city and it is quite a jolt. The street people, those who do not have a place to live, are the real

shock for me. They pose a problem for missionaries. We could devote all our time to talking with them. They are easily available, but we have to decide if that is our mission. It troubles me.

My companion is an all right guy. I was afraid I might get a dullard—but not Elder Bullock. He is a driver. We work from sunup 'til well after sundown. I'm glad we do. He is from New Jersey. His dad is an attorney who commutes every day into "the city." Their family is quite a contrast to ours. We would call them well-to-do but Elder Bullock says no. He claims they are average. Maybe it is just city living that contrasts with Laketown. I don't feel a bit deprived in comparison to him, especially in education. I'm glad I grew up largely out of doors with lots of physical work. He didn't have that chance. He is skinny but has a sharp mind. I can match him in math though.

The first thing I had to learn was not really a surprise but facing it every day is tough. The fact is that hardly anyone but street people want to talk to us. A few who answer our knock on their door are polite, but most are anxious to get rid of us and some are downright nasty. So our challenge is to keep up our spirits. We try every angle we can think of to match wits with these people. We don't want to be like a door-to-door salesman or like Jehovah's Witnesses. Many think we are JWs. Those people we meet are very suspicious. They think we will try to sell them something. Some belong to a church and they don't want to change, but most do not. They just want to avoid religion. They are the ones I feel sorriest for.

Each day two or three people let us give them a lesson. Then we make an appointment to come back for lesson # 2. Most of them disappoint us. Of fifteen such lessons in a good week, less than half are there when we come back. If we get one good contact in a week we consider it a victory. I have concluded that tracting door to door is an ineffective system. We could easily quit doing it and some missionaries do. But what do we replace it with? If we were in England we could hold street meetings, but that tradition hasn't caught on in this country.

I wish we could find another way, through the radio or telephone or something so we would only have to talk to those people who might take us seriously instead of considering us a nuisance. Several radio stations in New York carry the Tabernacle Choir, but that does not lead to chances for us to teach. The Palmyra Pageant is a super vehicle. *Some people hand in cards there and invite the missionaries to visit them. We have only received one such card since I have been here. When we went to visit those people, they were kind and let us in. I don't think they will join the church, but we have had a much fairer hearing with them than with others.*

Clearly the best way to do missionary work is to be invited. We are presently teaching a young teenage fellow. He is the friend of the Branch President's son here. The two young men meet with us each week. We had to get permission from his parents to teach him. That is often the end of the opportunity, but these people had no religion growing up and think their son could benefit from it. I hope we can get through the lessons and his baptism without some anti-Mormon preacher pounding on his parents.

One thing I didn't think about much before coming on a mission is rules. They give us a little white book. It fits in my pocket. It is the rule book. There are thirty-five rules. Some are obvious: no dates, no physical relationships with women. A missionary should never be in a room with women alone. Elders are not to teach young women alone or without their parent's permission. Companions are to be together day and night. Go to bed by 10:30 p.m., rise by 6:30 a.m. Study two hours every morning. Always dress in white shirt, tie and suit when in public. Write your parents every week. Do not travel out of your zone. And on and on.

It becomes obvious that there are two ways to be a missionary. One is to follow the rules and the other is to bend them, to nit pick at them or to just plain rebel at them. Elder Bullock does not deviate an inch. At first I thought he was going overboard, but since I have come to know several missionaries, I am joining the rule keeper camp. They are clearly the most effective and the most comfortable. The rule breakers have to look over their shoulder, keep things secret and justify their actions. So I guess I'm on my way to becoming even more of a square.

So much for now. Love, Elder Everett Proctor, Jr.

The very next day, after Junior wrote that letter, the missionaries had a memorable tracting experience. It stunned Junior. They were invited into an apartment by a man who appeared to be about thirty years old. Their enthusiasm was spiraling upwards as he listened to the Joseph Smith story and their lesson about the three members of the Godhead. Then he interrupted them.

"How much do you two get paid for this ministry of yours?" the man asked.

The question exposed a basic cynicism which he intended to use to discredit them. He was not quite prepared for the answer.

"Nothing," replied Elder Bullock. "In fact we pay our own support for two-and-a-half years while we are on our mission."

The young man didn't believe it. "Oh, c'mon, you may not be receiving a check, but some fat daddy is paying your way."

Pointing to Junior, who had been quiet up to that time, he said, "What about it?"

"Yes, my farming parents are contributing to my expenses, but I am paying part of it myself. I've been saving for this for over ten years."

The man sat back and gazed out of the corner of his eye. He stroked the small beard on his chin. "So you would classify yourself as an idealist, I suppose."

Junior was not quite sure how to respond so he said, "What do you mean by an idealist?"

"Oh, I had forgotten, you two are just kids. You are like my students. Every generation has to start from scratch. An idealist, my friend, is someone who thinks human beings are basically good. I used to think that until I found out that human beings are really trash."

Elders Bullock and Proctor just looked at each other, amazed.

"Oh, I can see you are essentially uninitiated. Have you ever heard of the Holocaust or the Gulags?"

Junior had taken a World History class in high school and responded somewhat confidently, "They had to do with World War II?"

"Well, I'm glad to see that we are at least on the same planet." The man's voice was colored with a kind of subtle sneer. "How do you explain the fact that human beings willingly slaughtered over ten million of their helpless brothers? Most of those butchers went home to their apartments at night and acted like they were decent citizens. It was not killing on the battlefield. It was the outright massacre of people because of their political opinions or race."

Elder Bullock countered, "So does that mean that we should ignore all the goodness that has happened or can happen?"

The professor retorted, "If there is a God, and He is all powerful, why would he allow these horrific acts? And it is not just these. There have been others before and since. Have you heard of the Cambodian Killing Fields?"

Elder Bullock looked ready to flee the place. But he held on to his courtesy.

"You ask good questions and we would like to come back and teach you some lessons that will include matters about man's free agency and God's plan for man," he continued.

The professor was more than ready to end it. "No thanks for now. You two go back home and get a Ph.D. and come back in ten years. Then I want to see if you are believers. As for me, I used to be naive, but I am not any more. I can't accept the idea of a God. There is too much wrong with this world."

Junior decided to jump in, "Sir, I respect your opinion, but I would feel dishonest to leave here without responding. I don't know a lot, but I have spent two decades with the same people in a remote mountain valley in the Rockies and I don't find them to be trash. I have seen much goodness, even amid family tragedy. I will not abandon the belief that my job is to be as good as they are."

The professor laughed. "Come off it. You fellows live strict rules and act like saints on the outside, but you know that inside are drives that you would love to enact. You would just love to find a prostitute and go wild with her. Admit it."

Everett was amazed at what came out of his mouth. "You are wrong sir," not knowing where the direct confrontation would take him. But he wanted to continue, "I have a girl friend at home. During our dates I considered it my job to protect her from my potential bestiality. If I am fortunate enough to marry her after a chaste courtship, I will be gentle and live by complete fidelity," he said. He had surprised himself with his personal candor. But he felt the pride and cynicism of the young professor needed an answer.

Everett's mind was reeling as they left the apartment: *Is Harriet trash? Is Hank trash? Are even the Thompson brothers trash? I can't buy that.* He thought he had settled the matter for himself, even though it was clear that the professor was not changed by his testimony. Nonetheless there was some haunting discomfort: *Is restraint the only thing that keeps us from being carnal? Why am I chaste? Because of fear of being discovered if I am not? No, I rather believe what Bishop Cannon said: "Being righteous is life's highest adventure."*

Chapter 14
Alan

Alan was a different son from either of his half brothers. His path of adolescence in Bear Lake County was his own. He was the offspring of Hank and Harriet, yet his determination was to outdo them both. It was Alan who started doing pushups as early as ten. By twelve he did fifty each morning, daring his brothers to best him. They sidestepped the challenge, refusing to recognize the legitimacy of the prod. They claimed it was just his way of compensating for being the third child.

Alan was also the brother who could spell. Somehow he had just inherited the gene for it. Here he was, four years behind Peter and two behind Junior and he loved to match wits with them. Spelling was his whiplash. They could hardly turn him down when he would ask them to spell a single word, even if they knew they would lose. Such encounters only took a few seconds. It wasn't a matter of playing a whole game, just respond to one query such as, "How do you spell 'picnicking?'" They knew it would be a tricky word and that he knew the answer. Who would remember to put the "k" after "picnic?" After losing, they would counter with their own challenge and often Alan spelled their word. It was uncanny.

These devices helped Alan, but it was not quite clear to him what his path should be. Peter's escape to the army was not an appealing option and it had little impact on him. More challenging was coping with Junior's status as an athletic star and as a straight arrow. These were two achievements that were hard to follow, but not something it was smart to rebel against. One factor was inescapable: Alan was six inches shorter than Junior. That nixed basketball as his road to fame.

Alan was nonetheless a high achiever. In actuality he outdid both brothers, and even Hank, when it came to work. Because of his muscular build, strong thighs and a well-developed upper torso, Alan had few physical limitations. He made sure that he and Hank put up as much alfalfa as when their crew included Junior, even when it had Peter too. Running back and forth on both sides of the wagon, he threw the bales up to Hank. They needed

Harriet to drive the tractor but when service called her away, they continued with the hay anyway, stacking it on the flatbed, layer after layer, criss-crossed to prevent the bales from falling off.

The youngest of Hank's boys ran almost the whole time they were gathering the bales, but Hank arranged for a relief when they had to hoist the hefty bundles into the barn. He splurged and purchased a roller track they could hook onto the tractor engine. Hank put the bales on at the bottom and the hoist dragged them up to Alan, high in the barn. That made it possible for two men to get the hay in when usually it had required four or five.

The farm work, including chopping wood both on the mountain and at the house, built Alan's muscles, prepared him for three seasons of football and three of wrestling at North Rich High. He carved out real success for himself in Bear Lake's main line—hard physical work. In that he was Hank's son.

His determination to excel extended well beyond muscles. Like Peter and Junior, he was not interested in being another Hank. The cattle and the farm were a fine launching pad. He never resented life in Bear Lake as Peter did, but he intended to excel in other ways. He did not know what these would be, especially because he did not have the math gene like Junior. Science was okay and he could do math and biology, but he did not become a devoteé of Mr. Bradley.

A minor matter at North Rich High had a pivotal influence. Mrs. Redd, the long-lived English teacher, asked Alan to be Casie Davis' debate partner. Each year Mrs. Redd hoped to field at least one debate team to guarantee that the school would be represented in local and state competitions. Casie was single-minded about debate, having done it as a sophomore and junior, but she wore out a partner each season. She was clearly skilled at the craft and in need of yet another partner. Her previous two were girls. Mrs. Redd thought that a mixed team might fare better. She knew that Alan had shown no previous interest, but his confidence and verbal skills were the raw materials essential for forensic competition. Besides, Casie was good looking, bright red hair and petite build.

Surprisingly, Alan took to the idea. It was something neither of his brothers had tried, an achievement a cut above Hank and Harriet. He was not concerned that his masculinity might be questioned. Wrestling had taken care of that, football too. Debate had nothing to do with science, which was good, and it offered travel opportunities to competitions against other schools. It meant lots of reading, but he was no stranger to books.

They were to prepare during the summer and early fall. The first competition would come in October so they needed to have an affirmative and negative case ready within a month of the school's opening.

The national debate question for the coming year was: "Resolved—the Electoral College should be replaced with direct election of the U. S. President and Vice President." Mrs. Redd provided a fifty-page booklet for them to read during the summer. It became obvious that if they were to beat teams from other schools, they needed materials beyond the handout, which all the contestants would have. Winners would have to search out more.

The school library had Britannica and Americana encyclopedia sets which they quickly mined. There were about twenty different magazines, the best of which were *Time* and *Newsweek*. The piles of back issues and the older volumes likely would have articles somewhere but there was no index to help them find the relevant pages. There was no public library nearby, so they decided to venture. They planned a day trip to the college in Logan and spent about seven hours in the library's big reading room. There they discovered the *Wilson Index*, which unlocked the world of periodicals for them. That led to *Vital Speeches*, which was a gold mine. In a set of the *Congressional Record*, they unearthed five or six full-length speeches on the floor of the U. S. House and Senate dealing with the dangers to small states like Utah, if direct election were adopted. One speech argued the opposite, saying it was an injustice to the large states not to have more representatives in the Senate (and in the Electoral College) because the small states got more than their population deserved. Thus the majority of the people could be overruled by the minority.

That one day was just a good start, so Casie insisted that they return the next week to extend their discoveries. "This is just what we are looking for—sound arguments on both sides," she pontificated. Casie made it clear that she was the senior partner. She had evidently been rather dominating with her previous female counterparts and they had tired of such pressure. She walked a bit more delicately with Alan but couldn't help herself. They did not have to solve problems, just argue persuasively for both sides. That was the luxury—no responsibility for solutions, just vociferous pleading, pro or con. The debater's mindset featured confrontation clothed in rhetoric. It was almost verbal football. In the end it was winner-take-all.

Alan was hooked. He could dodge Casie's occasional demands because he was not intellectually threatened by her and he liked her to take most of the responsibility. But the mental strategizing was something he would not abdicate. That required them to devise a convincing case on each side. It was like being in a courtroom and he had become a lawyer. Despite his excitement about the debate, he still wasn't sure he could match Casie in verbal skill. He was eager to try, not having been bested very often.

What appealed to him most was that for every argument, he created a counter case. It was a delight to argue with equal persuasion both pro and con. It wasn't entirely new because he had long thought up opposite views to his teacher's claims and his parents' instructions. Alan wasn't a contrary person; he just liked to argue. It was a mental sport. It frustrated Harriet to no end. She called it contention. Alan saw nothing wrong with it—it was just fun.

That fall Alan met Craig Pugmire when the Bear Lake debaters congregated in Montpelier, Idaho, for a regional contest. Craig attended Paris High School but he lived in Bloomington. His parents knew the Proctors well, including Harriet as a young girl. Alan and Craig quickly became kindred spirits even though they were opponents. Craig was a reader and already knew that he wanted to go all the way—get a Ph.D. in English and teach literature at a university. Alan was amazed. How could Craig come up with that? He had never even met an English professor. Craig just knew he wanted to read all of the world's great literature—even try his hand at writing some. He thrived on his high school English classes. His teacher in Paris fed him the idea of majoring in English and urged him to try for the doctorate: "Don't settle for being a high school teacher. Go for the top." Craig even wrote poetry for fun and shared it with his teacher. So Alan had met his match, one who elevated his sights.

The highlight of the season was the Weber College invitational debate meet. It had the reputation of being the tournament for champions. The big high schools fielded delegations with ten to twelve two-person teams whereas North Rich did well to send one team each year. Casie had been in the competition the two previous years and knew her way around the campus, three blocks east of Ogden's business district. She clued in Alan about how to appeal to judges and how to give an appearance of cool confidence. She had organized their file boxes so they could calmly pick out a response card to any argument their opponents might raise. Alan didn't mind following her lead in the preparation phase, but he knew that when it came to delivery he at least had to match her, living by his wit, thinking on his feet, pressing point for point. To be persuasive on either side of the question was sport, not insight. He had found his natural habitat.

Because he and Casie were the only two representatives from their school, they could not mount enough points to place in the inter-school competition. They managed to win three of their four debates and felt satisfied. Fortunately none of the four was against Craig and his partner. That was the best of Casie's three trips to Weber. Mrs. Redd's idea of a mixed team proved to be right and Alan and Casie reached the point of being equally matched. It was life's highlight for both of them. The sidelight was being with Craig between sessions. That presented a problem because Casie intimated that she would like their partnership to grow into a closer personal relationship. Alan sidestepped this, turning to Craig during the free time. This didn't leave Casie alone because she had made many friends with girls on other teams.

Alan and Casie were co-workers, but he and Craig became soulmates. It was a friendship of Bear Lake humanists. Had there ever been such a combination before? While sipping a malt in downtown Ogden between rounds, they decided to be roommates at college in two years. It was a way to keep directions straight—straight to advanced degrees in the humanities and straight to Bear Lake and back on weekends.

The following year brought a misfire. For some reason the State Board of Education objected to the national debate topic and banned it in Utah. That meant forensic teams in the state's high schools had to try different venues. They focused on impromptu speech competitions and on legislative forums. The same inter-school meets were held but no teams were created. Each student prepared independently, which was okay for Alan because by now Casie had graduated. Alan was on his own. At the meets they were handed a topic and given five minutes to outline their response. Then they had ten minutes to give a speech, which challenged in delivery but less in preparation. The argumentative strategy was gone and Alan lost some of his zest. Nonetheless, he repeated the competitions locally in preparation for the state meet, which was held this time in the State Capitol Building.

The main reason for convening there was to hold the legislative sessions in the House of Representatives and the Senate. Alan sat in the lower chamber, occupying one of the legislator's desks and keeping his copy of *Roberts' Rules of Order* close by. He had prepared a bill for the establishment of a state park at Bear Lake. Despite lobbying and logrolling, he hadn't been able to get the bill out of committee. It was a painful realization that the urban teams took no interest in the state parks idea because almost all venues would be out in the scenic mountain areas beyond the population centers.

Alan felt it would have been no skin off the city kids' noses to help rural development. The competition was just using play money, but the urbanites acted like their elders, having little interest for the outlying areas. A Bear Laker had only one vote to offer in logrolling and that wasn't enough to attract attention. Alan was dismayed to find out that the city kids thought Bear Lake was about the size of Silver Lake at Brighton or Fish Lake. They could care less about the great natural feature on the Utah/Idaho border. "That's what it means to live in the colonies," he concluded.

Alan and Craig chose a novel way to enter State College. They both received an invitation to an Honors Program retreat the week before fall quarter. Alan suspected that Mrs. Redd somehow must have been responsible. The one week "campout" was to be held at the Forestry Camp in Logan Canyon near Tony Grove. It would cost them $45 each, which seemed pretty steep, but it would mean living with fifty bright freshmen, a ready-made set of new friends with similar goals—an academic emphasis. There would be pre-meds and engineers but also fine arts and humanities types. So they scrounged the money, sent it in and arrived at the old barracks lodge that usually served to train forestry seniors.

It was their kind of week—frugal living, sleeping on army cot bunks, lots of hiking and volleyball, fun running games at night and plenty of chow. All this was interspersed with four daily seminars, many featuring faculty presenters. Brent Barker discussed the relationship between mathematics, art and music. Frank Fisher challenged Maxwell's Law in physics, Jim Kraus raised ethical issues about the environment. One memorable evening Sam Sanderson, a music professor, played a jivey guitar and asked for student reaction. They all fell into his trap, expressing their approbation. Then he showed them how simplistic that performance had been, how easily they had been won by mediocrity. He went on playing some classical guitar, to entice them to some sophistication, to something subtle that takes more than superficial skill, more than three chords and some rhythm. Instead it was the result of extended study. This was a defining experience; it raised sights to quality, to more penetrating appreciation.

The week was casual but crucial. It provided Alan and Craig a community. They decided the Honors Lounge in the library would become home, an easy locale for friends and action. Perhaps they would take an honors class each quarter as a window to reflection.

Alan's first year at State College, 1955, was a contrast with Junior's. There was no Mary Nelson calculus in his schedule nor a slide rule dangling from his belt. Alan knew his direction was to words, not numbers. The words resided in the English, History and Philosophy departments where a raft of new, young professors had taken up residence—Ted Smith, a nature writer, Cordell Sidwell, an American historian, Henry Robertson, a philosopher. These were his kind of men—reflective thinkers, scholarly writers, energetic physical men in mind and body. Alan was right at home. These men had grown up in small Utah towns, attended a Utah university and then gone to major national centers for graduate work—Wisconsin, Stanford, Pennsylvania. That was a most inviting path.

Craig Pugmire and Alan lived in that same Darwin Avenue basement apartment vacated by Junior and Kurt Kane. That put them next door to the LDS Institute, the student ward and the religion classes. Alan quickly figured out the faculty profiles there. He registered for classes from Dan Welch and Jack Kartschner, both men of quiet compassion, Alan's preference.

It was a fortifying year. Alan proved quickly that he could excel. He wondered if North Rich High or Paris High Schools could be a disadvantage but both he and Craig proved otherwise. Within a few weeks their professors knew them because of their cogent contributions in class and their correct answers on quizzes. It was a comfortable mesh—the young buck faculty and the aspiring Bear Lakers. They were quickly beyond freshman anxieties, either in class or out.

Those old debate skills helped out—how to outline, how to identify key arguments, how to look at many sides—but neither Alan nor Craig wished to continue with forensics, perhaps because they quickly discovered that their young faculty mentors had abandoned that mindset long ago. Just being able to win an argument seemed a past conquest. These scholars did not see things in a zero-sum model. The drive to best an opponent was fun in high school, but here Alan began to grasp that there is a huge gray area between the black and the white. The professors he liked most surprised him. One day they would build a convincing argument and Alan went from class convinced. The next day the professor took up the opposite argument just as convincingly. That was okay too. Alan had done that in debate. But then he noticed that the professor couldn't seem to settle on a solution. That was not okay. This was not debate; this was genuine learning and he wanted some closure.

Sometimes it came, but often the professor would intimate that the most important issues were unsolvable, such as "what can be done about poverty?" Or "what is the basic nature of man?" Alan was successful in classes and tests. But the faculty underscored how much more there was to learn and that it didn't all fit in files called "pro" or "con." Alan thought, "That's philosophy for you."

Certainly four years at college would be just a beginning at becoming learned. Men like Sidwell and Fisher embodied extended knowledge. Their ability to think was enticing. Ted Smith went on to prove that much great writing was yet to be done. He was at that very quest and wanted to entice others to join him. That won Craig to the task immediately; he intended to become a serious writer.

What a surprise this all was. Alan started out intending to be quite cautious about believing professors. They would have to prove themselves to gain his trust. He already knew what he believed. College was just to give him access to the evidence he needed to prove his beliefs. It was like one big debate case. Now here he was already trusting four or five men and thinking of becoming like them. What had happened? It was frightening because there seemed to be no limit to what there was to learn. That was a far cry from how Alan had intended to use college.

Did all this heavy academic view estrange Alan and Craig from the fun-loving college life? Hardly. Sigma Gamma Chi was a surprise. Alan knew a bit about fraternities and sororities, enough to know he didn't want to join one. They were selective—that is they could blackball anyone they didn't want in the club. They were expensive. They were soft on academics. Three strikes and you're out. So Alan was not invited to "rush" and he had no interest in it. But suddenly he found himself a member of Sigma Gamma Chi.

One reason was availability—right next door at the Institute. Another was the cheap dues and finally, it seemed safe, being affiliated with the church. The flag football team in campus intermurals and the bi-weekly exchanges with a girls' chapter of Lambda Delta Sigma appealed to him. Sometimes they played softball on the lawn behind the "tute." It was a comfortable home, a good place to establish a score of male friendships.

In November the chapter built a float for the homecoming parade. It took four afternoons. Since Alan lived close by, he was pulled into the project every day. He even drafted Craig to help for one shift. Saturday morning they maneuvered the disguised tractor and wagon down to Main Street. Alan drove and the chapter president, George Riggs, guided, sitting under the decorations, hidden from view, and peeking out a slit in the papier mache as they chugged past the stately Logan Tabernacle. Somehow they felt it was worth the week of work even though they did not win a trophy. There was a good crowd on three of the blocks, especially right in front of the judges. They made their point: the LDS fraternity was active and alive. Alan had come to be proud that Sigma Gamma Chi was "open to all comers," inexpensive, and was still lively, even without a keg of beer.

For the first few months at college Alan was so "psyched" that he could hardly wait to wake up in the mornings. He was in his element. Learning was so stimulating and the faculty so competent that he did not see a crack in the entire landscape. The concentration of several thousand people his age was exciting and even more was the fact that he could keep up with the best of them. Every day he just charged ahead with whatever he was doing at the time, making new friends or hitting the books. He was not the typical student at State College.

One day, early in December, he was sitting alone in the Student Union lounge right outside the cafeteria. Theoretically he was reading for his final exams but the sun coming in through the huge windows was so delectable that he was just allowing it to immerse him. At that moment Gregor Knapp sat down on the couch next to him. White-haired and obviously over seventy, Gregor was an anomaly here in the place where twenty-year-olds congregated. He leaned over to Alan and said, "I'm looking for someone to sell my Seventies priesthood to. Are you interested?" Alan didn't know what to say. *Is this old gent totally off his rocker?*

Knapp followed up, "Look, young man, I'm not as crazy as you may think. I was a professor of languages right over there on the third floor of Old Main for thirty years. I was active in my ward Seventies quorum until I discovered that this whole Mormonism stuff is a fraud."

Alan was looking for a way out of this confrontation. He didn't mind a good argument. In fact, that was his specialty. But old Knapp appeared to be demented. Knapp regrouped, "I can see you are an obedient follower of Joe Smith and you don't want any flak about it. But you are also a university student and your professors tell you to look at evidence, not just claims. I have some material here by Jerald and Sandra Tanner that shoots holes in the whole Joseph Smith story and the Book of Mormon. You need to read this. It's in the library or I can sell you three of these books for fifteen dollars."

So that was it. Knapp was a peddler as well as a defamer. Alan told Knapp he had no money and would look it up in the library. They parted curtly. The encounter disturbed Alan, particularly because it brought to the surface his own attitude of feeling threatened.

Friday evening he and Craig drove back to Bear Lake for a day of work.

They would return Saturday after a day of feeding cattle and chopping wood. At dinner Harriet had the ritual ready—another letter:

Hi folks in beautiful Bear Lake,

You must be in the heights of the season. Will there be two cuttings? What about three?

We are approaching the exciting time of our year—the Hill Cumorah Pageant. It runs for ten nights in late July. The advance cast and crew come a month early and are ready for major rehearsals July 10th. You will never guess what part they cast me in—Nephi, Moroni, Gadianton robbers? Nope, none of them. Someone saw the word 'engineering' in my papers and jumped at it. I'm working on the lighting crew. I don't know anything more than anyone else, but I'm learning fast.

Actually it is fascinating. Of course my companion, Elder Chambers, got stuck with it too. We climb poles and pull switches and follow the script for our cues.

It means we get to see the whole production every performance night and all eight of the rehearsals. What we miss though, is mingling with the visitors and giving out Books of Mormon. *I'd really love to do that because the people are so neat. They may never join the church, yet they come here with a good spirit.*

The message of the pageant is so powerful. It helps us focus on the ministry of Christ. Sometimes as Latter-day Saints we emphasize the unique elements of the restoration such as continuing revelation, the Book of Mormon, *the priesthood, eternal marriage, temples, the Word of Wisdom. These are powerful but the mission of Jesus Christ, which helps us focus on the redemption, repentance, faith and eternal life, is crucial. These we share with all Christians. People of other faiths feel at home here at the pageant because of that emphasis, and I have come to dwell more and more on these fundamental doctrines.*

So that is a quick report. I hope you get to see this great production some day. Love, Elder Everett Proctor, Jr.

When Alan had finished reading, Harriet produced another letter she had kept when Alan had not come home last week. So she handed it to him, expecting him to read it aloud, which he did:

Dear Folks,

Three weeks ago the mission president telephoned me to say that he was sending me a new companion. I thought that was odd. He didn't need to call just to tell me that. Then he went on to say that Elder Chambers claims he does not believe the gospel, does not want to stay on his mission and he does not want to proselyte. The president said he felt inspired that I was the right companion for Elder Chambers. I appreciate the president's confidence and realize that this might be the best contribution I will make if we can grow together. But it has been hard. I have thought dozens of times about how Hank came into the church, how Mom was patient and avoided confrontations and preaching. I don't think I have ever prayed so hard in my life.

An amazing thing is happening. We met a man named Kurt Guzzio a week after Elder Chambers arrived. We have taught him three lessons. He is a tough nut—smokes and drinks and swears. He is a plumber and wants to seem tough. The amazing thing is that he is interested. He particularly likes Elder Chambers. They are kindred spirits in a way. I've noticed a change in my companion. The most important thing is that he prays at length, silently, before we go to bed. Last night he gave me a big hug. He could see tears in my eyes.

Today we had our third lesson. Mr. Guzzio surprised us; he had read 1st Nephi and wanted to talk about it. He likes Nephi and admits he has been too much like Laman and Lemuel, the rebellious brothers. I can see a real sparkle in his wife's eyes. Elder Chambers gave the lesson. I didn't even have to coax him. We're not all the way there with either of them, but I feel divine power and am so thankful for this spiritual growth.

So much for this report. Love, Everett.

When they drove back to Logan, Alan told Craig about Gregor Knapp. Alan observed that Old Man Knapp had been on the "inside" once, but now he was on the "outside." He was proselyting others to join him in rejecting the church and the gospel. "He doesn't even believe in eternal life, much less the restoration," he said.

Craig was listening to Alan thoughtfully. "How did this happen?" he asked Craig. "There are two professors in the English Department with the same attitude. Once they were inside and now they are all the way out." He really wanted to know. "Were they insincere about their earlier convictions or did they find something that invalidated their belief?"

Alan could only add his own observation. "I was thinking about other faculty members. Most of the young bucks are believers. They know Knapp and are tolerant. Yet there are others on campus who join him or at least encourage him."

When Craig was silent, he continued. "You know, the other night I was looking around at the Sigma Gamma Chi fellows, forty of them, and wondering what three decades will do to our commitments."

He sincerely hoped to find some answers to these festering questions. *What is it that leads to devotion or to disenchantment? Are engineers more devoted than humanists? If so, why? Should one be careful what one chooses to read or to select as a major? Is it sin that leads people astray, which they then justify with long-held doubts? Or do the doubts come from knowledge? Wow! This is just too heady.*

Craig replied, "What does seem clear is that the score is about tied. There is an equal number of devoted believers to the disaffected Saints on the faculty. So what will happen to our current choice? Will we sustain our commitments or dilute them?"

In spite of such philosophical questioning, at the end of their freshman year both Alan and Craig returned to Bear Lake to work during the summer and save money for their missions. Craig accepted a call and departed for Belgium in late August. Believing he had thought things out thoroughly, Alan chose to wait a year. He told the bishop in confidence that he felt having two missionaries out at the same time would be too great a financial burden for Harriet and Hank. Furthermore, he argued that he and Junior could have six months together on campus after his return near Christmas, allowing Alan to complete his sophomore year before getting the harvest in and leaving next August.

Both the bishop and Harriet felt anxious about such reasoning. *Would there be another set of excuses next year at this time?* they pondered. Neither of them wanted to show distrust, so they went along with Alan's strategy. The result was that Alan returned to campus alone in the fall. He found a Sigma Gamma Chi roommate who would be leaving on his mission after Christmas, freeing the bed for Junior, who would return at that time.

Junior's return from his mission was not as threatening as Alan had feared. He did not ride into Bear Lake like a returning hero. He seemed normal, even solicitous of Alan's turf. The talk he gave in sacrament meeting was warm but not spectacular. In fact Junior intentionally seemed to avoid stories that would emphasize his accomplishments. Very quietly Alan was chastened.

Alan became more fond of Junior than he ever expected to be. He couldn't help but hypothesize that Allison might have had something to do with it. She had sent Junior one of those famous "Dear John" letters about four months before he returned, announcing her marriage to someone else. Junior certainly seemed subdued, but he didn't bring it up.

Both Junior and Alan knew these next six months would be a crucial time for adjustment and for decision-making. The older brother sensed Alan's questioning about whether or not he should become a missionary. Junior didn't know exactly why Alan was hesitant, but he sympathized because he had wavered too—over the issue of marriage to Allison. He had surprised himself back then. There had never been a doubt in his mind that a mission was essential for him, and then all of a sudden he had wavered. He could not begrudge Alan for his indecision. So Junior treaded lightly on the mission issue. He would let Alan bring it up.

Treading lightly did not mean Junior intended to compromise. Not knowing how Alan and Craig had arranged their apartment living, Junior paused that first evening they were together just before bed. He glanced at Alan, who then winked and said, "Your turn." They knelt and Junior prayed intently, but briefly. Then there was a new twist. When he finished, Junior remained on his knees and prayed silently for a full five minutes. Alan waited, motionless, until Junior arose saying, "That is how we do it in the mission field. We take turns orally for our companionship. Then we have a silent personal talk with the Lord to deal with our own worthiness and worship." Alan nodded, without comment, and the pattern was set. He admitted to himself that he had many issues he had not brought before the Lord. *These six months will be the time.*

Junior was not an intrusion in Alan's social life. He seemed wed to his studies—statistics, dynamics, engineering physics, advanced calculus. He spent five or six hours a day in labs and study groups. At home he tackled endless math and physics problems.

By spring quarter Junior found employment on a research project Professor Brown was conducting. Everett Jr. was hooked by the opportunity to be working with original engineering experiments. He had no doubts about where he was going. Alan watched with some degree of awe to see such singlemindedness, in contrast to his own wandering through several disciplines—political theory, history, literature, philosophy.

There was another dimension about Junior that Alan discovered upon close scrutiny. He was not surprised that his tall brother joined the ward basketball team and devoted two hours each Wednesday evening to playing in a game. It was his respite, one in which he excelled. He was still trim and quick. Alan had to admit that Junior was a great physical specimen—taut muscles, trim body, quick reflexes and tall stature. Alan couldn't help but envy him.

But there was something else that sobered Alan. He noted that early every Sunday morning Junior drove out to Hyde Park to pick up Arthur Jones and bring him to the ward meetings. Alan did not know how Junior came to know Arthur and didn't ask. Not much was said about it because Arthur was not the normal friend for a person like Junior, who had everything going for him. Arthur had physical limitations, a limp and a speech defect. It was not clear what his mental abilities were. He could not drive himself to church, but equally clear, he wanted to associate with people his own age, even though he was not a college student. Junior sat with Arthur in the meetings. He was also friendly to everyone else, and sought after by many eligible females who gathered around this duo. But they had to include Arthur if they wanted Junior.

Alan pondered—was he doing this to checkmate the girls or was he sending a message about Christianity? One of the first things Alan noticed about singles wards was that each of them included a handful of "disadvantaged" people, either in body, mind or spirit. It was a delicate situation and most people gently sidestepped it, greeting them by name but quickly moving on to another group. Not Junior. He befriended everyone, especially Arthur and those like him. Junior never mentioned it. Alan respected the omission.

Some evenings Alan and Junior went for a walk just before bed. So much of their life had been spent in the fresh air of Bear Lake Valley that they enjoyed getting outside. Almost always they took the same path—south along Darwin Avenue to the Institute, past the chemistry building, then behind Old Main with a view across the Quad to the mountains, then to the amphitheater, turning north in front of Old Main overlooking the grove of trees on the descending hill, pausing for a look at the lighted Logan Temple through the trees, past the block "A" reserved for kissing girls, then back to the "Tute" and down Darwin to their apartment.

It was not much more than a three-block walk, but the crisp mountain breezes and the clear skies with a view of the galaxies were medicine for Bear Lake boys. The exercise was a stimulant for a good night's sleep. They went only about once a week, but it bound them together more than anything else—even their prayers.

One of those evenings Alan finally confided his churnings to Junior. As they sat on the top row of the amphitheater, looking at the Wellsville mountains in the moonlight, Alan recounted his experience with Gregor Knapp. He went on to wonder about his mentors who had once been aflame with gospel convictions and who now were either not practicing and not commenting, or those who were actively critical, professed non-believers. How had this happened? He quickly admitted that others were as faithful as ever, standing as real models. But where were the two of them heading, and why?

Alan rested his case. It was clear he expected something profound from Junior. Both of them knew that the purpose of this six-month partnership was to help Alan in his decision about his convictions. They had both been careful not to press the matter, but now Alan had played his card, challenging Junior.

There was silence for two or three minutes. Junior looked at the stars before he spoke. "Remember when you and I took our sleeping bags and went up the hill behind the reservoir? We climbed to the overlook where we could see all of Round Valley and Laketown. We turned around and could gaze into Logan Canyon and take in a full view of the lake from the north shore to the south. At night we lay there and could see 180 degrees of sky with millions of stars. On moonless August nights the two layers of the Milky Way crossed the sky diagonally, testifying that 'there are worlds without number.'

"I didn't realize the full meaning of it all then and still don't. But when I was out in New York, under real pressures of faith, I sometimes went back outside in search of that sky. I have come to call it 'the big picture.' That awesome universe declares a lot. I know people who conclude differently, but I try to put my questions into that picture, the eternity of it all, the law that governs it, the natural processes that occur. I guess it is the physics and engineering that I love that now draw me to it. I see divinity in it. That is one dimension of my answer.

"The other is experience, from the blessings we witnessed when Hank was in accidents to the blessings I gave in New York. Through them I have again felt sacredness. One can debate the divinity in the universe. I no longer do. I just accept the celestial feelings I experienced in blessing lives and in watching people bless their own lives by faith. Similarly I have experienced what it means to keep the commandments. When I am worthy I feel the power of righteousness. I see the results in others too. I can feel virtue in them. To me there is no higher adventure than righteousness. When I am righteous, I feel its power. When I am not, I really feel its absence. This is experience that I cannot deny. I guess that's my answer."

Alan was so quiet that Junior began again after a sober moment. "Alan, you are way ahead of me. I'm not an intellectual. I don't have the equipment to be like you. You will find your own answers. No one else's will work for you. In fact, when one doubts, one becomes obligated to seek the answer. That's the only way it will work. That is what those silent prayers are for."

Chapter 15
Salzburg

Peter was astounded when he finally got his orders after a year of training. Was it Harriet's prayers or some other intervention? Helicopter crewmen almost automatically went to the new conflict in Korea once they were qualified, but his orders said, "Ninth U. S. Army Occupation Forces, Salzburg, Austria." Not only did that greatly reduce his chances of being shot down over the Korean war zone but it meant he would likely finish his four-year enlistment time in Europe. Peter didn't even know where Austria was, but he understood that it was not in Asia. *How have I—sinner that I am—deserved this?*

Following training at Fort Ord, he had gone to Fort Rucker, Alabama, to get 100 hours of flight time and lots of real life experience with the machines. At Ord he learned everything books could tell him about helicopters—operation as well as tactical uses of the amazingly versatile flying machines. At Fort Rucker Peter flew scores of flights where he was in charge of everything in the plane's body—rescue equipment, medical supplies, food. The pilot and co-pilot flew the craft. As crew chief he dealt with everything else—passengers, weapons, getting the mission accomplished.

Pete was in his element. Action was what he sought when he had escaped from Laketown. Fort Rucker gave him that intensity. Fort Ord was okay, but it didn't compare to Rucker. Within two weeks it was clear that this was the real thing. Life and death were at risk daily. Once they were in the air, not only was he busy with his hands, but he constantly had to think ahead. He was aware that within a few months he would be in the thick of danger somewhere in Korea.

Then the orders came. He couldn't imagine why they even had any helicopters in Europe. There was no war in Austria. Being out of the danger zone was a huge relief, but he wondered if he would be bored, just spending time in more training?

Camp Roeder, just outside of Salzburg, was at the foot of Untesberg Mountain, the first peak in the chain of the Tirolean Alps. Atop its southern side was the famed Eagle's Nest, Hitler's retreat. Roeder's airfield at its foot was home to the 10th Helicopter Squadron—ten machines and their crews. To Peter it was a surprise that their assignment was much like a combat unit. The surrounding infantry troops were often at encampments considerable distances from Camp Roeder. Many men were shuttled back and forth all hours of the day and night in simulated warfare.

Peter quickly learned about the "Iron Curtain." Less than an hour by air east of Salzburg, it was a real physical system of barbed wire and guard towers that separated the Russian-dominated satellite countries from the Western Alliance. On the news broadcasts "Iron Curtain" sounded like a boundary line. But here in Europe it was a fortified confinement that symbolized the confrontation between the communists and the American allies.

Frequently bullets were shot across those fences and occasionally some people were killed in their attempt to escape to the West. The Iron Curtain made the boundaries fairly clear. The "Commies" were in the East, armed to the hilt, and the Allies were in the West, meeting them weapon for weapon. However, in Germany and Austria, the occupied countries, the borders were less clear. Each country was divided into four occupation zones. Here the Russians and the Western powers (United States, France, England) were supposed to be maintaining some sort of cooperation with each other. It was perplexing. In the big picture the United States and Russia were deadly competitors, but in Austria they treated each other with kid gloves.

The American Zone in Austria lay adjacent to Germany. Fortunately the American Zone in Germany was in the south adjoining Austria. For those flying aircraft near Camp Roeder it was important because Germany was within a couple of miles of the airfield. Often, on their approach to Roeder, they flew into German airspace.

At first this was all fascinating for Peter. He never got bored in the air, gazing at the majestic Alps. But he soon found himself in need of friends and activities for his free time on the ground. There was a well-equipped gym on the base and he tried to keep in shape by lifting weights and running. Pushing pounds served as a substitute for hay bales.

The old city center of Salzburg was a real draw. Like the Germans, the Austrians made great beer and sold it in enticing ways. There were open air beer gardens which provided hearty meals served by buxom waitresses attired in Tirolean dirndl dresses. The servicemen flocked to these spots, sang with the accordion players and flaunted their extensive German language skills with "noch ein Bier bitte."

Peter could find buddies for such forays into town almost any time. It was not long before he was into the network of female companionship too. Many of the enlisted men knew the spots to find a partner for an evening's bundling. Others had established semi-permanent ties to Austrian maidens who would deliver service at whatever level was desired—once a week, more or less. Some even agreed to exclusive rights if the soldier could pay a steady $100 a month. That amount in dollars plus some cigarettes was sufficient to support a woman's keep. It was amazing to Peter. *What would the folks in Bear Lake think of such crass sale of sex?*

Peter's knowledge of history, architecture, music and art was cut short when he bolted from high school, so the old buildings in the city were strange to him. When he took his weekly excursions in the "altstadt" of Salzburg, this deficiency became apparent. He figured out that the 11th century castle on the hill was a military fortress intended to exact tribute from the river trade on the Salzach River as freight barges flowed immediately adjacent to the old city center. That the word "salz" meant "salt" became apparent, especially after he and some buddies took a military bus to nearby Hallein and acted like tourists, sliding on gunny sacks down into the salt mines that gave the city its wealth for several centuries.

Many of the soldiers never did figure out why salt was so important in past centuries. They were city boys who grew up with refrigerators, but Peter knew salt was the main way of preserving meat before refrigeration. He had participated in hog butchering at Bear Lake and they had salted the shanks to make hams. It was clear that medieval Salzburg had a steady income from that salt mine but had to have a fortress to control the river traffic transporting it.

The Salzburg Cathedral and the nearby St. Peter's Monastery were wonders. Religious worship to him was a completely different thing. At home it had to do with talks and lessons and endless projects to help people. Here he saw vaulted ceilings, dark side chapels with burning candles and incense. He heard priests saying mass in Latin and monks chanting liturgy. He was agog with amazement. This was an unfamiliar Christianity.

A stroll down nearby Getreidegasse always fascinated him—small shops cramped together, maybe fifteen feet wide, adjacent to each other along the street, their medieval signs hanging from second story windows announcing their wares—bakery goods, leather materials, jewelry, books, milk, butchered meat, each in a separate shop. Right behind that street was a plaza with a daily open market in front of the College Church.

"Bauernfrauen" were standing by their wagons filled with fruit and vegetables for sale.

The local "hausfraus" came with their shopping bags to buy a fresh loaf of bread, three or four carrots, a few oranges, some tomatoes and a quart of milk. Because they had no refrigerators in their apartments, they bought only enough for one meal.

There were stands where one could buy a wiener with a bread roll and some mustard. Apple juice was the appropriate liquid to accompany it, and oh, how the Austrians loved to get an American greenback for their pay.

Peter never tired of wandering the inner city. There was always action. But it was hard to find a fellow soldier to join him. They saw Salzburg as "weird." It was much easier to meander with Brigitte. Yes, Brigitte. She was one of those available young Austrian girls. Usually the GIs took the initiative, often quite boisterously, but it was clear that Brigitte had her eye on Peter for more than money. He graduated from the little widow in Los Angeles to Brigitte. So at first, it could be called an affair. That then extended into a weekly reservation and after not too long she maneuvered Peter into a full-time commitment. It impoverished Pete, but he had little else to do with his paycheck.

Brigitte was delighted that Peter could be won not only for lovemaking but for Austrian culture. She arranged outings into the farmlands, which fascinated Peter. It boggled his mind when he discovered that the barns and the homes were constructed in the same building, the animals occupying half of the main floor. Brigitte said it was to allow the animals' body heat to rise to the second story and warm those rooms. It was also convenient for the farmers to harvest the droppings and the urine to use as fertilizer, and it kept the animals from being out in the fields and overgrazing the small acreages. He had to admit they used their land effectively that way.

Sometimes the two of them took hikes into the foothills, often finding a Catholic pilgrimage church where Brigitte explained the healing miracles attached to artifacts in the chapels. Peter was skeptical about the beliefs that paintings could weep or statues could change colors. Once they took a bus out into the country and came across a huge Catholic monastery, St. Florian. They happened to be in the chapel just as the great organ was playing. The sound bounced between the walls and the pillars and the side chapels. As they sauntered around the inner courtyard, they noticed a plaque stating that this was where Anton Bruckner lived and composed his famous organ symphony. Neither of them had heard of Bruckner, but now they had heard the glories of organ music in a majestic setting. This was more believable, even reminiscent of the Salt Lake Tabernacle.

Brigitte decided to show Peter what a real mountain lake was like. She had heard so much about Bear Lake that she wanted to give this American some appreciation of genuine lake country. Peter found another military tour bus, this one scheduled for the Salzkammergut on Saturday and so they were off to Wolfgangsee. He had to admit that it was scenic. The huge pines covered some of the surrounding mountains interspersed with Alpine chalets. Lush meadows adjoined the lake. At St. Wolfgang there was a town that looked just like a travel calendar, complete with a village, church, and many lakeside hotels.

Brigitte pulled Peter into a rowboat and challenged him to show off his lake skills. They rowed for a while but Peter was frustrated. The lake was only a tenth the size of Bear Lake and there were hundreds of boaters on it. One could not glide for any distance without having to tack to avoid another craft. He thought back to his home—that huge lake with maybe a dozen boats on any given day. America was a land of space, while Europe was a land of compact beauty, especially the Alpine kind with its rich green colors.

Turning to Brigitte, Peter said, "You Austrians really know what to do with a lake."

"What do you mean?" she asked.

"Look at this place. It is alive. It has zip. There are gondola boats waiting to take people for a ride and trams to lift people up to the mountain overlooks. There are dozens of hotels and outdoor restaurants. Hundreds of people are boating. Visitors of many nationalities are walking the streets. Shops are everywhere. This is excitement. Why can't Bear Lakers get something going, something like this?"

"Well isn't it as beautiful there?"

"Not a beauty like this. This is alpine and ours is a dry climate, but that is not what I mean. The natural beauty is wonderful at Bear Lake, but the people aren't as dynamic as here. The place is bland and certainly without the classy buildings and hotels and restaurants. It is just very slow."

Brigitte didn't quite know what to say.

On Christmas Eve Peter initiated a trip. He had heard about a GI tour bus that would take them to hear an Armed Forces Christmas Eve broadcast. So they hopped the bus at Mozart Platz and rode out to the village of Obendorf. There the snow on the ground crunched under their feet as they walked past the village cemetery, decorated with glittering candles on each grave. It was stunning, the flickering flames in the snow illuminating the headstones. Peter thought of the lonely windblown cemetery at Meadowville, almost always silent on the dry hillside.

When they reached a little memorial chapel they saw a small choir of boys and two people with guitars. There were microphones for the broadcast. The boys then sang "Stille Nacht, Heilige Nacht," the famed carol that had been first sung on that very spot one hundred and fifty years ago. Brigitte had never been there, but she knew the words of the song and attempted to teach them to Peter in German.

This Brigitte affair did not occur without Peter feeling guilt. Naturally he could not mention her in his letters to Harriet and Hank. That alone made it clear that this was sin. *If you can't tell your parents, then it can't be right.* Harriet and Hank didn't know how much they were in Pete's mind. His rare letters gave the impression that he was cutting his ties with them but that is not how he saw it. He thought of them often. Yet he was living in a different world, in a different set of values.

Peter began rationalizing. *There is nothing wrong with sex. It is natural. Everybody my age has sexual cravings. It comes with the human body. It is just not natural to deny such feelings. They are wonderful.*

He and Brigitte were great partners, both feeling the ecstasy of physical love. It made no sense to be chaste when lovemaking was so thrilling. He kept going at that argument, over and over, but the guilt would not evaporate.

That Mormonism stuff still had its claws in him. Peter could have churned up a lot of bitterness, enough to spit out everything to do with Bear Lake. He had tried that and it didn't last. It wasn't the valley he was linked to as much as to the people. He would give anything to find a way to heal the breach with Harriet and Hank. Why had he come to love Harriet so much when she was just a stepmother? As her letters kept coming he realized he just couldn't untie himself from his parents. His brothers were also icons for him. It hurt him so much that he had eventually pulled out of their lives. How could he rekindle those ties? He realized his brothers would be very different from him, now that both Alan and Junior had been on missions. They had probably become narrow-minded monks who would judge him a sinner. They were right, of course. But how he would like to throw bales with them.

Try as he may, Peter could not totally duck the Mormons. Within a week of arriving at Camp Roeder he noticed an announcement on the bulletin board telling where the Serviceman's Branch of the LDS Church met. It was in the downtown USO each Sunday at two p.m., right next door to the elegant gardens of Schloss Mirabell. Seeing that sign was fairly safe. No one had to know he had actually read it. The problems arose when his buddies began talking about his home state. There was no way he could disguise where he came from. It was on all the records and came up in most conversations. Everyone talked of home and the mail call brought letters from there, so it was common knowledge that Peter was from Utah. And they could tell by his lifestyle that he was a "Jack Mormon"—the non-practicing variety.

As soon as that became clear, the active Mormons on base began laying their nets for him. No one in the helicopter squadron was a Mormon, but there seemed to be a dozen or more on base who knew he was fair game. One fellow, named Charles Bartt, was over thirty. He had been in the Merchant Marine and was fairly hardened. Every two or three weeks he showed up at Peter's barracks, befriending, almost harassing him.

"Pete, I've been down your road. Four years of being in the Merchant Marine made it possible for me to slip away from the Mormons. I got into it all—tobacco, gambling, alcohol, sex. It was supposed to be freedom. But after a while it was downright depressing."

Peter tried to ignore what was coming. "Do you see me depressed? Not a bit."

"If you aren't, you soon will be and I think you are covering it up," Charles said.

"You will be the first to know, if I get down."

On another occasion Bartt took up the lecture again. "It wasn't easy; I determined to go straight. That didn't happen until I had re-upped, this time in the Army, and landed here in Salzburg. Perhaps it was the fact that we have an LDS serviceman's branch, thirty of us. Those guys inspired me. Here I am ten years into sin and I decide to change, change big."

Charles paused, hoping to see some effect on Peter. Then he continued, "I feel like their dad yet they are leading me and I am proud of myself for the first time in a decade. Come on, Peter. Save yourself the years of waste. You are going to change. You know it. Do it now instead of waiting like I did."

Charlie did entice Peter to go on an outing in the countryside with him, not telling Peter. When they got there he discovered it was a 24th of July celebration put on by the Austrian members for the American soldiers' branch. It was so funny to see the Austrians in makeshift pioneer costumes learning to dance the Virginia Reel with the soldiers. It was a dose of American culture imposed on them. They had brought a wonderful Austrian meal and Peter found himself feeling right at home. None of the Austrians knew who he was nor of the guilt he felt. They just enjoyed him. Some of the soldiers knew that he was the fellow from Bear Lake, but they seemed to feel right at home with him, too. Charlie had made his point. Coming back would not be as hard as Peter feared.

The next effort to ensnare Peter was the Berchtesgaden Conference. LDS military personnel from all over—England, Italy, North Africa, Germany, Austria—got TDY orders to come to the resort hotels just a few miles from Salzburg for a three-day conference.

Many brought wives and children. President McKay's counselor, Hugh B. Brown, was to attend and be the major speaker. Charlie urged Peter to join him. He twisted his arm several times. Peter resisted and was successful in getting himself assigned to flight duty to justify his absence.

One day Charles Bartt described a project he and his fellow members were doing. "We've decided to help the Austrian members build a chapel. The thirty of us are trying to raise $5000. My new lifestyle means I'm not spending dough on women or drink. I challenged my buddies to put in $25 a month. If they do, I'll pay the same plus toss in the $500 I've saved. You know what? President McKay heard about it and sent a message that if we reach the goal, the church will raise the rest to construct a small chapel. The mission president came last month and bought a lot for the building. We are going to make it."

Charlie didn't give up. He hoped to tackle Peter when he was in the USO snack bar and pull him into their Sunday meetings, which were held upstairs. He knew that Peter liked raspberry malts and they were available at the favorite hangout. The problem was that Brigitte liked them also, so the two usually visited the place as a couple when they spent each weekend together. The last thing Peter wanted to do was take Brigitte with him to that meeting.

Realizing that the afternoon services would not work for Peter, Charles invited him to the evening session for the Austrian members, held in the old Gasthaus Hoellbrau right near Getreidegasse in the historic district. "Bring Brigitte with you. We need your help. We Americans bless and pass the sacrament, even though we don't understand German. They give us the prayer in German printed on a card and we learn to read it. Brigitte could help you practice."

Passing the sacrament was the last thing Peter wanted to do. It would be fascinating to attend and would be something big to report to Harriet, but he was not about to pass the sacrament. It would be a travesty. He was not worthy; both he and Charlie knew it. What Peter didn't realize is that Old

Charlie Bartt knew exactly what he was doing. He had experienced the same unworthiness about participating in ordinances. How could he pass the sacrament and then not be worthy to partake of it? Charlie knew that down deep Peter would want to partake. That was the important start. It had to start somewhere, and this was as good as any.

Pressure seemed to be mounting where Brigitte was concerned. She had already told Peter that she would gladly become a Mormon, but only if he baptized her. Where had she learned all of this? He didn't know, but he was petrified that he would come to her place some time and find out that she had been meeting with the missionaries. It was clearly apparent that Brigitte had decided they were to get married. It was not a question for her; it was decided. She was clever enough not to talk much about it. That amazed Peter, because if he were to marry her here in Austria, he needed to be about it. It would require a major bureaucratic clearance. The U. S Government was hesitant because so many young Austrian girls had hoped to become American citizens that way. An equal number found themselves dumped by their live-ins who returned to the States with only weak promises about sending for them. Some of those women had children by their GIs. Fortunately that was not Peter's problem.

Suddenly the distant crisis became immediate. A diplomatic breakthrough brought about the unexpected. The four allies came to an agreement with the Austrian government. They agreed to leave Austria if the Austrians declared themselves "neutral like Switzerland." The Russians could save face that way because then Austria could not join NATO or the Common Market. The Austrians agreed, so the Russians decided to depart if the Western Allies would do the same. On May 1, 1955, a peace treaty was signed with great fanfare in Vienna and the military troops had just three months to leave.

That created a huge problem for Peter. *What about Brigitte?* He churned and churned. *If I marry her, will it be just a convenience? Do I really love her? Will Harriet and Hank accept her when they find out that we have been living together and that she has had other men before me? How will Brigitte fit into America?*

Peter tried to wind down the romance. Although he skipped a few weekends, he found himself going back. Why? Was he sex-crazed or did he love her? He couldn't decide. But it was so comfortable to be with her. They had grown together. He was like a married man already. His life centered around helicopters and her. But then so much of their life was Salzburg. She had planned adventures for him almost each week, adventures that wouldn't be the same in the States. She would not be the culturally advantaged teacher to bring him along. It would be the reverse, and Peter didn't see himself as a good teacher. Every day he thought of another angle, but the issue would not die down.

Soon it was too late. It would take longer than the remaining time they had left together for her to gain a clearance to marry him, so the question moved to how soon they could marry if she came to the States.

That was the point where most Austrian girls got the ax, but Brigitte would not entertain the thought. They were going to marry and so the problem was simply raising enough money to get there and getting a visa for a visit. She assigned Peter the job of raising the money for the ticket while she applied for the visa. There was no discussion; it was a final decision as far as she was concerned. Peter did not mount an opposing case. Brigitte intended that they get most of the money together before he left. She knew her chances.

By the time she bade Peter adieu at the Salzburg Bahnhof, Brigitte had all but $200 of the money for the ticket. She expected Peter to send her the rest, but he knew she could raise it alone if necessary. So she was coming as soon as she had a visa. They didn't even know where she would be meeting him, but Peter knew there would be no escaping it.

There were hundreds of women at the railroad station tearfully saying goodbye to GIs. Many of them had some kind of "understanding" with the soldier they were kissing. But everyone knew that most of those arrangements would fall through. It was like Pinkerton in "Madame Butterfly" that Brigitte had taken him to see at the Salzburg Opera. Both of them were rather subdued after the performance—which depicted an American naval officer who lived with a Japanese beauty and then sailed away with little intention of loyalty. That railroad station was packed with Pinkertons.

Peter had despised Pinkerton after the performance and couldn't get him out of his mind now. It wasn't so much a question of being unfair to the women here in Austria. As soon as the train left the station, Peter realized that he missed Brigitte. By the time he boarded the troop ship which would take them back to the States, he was sick with loneliness. The talk among many of the soldiers was one of relief to be free from their co-habs and the excitement of starting over with an American girl. Such talk sickened Peter. A few months ago, when Brigitte began overtly planning for marriage, he felt the pressure, the embarrassment, that would come in bringing a bride home from his tour abroad. Most people would think that she was one of those street girls who chased after soldiers. He would see that sentiment reflected in the eyes of many folks he met. He wasn't sure what Harriet and Hank and all of Bear Lake would think. But then he might not even give them a chance to see her.

By the end of that awful troop ship voyage, with several days of seasickness, Peter was resolved in his mind. He would not be like the rest of the guys. He would not doublecross Brigitte. He would send for her and keep his chin in the air, acting as if he had to talk her into coming.

Their marriage occurred in Atlanta four months later. In a way, Peter was relieved. As far as his Mormon conscience was concerned, he could now pretend that they had been partners for over a year. He had never been disloyal to her and now he had sworn fidelity in a marriage ceremony. True, it had been conducted by a Justice of the Peace, but that was enough to make it legal. It would satisfy Harriet and Hank. Brigitte could be seen in Laketown respectably, and Harriet was lobbying for just such a visit as soon as possible. His stepmother knew that for Peter, such a return would be a psychological mountain, to face the folks he had so blatantly rejected. Having a bride to introduce would make it much easier.

Now that he was a married man, Peter had to think long range, even if he was only twenty-two years old. It was clear that he would not become a college graduate like his brothers. He needed full-time employment instead. Because Brigitte became pregnant shortly after she arrived, he could not take time out for the luxury of college. So he made the choice. He re-enlisted in return for the chance to attend ground school. Learning to maintain helicopters would get him an employable skill that he could carry into civilian life. Not being a crewman in the air was a big sacrifice. He loved the flight time, but fatherhood and being a husband had responsibilities he was coming to enjoy.

Then it happened. Just what he feared. He came home one evening to the news that Brigitte had accepted an appointment with the missionaries. They just showed up on her doorstep that morning. She was savvy, not accepting their request to come in. Instead, she put them off for an appointment until Peter could be home.

"*Damn that Charles Bartt.*" Peter just knew he was to blame. He most likely sent a note to the Atlanta missionaries with enough information for them to end Pete's newly-won isolation. So on Wednesday night they would be there.

In the intervening days Peter churned. He knew that he was unworthy to baptize Brigitte and she would insist that he do it. Likely, he would have to face some kind of inquiry, the very thing he feared most. *Damn, no one has a right to inspect my private life*, he thought. *If that doesn't happen or if I somehow get past it, then there will be the Word of Wisdom that will steal away our coffee and beer, too. There will be tithing to pay and worst of all, they will assign me to some kind of ward job like being scoutmaster. Man, what an invasion!*

The six weekly discussions were a rigorous review for Peter. He knew about much of the gospel casually but not systematically. He could hear Junior and Alan as though they were giving the lessons, which were actually presented by a pair of young elders, neither of them from Utah. The information was not new for him, but the idea of commitment was demanding.

Peter was awfully glad that he got the wedding taken care of before the missionaries came. It would have been humiliating to have to explain their "living in sin." The wedding had not originally been designed to resolve that conscience issue, but more, it was to guarantee Brigitte's ability to stay in the United States. The side benefit was that they could deal with the missionaries on the up and up.

Brigitte was quick to convert. She intended to weave her life into Peter's and saw this as a natural step. The real issue was Peter. He would have to do some measuring up if he were to baptize Brigitte. Before leaving Bear Lake he had been ordained a priest, so he was nominally qualified to perform the ordinance. Worthiness was another issue. He would have to obtain a bishop's recommend prior to baptizing Brigitte. That would mean a private interview.

That first Sunday, when they attended the Atlanta First Ward, Peter kept his eye on the bishop. Here was the man he must quickly learn to trust. Wow. This was pressure. If it were Bishop Jaggi, he could probably do it because Peter suspected that the Bear Lake bishop had already deduced what Peter was doing. The Atlanta bishop knew nothing of Bear Lake nor of Salzburg. He had certainly dealt with lots of soldiers, especially those who were returning from Jack Mormon status. Maybe Peter could eat humble pie and talk with this man.

As Peter and Brigitte proceeded through the missionary lessons, Peter had to decide. Was he going to terminate the meetings and spend his life denying who he was and keep Harriet at bay? Or was he going to get his life in order? Each week that issue resounded in his mind. He refused to be talked into something by the missionaries, knowing that would have little staying power. Similarly, he was not going to do it just for Brigitte. As the weeks included lessons four and five, he came to his decision.

The conversation with Bishop Gilbert would be tough. Peter delayed asking him for a week. But he got up his courage the third Sunday. As a soldier Peter prided himself in facing danger head on. He didn't like ducking threats. He'd done enough of that concerning the church in Salzburg.

The hour he and the bishop spent together was painful but amazingly uplifting. The bishop seemed deeply hurt as the story unfolded—Peter's rejection of his family and home, gradual steps at Fort Ord culminating in the little widow escapade and then two years of an illicit relationship with Brigitte. The bishop just listened as Peter spoke with tight lips and tense muscles.

Then there was a pause of silence.

The bishop looked at him, stood up from his desk and came around next to Peter's chair. He put his arm tightly around Peter's shoulder, saying, "Congratulations on having some real guts. You didn't have to do this. You chose to. Most people don't. They justify their actions. They duck the humiliation of confession—avoid rejection. You have done the opposite. It would have been wonderful if you had done it the day you arrived in Salzburg, but now you have done it. Somewhere down deep you have called forth real courage. I can tell that you have been honest, withholding nothing, and I envy your integrity."

They talked for another half-hour about the consequences—both of his sins and of his confession. The bishop said that the test of Peter's admission would be whether he felt forgiven, whether the weight of his misdeeds would be lifted from him by Christ. That would take some time. Peter needed to sustain good intentions, mend some fences and build self-respect, but he was finally on that track. They should talk every three weeks for a while, the bishop suggested.

Peter was surprised that he didn't feel humiliated. The bishop had been accepting, though he had not minimized the matter. Peter could see the same kind of firmness in the bishop as he had seen in an army commander, but there had been much more personal concern. The bishop's focus had been on Peter and his future, not on getting a job done. It was the kind of masculinity he admired.

Peter began tackling the things he needed to change—things he needed to quit and things he needed to start. One of those bridges to be mended was Bear Lake. It was on the calendar anyway, but now a trip there had more purpose. Brigitte would think the return was to introduce her as his wife. She was right. There was another reason, though. Peter knew something of the pain he had caused Hank and Harriet. What could he do to compensate for that?

They would have a whole week in Round Valley. Peter chose August so he might throw bales. But he chose it also because it was just three weeks away and fortunately he could arrange a furlough. They needed to travel soon, before Brigitte was too far along.

Peter had never thought this way before—pregnancy, birth, babies. Somehow he had still been considering himself to be seventeen, a kid with no responsibilities beyond himself. The last months in Salzburg, the time awaiting Brigitte's arrival in Atlanta and the weeks with the missionaries had ended his flight from responsibility. Five years ago he had insisted on asserting his independence—thinking of no one else. Now it was the other way around. He had to admit that youth was over. Neither Junior nor Alan had been forced to face adulthood quite so bluntly as Peter now was. In some ways though, he liked it. It confirmed he was the senior son.

Brigitte did not know what was going on in his mind. Even he hardly knew. This trip, for instance. It was not a return to the starting point for a second round. He had no intention of being part of Bear Lake again. It had no real draw for him. He liked helicopters too much. And he wanted Brigitte to have her own world, not to fit into his. He liked Atlanta, even the church there. People accepted them as Peter and Brigitte, not as descendants of pioneers or relatives of Wyoming ranch hands. Many of them attended Brigitte's baptism, congratulating Peter on his dignity in performing the ordinance and welcoming his bride into their ward family. No, the break with Bear Lake was final.

Harriet and Hank were another matter—how to make things right. There wasn't a lot one could do about how badly he had hurt them. It wasn't like paying a farmer for watermelons one had stolen. The past pains had taken their toll. Gifts or money weren't the solution. Hank and Harriet made it clear that rekindling the ties was what they wanted. The coming baby would make a huge difference. But Peter had no intention of returning to live in Utah, the action that would fulfill Harriet's dream.

Brigitte spent many hours with Harriet. They hit it off, dealing with domestics and crafts. Harriett took her to meet Abigail Allen and some of the other Laketown women. She introduced her to quilting. They had a grand time and it was decided that Harriet would come to Atlanta for the birth of the baby. Harriet had never been outside of the Rocky Mountains but she would make it no matter what, for that first grandchild.

Peter and Hank put up a whole cutting of hay. That is how Peter wanted it—not a lot of talking, but a lot of muscles. Hank really needed the help because both Junior and Alan had graduated from State College and were far away. It was a fortunate arrangement. Peter thrived in the cool air, something he had really missed in Atlanta. He loved looking at the lake but realized it did not impress Brigitte at all—dry hillsides, brown grasses, no pine trees. Not surprising if one thought of the Salzkammergut.

On Sunday they attended the Laketown Ward. This was a chance for Brigitte to see the inside of the community, neighbors all bound together. It was much different than Atlanta where the members only saw each other at church. Here they were with each other all week and then on Sunday they formalized the values that bound them eternally. Brigitte had roots in an Austrian village not far from Salzburg; she could sense the close similarity. Both were a place where people's lives were interwoven with concern for each other.

Not much more was said. It was a matter of actions. Harriet and Hank were renewed. Their love flowed. Peter could now quit looking back over his shoulder.

Chapter 16
Academe

Alan's freshman and sophomore years at college were a contest between two world views, one a gospel of Christianity, the other a canon of secularism. He wandered between the two with considerable sensitivity, being pulled each way. It wasn't comfortable, especially because most students didn't concern themselves with such issues. He refused to opt for simple solutions, sensing significance in both ways of looking at things.

There was nothing sudden or even noticeable that brought things to a head in his paradoxical debate, however. There was no announcement, no discussion. Alan simply went to the bishop in Laketown that spring and said, "I'm ready." By late August the hay was in and Alan had left for Geneva, Switzerland, a fully-ordained and endowed missionary.

His French classes at State College were a boon. They cut three months of struggle off the usual six required to learn a modicum of conversational French. By the fourth month he was giving lessons when he and his companion could find someone to listen in Lausanne, his first field of labor.

Because the missionary force had been greatly reduced during the Korean War, it seemed as though they were re-opening the entire area. Members in the small Mormon congregations were thrilled to see the elders again. Some of the older Saints could clearly recall what it was like during World War II when the vibrant young proselyters were withdrawn for nearly a decade. Alan thrived on their welcome, energized to master the language. He shared their pride in knowing that the first LDS temple to be built outside North America was under construction in nearby Bern. Reflecting on that fact helped him remember that four generations ago his progenitors on his mother's side participated in the opening of a temple in Logan, just as he would soon do in the Alpine land.

The intense occupation of the Swiss land caused some culture shock. European cities were mostly apartment houses, clustered closely together. Mountainsides had small farms packed tightly in every spot that could be cultivated—some even terraced to produce a plot the size of a swimming pool where they could plant grape vines. There were lakes almost everywhere in Switzerland, but they were also populated—visitors crowding the shores, vendors busy at their trade among them, boats by the scores, hotels and hostels and restaurants nearby.

Most challenging to Alan was the lack of open space. He remembered Utah truck drives from Round Valley to Randolph and Woodruff to deliver calves. One could look over the landscape of Rich County for miles and miles without seeing a single structure, just open range and low mountains. The Swiss likely would want to put ten thousand five-acre farms with colorful Tirolean homes and barns there. They certainly were incredulous when Alan told them that the population of his county was less than twelve hundred people for 650,000 acres.

Alan had to admit though that the overpopulation issue he had heard so much about on campus didn't match Switzerland. Yes there were nearly six hundred acres per person in Rich County in contrast to half an acre per person in "la Suisse." Nonetheless, all was order here—no slums, no unemployment, no overgrazing, no abuse of the forests, no traffic jams, hardly any crime, and the world's highest income level. Was it the favorable weather, the great mountain resources or the industrious people that caused this plenty? Alan had sufficient to think about.

A new experience for Alan was keeping a journal. Missionaries were urged to do this as a reflection on their efforts and as an historical record for their offspring. Abigail Allen had given him a handsome volume of blank pages with an embossed binding including his name in the right-hand corner and large letters at the top: "Missionary Journal." His initial reaction was that such writing would be too self-serving. On the urging of his mission president, however, he gave it a try. He quickly found in such reflections a chance to go beyond mere narrative and do some analysis, such as this entry:

> *Missionary work is exciting, disappointing, rewarding, tiring. It deals with heart things. It's them all. I've fallen in love with it. The people that I've worked with, seen baptized, watched grow seem part of my life. I'm not sure which is my life and which is theirs.*

A few weeks later his entry from Montpelier, France said,

> *I've been able to work with quite a lot of people from the French colonies around the world. We've met with people from Southeast Asia and all parts of Africa. Western, Christian culture really seems to come under fire when we see people from these lands. They have*

so many things naturally that we have to be taught and have to learn from long years of experience. I almost feel that we've all had deprived childhoods. They are such fine people.

Alan's habit of hard work came out in this entry from Marseille:

This week my companion and I set a goal to have fifty hours of tracting. The number asked by the mission is twenty. We went ahead and got the fifty hours, but more important to me, we got into one hundred doors. The most that I have ever had in any previous week has been twenty-eight. I feel good about the week and am really getting into the work. I like talking to that many people. It fulfills spaces in my childhood that had never been filled before. That's one thing that I'm finding: fulfillment. I'm losing myself in the work here and enjoying every minute of the loss.

An unforgettable experience for all the LDS missionaries in Europe was the dedication of a temple, the first on that continent and located near Bern, Switzerland. Mormon apostles, Spencer W. Kimball and Henry D. Moyle, toured the continent the preceding six months visiting congregations and missionaries. Then the climax came with a week of dedicatory sessions, each for a separate language: English, French, German, Dutch, Norwegian, Swedish, Finnish—the lands where missionaries were legally allowed to proselyte and where Mormon branches had existed for decades—or even as long as a century.

On Tuesday morning of that week the Swiss and Austrian missionaries, nearly three hundred in number, gathered at the temple to have a picture taken outside, including the church president, David O. McKay. Following the photo the prophet agreed to address the group inside the sacred structure. It was an unplanned event but memorable. For two hours he opened his soul, mesmerizing the hundreds of twenty-year-olds. He spoke of the temptations of Christ, applying them to the youths, first the temptations of the body, then of wealth and power and finally of pride.

Both subdued and elevated, Alan resonated to the message. Perhaps because he had held to the standard of chastity prior to his mission and had become ever more converted to it through his many experiences with Europeans, he was convinced of its validity. Wealth and power had declined in importance to him as soon as he left Laketown. The austerity of farm life could have drawn him to desire wealth but studying the humanities quickly diluted that goal. The problem that hit Alan in the talk was exactly what

President McKay intended should strike the stronger chord—the danger of pride.

Alan's mission had been a booming success. He found people to baptize, a rarity in Switzerland; he gained the approbation of his president which led to increasing responsibilities, and he won the respect of his co-missionaries. He was a sitting duck to be tempted by pride. The message cut him to the quick.

Natural talent and his work ethic are what undoubtedly led to leadership assignments. While in Lausanne, Switzerland, the Bear Lake Elder was assigned to be in charge of the missionaries in that district. Later he was moved to Marseille, France, to be a zone leader, coordinating several districts. And then finally the president called him to the mission office in Geneva to be his assistant. This required him to travel throughout the mission with his co-assistant and to recommend all the transfers and missionary assignments to the president. They encouraged and counseled all the hundred missionaries located in French-speaking Switzerland and Southern France. It was heady and spiritually demanding, occupying the concluding six months of his missionary service.

Then the thirty-month calling was over. His mission president interviewed him, expressing deep appreciation for his service. "I don't pretend to see the course you will pursue from here. You know I am a businessman. I never took a philosophy course. Some of my colleagues are critical, if not cynical about academics. As I look at many scholars I know in Salt Lake City, I find a portion who discard the gospel and a portion who are devoted to it. I conclude that it is a choice, not a pre-determined outcome." Alan recalled that his friend, Craig Pugmire, made the same observation.

"So I think it is up to you. Your challenge will not be money or power. We both know that. It will be maintaining the fervor for the gospel you have developed here." Alan did not pursue that topic. Rather he replied, "President, I'm not absolutely sure I'm going to be a professor. I could end up in business. Wouldn't that be ironic?"

"I would be surprised, and in some ways disappointed. You will be a positive influence on students. Yours should be the life of the mind," the president affirmed.

"I hope you are right and I appreciate your confidence, but I worry about finding a harmony between scholarship and faith," Alan responded.

The train ride from Geneva to LeHavre to meet his transatlantic steamer was poignant. In two-and-a-half years this was the first time he had been alone. As a missionary he had always been with a companion. It was a mission rule that became a way of life, a wise rule that impeded many preventable problems. Now he bade those comrades adieu and was honorably released. He was a civilian again and it was not comfortable at all.

During the six-day voyage of the *S. S. United States* to New York he had time to contemplate. He wrote in his journal:

> *I have been completely absorbed in the convictions of faith and know that such a luxury will never be afforded me again. I am heading back to an encounter with academia, not sure I want to leave the comfort of certainty and return to ambiguity. When I came the opposite direction toward France, I was filled with apprehension because I loved the secular world so much. From Jefferson to Kafka, I was drawn to the clashing ideas of the contemporary life. Now, after thirty months enclosed in the absolutes of Christianity, I have to admit I am deeply attracted to religion.*
>
> *It is not so much the dogma as the divinity that engages me— prayer, blessings, repentance, faith. I have been all the way inside them, first for myself and intensely with others. Much of my doubting has been calmed. Will arrival in New York and a full-time return to the humanities afford such calm? Not likely.*

Outwardly the campus had not changed. The professors were all there as if awaiting his return. The buildings, the library, the LDS Institute, the student ward, the drive back and forth from Laketown, Harriet and Hank and Bishop Jaggi, and yes, Craig Pugmire. They all welcomed him with genuine warmth. And within a week he was right back in the conflicts of convictions. This time his hair was short and his face was shaved. His academic skills had actually improved—perhaps the result of his daily study routine in two languages.

His arrival at State College this time presented a different Alan, not just in appearance. He was less willing to be an uncritical disciple of professors and of competing world views. There are so many of them—Absolutism, Enlightenment Rationalism, Utilitarianism, Liberalism, Conservatism, Communism, Existentialism, each with its cadre of giant minds —Aquinas, Rousseau, Bentham, Mill, Burke, Marx, Camus. And there were so many more—Kant, Leibniz, Locke, Hegel. The list went on and on and few of them were disciples of what he had been professing in Europe. There he had been very much the person with the answers, though not of his own making.

He was the prescriber of solutions and he had seen such positive results. Now he would be very much the junior, not only to professors but to the major thinkers of Western Civilization. Nonetheless, he would not be as pliable during his second two years as he had been the first.

That fall the most famous Mormon scientist, Henry Eyring, visited campus to give an address sponsored by the LDS Institute. An overflow crowd came to hear the renowned chemist who had known Albert Einstein at Princeton. He was an easy person to enjoy, speaking about big ideas but in memorable narratives. His major point was: "Don't be afraid to study any subject, because the gospel includes all truth. In the long run the gospel and truth are compatible. Remember, science is always in flux so we don't always know what truth is. Don't hesitate to be a physicist or an anthropologist. Be the best one you can become. But don't set the gospel aside while you are becoming a scholar. Continue to pray, to read the scriptures, to be involved with the community of Christ and to keep your covenants."

It was obvious to Alan that Eyring had done just as he advised, always living the gospel while becoming a world-level biochemist. Between President McKay's words in Bern and Eyring's in Logan, Alan felt he knew his direction.

Those were the highs. But the doubts didn't quit. They seemed to intensify. What frustrated him was that he seemed almost alone. Other students were aiming at a vocation, not at great issues. Their strategy was to memorize and answer the test questions. Once out of class or the library, their minds were carefree. That's when Alan's began to churn.

One afternoon as he sat in the Honors Program Lounge, his old stomping ground, he saw that the director, Professor Anderson, was in his office alone. Alan knocked on the open door and the professor waved him in. The two of them had talked often in previous years so both knew each other's values. Alan reasoned that the director, historian that he was, must agonize about the same issues he was pondering—evolution, relativism, communalism versus individualism, the limits of freedom, war, poverty, overpopulation, crime, communism—the list went on and on.

Alan indicated his distress and the professor belly laughed saying, "Welcome to the club." Somehow that response relieved Alan's turmoil and the two of them dove into the problem with delight. The director said, "You are experiencing what I call tension. If you would move either left or right quite a ways, you could embrace dogma that has all the answers, allows no ambiguity and rejects any tentativeness. The Nazis on one extreme and the communists on the other fit that mold. We live in the middle—a democracy where much is compromise and speculation. That can be troubling. The same exists with your faith. On the one side are those who are adamant about literal meanings and call doubt a sin. On the other extreme are those who deny God's existence and see religion as an illusion. In the middle, most conclusions are tentative. That creates tension and that is where you and I sit."

Alan took a long breath. At last he felt somebody was making sense. Anderson continued, "I believe such tension is what produces the greatness of life, of Western Civilization. We inherited it from the Greeks and it has been our glory ever since. It is at the basis of literature and philosophy and history—even science—where all issues are open to doubt. It fosters change and growth. One can develop a tolerance for this lack of absolutes but I feel such tension is far better than false finality."

However he was still perplexed. *How can Anderson be such a committed Christian and still doubt?* The thought seemed discomforting but Alan had to admit he was in exactly the same boat as his professor. So was Eyring for that matter. On reflection he could see that Aquinas and all of Medieval Scholasticism was an affirmation of both faith and doubt. *Oh man, this is going to be something. I could spend my whole life and not find final answers. Will going to graduate school settle my questions or just create more?*

The next weekend in Round Valley Alan saw a book on the kitchen table. He was amazed. It was a thin paperback titled *Screwtape Letters*. He asked Harriet how it came to be there.

"That's the current reading for our book group."

Alan thumbed through it. "You're serious? How did you hear about it?"

"One of the ladies in the group found out we can borrow several copies of books from the Logan Library. The librarian suggested this one."

Alan had no idea his mother had ever liked to read much. "Are you reading it?" he asked.

"Of course, do you think I'm a freeloader?"

Alan was amused. But he responded with a question. "Well, what do you ladies do when you get to the reading group meeting?"

Harriet was washing a platter in the sink. "One of us writes out questions in advance and shares them with the others before we meet. Then we discuss them. It gets quite heated at times because some of those good sisters get threatened. They aren't used to open-ended thinking."

Alan's mouth dropped in amazement. "You're serious?"

"Yes, my boy. You must understand that we are becoming liberated women," Harriet said with a hearty laugh, her hefty waist bouncing and her eyes twinkling.

"Well, what do you think of the book?"

"It's lots of fun. Have you read it?"

"Sure, it's a staple on campus. C. S. Lewis is especially appreciated at the LDS Institute."

"His tactic of having Satan as the fall guy keeps us old ladies reading," Harriet smiled.

"Do you think Lewis proves his point?"

"Well, he is obviously a defender of the faith."

Alan took the platter from his mother, dried it with a towel. "My gosh, Mom, you should be over on campus giving lectures. I'm impressed. Just wait until I get back to campus and tell my professors that philosophy and theology are in my genes. There is nothing I can do but be a scholar. It has been predetermined by my mother."

Harriet laughed, "Just you remember some of us ladies can do some thinking. It wasn't your father's genes that put you into books. And though Hank is smarter than most folks think, I've just never seen him engaged in a novel."

By Christmas Alan had sent for applications to various Big Ten universities. Three months later he was accepted and after six more months he was on his way. He made sure that he and Junior got the second cutting of alfalfa in the barn before departing, and he promised Hank he would be back at least two more summers to do the same.

Arrival at Midwestern University seemed ill-timed. The humidity in Bloomville was near 100 percent, something totally new to Alan. As he carried his bags into Memorial Hall—the men's graduate student dormitory—he found himself sweating profusely. He settled down on the bed, despite its bare mattress, thinking he could turn off his perspiration, but the muggy, sweltering air of August coming through the open window was no help. He wondered why anyone would freely choose to live in such a humid land. Yes, there was heat in the Great Basin, lots of it, but the breezes in Bear Lake Valley each day had kept the atmosphere constantly fresh and his upper body dry as he hefted the bales of alfalfa. He hadn't really thought about it until now: how much he missed arid heat.

A solid thunder clap shook him awake from a snooze, announcing the arrival of rain. Its coming was welcome relief. Getting up, he stood by the window to greet the change. Hurrying outside, he stood under the building's eaves and questioned his choice to become a midwesterner. He was too sophisticated by now to admit being homesick; nonetheless, he sensed his isolation. He knew not one person in this town. The oppressive weather only underscored his loneliness. Because he had arrived a week before the fall semester would begin—as the Philosophy Department had requested—he was almost alone on the quiet campus. So far he had met only the dorm supervisor, who issued him a key to his room.

Unpacking his two suitcases and the duffel bag didn't take long. Soon the clothes were in the closet and chest of drawers. From the bottom of the duffel he extracted his French dictionary, his German Duden, his Webster's and even his French triple combination scriptures, all to adorn the small writing desk in the room. As he arranged them, a card fell out of his triple, containing two addresses, one of Professor Harris, a scientist on this campus. Professor Robertson in Logan had sent it with him. Two years ago he had met Harris at a BYU symposium on science and religion and hoped Alan could strike up an acquaintance with him. Another contained the address of the LDS ward in College Town. Bishop Cannon at USU had looked that up for him. Now they might both come in handy.

Saturday brought a chance for reconnoitering, exploring the formidable campus where twenty thousand students would arrive next week. The sprawling Student Union Building with its substantial bookstore, cafeteria, billiard room and student lounge was an obvious attraction. The nearby library consumed his attention for three hours while he caught up on newspapers and magazines. Wandering through the philosophy shelves he felt intimidated until he finally decided to look into religion, focusing on the Dewey Decimal number of 973, which contained the Mormonism titles in the Utah libraries. It was absolutely amazing to discover that this library, a thousand miles from Bear Lake, had a rather substantial collection of books on his religion, even the most recent works of the New Mormon History scholars that Professor Robertson had introduced to Alan. That won his respect for whoever was in charge of building the collection here in Bloomville.

After passing through a lovely grove of dogwood trees near the library, he crossed the street to the small stores on Elm Street, discovering coffeehouses that were obviously the hangout and talkathon spots for many students, as well as folks who clung to the campus even though they were not registered. There were small groups of them, scantily clad, bearded, barely awake even at this afternoon hour. A block away was Fraternity Row—a collection of a dozen huge, three-story houses, obviously homes to undergrads and their freewheeling lifestyle. The windows were open, drapes blowing out into the air from rooms that wouldn't know air conditioning systems for another decade.

Admitting that he had consumed a whole day with dallying, Alan was compelled to end his isolation. He dialed the phone number of the Harris family, introduced himself to Dr. Harris and asked directions to the LDS meetinghouse for tomorrow morning. It was good he did; he would have walked a long way trying to find it. Even then he could have mistaken it for a Protestant church, which it had obviously been prior to its purchase by the Mormons. Professor Harris insisted on picking up Alan, setting the time at 7:45 a.m. When the hour arrived the next morning, Alan was surprised to find Sister Harris driving with three children; the father had long been at the church holding planning sessions with his counselors.

That Sunday opened many doors for Alan, particularly to Bishop Harris' family. Alan had no idea that the well-known astronomer was also presiding over the Bloomville Ward. This could make his stay akin to the years in Logan where his bishop was clearly Alan's intellectual compatriot. It was so comfortable to have a bishop who could read and doubt and live with intellectual tension. Perhaps Dr. Harris would understand him. Dinner at their home that day seemed to weave him into their family.

On Monday Alan presented himself at the Philosophy Department and he was surprised to be told that he would need to take an oral admission examination. The letter he had in his pocket said he had been admitted to do graduate study in the Philosophy Department. The secretary explained politely that the letter was correct, but admission to candidacy for either the master's or doctor's degree depended on the recommendation of the faculty following this oral entrance examination. Alan asked her what he could expect. Should he bring anything with him? Would there be content questions? Was it common for people to be rejected? She tried to calm him, but obviously she had no idea what the faculty might ask.

Thursday afternoon Alan met three professors seated around a table; he had never been the object of such an inspection. And frankly, it was intimidating. They seemed aloof and unimpressed with his undergraduate university. When they asked him to name some twentieth century philosophers, he listed such names as William James, Rhinehold Niebuhr and Albert

Camus. They were using an old oral examination trick; they let him choose the subject and then they would penetrate it, discovering whether he knew anything in depth or was just posturing. So the follow-up question came quickly: What have you read from them? Alan quickly strategized: *James was really a psychologist, Niebuhr was a theologian, so I will go with Camus. Besides, Camus was French.*

The faculty responded and the debate began: "Did you discover the essence of existentialism by reading him? Is Camus a conscious proponent? How reluctant was he as an advocate?" Alan felt he was right back in John Meyers' office at USU. The Dutchman was hooked on Camus and was determined to loosen Alan's Christian absolutism, to broaden his sensitivity to secular thinkers. They went round and round. Alan didn't really like Camus but he had read him thoroughly to defend himself with Meyers. Now it all came in handy.

One of the three professors, the younger one, sensed that Alan's pronunciation of French phrases was better than the normal grad student, so he asked a question in French. Alan replied fluently, acting as though he didn't notice the switch. Then there was a French follow-up and a French reply. The senior professors dropped out. That did it. Alan had earned his way. They welcomed him. The senior professor said that the two French speakers should meet the next day and decide on the courses for which Alan should register.

He thought back to the small cubicle in the Old Forestry Building at State College where he and Meyers had argued about Camus in the nice dry air of Cache Valley. He chuckled to realize that such modesty had sustained him in this plush seminar room and the humidity of a Big Ten university.

Alan's enthusiasm went up a few notches. Promptly at ten a.m. the next morning he knocked on Dr. Thorne's door. The meeting was more formal than he had hoped. And brief. Thorne suggested eight courses he should take over the next two semesters and noted which professors he should select. Then he dropped his guard saying, "One bit of advice. Get over to the language department and take the doctoral exam in French. You will pass it and thereby make some points around here. Then start boning for the German exam for next semester."

The first week of classes was humbling. There would be major papers based on original sources expected in all four courses. He was to propose topics and add a bibliography within two weeks, requiring almost permanent residence in the library, especially Tuesdays and Thursdays, when the classes did not meet. Most of all Alan felt intimidated by his classmates. Several were from well-known liberal arts colleges—Antioch, Grinnell, Macalester. Others came from the Big Ten—Minnesota, Ohio State, Michigan. Three were from UCLA, Pepperdine and Stanford. Absolutely no one came from or had heard of anything between California and the Mississippi. He felt his obscurity, particularly the humble stature of his undergraduate department with but three philosophy professors. How the Hoosier professors would have laughed if they had known about North Rich High School and its fifty-six students.

He felt estranged among students he did not know, and who seemed to be unapproachable. Soon, however, he found an affinity with some of them in his Medieval Philosophy course. Three fellows were from Lutheran colleges and were being prepped for positions there. Two were from Nazarene campuses and they had already been hired by them. One was from a small Catholic college in Oregon. Then there was Alan. They all met in Professor Keene's course and came under the influence of this Calvinist minister who also served as the university chaplain. He was a scholar of wide reputation.

It was amazing how quickly these believers developed a friendship, setting their dogma differences aside as Professor Keene led them into the documents of Thomas Aquinas, Duns Scotus, Anselm, St. Bernard and Peter Abelard. The scholasticism of these giants, that would later be denounced by Enlightenment thinkers in the 1700s and ignored by secular rationalists of the twentieth century, suddenly appeared substantial. It was amazing to Alan. He had not previously given the Middle Ages much thought—and certainly not scholasticism, the intellectual fervor of the period.

By the third week Alan remembered Dr. Thorne's advice about the French exam. He made an appointment, went to the Language Department and was given a volume of French philosophy. He was to translate a page from two different writers in one hour, then read his translation to a female professor who did not give him her name. After hearing him, she made some notations on his translations and attached her signature. She said the results would be sent to the Philosophy Department within a week. They were. The secretary handed Alan a note saying that he had passed. It seemed completely routine—rather anti-climactic.

His professors suddenly knew his name. Even some advanced grad students said hello. He became aware that a few of them were being held up because they had not passed their language exams—a pre-requisite to taking the written doctoral examination. Into this situation came Alan, who passed one exam within the first month and was preparing for the next. He felt quite sensitive, admitting privately that his fluency in French was a gift created by his mission. German was going to be a much more difficult matter, yet he needed to deliver on the positive attention he was getting.

Before long Alan was well into the grad school mentality. He was determined to achieve. If he did so, he could qualify for an assistantship next year. That would end his money woes.

Bishop Harris read between the lines and offered him a Saturday custodial job at the church, even lending him a bicycle to get there. He was to maintain the lawns and gardens, paint the exterior wood trim on the old stone building, and set up and take down chairs for the Sunday meetings. Was Bishop Harris being compassionate or sly? That meant almost a full day's job on Saturdays and an hour on Sundays. It produced enough money for Alan to pay for his dorm. He had banked enough for tuition and Harriet sent about $40 a month, which he used for food. It was austere, but it worked and he did win a fellowship for the next fall.

In the summer Alan returned to Bear Lake, and worked for Wendall Allen, who rented boats and other play equipment to lake visitors. It was a lucrative business and Alan made a substantial sum. In addition, he helped Hank put up bales. There was no brother to help throw them onto the wagon this time because Junior had taken a job with an engineering firm in Chicago. That meant the two of them would be close to each other in the fall. He looked forward to a reunion even if it was in humidity.

Somehow Alan's second year was not as successful. The fellowship income solved lots of problems—eliminating Saturday custodial work. That fall he finally passed the German language exam, after two failed attempts the previous spring. On the surface he seemed to be a promising candidate.

The more he conquered the benchmarks, the more he worried about unsolvables. For one thing, he became increasingly angry about war. The Korean conflict seemed brutal, dogmatic, unnecessary. The influence of the "Military Industrial Complex" appeared unchallenged. The Cold War mentality of anti-communism revolted him. It pervaded much of America and even found loud spokesmen in the church, both at the top level and the ward level. It turned him off. He had never thought of being a draft dodger before. But now the possibility began to stir within him.

He hated the idea of war, knowing too much history and too much philosophy. *Arguments can be twisted to justify any war. It is painful to admit that intellectuals often do just that—twist ideas to justify almost anything. They reason like high school debaters. Is that what I am getting a Ph.D. for? Why do I focus on such unsolvable problems? Why not just aim at the task of obtaining a Ph.D. for the next two years? That's what some of my colleagues do.*

It is the same with religion, any religion. There are credible arguments to undermine faith. How hard Aquinas worked at resolving such questions— thirty volumes aimed at answering any doubt. Yet in the end he turned his back on it and depended on a leap of faith, on dogma instead of scholasticism. There are similar doubts about the Book of Mormon *and church history.*

Alan despaired of ever solving them. Bishop Harris seemed to ignore them, focusing instead on pastoral matters, with considerable benefit to many. *Is that valid?* Alan asked himself. He could not judge. His thoughts drifted naturally to Everett Junior. He also seemed unconcerned by intellectual doubts. Why? *Does Junior know something I do not? He is a lot like Bishop Harris. I wonder if I will ever be acceptable in this profession, or whether I should even continue to try for it.*

These feelings within Alan moved up another notch in Chicago. The American Philosophy Association had chosen the windy city for its annual convention. This gave Alan a double opportunity, one to see inside the profession at its heart and, second, to visit Junior and observe the reality of a beginner in his particular profession.

Several of the grad students carpooled together to the city, just a four-hour drive, leaving very early and arriving in time for the beginning of the meetings. Some of the paper sessions were stimulating, some seemed too esoteric, irrelevant. Alan noted that the scholars read their papers, certainly not an exciting delivery mechanism. Then they were followed by a critic who commented on the scholar's effort. That provided some excitement, but it was all done with a deliberate, if not bland tone. This was a far cry from high school debate, but he could see the intention of precision and quality. He could live with that even if it was bland.

The letdown came with a side matter. There was a job interview clearinghouse sponsored by the association, an appendage to the national meetings. Alan knew two candidates from his department who had completed their degrees and were seeking positions. They were depressed. It appeared that there were eight possible vacancies nationally and some eighty people seeking interviews. Although both had interviews at the convention, neither received invitations to visit campuses for local interviews, even at their own expense.

Perhaps the best benefit of the meeting was that he had a chance to visit Junior at night. Junior's apartment was right inside the so-called Loop, the heart of the city. It was a one-room flat in a dilapidated building, but it was all Junior needed and it was close to his work. The old double bed reminded Alan of life in Meadowville and the "price was right." Alan wanted to see firsthand what Junior's life was like as a budding professional, a status Alan hoped soon to achieve, if he ever made it to a job as a philosopher.

"How did you pull this off?" Alan inquired.

Junior looked surprised. "What do you mean—this dingy apartment, this loud city?"

"Well, that is part of it. I would never have expected you to choose Chicago. Living right next to the elevated railway sure doesn't seem the right habitat for a Bear Laker."

"You know, it seems crazy," Junior responded, "but after two months I don't even hear the noise anymore. Those old banging rail cars go past my window at night and I don't even stir. I can catch one in the morning and be at my office in fifteen minutes. It seemed just too convenient to pass up this place. One of the fellows in our office was being transferred so he left it to me—it works just fine."

"Is this really my brother, my calm, bale-throwing partner?" Alan questioned with a grin.

Junior replied, "You know, I don't feel a lot of difference. My daytime job is just a more intense version of the research project Professor Brown and I were doing in Logan. It is still civil engineering. It is designing ways to move water long distances from reservoirs onto farm land. So I don't feel strange."

Alan looked at Junior's progress with awe. "How did all this happen?" Alan inquired. "It seems like magic, you finding a big-time job like this."

Junior responded, "My company really wanted Professor Brown. They offered him big money. But he turned them down. They were in a pinch because they were using his patent on a big contract and they needed him. But he wouldn't leave his professorship. So he offered me as a substitute with the promise he would continue as consultant. He argued that I knew the research as well as he did. They were reticent, but they could get me cheaper and pay him as a consultant and it would all still cost less than hiring him full-time. Of course I'm having to prove myself. And that causes pressure. But so far I'm able to produce."

"Man, this just takes my breath away," said Alan. "This is just the opposite of the philosophy scene where jobs are so scarce and candidates are scrounging in every direction. Sadly our professors aren't tied into firms like yours. We seem to be on our own."

Junior heard the stress in Alan's tone, "That does sound frustrating," he said. "Engineers are in demand, probably because our training is so rigorous. The fallout rate is huge. If we make it through the advanced courses and the research projects, we are almost guaranteed employment. My concern is not finding a job but whether I want to stay in a big city."

"Will it turn you into a secular sinner?" Alan joked.

Junior didn't hesitate. "Oh no. It's a lot like my mission days. Our ward here is a real home. The members are my friends—really devoted to gospel living. And they look to me as an example. That's scary but they keep me on the straight and narrow path. They won't let me slip. We do a lot of things together; we are a family."

There were other things Alan intended to ask. "But Junior, you have said nothing about the really big question."

Junior outguessed him. "Well, yes, there are women. But so far none in my life."

"No one can compare to Allison. Is that the way it is?" Alan wanted to know.

"You know," Junior replied, "I don't dwell on her, fortunately, but you are right, it is hard to find anyone quite that spectacular. So the answer is, yes there are women here in the ward. And there are folks who want to be the matchmaker. So far I'm still new and I haven't made any serious contacts. That is my report. But what about you? You are as eligible as I am, Mr. Bale Thrower."

Alan laughed again. "I wouldn't say that. I'm still a journeyman," he admitted. "You are all settled down with a salary. But there is a little school teacher in Logan who has let me have a couple of dates. I call her affectionately 'Miss Coombs,' to make sure I am one of her class. We have no understanding, but I hope she will be around in a year."

"Wow. This is big news. Do the folks know?"

"Gosh no, this is just in my head."

Alan left it at that. It was clear that Junior's life was fully occupied but seemed unassailed by wrenching issues. It was a practical life and a full one. He had clear purpose, both at work and in his private life. There was no ambiguity. Alan didn't want to mess it up.

The visit to Chicago forced the question: *Why am I doing this? The other grad students in the department seem ahead of me, sophisticated, widely-read, confident. Yet will they fare any better at next year's job fair?*

Eventually Alan discovered that the other grad students felt just as inadequate as he did; his trick with the language exams had them fearing him even as he had been intimidated by them. Was this all a game of posturing? His feelings of disillusionment returned, the fear he felt the first two months.

A further blow was the realization that he had earned half as much each summer renting boats as the starting salaries to teach philosophy at some modest college for a whole year. Such reality was disturbing, so he tried to justify finishing the degree, even if it did not lead to a faculty appointment anywhere. Perhaps he could use it as a base elsewhere—in government, in journalism, in educational administration. There was a lot to argue for finishing the degree just to establish professional status. As Junior said, the dropout rate was high because the study was rigorous. So what was Alan to be—a finisher or a dropout?

Alan decided to probe the matter directly. He went over to the quonset hut where the grad assistants each had a desk. It seemed like *"terra incognito"* to him because he was not a teaching assistant and all the occupants there were. But Alan mustered his old mission tracting skills. Fortunately, one of the four job seekers, Rob Schastel, was there.

"Hi Rob, I'm Alan Grossberg, one of the second-year grad students."

Rob looked up. "I know you. You're the foreign language whiz."

"Well, I know French. *Comment allez vous?*"

"I wish. I can read just enough but can't converse. How are you doing in this meat grinder department?"

Alan tried to act casual. "Well, some days I'm excited. Others I get depressed."

"Welcome to reality. Being depressed is very fashionable here," Rob sneered.

Alan wanted to follow. "Do you mind if I ask a couple of questions about this program?"

"Not at all, but I only know things from my perspective."

Alan began, "What frustrates me most is what happens after our battles on this front. Suppose I survive and receive a doctor's degree. Then what? How can I go about finding a teaching position? Obviously I ought to ask the faculty around here because they did, in fact, find a job. But I thought I would start with you because you are in the searching phase."

Rob seemed ready to talk, "Man, do you want to learn about pain? I'll spill my guts all over the desk if I get started on it. I had no idea it would be such a mess. I didn't really do my homework before I came here. I knew I wanted to be a philosopher. My undergrad teachers beamed with pride when I declared that. They enthusiastically helped me get accepted here, and we just didn't talk honestly about the job market."

"Would you do it over again?"

Rob began to shake his head, "At this point I doubt it. I am so discouraged that some days I wish I was just an auto mechanic."

The real issue was more fundamental, not just the question of finding a job. Perhaps it was the two courses he took in twentieth century philosophy that brought the matter to a head. Through them he gained insight to the values of some faculty, their lack of idealism, their cynicism. It repulsed Alan; he did not want to become a cynic.

These philosophers of modernity seemed to laugh at medieval thinkers like Aquinas, at their absolutism, their assumption that truth existed. The relativism of the moderns claimed that truth was not absolute, if it even existed. In their ambition to be unfettered by any assumptions, these modernists rejected the insights of the past. Taken literally, their disdain for any established truth undermined the validity of a commitment to Christianity or to any written code, asserting that religion was an emotional delusion. One professor argued, "Man is not rational; Nazism proved that." They were similarly critical of the belief that science would lead to truth. That idea had reigned for two hundred years, and mankind was worse off for it, in their estimation.

Going out of class one day a fellow from Asia said to Alan in an undertone, "Notice that he drives a new car, lives in an elite neighborhood and denies himself nothing. Do they call that cynicism?"

Alan had heard that these two professors were considered to be philosophical anarchists. He gradually saw why. They were convinced that governments and institutions were dysfunctional, creating more problems than they were solving. All of this was leading to despair. "Despair is the only intelligent explanation of man in modernity," one argued.

This Nihilist attitude was often brilliantly written and argued, but Alan did not jump in. He knew anguish, because he was deeply troubled about war. Time after time in southern France he had run across people who were isolated and bitter. They had participated with the Vichy government. They reasoned that cooperation with the German government was far better than allowing a Nazi occupation as was underway in northern France. After the Nazis lost the war, these people were accused of being traitors. Their neighbors turned against them—the same ones who had accepted their help during the Vichy regime. Cynically they laughed at the missionaries who tried to entice them to a new idealism.

War had torn at him deeply and would continue, but he was not ready to discard all meaning in life. Those doors he had knocked on in Switzerland and France loomed in his mind. There he was, telling people that life is eternal, that righteousness is primary, that virtue has its reward, that man has a divine destiny. It was entirely possible that he was deluded in peddling such a gospel, but he still responded to that hope—Nietzsche or not, Nazis or not.

Alan was not convinced of the modern arguments. The message of Bear Lake may be obscure, insignificant to a larger world, but the heralded philosophy of modernity was less than moving.

Instead of winning him to cynicism, these modernists reminded him of an alternative view. He recalled the seminar about utopians that he had taken at State College in the Honors Program. For five centuries these idealists had forged attempts to change society. They tried to create new societies, to write a new revelation as their base. Some were religious, but most were secular crusaders, intending to create an ideal society. That study of utopias now became an intriguing option. Maybe this was the time for Alan to become a utopian, to seek renewed idealism, to escape from impending despair.

He had to be cautious about such idealism. Would his faculty advisors scoff? His professors at State College had stuck their necks out to get him accepted at Midwestern University. He didn't want to disappoint them. Alan also realized that he would let down Harriet and Hank and maybe hurt himself if he just left his graduate program in a temper. But his feelings were intense.

He often had a hard time going to sleep. His mind wandered from his reading. He daydreamed what he had always thought to be irresponsible fantasies. One of those fantasies had always been his desire to hike the mountains in Nepal. He found himself thinking that it could actually become a reality. His experience in climbing had been limited to the Tetons with Craig Pugmire, who was an avid mountaineer. But the idea of climbing in Nepal began to occupy his mind until he couldn't put the thought away.

He knew he couldn't just walk away from philosophy. He would be branded as the scourge of failure, as bad as Peter. He wasn't failing—quite the opposite. Clearly he could finish this Ph.D. within two or three more years of effort. It seemed to be two more years of investment with little potential yield.

Then finally out of this frustration came a fantasy compromise. He would write a master's thesis. The philosophy faculty offered two tracks, first, the traditional master's, then a doctorate. That was standard around the nation. One had to be invited to the other track—to skip the master's and go directly to the doctorate. It was riskier because one had nothing, should he fail the doctoral exam. But it saved a full year and was a sign of distinction, of higher achievement.

Alan sensed that the faculty would soon invite him to track two. The successful language tests and three of his term papers that received "A" would likely bring the invitation. Alan decided to short-circuit their option by proposing a master's topic. What he had in mind was more applied than they would accept for a doctoral dissertation.

Winding an idea together that justified what he really wanted to do anyway, he proposed a philosophical thesis examining the idea of equality as practiced by the Buddhist monks, the Israelis living in a kibbutz and the Mormon village. This would necessitate and justify his travel to the exotic sites. That way he could defuse his fury and give himself an option. If he overcame his discouragement and if his thesis aroused any interest, he could return to complete the doctorate. If not, he could turn elsewhere with at least something credible in his hand. So before the faculty initiated the "direct to the doctorate" option, Alan made an appointment with his advisor, Professor Thorne, and handed him a four-page precis entitled: "Equality in Communal Experiments."

Chapter 17
Utopia

Making arrangements to actually trek in Nepal and to visit a monastery there was another *terre incognito* for Alan. He hardly knew where to start. He went across the street from his dorm to the coffee houses where the "hangers-on" congregated. Alan thought he might find a peacenik or utopian among them who knew mountain climbing. His inquiries about Nepal drew sympathies but no specific contacts. Then Alan hit on another idea. He headed for the office of the Graduate School Dean. Approaching the secretary there, Alan inquired, "Is it possible that we have a graduate student on campus from Nepal?"

"It sure is," she replied. "I'm not up on the citizenship of all of our international students but I do know Rano. She is doing doctoral studies in chemistry."

"How would I contact her? I'm planning to travel there for a research project and need some tips," Alan explained.

"According to my files, she is living in Strawn Hall."

"You say her name is Rano? What is her family name?"

"That is her family name, but everyone calls her that because her first name is a mile long."

"Thanks so much," Alan smiled. "You have given me a crucial link. It will be vital to my thesis."

From there on it was simple. He went directly to the dormitory and left a note for her at the reception desk stating his purpose, indicating that he would be back at 7 p.m.

When he arrived that evening, a lively Asian woman about his age was standing at the desk, books under her arm.

"I am Alan Grossberg. Are you Rano?"

She was dark, with straight long black hair, her eyes large and her face bright.

"Yes. It is a pleasure to meet a philosopher. I hardly know what that is."

Alan smiled, "Well, I often wonder if the philosophers do."

She looked quizzically at him. "You are really going to Nepal. Why?"

"My thesis topic compares three communal societies and I would like to visit a Buddhist monastery."

She paused. "That is amazing to me. Most people here know nothing about Nepal, much less our monasteries."

"I know the feeling. I am from Utah, even a remote part of that state. People here can't imagine how anyone could live there. They think it is a desert with blowing sand."

Rano was quiet. "I'm embarrassed to say that I've never heard of Utah." She paused again. "So we are both from 'the sticks,' as Americans say?"

"Yes, we are," Alan agreed. "Maybe that is what attracts me to Nepal."

Rano continued, "I've talked to lots of people recently about Nepal because of the Mount Everest climb by the first American to reach the summit—that Mr. Whittaker. Are you a climber?"

"Not really, more a trekker," Alan admitted.

"How interesting. I've never met an American who knew the difference."

Realizing that Rano had books under her arms, Alan said, "It looks to me like you are anxious to study."

"I plan to go to the library after I talk with you."

"Let's go. That's almost my home. You see, philosophers don't have laboratories. We live in the library stacks. I even have an assigned desk there."

If it were possible Rano's eyes grew wider. "That sounds interesting. How about showing it to me? I'd like to observe the philosophical methodology."

"All you will see is sweat on my brow as I ponder unanswerable questions," Alan half joked.

Rano caught the irony. "Why spend your time on such issues?" she asked.

"That's another question I think about often," he sighed.

While Alan and Rano walked the two blocks to the library, he asked about her name and family.

"The Rano clan is huge. Two centuries ago our family was royalty, but a palace coup ousted us. After some decades we re-emerged as the leading commercial influence. There are now several thousand of us. My father is a businessman. He is an advocate of opening up our land to international trade. That makes him highly suspect to many."

Alan was very interested. He didn't know a lot about Nepal, but he was excited with the possibility of learning. "I am aware that until recently Nepal was a so-called closed society. We in the West don't understand that," he began.

Rano didn't elaborate. "By the time you return, I hope you will find an answer."

So he changed the subject, "What about you?" Alan inquired. "You are here in the West. You are not shunning the West. Do you plan to return to Nepal?"

Rano grew firm, "Without question. I am realizing our limitations every day, but I wouldn't live anywhere else. My identity is totally linked to Nepal and I love it, drawbacks and all."

"You have something to teach me on that account," said Alan. "How come you are here then?"

When Rano smiled, two dimples appeared in her cheeks. "My father feels that my knowledge in chemistry could be a boost to one of his health businesses. He is willing to pay the costs and I am thrilled to be a scientist. I will be one of the few women in our nation to be a professional."

"Are you sure you are not being corrupted by materialism and the sensuality of the West?"

"I can see how it could easily happen," Rano said unevenly. "But I love my religion and my family and they sustain me."

Finally Alan wanted to ask about his thesis. "What advice do you have for me about my plan?" asked Alan.

She was direct. "Oh, go by all means. The monastery will teach you much, and the land is beautiful beyond compare."

Alan was very grateful for Rano's positive statement. "I'm glad you are encouraging me," he smiled. But he needed more. "I need to know how to make arrangements for such travel. Do I need to go through some travel agency?"

"As I said, our country was nearly a closed society, so Americans are a rarity there. You will need a visa, but can get it at the airport at Katmandu. Of course you will need your passport."

Alan knew he could arrange for that, but he wanted to know other details. "What should I do when I get off the airplane at Katmandu? How do I find a way to trek up the Dudh Kosi River toward Everest?"

Rano nodded. She had many of his answers. "If that's the route you have chosen, it will be simple. You may find this hard to believe, but once you get into the airport, a Sherpa tribesman or two will approach you and ask to be your guide. Your destination is well-known, so they will be informed. You can trust them."

"What do I need to pay them?" Alan kept up the questioning.

Rano didn't seem to mind giving him the answers. "They will probably ask for $5 a day for them and $2 for each porter. You can talk them down, but I wouldn't go below $3 and $1.50 or they might strike midway. You will need to pay them each day."

"Won't it be dangerous to carry that much money with me, especially in small amounts?"

"No, both the Sherpas and the porters will be honest," Rano answered. "You can trust them with your camera or any belonging. If you accidentally leave money lying about, they will bring it to you. You must understand Nepal is a land where almost all the people live their religion. It is their highest value."

Alan at once appreciated her evaluation. "What about the monastery? Should I write in advance?"

"No. They have a hospitality tradition similar to Christian monasteries. They will welcome you for a week or so."

"How long will it take to complete the trek to the foot of Everest plus a week at the monastery?"

Rano pondered as though studying it out in her mind. "I don't know much about trekking," she paused. "But I'd say two months are a minimum. You understand about acclimatization, don't you? It is not possible just to go from 12,000 feet to 18,000 feet without several days of gradual adaptation to the altitude change. The trip from Katmandu to the starting point will take at least a week."

Alan was impressed with Rano's answers. "You sound like a guide yourself," he said quietly.

"Well, the mountains are a very central part of our society," she smiled. "What I've told you is common knowledge, but I've told you almost more than I know. I just suggest that you arrive without a deadline. Plan on one or two months and just enjoy the wonderfully simple lifestyle."

The conversation with Rano charmed him—her kindness, simplicity, knowledge. It was vital advice as well as an introduction to Nepalese wisdom. It confirmed Alan's plan.

First there would be a summer of hay hauling before the trip. He would schedule at least one climb in the Grand Tetons to add to his conditioning. It would give him three months of hard physical work at 6200 feet and then some strenuous effort up Skillet Glacier on Mount Moran at the 12,600 foot elevation.

Hay hauling would be a sideline that summer at Bear Lake because another season of managing rental boats could net him the funds for the fantasy trip. The thousand dollar stipend he won from the Philosophy Department for his research would pay his airfare. It was a simple plan.

Alan arrived in Katmandu just as the professional climbers were beginning the season. The city was teeming with Nepalese and Tibetans as well as many from local cultures and languages he had never heard of: Gurung, Rai, Chetri, Newar and Sherpa. Rano was right. A Sherpa, speaking a modicum of English, approached him and inquired of his proposed destination.

Alan responded, "I want to trek to Everest, no climbing, just trekking to the base with a stop at Thangbok Monastery."

"You want Everest?" the Sherpa looked askance. "I guide you. That is my homeland."

They proceeded to negotiate. The Sherpa looked over Alan's luggage, figured the need for food and estimated a month plus. He said they would need three porters. When it came to setting a price, Alan let him know he understood the market, and he talked the price down to $3.50 a day for the guide and $2.00 for each porter. They were to be paid daily and Alan offered a bonus at the end, if they stayed with him all the way.

The Sherpa then asked Alan if he would agree to traveling with six other Americans he was leading to Everest. This took Alan aback, but his reflex was to stay on the Sherpa's good side; he knew $3.50 was a pittance, so he said yes. Obviously his Sherpa was a real entrepreneur.

Alan had never experienced extremely high altitudes. The Tetons were impressive to Bear Lakers, but he had reached the top only three times and only for a few hours. He had heard how one's strength was sapped and one's heart was taxed at anything over fifteen thousand feet and one's brain could be deprived of air. At that point going would be slow, especially for first-timers like him who didn't really know how their bodies would respond.

Getting their group equipped took nearly a week. No one seemed to worry about schedules, which made Alan grateful that he had set no departure deadline. This gave him an opportunity to stroll around Katmandu and its valley. Somehow he had misjudged Nepal before coming, thinking it was a third world country, one of the so-called "underdeveloped" nations. Just an hour's walk in the city dispelled that notion. Here were thousands of multi-story homes built with fine-crafted wood and decorated with detailed carved figures, many painted with gold.

These were not humans living at a subsistence level, rather a people enjoying a heritage several millennia old. Alan's eye for agriculture quickly perceived that the nearby farms were finely manicured by expert labor and precise hand tools. What most amazed him was the surrounding valley, its rich green growth, hills in all directions, encircling an area similar to Cache Valley. And most amazing, in the middle of the valley was the Buddhist Swayambu Stupa, its white stone walls and gold roof blazing a spiritual influence on all inhabitants. What a parallel to the Logan Temple. Alan was in awe.

Once underway the expedition sustained a moderate tone—no peak-scaling. Alan knew he could not start at the professional level. He did not consider a career at this; it was a one-time probe, searching for something as much of the mind as of the body. Mainly it provided a legitimate excuse to be near a Buddhist monastery, the one their crew would visit on the way. His group would rest there for only two nights, but he hoped to open a door then. It was the only contact he would have for his real objective—an intensive look inside the Buddhist community.

When they were finally underway Alan sized up the group. Three of the Americans were college dropouts, sons of wealth. They were at loose ends, seeking adventure. It was obvious they were more brag than brawn. The guides had seen many of this kind and knew they wouldn't make it to eighteen thousand feet.

The other three were more difficult to assess. A young married couple were well-equipped and intent. The third was a forty-five-year-old-man, lean, bearded and quiet, Alan had not been able to open up but suspected he might outdo them all, despite his age.

It didn't take Alan half a day to realize that he was in better shape than all but "Dad," as they dubbed the older man. Even the guides were slow. Of course they were carrying heavier loads than the Americans. Maybe they were conserving their strength. Certainly they knew a lot he didn't.

Alan could feel the exertion on his leg muscles and the strain on his breathing, but the slow walking protected him from exhaustion. He was pleased that his body seemed to be adjusting to this test, the longest one of his life. Even high school wrestling hadn't demanded as much. So when the group made longer rests, Alan was ready for refreshment.

The Sherpa seemed to have his greasy tea readily available. At first the tea was unpalatable to Alan, but "Dad" drank it saying, "You will need the grease in your gizzard."

The trail was almost a highway, marked by logs set as steps in convenient spots. There were locals and foreigners using it in both directions. Their group, however, seemed to be the only outfitted party on the sustained ascent. That was worrisome. Were they heading into snowstorms? The guides did not appear to worry, so Alan took on that assignment.

Each evening they would stop at a nearby farm dwelling where a meal was quickly prepared by the host family. Of course they had to be paid, but it was a pittance. The packed food seemed to be stored for later when they were at higher levels. Each morning the porters mixed up a hot mush with some sort of grain. Lots of salt provided the seasoning. It was anything but appealing, but it was the only choice. After filling their water bottles and packing their gear, the party took up the trail again, walking casually to prevent pressure on their hearts. This routine continued for ten days with plenty of rest.

After two weeks of trekking they reached the monastery of Thangbok, located at about fourteen thousand feet. It seemed like a small city because there were many buildings, some clinging on the side of a rocky hill, each seemingly built in a different century. It wasn't clear whether all of the structures were under religious control.

Fortunately for Alan, the itinerary called for a day layover at the monastery, just for recovery, in case anyone was experiencing breathing problems. So far none of the party was in difficulty but they rested anyway, allowing their bodies to acclimatize to the elevation.

The stop gave Alan a whole day to wander, looking for someone with whom he could negotiate a longer stay on the return trip. He had already decided earlier not to let his fellow trekkers know that the monastery was his real objective. He knew their group needed the cohesiveness of one goal. Their safety, maybe even their survival, could hinge on their support of each other. So far the group had taken him seriously as a hiker and he wanted to keep it that way. Maybe he was trying to prove something to himself, something about prowess, about manhood. Or perhaps a successful trek would confirm that he had options that required such stamina. He had already decided his life's goal would not be to throw fifty pound bales in Round Valley. Those bales had shaped his body, but he was intent on finding another venue. For a long time he had thought his life's best option would be to teach philosophy. This trip was to probe other possibilities.

Surprisingly, it took no sleuthing to find the host of the monastery guest house. He was in his red robes, sitting silently in a cubby hole office at the foot of a trail up the mountainside. There was no mention of the man's name, but he seemed to understand Alan's request for a guest room inside the monastery upon the party's descent in about a week. The monk was cordial, responding with limited English, but he did not seem anxious to show it off. He made no notations about a reservation, which unsettled Alan. In fact, there seemed to be no evidences of an office, no files, no papers, just his quiet presence which seemed to be expecting Alan to come by. Was Alan to be charmed or worried? He couldn't easily ask anyone for confirmation. He would just live in suspense until their return.

The next morning the party left to begin more serious trekking. It was necessary to rest every half hour. Alan didn't complain. They reached a thousand feet above their previous day. It was apparent that all of them were feeling it. Even "Dad" was quick to retire. Only the porters stayed up, playing some sort of a gambling game. Alan was experiencing vertigo, having a difficult time sleeping. He realized that by the time they reached Everest's base camp there would only be half as much oxygen as at sea level.

Shortly after their departure the next morning, they faced their first crisis. The three dropouts were about to drop out again. Gasping for breath, they argued over breakfast, even with some fisticuffs. Tempers flared among the trio. Within an hour they headed downhill, their porters following them almost as if it were scripted. The remaining four Americans, the Sherpa guide and all of the rest of the porters continued the trek, clearly relieved. The reduced number did not, however, mean a faster pace. The porters and the Sherpa were stolid. They almost plodded; the four trekkers accepted the reality, assuming that the ever-thinning air must be rationed for their lungs.

Once the young rebels had departed, the foursome began more serious conversation. Dad admitted that he had never been this high, but recounted many seasons of climbing throughout the Rocky Mountains and in Glacier National Park. The couple, Hugh and Sophia Donahue, claimed to be rope-and-pick specialists for more than a decade. Alan could only recount his time in the Tetons, certainly a lean legacy.

They toyed delicately with the issue of when to quit. No one wanted to initiate the decision. It was obvious that none had the intention or equipment to begin seriously scaling the rock cliffs. Finally they decided that one more night would finish it for them if they could get a good view of the face where the professionals undertook the serious scaling. Hugh and Sophia insisted on that. Dad agreed reluctantly, but urged caution. Alan was glad to ally with him. It was a delicate consensus, one the guides appreciated. The main factor was to preserve their good fortune. They had not encountered storms and hoped to get back below twelve thousand feet before snow came their way. They were also pleased that the pace set by the guides had prevented any of their foursome from developing heart problems or brain difficulties caused by oxygen deprivation.

There was no rush; the descent was comfortable. But once they reached the junction of two trails, a dispute arose. The Sherpa wanted to direct them to a secondary and shorter route that would bypass the monastery. That was unnegotiable for Alan. Their relations had not faced a serious disagreement until now. Alan could not accept a majority vote. He was hesitant to take to the trail alone, even though it was well-traveled. Finally he had to level with his party, telling them he had reservations for research there. It took some bribing of two of the porters to accompany Alan. Then it became clear that the Sherpa and porters had wanted the other route because it took them closer to their homes. Finally, Alan, alone with two porters headed out to the monastery—three days' travel away.

Alan's apprehension about having a place to stay at the monastery was unfounded. He knew there were rooms for visitors and hoped the host had his name on one even though he had no ticket. The gatekeeper monk recognized him when he and the guides returned. Alan paid and dismissed his porters, not knowing how long the monastery visit would last.

As if it had been planned, the host led Alan to a trail, inviting two young monks to help with his bags. The four of them wound upwards, behind walls his expedition had not penetrated. They passed several courtyards and a gold-domed temple, then reached a steep trail which led them abruptly upward to three small caves. There were no doors, merely a cot and desk and chair in each. The monks left Alan's belongings in the enclosure and departed without comment.

Trying to be as sensitive as possible, Alan asked nothing. Was there a fee? Where could he obtain food? What about a latrine? Was he allowed to walk about the monastery? Were any places off-limits? When his State College Honors class on utopias visited the Trappist Monastery in Huntsville above Ogden, Utah, they were greeted by the guest house monk and shown how visitors were housed in complete simplicity when they came for a religious retreat. Like the Trappist monastery, this was not a tourist facility; it was a scene of religious experience.

Alan knew that a vigil in a holy place such as this was for contemplation. The monks had not agreed to be studied and Alan had not proposed it. He had read volumes about Buddhism before coming, so that was not what he was here to do. He intended to observe sensitively, but also to seek personal enlightenment. Yes, he had not long ago been a purveyor of religious doctrine, but here he would be the seeker, suspending the dogma he had so long internalized.

The two other caves were obviously occupied, but no one was present. Guests, therefore, must be allowed to move beyond those limits. So after an hour of quietude Alan decided to venture. He cautiously descended the wooden steps that had led him to the cave.

When he reached the host's closet, Alan found no one. There seemed to be no gatekeeper to the courtyards and temples. Monks of all ages, including very young ones, were traversing the plazas in their red robes. Here and there he saw obvious Westerners in European attire, but they too seemed to know where they were going, even though they had chosen a slow pace. He followed this example, posturing as though he had an errand, trying hard to avoid gaping like a tourist.

He wandered through three courtyards adjoining separate temples which seemed to represent different centuries. Trying to keep his bearings, he circled back and sauntered to the entrance of the trail to his cave. This time the monk he had been calling his host was there and seemed to expect him. Alan began again. The conversation seemed brief.

"Do you understand my English?"

"Some. My name is Novbu."

"Mine is Alan and I will need your help."

"No, I need yours."

"Why?"

"You came here to improve my English."

"I did?"

"Yes, why else?"

"I came to learn Buddhism."

"Then we make a trade." It seemed a faint smile played around Novbu's lips.

"How can I teach you English?"

"You talk. I listen."

"First I need to eat."

"Follow me."

The two of them walked about a block, through a narrow alley, into a low room where a score of men were sitting at long tables drinking tea. Alan was delighted to see a door with a sign "W/C" on it. How many hundred times had he seen that sign in Europe? To find it here was amazing but welcome. He excused himself, pointing to the sign, grateful to find a toilet.

Their meal was modest—some kind of meat with rice—and the ever present tea. It was clear Novbu didn't intend to miss any opportunity to absorb English. Alan started right in on Buddhist topics.

Their visits lasted for two to three hours each morning for ten days, right inside Alan's cave. First they talked of meditation, something rather new for Alan. His religion was more of action, less of contemplation, so Alan applied the concept to his afternoons. He wiped his mind clean, set aside agendas and topics. Then he pondered for up to an hour. He kept at it every day, though he did not experience a transformation. Perhaps his spirit had just needed calming.

The inner peace Brother Novbu spoke of could replace tension, Alan thought. He had known inner peace as a missionary in Switzerland but then consciously chose academia, the source of his turmoil. When he and Professor Anderson decided that the resulting tension could be desirable, Alan had abandoned his need to be rid of it. He had come to accept it. Then in the doctoral program the tension had grown beyond a desirable balance. That had led him here where he was considering meditation as a replacement.

They spoke of inner light, again a product of meditation. "Self-realization comes from inner light," Novbu said, "not from achievement." That one was hard for Alan to swallow. *Achievement is the cherished goal in Western Civilization. The Bible teaches man to "subdue the earth." From the Greeks to the industrial revolution Western man has been a worker, a creator. The results are clear from cities to airplanes. The fruit of man's labor has transformed the earth. Would that have come to be if inner light rather than productivity was the goal? Manhood itself seems to come from a sense of achievement.*

Alan would have to chew on that one for a while.

Novbu brought up the concept of celibacy. They had a lively exchange because Alan's convictions were as strong as the monk's. Yet it seemed their assumptions were different. For Alan, chastity was preparation for marriage. He saw the human body as created in the image of God and a positive good, quite the opposite idea of medieval Christians. So permanent celibacy, such as this brother was living, seemed misguided to Alan. The monk argued that celibacy was essential to enlightenment. The two of them decided they were fairly close, so they would just let the issue rest.

Reincarnation was a given for the Buddhists. Alan saw it as an affirmation of the eternal nature of human life, but found himself attached to his concept of the eternity of the distinct individual. The brother argued that life comes in cycles and humans start anew endlessly, not only humans but all living beings. Alan sensed that he was really on foreign turf with this idea; there didn't seem to be a meeting point.

The toughest concept for them was destiny. Novbu said everything that happens is God's will. Man's glory, according to him, is to accept divine determination. Man may learn about destiny through oracles or by reading the stars, but it is not his role to direct or control his or anyone's life. Alan reflected, *That argument is one the ancient Greeks wrestled with. From Homer to Alexander the Great they debated whether the gods controlled man's fate. They told of Ulysses, who defied the gods and actually won on occasion. To accept the Buddhist view of destiny would move me all the way out of the civilization of the West.* Alan was not drawn to the invitation—even through meditation.

Those hours together welded Alan and the Buddhist brother beyond what they expected. Each morning Novbu came up the trail to the cave in his red robes and shaved head to share beliefs with Alan. Their talk was basic, in English, each struggling to penetrate the meanings of short words. Within two days they advanced beyond words; feelings bound them even though they were worlds apart. It was moving. The monk was surprised to find spirituality in a Westerner. Alan felt respect, even love for him.

After their sessions Alan remained in his cell to honor their time together. In the late afternoons he wandered freely, observing the practice of the community surrounding the beliefs. He saw much ritual—monks prostrating themselves before statues in temples.

Others turned prayer wheels as they entered and left the rooms. Many carried prayer beads which they activated as they walked by the sacred idols.

Monks of all ages gathered for their morning puja each day, a two-hour prayer ceremony. Then the young monks went to school and the older ones memorized religious texts and learned languages. This schedule was rigidly enforced; those who missed the appointment were beaten with a whip. The entire community was run on a tight authoritarian system but Alan could not really discover who the leaders were or how the whole enterprise was financed. There was no doubt in Alan's mind that religion pervaded every aspect of life here at the monastery. There was nothing hidden; rather, their religion was completely open and he felt no limitations in observing it.

There were other monasteries elsewhere for females but here at Thangbok there was one group of women who were wearing leather aprons. Their grey hair was woven in braids, hung down their backs. They used prayer beads as they walked into the temples, turning the prayer rolls as they entered. Other than temple worship the women were seldom seen. This contrasted with Alan's Bear Lake experience where women were central to both worship and community. He thought of his mother and the activities of their family's life that had been guided by her—how she was so involved in the ward, as were other women. He was not averse to such female anchoring. In fact, his contemplations brought him back to that need in his life, to thoughts about Miss Coombs—the teacher he had left behind at State College.

On the eleventh day Novbu did not arrive. At first Alan was worried. Had he offended the monk? Was this a message that his welcome had ended? Then he had to admit that Novbu was probably responding to Alan's need to conclude the encounter. Perhaps the monk was aware of Alan's growing restlessness. Novbu could sense that Alan was sympathetic to this Buddhist life but knew it was not for him.

The time had come to leave the monastery. Alan was anything but eager to go. On the last afternoon he wrote in his journal:

My Buddhist Brother is one of the finest men I have ever known. It is his inner self that commends him. We have come to share our very souls with complete trust. The Buddhist dogma is fulfilled in this man. He has set the world aside, no possessions, no desire for them. There is no inner tension, rather he is at peace. He could just as well be living in the 10th century as the 20th.

As I have wandered through the monastery each day, I have seen much to admire, but I am troubled about other matters. In comparison with the Trappist Monastery in Huntsville, Utah, where the brothers raise much of what they consume, I see little production here. In both monasteries authority is paramount. The freedom and individualism I am used to in secular America is gone; I'm not sure I could submit myself to such a life. My time as a missionary was regimented, but not as much, and only for a short period of my life.

These monks have no concept of progress. Most likely they would brand it as presumption. Being with them has clarified what it means to be a Western man. It has taught me that my mind and being are linked to individualism, freedom, progress and achievement. Men like Professors Keene, Robertson and Harris have not been diminished spiritually by scholarly learning. They continue to inspire me, but Novbu is equally admirable. These monks are doing just fine without the West. They also show me the shortcomings of our culture, our intense materialism, selfishness, crassness.

The descent from the monastery to Katmandu was rather easy for Alan to arrange. In fact it was a pleasant surprise to discover a party of eight French trekkers who welcomed him to walk with them for the two-week trip and share their porters. What a delight to be speaking French again. They brought him back into the twentieth century, their jivey talk, their casual attitudes about sexuality, their scanty attire, their innuendos about the poverty of Nepal, their jokes about the monks.

Alan wondered if he belonged in this century. *Perhaps I have become one of the monks without realizing it. While I was there I could be critical of a doctrinal point or two. But from my time with them I learned to admire their internalization of beliefs that seem to pervade the community. No one is forced to stay. They seem to believe in their mission, even though they are strictly disciplined. The simplicity of their lives is admirable. They possess nothing except clothes, yet there appear to be no unmet needs. The study of their beliefs occupies much of their time. They are literate and appear to be satisfied in their community that has endured for centuries. They are so gentle.* Clearly, Alan had plenty to write about.

The next phase of his field research was going to be quite a different matter. He had no contact point in Israel. Despite all the diversity in those coffee houses next to the campus, he found no one who had lived in a kibbutz. From his reading it was clear that visitors were welcome if they would stay a while and do physical work each day. Alan knew his Round Valley skills would qualify him in that area.

When his plane landed in Tel Aviv he was relieved to find that the information desk attendant in the airport responded to his question easily, as if it were a daily inquiry. She referred him to a government tourist booth just down the main hall. There he obtained a list of fifty existing kibbutzim and their requirements for visitors. It was a fairly simple matter to decide on one. He soon headed in the direction of the Gaza Strip to the community of Erez, being one of the earliest to be established. With three hundred occupants, it was directly comparable to the historic Mormon villages.

Getting there was another matter. Tourists seldom went that way, likely because they wanted to avoid a politically sensitive boundary. He rode on three different buses, easily finding speakers of English who were delighted to get him to the last stop. Knowing the kibbutz would be quite isolated, he expected to have quite a hike to Erez.

One elderly man he asked for directions happened to speak French, so they felt like comrades. Calmly responding as though he were in charge, the man instructed Alan to sit in the shade and await his return. Soon he rode up in a twenty-year-old black sedan, got out and helped Alan into the back seat with his backpack and suitcase. Then he bade Alan adieu. The young driver, who spoke neither English nor French nor German, headed the car down a gravel road. They soon arrived at a gate. Alan tried to pay the driver but he would not accept the money. That was a quick reminder of both Bear Lake and of the Nepal monastery.

Alan passed a man setting the water in a field. When Alan questioned him, the farmer simply pointed up the road, evidently used to the same inquiry. A house came into view, bearing a simple sign stating "Erez." Alan knocked and a middle-aged woman welcomed him inside. She spoke some English, even more German. Alan's German was fairly sparse and she had no French. It didn't matter. She handed him a one-page explanation form, outlining the rules and stipulations applicable to the kibbutz. Two weeks was the minimum stay; no maximum was mentioned.

Obviously the residents were not interested in tourists. Work was their agenda and visitors must expect to do physical labor eight hours a day with Friday afternoons and Saturdays off. There was no charge for room and board and no pay for the labor.

Alan filled out the form. He expected some sort of interview to find out his qualifications and motives. But it was obvious that his hostess' language skills limited that. Down the road about a half-mile, they came to a large rectangular two-story building that looked like an army barracks. Inside was a large meeting room with old folding chairs. A dining hall of similar furnishing adjoined. His guide led him upstairs to a row of cell-like rooms. He placed his gear in an empty one. There were about nine other rooms which appeared to house other visitors. He followed her again, this time to a barn nearby where she introduced him to Ben Salik, who was repairing a tractor.

Ben, appearing to be at least forty years old, let out a belly laugh: "So you've come to work have you? That's what we do is work. Let's start right here on this tractor." Alan was amazed; the old vehicle was a John Deere, even older than the one Hank kept running in Round Valley. *How did it get clear across the Atlantic and Mediterranean?*

"You see the problem I have," Ben said. "This clutch lever is broken. I've welded it twice but it keeps breaking. What do you suggest?"

Alan wished he had paid more attention when Hank hammered and twisted the parts on that old tractor. Alan was good at lifting bales, but he had gladly left the engines to Hank.

"Where I'm from we just drove over to Evanston to the John Deere dealer and he usually had the part."

Ben looked at him intensely. "I think you ought to try it. First go to Ashdod. If you can't find anything there, then try Tel Aviv."

Alan looked at him in amazement. Ben was serious. So Alan took the broken part and headed down the road, picked up his back pack and reversed his trip, presuming this was a test. If he could pass it, Ben might open up this community to him.

In some ways Alan now felt the school principal had sent him on an important errand, such as when Craig Pugmire went to a print shop in Logan for two days to put out the school paper. He hadn't needed a hall pass. Alan was similarly a trusted link in the system after only an hour.

In fact, it took three days, but Alan found the part. It only cost the equivalent of $10, but it challenged his wits—dealing with buses again and languages and parts, catalogues, and youth hostels. It was a delight, though, to be part of the daily life, not a tourist—to see the country through the eyes of a functioning worker.

The highlight was returning with the prize. Ben hooted with laughter and gave Alan a big hug. He was now part of the family. Alan wouldn't even take reimbursement for the part.

That evening, after a meal at the common dining hall in his building, Ben invited Alan over to his home for a talk. He included Etti, his wife. There Alan spilled out his questions. They talked on late into the night as though they had always been friends. His modest contribution had opened a door that might have taken weeks to achieve. He noticed that other visiting workers were not as engaged in community issues.

Ben and Etti were in their forties and had come to Erez as small children. Their parents were reformed Jews from Warsaw who felt rejection from both the Poles for being Jews, and from the Jews for not being orthodox. Earlier they had abandoned the Hassidic tightness in favor of Zionist liberalism. A successful tailor, Ben's father had been able to save enough money to buy their fare to Jerusalem.

They settled in Erez when it was a frontier, attempting to wrest a living from the desert. This was before the Yom Kipper War and its impact on the Gaza Strip. Ben learned to farm, even though his father hated the physical work. Their crusade to create a viable Jewish state kept them at the defying task of raising cotton in the desert. It consumed them. Their loyalty was to the movement, to the community, essentially a secular crusade.

Ben inherited all of the values—the belief in equality, in simplicity, in shared property, in the goodness of man, and in community. As he talked of these concepts, he radiated. He loved the message and lived the destiny. Etti was less ideological. She threw in witticisms about how tough it was to keep believing all this idealism, about getting people to do their share of the work. Ben had met her in the army. She had no kibbutz heritage, but she loved Ben. Their two children, already late teenagers, were living in the community youth home; both planned on living in Erez after their military service.

Alan knew that Zionism was a political crusade and not a spiritual quest. It was obvious that the Jewish calendar was observed at Erez, but if there was a synagogue life, it was not apparent.

He stayed for a month, learning about cotton, a crop very different from alfalfa. Irrigation water was directed through tubing instead of through sprinklers. The tubes had to be inspected and repaired daily. Everything depended on water; it was as precious as gold and more scarce than in Round Valley.

The farmers of Erez planted their cotton in huge multi-acre fields, spacing the harvest over two months—each one planted two weeks later than the former. The good weather allowed that because Erez was located just seven miles inland from the Mediterranean Sea. A desert land, it could only produce if regularly irrigated, but the air was cooled somewhat by the sea breezes.

The pipe irrigation apparatus impressed Alan. It was obvious that the system which enclosed the water resulted in a major savings of flow. In contrast with his Round Valley garden, there was no seepage into ditchbanks and no evaporation. It appeared to Alan that they saved as much as fifty percent of the water they would have to use in the primitive ditches and canals of Bear Lake. It was labor intensive in comparison. That was all right because labor was unpaid in Erez. So the workers walked up and down the rows all day, checking the tubes to unclog or repair them and to chop out weeds.

Alan and the eight other workers did most of this unskilled work, reminding him of the Africans who tended the cotton plants in the "Old South." Most of them were younger than thirty and seemed to have a wide spectrum of motives. They were pretty much alternative lifestyle people but did not really let on whether or not they were serious about joining the kibbutz. It was not easy to be admitted and this work was just a casual window. Were they to become serious and request more attention, they would be transferred to weightier assignments and to meetings and reading. The nine of them were pretty much neutrals. They felt the necessity to prove their rigor as they contemplated their next move.

Alan was shifted to harvesting, not because he expressed interest in joining the commune, but because Ben knew of his skill with the tractor. He and Alan took turns driving the tractor, activating the very sophisticated cotton picker. They had to drive up and down the rows with precision. Sometimes Ben would drive and let Alan help two other men guide the huge cotton bales as they came off the rack. They needed to be positioned so that a forklift could get its tongs under them and deliver them to waiting trucks. That was another assignment Ben gave Alan, to maneuver the forklift. Once the bales were on the truck they were delivered to the ginning plant next to the dining hall.

One of the most outstanding achievements of Erez was that they did their own ginning and could market their cotton themselves. They even gleaned the cotton seeds, crushed them and used them to feed pigs and cows. Alan could see that this was a first-class operation, far more sophisticated than those in Round Valley.

What a puzzle all this was. So different from Nepal. Non-theological. It was a mission of communality, but for totally different reasons. Simplicity was valued in both, but contemplation was central in Nepal and labor drove everything here. Erez was this-worldly and had one main point, a political statement—*we are here, here in this land, in this desert. We will not be driven from it, militarily, but even more economically. No one else can make it bloom. We are doing it against all odds. Our muscle is the might of Israel. We are doing it because we work together, communally.*

One Friday evening at yet another chat session with Ben and Etti, Ben mentioned that he had to travel to Tiberius for a national water users' convention. Evidently the several kibbutzim cooperated on such matters and had designated him as one of their delegates to the organization that recommended national water policy. When Ben looked at Alan he could see the calculations going on in his mind. Tiberius was on the shores of the Sea of Galilee.

Ben had guessed that Alan could be easily enticed to go there. So Ben went on, suggesting that Alan could ride with him in the commune's old truck. They could do some equipment business along the way. Alan would have to find a youth hostel to accommodate him for the three days, but that would give him time to explore the northern part of Israel. Alan jumped at the invitation, sensing that it was Ben's way of rewarding him for his able service to the community.

As they drove across the summit and saw the lake vista spread before them, Alan gasped. He once heard an old neighbor in Round Valley say that their lake had a similarity to the Sea of Galilee. He had dismissed such talk as just a flimsy miracle-type story. Now he repented quickly. The vista just slammed at him. It was indeed so much like Bear Lake. The dry hillsides with very few trees dropped sharply to the lake shore. It was uncanny that the two lakes could be so similar, a respite in an arid land.

He had to choose between visiting the historic sites that were so important in the area, or being Alan the philosopher. He chose the latter, wandering each day among the hills, finding spots where he could sit in the shade of a tree and write, capturing the feelings and the atmosphere before he returned to a typewriter. He conceptualized what he was going to write in that thesis. The contrast between Nepal and Israel was fodder for stimulating prose. Then he realized that he must devise a chapter on the Mormon village and its elements of communality and equality. Sitting on those hillsides and gazing at the Sea of Galilee, he concluded that he must go back to Bear Lake and look at it objectively, conduct interviews, examine the ideology, participate in decision-making instead of just relying on his memory. He must observe as a scholar.

Alan was beginning to feel already that the result of his activities might easily be a permanent residence in Bear Lake. The place was natural to him. He had found that out. To his surprise Bear Lake had stood up well in comparison to the academy. He had been respectful of his home valley, but had always assumed he would graduate from it when he got into the "real world." Peter had done that, and Junior also, though in a different way. The third son had not anticipated that academia had its own dose of liabilities, despite the allure of sophisticated knowledge. Yet he still might become a professor in some distant setting; it was possible.

The Mormon village also had elements of Nepal and Israel. It could not be easily dismissed, intellectually or socially. Peter had dismissed it, but Alan could not. Junior too had left the village but had adopted a different kind of Mormon village, an urban one. Though the Saints were not neighbors, they had been bound together in another way. Junior had been a vital shepherd in keeping them together. Of the three brothers, Alan was unexpectedly considering the rural option. Besides, Alan had concluded that the drama teacher in Logan, Miss Coombs, needed a husband like him. She was bright, creative and independent. His intellectual flights had not intimidated her a bit. Serious courtship could fit right in with his "research" on "equality in the Mormon community."

Chapter 18
The "Old Fart"

Several things about Hank's heart attack were fortunate, at least initially. It happened at home, just as they were sitting down to dinner. His eyes bulged; he gripped his chest as he slid from his chair to the floor. Harriet ran to him, knowing instinctively what was happening. Hank never lost consciousness, nor did he stop breathing. Harriet grabbed the telephone, remembering that the county now had an ambulance service—only a year old. But she didn't know the number. She called the sheriff instead and he radioed the volunteer driver. It took about fifteen minutes for him to get to Round Valley. She kept a cool cloth on Hank's forehead, loosened his belt and held his hand, talking calmly to him. He did the rest, keeping his breath coming.

The next good fortune was that the ambulance took Hank to the Logan Hospital. Montpelier was about the same one-hour distance and a safer, lakeside road, but the ambulance was a service of the State of Utah and that meant going over the mountain to the larger city of Logan instead. The result was that a heart specialist, Dr. Budge, awaited them when they arrived. Radio contact between the ambulance and the hospital delivered vital information.

A second volunteer was not available for the ambulance drive, so Harriet had to ride in the back beside Hank's stretcher. It was she who faithfully administered the fluids the driver initiated before he slipped behind the wheel. The driver hollered instructions as he drove down the canyon. The combination of medications and Hank's strength kept him alive.

The first few hours at the hospital were critical. Being cautious, Dr. Budge said there was a danger of a second attack. The damage to Hank's heart was substantial. The seasoned surgeon wouldn't assure them for twenty-four hours that the sixty-three-year-old farmer would survive.

Harriet called Peter in Atlanta. She told him to wait a few hours before coming. He couldn't arrive in less than a three-day train ride, and that would be either too late or unnecessary. She reached Junior at his Chicago office with a similar suggestion. Alan was in Israel and unreachable.

Within two hours a Laketown delegation arrived—Woodruff Kane and Bishop Jaggi. Though he was no longer bishop, Brother Jaggi joined "Wood" because they were both Hank's confidantes. Their friendship had become deep. This part of the ward family would have to suffice for now.

The blessing they administered set Harriet somewhat at ease, but Hank was so sedated he was unaware that his friends were with him. It was a long way for them to come for just five minutes with the patient, the limit in the Intensive Care Unit. Nonetheless, it symbolized a lifetime of meaning for Harriet. She assumed they would come; it had not been necessary to ask them. It was a matter of belonging. She had made scores of similar support visits because people cared about each other. That was what it was about.

Then the fortunate occurrences ended and the problems began. The first complication came with Dr. Budge's assessment that the recovery would be slow. The doctor said Hank needed to be within ten minutes of the hospital for several months. Additional attacks were possible and Hank's heart no longer had the strength to endure a long ambulance drive. That meant residing in Logan, at least temporarily.

While she awaited Hank's release from the hospital, Harriet had lots of time to walk through the neighborhood and digest the doctor's judgment. At first she went around the Logan Temple. It was across the street diagonally from the hospital, nicely framed in the window of Hank's hospital room. She even took time to attend a few sessions there, a real bonus that Round Valley folks seldom had. It was a perfect place to ponder.

She walked around the blocks nearby in a lonely search, without the help of a local network. Then one day she saw a woman putting up the sign she needed. After a quick negotiation they reached an agreement. The Grossbergs now had a tiny but furnished student apartment and could move in immediately.

When Woodruff and Bishop Jaggi came for that next visit, they thoughtfully brought Hank's car. This meant Harriet could drive back to Round Valley to get the blankets, sheets and housewares they would need. The next day she made the trip through Logan Canyon. Pulling up to their place, she noticed a hay wagon in their field with three men putting up Hank's alfalfa they had baled. In another field someone was driving his threshing machine, getting the rest of the cutting done.

It was somewhat of a shock, not only to see them doing Hank's work but they were simply acting out their concern for the Grossbergs. She didn't know how to feel about it—humiliated or appreciative. Sure that was the way a ward should work, but dependency was not something that could be easily sustained over a long time. She learned this lesson three decades ago. Nonetheless, she was grateful.

Just being in Round Valley again subdued her. There was so much to be done. In a month the cattle would have to be brought down from the range. That would mean daily feeding would soon begin. With good luck there would be one more cutting of alfalfa, consuming scores of man hours. Their three sons were not likely candidates for that work. They had established their own careers, which meant no more quick drives from State College to lift the bales. Suddenly the farm seemed like a huge burden, even though it was their only means of sustenance.

Once established in Logan, Harriet found employment at Sunshine Terrace, a nursing home next door to the hospital. She walked to work, arriving at six a.m. to prepare the breakfast. By two p.m. her shift was over, the evening meal in the oven. That left Hank the freedom of their car which soon took him to a daily appointment at Royal Bakery, located on Main Street.

All morning men dropped into the bakery for their coffee and donuts and talk, talk, talk. One corner was for the town fathers—a cabal of insiders, about six or eight men, who carried many of Logan's decisions in their pockets. Candidates for election were often chosen there.

The opposite corner was where Hank met several outsiders, the "old farts." That is what they called themselves. They liked to chum with the waitresses, knowing each by name. They knew how to catch the girls into a conversation. The "old farts" spent very little money and got lots of chair time for the price of a cup of coffee. But no one drove them out. Hank soon had a morning ritual.

Harriet and Hank risked a trip back to the farm in late October. Razzle Thompson had driven the Grossberg herd to Round Valley and turned them over to Woodruff Kane, who had mixed them in with his cattle. Hank was alarmed. It looked as if he would not be back all winter. A chat with "Wood" confirmed that his neighbor was prepared to feed the Grossberg herd until spring. There was enough alfalfa put up in Hank's barn to support them, but it wouldn't be sensible to keep separate corrals. Hank saw the logic but it hurt.

It seemed like folks thought he was through.

Once back in Logan they had to face some realities. Obviously Hank could not farm forever, though Wayne Allen in Pickleville was still doing it at 75. What was to happen when they did quit? Hank was trying to believe that he could farm again by spring, but his strength was not coming back. Gently but firmly, Harriet pressed him to consider the possibility of not returning to his land. Hank had to admit that sometime he would have to quit, though he had always assumed he could keep at it part-time—driving the tractor at least. If they never returned to Round Valley, but stayed in Logan near the hospital, he felt his whole world would crumble. He had never lived in a city.

That brought up the issue of Peter. Grandpa Ridges gave the farm to Hank as a way to get it to Peter when he grew up. Should it belong to Peter? Harriet was adamant: "Only if Peter will come here and farm it. The farm is not for him to sell. You have put your whole adult life in it. If it is sold, the proceeds should support you."

Hank often agreed with Harriet, but mainly in silence. This time he was hesitant to show it. But he was strongly of her view. The question was how to go about it. How could the question be put to Peter? Harriet pointed out that a legal document would have to emerge, one way or another, in order to prevent later litigation.

The other two boys were less of an issue. Junior was well established with an engineering firm in Chicago. He was not married, but would certainly not be returning to Round Valley and was not even an heir of Grandpa Ridges. As a counselor in the bishopric of the Logan Square Ward, where many professionals and singles congregated in the downtown area, his free time was pretty much occupied and tied to the "windy city."

Alan's situation was less clear. He was not related to the Ridges by blood, but he certainly was to Hank. Yet he had given no indication of taking up farming. His graduate work seemed stalled while he chased after utopias. His letters from halfway around the globe did not seem to indicate any firm direction. And his return could be temporary.

The matter needed to focus on Peter. Then it could be discussed with the other two. But how to get Peter into that conversation? Could it be done by letter or must it be face-to-face? Surprisingly a letter came from him simplifying the whole matter:

Dear Dad and Mom,

When Brigitte and I returned from our visit to Round Valley two years ago we were so glad to be in Atlanta that we realized we were home. There is no way I could stand to live on the farm. It is just my quirk, but it stirs up all the wrong things in me. I can't fathom how you and others can hack living in such isolation, unaware of the exciting world beyond the mountains. You are missing the whole twentieth century. I don't plan on moving back to live in Bear Lake Valley. Helicopters are my life and the ward here is so much more exciting; the people are dynamic. We would invite you to come here, but I doubt you could handle Atlanta. It would be best for you to sell the farm and live in Logan. It has the mountains but not the isolation. From what I hear, Logan is no hick town.*

Hank feared leaving the farm but knew he would die lifting bales. But if he didn't farm, what would he do? He knew how to fix engines, but he wasn't really a mechanic. What if he couldn't maintain a job at all? "Retirement" wasn't a word anyone in Round Valley had even used. He felt panic coming on when he thought of staying home while Harriet earned their keep.

The choice was tough but clear, especially when Woodruff Kane drove over to Logan to convince Hank to sell. He made them an exciting offer and they accepted it without waiting even a day. "Wood" was surprised, but realized that they had edged themselves up to the point. So it was done. Hank was amazed that he had been a willing party to the decision.

It was no surprise that Junior arrived. A consulting trip to California afforded the opportunity. He knew they needed hugs, so he had made the side trip to Logan. Fortunately, the big decisions had already been made. Otherwise he would have undertaken some plan to be available regularly to help with the farm. That would have been senseless. The price of travel and his missed wages could have easily hired all the work done, but Junior thought his presence was obligatory. He was quietly relieved when Hank and Harriet settled everything without consulting him. He agreed it was better for them to "cut bait" now and get away from the farm.

Nevertheless, Junior's visit was important—to feel close ties and real concern. Naturally, Junior worried about Harriet first. Hank couldn't help but notice that his questions were about finances and housing. Seeing his mother as a kitchen employee was no surprise to Junior since she had spent a lifetime with stoves and pans. And being at it by six a.m. was also not new. Nonetheless, Junior was uneasy about her having to work. He didn't offer to go with Hank to the morning bakery gathering, nor was he invited. The decision to sell the farm hadn't involved Junior directly, but he supported it with zest: "You did exactly the right thing. I admire your gutsiness."

Junior wanted to talk about Harriet and Hank initially and what they had given him in his life above and beyond any inheritance. In addition he had a tale to tell Harriet, something that had helped him realize how blessed he had been. "Last week in our Logan Square Ward in Chicago we had a sobering experience."

Harriet was anxious to hear about his big town experiences, hoping her mind could focus on something else other than her concerns.

Junior told about a young father who had died, leaving his wife and two sons, ages four and six.

"Was he in an accident?" inquired Harriet.

"No. That's the frustration of it." Junior continued. "It was worse than an accident. They took him to the hospital on Saturday evening with pains in his abdomen. The emergency room doctor diagnosed appendicitis but felt an operation was not urgent. Monday was a holiday so they scheduled the surgery for Tuesday morning. His appendix ruptured Monday morning and he died a couple of hours later."

"So it could have been prevented?"

"It was a complete bungle—medically inexcusable—a real tragedy for his wife and boys. He was a man of virtue. I looked to him as what I could be now and want to be soon. I am so down about it all. I just can't get it off my mind."

"This may be your first tough one but there will be more as you serve in bishoprics," Harriet commented. "This is when your gospel insights are so essential."

"You're right of course, and I have no difficulty understanding about eternal life. But it is that young wife and two boys I'm focusing on right now. The bishop and I had a chance to talk as we were waiting to help the family plan the funeral. At one point he looked at me and spoke with direction. He told me to look at the results of this situation. The young father made one important decision in his life, choosing the girl he married. How was he to know that she would have to be both father and mother to his offspring? Yet he chose a woman of spiritual strength exceeding his, just as if he knew. Those boys are going to be all right."

Harriet was touched. "How fortunate."

Junior continued, "It hit me as though he dropped a bale of hay on my head. Obviously he was instructing me to do the same. Then I suddenly realized what my father did."

There was a pause. Harriet's eyes filled with tears. She took Junior's hand: "So continue the pursuit for another Allison. She's out there. And you know the criteria."

Junior's visit was brief. Soon he was off, back to the career world, his consulting trips and his Chicago flock, relieved that his folks seemed in control.

When Junior's follow-up letter came a week later, it brought quite a surprise:

Dear Mom and Dad,

My visit with you was a great relief. I am proud of how you have made some tough decisions. You are obviously trying not to burden us boys and that is just like you. I know that you worry about me because I am not yet married. I worry about that too. It will come. I am determined it will, but I have not yet found her.

No, I am not pining about losing Allison. She is doing just fine, and I will yet find the right girl. In the meantime, I am reaping the benefits of singleness. There aren't many, but one of them is financial. I am amazed at how well my career is coming. Perhaps I have just learned your lifestyle because I really don't spend much money. The result is that I have saved quite a bit. Two years ago I started a little stock account that is doing very well. Yesterday I transferred it to your name. You will start receiving the quarterly reports. Right now it has enough money that you could take out some each month for the next ten years. If you don't need it right now, just let it grow. I will continue to put funds in it, and I expect it will be worth considerably more in a couple of years.

Don't hesitate to spend it. I am experiencing very good opportunities right now and I don't need the money. My job benefits will only increase, so I will be able to handle my needs when the right woman walks into my life. This is not welfare. It is a very small payment for the great upbringing you provided for me. You invested in me and it is paying off. What you have given me is incomparable. I use the work ethic, the gospel principles, the feeling of belonging to a wonderful family every day. I am so proud to be your son.

Love, Everett Jr.

Within a month of the farm's sale Harriet and Hank purchased a modest tract home in a new development on the hill behind the university, midway between the cemetery and the Logan Irrigation Canal. Their backyard was large enough for a substantial garden, so Hank took up its care—the job he had previously assigned to Harriet. Generally he sat on a stool or slid onto his hands and knees to pull the weeds or channel the water coming from the hose. Every morning Hank went outside to inspect the place. He had a hard time accepting the idea of houses lined up in a row just twenty feet apart. It was crowded—so different from Round Valley, where hundreds of acres separated the homes. He felt penned in by the backyard fences. Yet he was glad to keep the dogs from both neighbors out of his garden. This thing called suburbia was not Hank's idea of how to live. At least he could see the mountains just four blocks away and smell the crisp air each morning and evening.

The new home meant a new ward, something quite different from Laketown. On their first Sunday, members were eager to meet them, knowing the empty house was now occupied. In fact, the neighbors had rallied to help unload the truck they used to move their furniture. It was a custom—the men of Laketown ward had loaded it, assuming the Logan ward men would complete the task.

Hank and Harriet surveyed the membership, determining there were only four other grandparent-age couples. The rest of the two hundred people attending that morning were parents and children of all ages, lots of them. The Grossbergs found themselves surrounded by young families. It was a vibrant group, exciting for Harriet, but unsettling for Hank.

Within two weeks Harriet's stitching skills were discovered and she became completely involved. Many of the young mothers knew nothing of quilting, so a class was held on Tuesday nights. She could see a role for herself there. In addition, there were ward dinners to cook and visits to make and neighbors to get to know. It was the same as in Round Valley—just new people.

Hank didn't see it that way. His stake Sunday School job in Bear Lake Valley had been a great boost to his ego. He had visited the wards all along the lake's west side and found many a Sunday School presidency with men much like him—farmers with sun-baked faces and rough-hewn vocabularies. He had come to feel needed and certainly welcome in each village.

The Logan ward was a completely different matter. Several of the men were professors, others businessmen. Their white skin and clean fingernails proclaimed a lifestyle he could hardly imagine. *How could they get paid for just words instead of muscles?* Certainly he would have nothing to offer this

Sunday School—even the entire ward—unless they needed help fixing their lawnmowers. That he could do without attending meetings. The machine owners would search him out, once the word got around.

There was no Woodruff Kane in that ward, a well-established leader who would invest himself in Hank. It was easy to stay home and let Harriet attend alone. It hurt her to leave Hank behind, but she refused to disengage from the church. In fact, she was quickly enlisted in regular service.

Harriet discovered a store in Logan that would sell as many quilts as she could produce. She decided on a home industry instead of continued employment at the rest home. That meant four or five hours of sewing each day. Before long, the neighbor ladies dropped in regularly to join her, not as much for the craft as for the conversation. For all of them it built close ties. There were also bedspreads to make at the ward Relief Society days, coverlets to donate to the Asian refugee families moving into Logan. Harriet became one of the handful of quilters to engage all the women in that project.

Within a year the pattern was set: Harriet was at home in the ward and Hank was on the periphery. He knew that the "old farts" were good for a morning conversation but that was all. He wouldn't think to call on them if he needed help to lift lawn mowers or ladders. Harriet was caught up in the community where everyone depended on everyone else. The question was whether the different levels of church activity at the Grossbergs could last.

The first night Hank came home drunk Harriet was devastated. The lingering danger of the Thompson brothers had always stirred fear in her. Somehow Hank had maneuvered past the wild duo. For thirty years he had moved, one step at a time, closer to a steady, even respectable, life. She had felt rewarded by him as he had supported her effort with the boys and with the ward. She had returned the compliment by her labor— both in the house and on the land. They were a good team, not flourishing, but solid. Their sons were launched. She worried about each—Peter's distance and coolness, Junior's singleness and Alan's wandering. Yet there were substantial positives about each.

Now alcohol had re-entered the scene. Harriet asked herself many hard questions. *Is it an act of depression, a flailing about because Hank feels so unneeded? Is the loss of the farm destroying his identity? Has my quick acceptance into the ward and neighborhood driven Hank to feel isolated? Is his drinking a way of calling for help?* Harriet was trying to play psychologist, but the alcohol also caused her to feel defeat. *Will the neighbors and ward members find out? How will they react?* She kept her temper, but delivered a strong lecture the following morning.

The next time he didn't come home on his own, the police brought him about ten p.m. The officer said they didn't want to arrest him, but would have to if Hank drove "under the influence." So they brought him home instead, leaving the car downtown.

Though it was kind of the police, it was shattering to Harriet. Obviously what Harriet said to Hank the first time had no impact. *Where was this leading?*

She dared to ask him, "What happens if they arrest you?"

But Hank seemed undaunted. "This is stupid," he answered. "They have better things to do."

Harriet tried to hold the sharp words that wanted to come, "That's what you say. Shouldn't they prevent accidents?"

"I can drive perfectly well."

"It's against the law. You know it—drunk driving."

"I wasn't drunk."

"All drunks say that. Drunk doesn't mean you are unconscious."

"They never would have known if someone hadn't called them."

"Who called?"

"I don't know, maybe the bartender. He asked if I could ride with someone." Hank paused and when Harriet did not say anything, he added, "Quit worrying about who knows."

Harriet felt helpless as well as angry, "You realize it will be printed in the paper, if you get arrested."

"Oh hell, who reads the small print?"

Harriet felt a stab of pain in her heart, but she could not leave it alone. "Have you thought of what will happen if you are put in jail? Do we have money for a lawyer?"

"They can give me a public defender."

Finally, Harriet, still hurting, confronted the truth. "Don't you care about me? Can't you see where this will lead—the ruination of your three decades of hard work."

But all Hank offered was, "Oh, get off my back."

During those fearful weeks Harriet tried to understand. *Is Hank rebelling? Is he mad at me?* She probed it once with him.

"Drop it, Mom," Hank replied. "My problem is me, not you."

"Your problem—what is your problem?"

"Just drop it." That's all he would say, retreating into himself.

For two months almost once every week the police brought him home. Then came their ultimatum: "Next time it's jail. We can't keep this up unless there are some positive changes."

The crisis had arrived.

Somehow Bishop Tom Bitner got wind of the situation. As a neighbor, a block away, he could see Hank's decline, his unwillingness to attend ward meetings, his lack of contact with neighbors. Over a year ago the bishop began bringing his garden tools to Hank for repairs. That opened the door for some visits—about gardening, about farms. The bishop had grown up in a small southern Utah farming town. He knew the inner workings of a farming ward society. His father had been the bishop and the mayor, and then, feeling unneeded, he had fought depression when he reached his seventies. Perhaps that is what drew the bishop to Hank. He assigned himself to be the Grossbergs' regular monthly visitor. He came by persistently for a formal contact, bringing his son with him. In addition, there were the casual chats about tool repairs. Harriet took the cue and left them alone.

So that is how he and Hank had stumbled into a night of sitting in the car together. Harriet had asked the bishop to pick up Hank at the bar. She was desperate, so she had turned to the bishop, hoping the two of them could make a breakthrough.

Hank was embarrassed when the bishop took him by the arm and led him to the car. "Oh bishop, this is stupid—you retrieving me. I can drive home."

The bishop opened the door and helped Hank sit down. "The police don't think so," he said, shutting the door and going to the driver's seat.

"They've got better things to do than trail run-down old gents like me."

"They think they're protecting you from yourself," the bishop said, starting the engine.

"I can hold my liquor," Hank said. "I've drunk kegs of it in my younger years and then put in a whole day's work."

"The police don't want to jail you. You can imagine how Harriet would feel if that happened."

"Well, they could just ignore me."

"Imagine how that would look in the paper. It would rate a headline instead of a back page notice: 'Police to ignore drunks over the age of sixty.'"

"I'm an embarrassment to everyone. Harriet would sure like to dump me."

"Has she said that?"

"Nope, but I can read her."

For a moment there was silence in the car. The bishop had told Harriet and Hank about his father in his meetings with them. He couldn't get the comparison out of his mind. "My dad told me that growing old was tougher than he thought it would be," he commented.

Hank wanted to talk about it too. "Well, we have plenty of warning that it's coming. I've survived three brushes with death."

"But somehow we postpone thinking about actually dying."

"Not me," Hank said. "I've thought about it a lot." He paused. "But that isn't what drives me to drink."

"I didn't think so. My dad just couldn't stand being so unneeded. He had worked every minute of his life. He supported us and led the ward and the town. Then gradually we all went away. Other leaders appeared and he was soon alone in his thoughts. He felt he was being put on the shelf."

"Well, bishop, that is getting closer, but it still isn't square on." Hank opened up now. He had a lot to say. "You see, Harriet and the boys think they understand my situation. They say, 'Hank is a farmer and now he can't farm. He feels useless.' On another day they say, 'Hank worked himself into acceptance in Laketown. He gradually got inside our tight circle. But the move to Logan cut those ties without creating new ones. He was left out.' Or finally they pull the clincher by saying, 'Hank can't be married to Harriet in the next world because she is sealed to Everett Senior. He mourns about losing all he has worked for.' Wow, that sounds like the full explanation. But they are creating solutions to their own mysteries. They don't see the real situation because they don't know the facts. They feel secure in their own thinking and their own priorities. It's not the farm, even though I miss it terribly. It's not the new ward, and it's not even Harriet's first husband. I've come to terms with all that." He paused but the bishop let him talk.

"I've lived with an awful memory haunting me," Hank continued. "Bishop, I haven't dared to share it. Not with Harriet. Not with anyone. It haunts me. I am so ashamed."

"It's your choice, Hank," Bishop Bitner replied. "You have your agency, but I think you intend to unload it. Am I right?"

"I guess, but why am I telling you? You were not involved."

"Because you have tried the other alternative of suppressing it. Sometimes people tell themselves: 'It's water under the bridge. There's nothing I can do to rectify it now.' The problem is that it festers. If you don't smother your conscience, your guilt grows and grows with nowhere to escape."

"Well Bishop, this is so awful that I can't unload it because I can't defend it. It is just awful. I am so ashamed. You see I was the undoing of my first wife, Carmen. I am responsible for her death."

Silence.

The bishop's mind raced. Hank's eyes dropped.

"What do you mean 'responsible'?"

"You see, she died during a miscarriage—she bled to death."

"What was your role in it?"

"I drove her to it. She wouldn't have had that miscarriage if I hadn't abused her."

"Abused?"

"I didn't beat her, but I beat her mind."

"Her mind?"

"Yes, I was in a fury for four months. I moved out, camped in the bunk house to punish her. I refused to talk to her and got madder and madder."

"Madder?"

"Madder because she wouldn't tell me."

"Tell you?"

"Tell me who the father was, the father of that baby to be born."

"Oh."

"Right from the start I was perplexed. The calendar wasn't right. I wasn't sure exactly when the baby would be born. So for two months I just wondered. She could see the question in my mind."

"How did you find out?"

"She told me. One night after she had not said a word all day, she told me that I needed to know I was not the child's father. It wasn't a complete surprise, but I blew up anyway. I demanded to know who the father was. I acted like a damn teenager. If I had the slightest amount of maturity, I would have seen how she was suffering. I would have admitted that in her situation I would likely have kept it secret.

"The fact that she decided to admit it went past me. It took me months to realize her greatness. I just acted like a damn ass. I thought only of myself—how I had been insulted, how I had been assaulted. It must have happened while I was up on the mountain with the herd. I was livid that she would not tell me who the offender was—who it was I should hate, accuse, beat up. I even talked of an abortion.

"There were ugly scenes almost every day. We tried to keep them from her father and Peter, but they felt the bitterness. I thought very seriously of leaving; I even made plans. Carmen knew it. It petrified her. It was Peter I couldn't leave.

"But I had no mercy for Carmen. She suffered with guilt, with rejection. Soon she would not leave her room. Grandpa tried to sustain Peter. I brooded. I was no help to anyone. Worse still, I suspected every possible male, even Grandpa. It was awful.

"Then she started to bleed. At first it was slow, but I wasn't staying in the house. I could have acted sooner. By the time Grandpa hobbled to the bunk house at three a.m., it was serious. I put her in the car. I was in a panic. Stopping at Kanes' to use their phone, I called the doctor. I told him we were coming at high speed to the Montpelier Hospital, nearly an hour away. Grandpa wanted to come, but he had to watch Peter.

"Carmen was so weak on the way up that she couldn't talk.

"She bled to death an hour after we arrived. We were way too late leaving, probably a day late. Damn ass that I am. I caused it all, the depression, the isolation. All that led to the bleeding."

Hank continued talking through the stress of his voice—as though his life depended on it. "The drive to the hospital was worse than hell. I realized it suddenly. It showed me that my sin was as great as hers, yes, greater. She had tried to make up for it. She told me. She didn't have to do that. She could have carried her secret to defend the child, but she risked admitting it. Risked it, knowing how stupid I would be. She decided to protect the guilty for fear that I would take my rifle and shoot him. She was probably right. I forgave her ten times on that hour's drive. I told her but she was too weak to respond. I don't even know if she even heard me."

Listening to Hank's amazing confession, the bishop slowed the car as they rounded the corner to Hank's home. Hank's voice sounded on the edge of sobs. "But why couldn't I get enough manliness to do it before? During that awful hour I even forgave myself for the first week of my temper. Those tantrums were understandable, but drawing them out was stupid. She knew how I would act. The awfulness about it is that I compounded the initial week of temper and shame and self-pity. I should have looked for a way to calm down. Forgiveness didn't enter my mind, just self-righteousness. It was all so stupid. Here I was, a man of a thousand sins and I was stomping around being offended.

"On that terrible drive to the hospital it all poured out on me. I realized what I could have done, the awfulness of what I had done and that I wasn't willing to admit it. The consequences were playing out before me. The weight was horrible—two lives were slipping away with every mile. And it was my fault. Not hers or her partner's.

"By the time we arrived at the hospital I felt my punishment was just. I so wished that she had told me who the father was, but for a different reason. I have forgiven him a dozen times and only wish I could tell him. But I forgive him now out of weakness. Why couldn't I have worked my soul as Carmen did? Why couldn't I have initiated a mite of goodness? No, I just played holier-than-thou until the consequences fell in on me and at the price of Carmen's life and the baby's.

"I know that the miscarriage could have possibly happened anyway. But it would not have happened in bitterness, in agony.

"Why could I not have accepted that child? The irony is that I later accepted another man's son, Everett Jr., all to my benefit.

"Why could I not see that I could forgive Carmen? I didn't even consider it. You see, I didn't have the faintest seed of Christianity in me, not even of decency. No one knows the real story. The doctor didn't suspect. Grandpa could hardly talk. It was possible to duck the responsibility. But I have hated myself ever since, while still continuing to duck it. This feeling won't go away. I remember it every day. I've taken lots of steps to become decent. I've supported Harriet and even joined the church, but the feeling of guilt resurfaces time and again."

Slowly the bishop offered: "Hank, I suppose you didn't discuss this with the bishop when you were baptized."

"No. I was a coward. I ducked it again. He didn't probe. He asked if there was anything I wanted to tell him from my past. I could easily say no because I didn't want to talk about it."

The bishop slowed the car and parked it in front of Hank's home. He did not move to get out. "You know," he began. "Hank, you have been carrying these awful feelings a lot longer than God wanted you to. Your guilt is justified, but it has nearly paralyzed you. That baptism would have been a great time to unload it. You know that is exactly what Christ is for. You have now confessed the matter. It could have been done a decade or two ago. Those mistakes are over—gone."

"Maybe, but there is no way I can pay back for it."

"That's the point, Hank. That is what Christ does. You can't, yet he can and will. But it is not casual. In order for you to feel the guilt and responsibility lifted from your shoulders, there are things for you to do. You need to have some long talks with God. So do I. My role in all this is being the Judge in Israel. Both of us need to seek his will."

"I'm not much of a praying man, Tom."

"It will come, Hank, but this much I can tell you: we insiders have a lot more to learn from you than you do from us—all of us in the ward and particularly Harriet, Peter, Junior, Alan and I."

The second heart attack, a year later, was not so fortunate. It happened right in the Logan living room, Sunday afternoon. Harriet and Hank had finished dinner and Hank was settled in his recliner for a snooze. All of a sudden he grabbed his chest and tried to get up. He fell backward into the chair, unconscious. Harriet was right there in the room with him. Kneeling by his side and grasping his head, she reached for the phone and called the paramedics. In response to their question, she replied that he was breathing lightly. They were at the front door in five minutes and applied their equipment while placing him on a gurney and rushing him out the door to the ambulance. Harriet climbed in beside him, but by the time they arrived at the hospital it was clear that his breathing had stopped.

Without hesitation, Harriet dialed Bishop Bitner. He was at the hospital within minutes and took Harriet in his arms. They cried together, unrestrained. He told her that Hank had won his highest admiration and was a man who had come to the deepest insights on his own. They sat for many minutes and then went back to the Grossberg home. The Relief Society president was already there. Between them they took on the job of many phone calls. The bishop got each of the boys on the phone and then let Harriet have some time alone with them.

Word of Hank's sudden passing rapidly spread through the ward—within minutes it seemed. Harriet's friends all wanted to do something, anything, to express their deep respect. Many felt it was important to wait a day or two, but a few could not wait and soon there were close neighbors dropping in for a quick hug. Harriet couldn't help but remember the many times she had grieved with neighbors and friends, and she felt comfortable with this outpouring.

Alan arrived from Bear Lake an hour after Harriet had spoken to him by phone. Fortunately he was living in Garden City doing his "research" on the Mormon village. He did not allow anything to keep him back. Harriet was so relieved to have his arms around her, reciprocating the many times she held him as a child.

"Oh, Alan, I need you so. Many dear friends have been here but I need my own family. My own can sustain me."

"I came as fast as I could," Alan told her. "You know how tough the canyon road is. I didn't dare drive faster. Was this attack like the last one?"

"Almost exactly the same, but he was different. He didn't have the taut body to fight back. He was gone in minutes, without regaining consciousness."

"It is probably better that way, no painful lingering."

"Yes, but he wasn't really old," Harriet protested.

"That's true, but his body had aged," Alan said.

"And his spirit was so troubled," added Harriet.

"Troubled. What do you mean he was so troubled?"

"I wish I knew," responded Harriett. "He seemed to be churning, anguishing these last few weeks. But he would never volunteer anything. We have lived together so long in silence that I didn't know how to help."

"Silence. What do you mean silence?"

"We talked, yes, but not soul to soul. We spent thirty-one years together, toiled at that farm, survived three near-death accidents, raised three boys, shared the same bed. But we talked little about things that mattered."

"Yes, I was there. I witnessed it."

Harriet continued in a subdued tone. "He seemed to respect me. Certainly he never demeaned me. Of course, I didn't allow that. He trusted me and I increasingly trusted him. But he never really let me inside of his thoughts."

"Don't be too hard on yourself," Alan reprimanded her. "You certainly knew my insides, even when I didn't."

"I couldn't figure out why he wouldn't open up and I didn't press it. I probed but I never got a response."

Alan queried, "Was he afraid you would find something forbidden in there?"

"At first I took it as a lack of acceptance but that soon abated. He allowed me to handle the finances and make decisions about you boys so I knew I wasn't being forced into inferior status. Yet he wouldn't confide his inner feelings to me."

"Was it guilt for abandoning his parents? Was it some dark secret?"

"I gave up on those possibilities because he was so consistently good to us. I just never figured it out."

"Maybe he just had a different personality from the rest of us," Alan offered.

"I don't really believe that. All humans have an inner self, an inside."

"Yes, that is what I felt with Novbu in Nepal." Alan had described some of his experiences there to her.

"I don't mean we were strangers," Harriet continued, still feeling compelled to share with Alan, "We were genuine friends but I never experienced with Hank what Everett Senior and I knew almost daily. Our very beings melded together."

Alan knew this. "Is that why you were so close to the people in the ward, as a substitute?"

"Perhaps," she mused. "I felt one with them. Not all of them. But many. I needed to share my innermost feelings even if it was unspoken. Sometimes in a meeting or in the choir or on a visit, there would be a feeling, a harmony, a knowing. Words were not necessary. Often tears expressed the joy, the love. I longed for it with Hank, but we never achieved that real harmony that transcends words."

Alan gazed at her for a long moment, waiting to hear if there was more. "Well," he hesitated, "we better get on with our tasks here. Have you reached Peter and Junior?"

"Yes. They will be on their way tomorrow. It will take them each three days. So that means you and I will need to do all the planning."

"We can postpone that until tomorrow, can't we?"

But Harriet was not in a mood to postpone anything. "Not easily. People need to make plans; they need to know when the funeral is. Those who will be performing also need to plan. So I think we should get right at it. Your brothers will accept your decisions."

"I'm clearly not the senior son. I don't want to pre-empt Peter's rights."

Harriet was not worried about that. "Well we haven't any choice. I will take the blame if necessary. I haven't really had time to think yet, partly because I wanted your support."

Alan began to take the leadership at this point. "I did some thinking on the way," he said.

"You had the luxury of being alone. I didn't, and actually, I'm glad," Harriet added.

"Well, it seems to me that there are some givens. First, he should be buried next to Carmen in the Meadowville cemetery. Do you agree?"

"Yes," affirmed Harriet. "There is no question about it. Peter may think he will have to convince us, but let's surprise him."

"Next, then, is where the funeral should be. Logan is most convenient and your most recent friends are here, but I vote for Laketown."

"Definitely," Harriet agreed. "The people there are the ones who gradually adopted him. He loved them—and the place. Maybe we could have a viewing here the night before."

"Okay. Then comes the question of speakers," Alan said. "I vote for Woodruff Kane."

"That's a natural, but I choose one too, our bishop here in Logan. He and Hank became even closer than Hank and Woodruff."

Alan paused and then concluded: "It sounds to me that most of the decisions are made."

"Well, there are a few little touches. Let's see if Peter's sons will sing a primary song. Their mother says they have good voices and they are old enough to be a good duet. And then I want you boys to participate too. You three are Hank's greatest joy."

"Okay. Junior and I will give the opening and closing prayers at the funeral, but Peter should dedicate the grave."

Harriet's eyes moistened. "The symbolism of that is wonderful."

Alan wanted to keep it lighter. "There you go, Mom, sounding like a philosopher."

Harriet's response surprised him. "Well, I'm still reading, are you?"

"Probably not as much as you are," Alan teased and he squeezed her hand. "I think we've done a day's work in just fifteen minutes," he said. "I'll take it from here. You greet your friends. When you are exhausted just give me a signal and I'll intervene and send them home so you can sleep. Okay?"

But Harriet still had more. "One additional thing, Alan. Will you go to Hall's Mortuary and pick out the casket? Dad would choose oak, not metal. And arrange for the clothes. Take this picture of Hank with you. They may want it, and help them get the program and obituary printed."

"Yes, dear Mom. That is what I meant; I will take care of the details. You've given me the broad outline. I can fill in the rest."

"How do I ever deserve this?" Harriet asked.

"Do you want me to count the ways? 'Tis I who am in your debt. You put up with my wanderings, my indecisiveness."

Before going to Hall's, Alan wanted to act on one more idea he had hatched on the way through the canyon. He went to Harriet's and Hank's bedroom where they had a phone by their bed, closed the door and dialed Junior's number in Chicago.

"Hey Junior, this is your junior."

"Alan, where are you?"

"At Mom's in Logan."

Junior's voice brightened. "Thank you, thank you. I feel terrible to be days away. How's Mother?"

"She is amazing, as usual."

"So, is there something I can do before leaving in the morning?"

"Well, I want to run something past you, something unusual."

"Shoot."

"Mom has asked me to arrange the details—and by the way you are to give the opening prayer and I'll do the closing. We'll reserve the dedication of the grave for Peter."

Junior responded: "He will like that, I think. It recognizes his role and our respect of his worthiness."

"Exactly."

"Is that all?"

"No. I want to do something unusual, something to do with us three. I propose that the three of us prepare the grave. We can do it the day you arrive. I'll get a backhoe from Woodruff, and I'll have a cement vault delivered. I think being in work clothes, using shovels and directing a machine is what we should do for Dad."

"Man, does that sound like a thinker—full of great meaning. I hope we can do it without tears."

"Does that mean you agree?"

"Alan, I love you. That is one of the best ideas I've ever heard of, giving a part of us." There was a short pause on the other end of the line. "But can I add one twist to it?"

"Sure."

"I know this is a bit fast, but would you go to the fellow next door to Hall's Mortuary, you know the one where the grave headstones are out in front of his store? Ask him to make a joint headstone with Carmen and Hank's names and dates on it. You can get the correct information from Harriet's genealogy charts. I want to pay for it. Ask him if he can have it done in four days. Then shortly after the funeral let's put those old clothes on again and shovel the dirt back into the grave. We will surprise Peter and install the headstone right then. Get a couple bags of cement so we can do it."

Alan was moved. "Well, Engineer, you have one-upped me again. I love you, too. That is a great plan and I'll have it ready to go, Boss."

Her other two boys, Peter and Junior, were the last to gather at Harriet's side. They headed home as soon as they could, but it took time to cover the distance of a continent.

Peter and his family arranged railroad tickets and were soon on the way. The clicking of the train wheels should have lulled them into sleep; the Pullman car vibrated in sync with the rail connections, but Peter was in a talking mood. It would take nearly three days on the train from Atlanta to reach Ogden, Utah, and then a two-hour drive to Laketown where the funeral was to be held. There would be plenty of time to talk. Nonetheless, with Brigitte nestled by his side in the lower bunk which the porter had so nicely fitted for them, Peter was in a reflective mood. Their two boys were settled in the upper bunk, like a campout, and the parents could finally have some quiet time.

"I knew this day would come, but I have postponed considering its meaning," Peter said.

Brigitte's voice was so soft he could barely hear it above the noise of the wheels on the tracks. "Well it is natural, and your father had already survived one serious heart attack."

"Yes, dying is part of living. But that is not what I'm thinking about. It's the meaning of Hank's life. I have not wanted to admit it but we are quite alike, Hank and me."

"I sure don't see the similarities. You are a big city boy. He lived in the open spaces. He clung to a remote corner; you ran from it."

"It's true, but you see, he ran away from his boyhood home, too, and never went back. I have resisted the return. I know Harriet has grieved endlessly that she and Hank could not be real grandparents to our kids. And Hank has felt rejected. It is sad to me, but not sad enough that I ever took any action to remedy it. I just kept thinking there was lots of time yet."

"There's more to it than that, Peter," Brigitte maintained. "You feel guilty and you know it. You won't forgive yourself. Why?"

"Because I never should have gone to Fort Ord. I should never have jumped into that kind of life. Why resist admitting and try to cover it up? It was stupid, pigheaded, and it led to debauchery. Yes. I guess it is guilt. I just hate to call it that."

"But Peter," Brigitte continued, "it is past. You are miles ahead of that. No one in Bear Lake even knows about it. You are the only one who doesn't respect you. Even God forgives you."

"Harriet and Dad could read between the lines. They knew what I was doing."

Brigitte's rejoinder came: "You know, I thought that would change. It seemed to me that once you reached a reconciliation with the church, you would also build your family ties."

"I'm sure Harriet and Hank thought so too, but I didn't want to go back and have people see me and wonder how I had been reformed."

"Or was it that you are ashamed of introducing me—a woman of the street who latched on to you?"

"Stop that. You knew darned well I could have left you in Salzburg. Most guys did. I wanted our marriage as much as you did."

"Well, I just like to hear you say that," she grinned, then asked, "What about the church?"

"That's another way Hank and I are similar—we were both reclaimed by our women. From Fort Ord to Salzburg I dodged the church, yet the woman who was my downfall dragged me back in."

"I didn't know much about the church until we got to Atlanta, so it was not my scheme."

"I was more fortunate than Hank because I couldn't hide my seamy past from my wife. People thought I was running from Bear Lake like Hank had run from Wyoming, but I was running from the church as much as from Round Valley."

There was a pause, then "Why do you love it now?" Brigitte asked.

"Partly because it has brought me relief from my guilt. Now I'm living like I always knew I should but refused to admit."

Brigitte smiled warmly. "I think you are more of a straight arrow now than Junior. You want to whip everyone into shape."

"Yes, I admit it. I just hate to see people make the mistakes I did. I can't help myself. It is so stupid to rebel so irrationally. It bugs me."

"Sometimes I wish you had more of your parents in you. They were furious with you but didn't say so."

"I guess I'm just reversing my rebellion into intolerance," Peter muttered.

"You said it; I didn't. So you understand why I'm trying to get you to be gentle with the boys and everyone else instead of being a top sergeant." She snuggled closer to him in the berth.

"You are right. It is just hard for me to admit it. One of the things I cherish about the church in Atlanta is that people love me and say so. I know they understand I had a long way to come back. But they act like I am their equal. That's what I don't think the folks in Bear Lake will do. They know too much about me. I will be the talk of the valley. I've watched them gossip. They can be so petty."

Brigitte had a comeback, "Aren't you being as judgmental of them as you fear they will be of you?"

Peter didn't accept it. "You don't know them. Their lives are so narrow that they have little else to talk about."

Now Brigitte pleaded with him. "Let it go Peter. It is past and forgiven. Harriet has her hopes up so high. I just know it."

"Well, we are headed for the showdown. I'll try and be humble—but you know I've postponed that so often." He was being ironic.

"Okay. I promise not to say 'I told you so.'"

Peter wasn't finished with his pondering. "But you know the thing that unsettles me the most is my own mother. Will anything be said about Carmen Hodges? Everyone loves Harriet. It will be a grand homecoming for her. Who even remembers Carmen?"

"Do you?"

"Well yes, just a bit. I can remember her rocking me and singing to me, but that is about all."

"Did Hank tell you about her?"

"A few times I asked him about her. He answered with a sentence or two but no extended stories. It puzzles me. Why?"

"Well, it must have been awkward with Harriet right there."

"Yes, but I longed to hear about her. It seemed so odd that he almost hushed her up. I still want to know more and I am determined to do something about it."

"Now wait a minute. Don't use this funeral to upset Harriet."

"I know. I know. But it seems unfair. We always knew that Harriet was sealed to Everett Senior. Does that mean Hank is left out?"

"Of course not."

"It sure does unless he and my mother can be eternal mates. And that is what I am going to do."

"Are you sure that Hank and Carmen want each other that way?"

"I can only hope. Now I wish so much that I had somehow talked with Dad."

"Peter, you have been away from home nearly a decade. You and Hank have changed a lot. Did you ever try to talk with him recently?"

Peter felt certain of his feelings. "Somehow I just assumed that he would respond briefly as he always did, dodging whatever it was he was not telling me."

"Maybe he hoped for another chance," Brigitte said.

"I wish he would have given me a signal."

"But you know, as the years pass, our role as offspring changes. We are supposed to initiate the caring."

"Maybe so, and like in so many things, I have ducked it."

"I didn't mean that. It is not a matter of guilt. It is a question of understanding."

Peter was puzzled. "I just wish I knew how Carmen felt about Hank. We all knew clearly how Harriet felt about her first husband. He took priority over Hank. She never said so. She was diplomatic about not mentioning him, but we knew that Harriet and Everett were to be together for eternity. She respected Hank a lot, but for this life only. She wasn't a lot better in understanding Hank than we boys were. We sort of ignored him and went along intending to pass him up.

"If only I knew that an eternal feeling was binding Hank and my own mother, Carmen, then I would feel I had deep roots. It would mean a lot to me."

"That's great to hear. Sometimes you seem so confident that you are dependent on no one."

"Well, it is absolutely basic to me, and I hope it is to Hank, too. I intend to act on that premise at the temple."

Driving his car through Iowa and Nebraska was tedious for Junior, the boy from the Rocky Mountains on his way home for his stepfather's funeral. Everything is flat and rectangular on the Great Plains. The fences and by-roads are built along the straight lines of 640-acre sections dictated by the Homestead Act. *It frustrates me that everything is green here. It seems unfair—every inch of ground is growing, and no one has to stand by and water it. When I think of how many thousand times I moved sprinkler pipes in Utah to get water onto our fields, I'm just not very patient with these Iowa farmers. Look out there. As far as I can see fields are lush with growth, and there's not a farmer or tractor in sight. I wonder if they can develop character without fighting for every inch of yield like Hank did in Round Valley.*

That brought Junior back to Hank.

He raised me; always supported mother's direction for me. We worked side by side for hundreds, even thousands, of hours. I felt he was as devoted to me as he was to Peter and Alan, his own blood. Interestingly, when I almost wavered, it was Hank who pointed me toward my mission. I owe him so much for that.

Especially since they moved to Logan, he needed me. Sure, I wasn't in town very often, but we could have talked on the phone or in letters. I knew he was desperately lonely. I don't think he was really put off by my education and salary and living in the fast lane. We could have talked. I know it was hard to leave the farm. It was a snap for me to leave, but I'm just as addicted to work as he was and I don't really talk any more than he did, especially without a wife. I so want a wife, one of goodness like Mom, but in contrast with Hank I want a wife who will make me talk.

Mom thinks I am mourning about Allison and can't get over it. I try to deny it, but she is probably closer to the truth than I want to admit. It is paramount that lovers talk and loved ones too. Look how little Hank and I knew each other because we didn't confide in each other. I'm afraid he felt that I didn't care. I invest myself in the spiritual needs of my ward members in Chicago but have not done the same with Hank. Harriet knows I am concerned about her. She gets some benefit from my career and church life. Even though she is worried about my not being married yet, she enjoys my many blessings. I somehow left Hank out of that feeling—marginalized. Why have I not attended to him, at least as much as I have to people in our Chicago ward?

On Thursday everyone had gathered at the chapel on the Laketown square, the people of Laketown and Meadowville, Harriet's extended family from Ovid and St. Charles, three carloads of Logan friends and the three sons, Alan, Junior and Peter, his wife Brigitte, and their two sons. It was a grand reunion of the people Hank had touched and those who had touched him.

Woodruff Kane spoke of how Hank devoted his life to his family and his land, of how he loved two wives, Carmen for four years and Harriet for some thirty. He said that Hank had an inner spiritual life that he, Woodruff, had observed over two decades. "He put up with our eccentricities and then he jumped inside our commune and joined our efforts to become Zion. Now look at these sons, each having worked out his own positive path in an admirable way. Their convictions came with major effort not just by following the crowd. Hank did the same even though his family was not aware. I know because he allowed me to join him."

Bishop Bitner continued the saga Woodruff began. He was the Logan part of the story: "I am speaking today because I know Hank from inside his soul, the soul he chose to share with me. He chose to confide in me, not because I had been his long-time friend like Brother Kane, but because he had reached the point in his life where he was ready.

"I want you to know, all of you—Harriet, the boys, Brigitte and your boys and all of you who were close to Hank—that I learned insights from

Hank, insights into principles of the gospel that surpassed my understanding. I learned how Carmen and Harriet and you people taught him things he pondered and put together in a way that exceeded his teachers. He was slow to act on them, partly because he was suffering with guilt. In that he was like us all. We all have sins as serious as his. He knew us well. He watched us closely. He knew our imperfections, but felt his were more overwhelming that anyone else's. We have all felt the same about ourselves.

"I just want to witness to you that this man, Hank Grossberg, has earned my deepest respect, has taught me about what I was supposed to teach him."

Following the formal session, the whole group, including relatives and Logan friends, went the four miles to the Meadowville cemetery where Peter pronounced a fitting dedication on that plot of ground the three sons had prepared. The people milled about for a few minutes and then returned to the ward cultural hall where a dinner was provided by the Laketown Relief Society, so much like what Harriet had done often for others. Many members contributed food items to the smorgasbord.

After the essential greeting of the many there who longed to see them, the three brothers slipped out the back door, leaving the women, including Miss Coombs, in the church kitchen. She had surprised Alan by coming unannounced. The brothers drove back to the cemetery. There they put on the old clothes and packed the dirt into the grave.

It was nearly dusk. The welcomed breezes came off the nearby hills of the mountain range, cool, dry, invigorating. They surveyed the cemetery on the western foothill, only ninety graves. Wildflowers and bunchgrass nearly overran the headstones. It was not a city cemetery where someone could mow it like a lawn. This preserve was dry and natural. Most importantly, it was silent.

Alan and Junior went back to the truck and hauled the marker to the grave. Peter was surprised, and could not hold back tears as he read the words memorializing both his parents. They mixed the cement and put the marker in place. The three of them looked over the whole circle that was Round Valley, holding shoulders, engulfed in that silence.

As they stood there, bound together, a car approached. Brigitte and the boys and Miss Coombs stepped out, arms filled with blankets. Peter signaled them and then said, "Junior and Alan, you have each had your wonderful surprises for me: Alan's idea to prepare the grave, Junior's to have the headstone ready. I want you to know that they mean all the world to me, especially that you would accept me as your equal, something I dared not hope. So I would like to share a little surprise with you and especially my boys who are near the age now as we were when we first did this. Let's each take a blanket and walk over there about a hundred feet, just above the grave lines. Spread out the blanket and lie on it. Wrap it around you and then follow my instructions. Be absolutely silent. Don't move even to swat a fly. Just listen.

"Close your eyes but don't go to sleep. Be absolutely silent until I give you a signal, three light clicks. You two brothers already know what to do but the ladies and the boys will learn. They will become Bear Lakers."